PINION

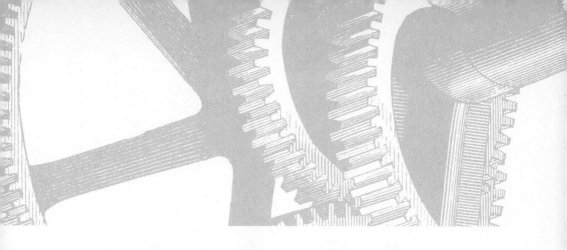

PINION

JAY LAKE

TOR®

A TOM DOHERTY ASSOCIATES BOOK
New York

This is a work of fiction. All of the characters, organizations, and events
portrayed in this novel are either products of the author's imagination or
are used fictitiously.

PINION

Copyright © 2010 by Joseph E. Lake Jr.

A Tor Book
Published by Tom Doherty Associates, LLC
175 Fifth Avenue
New York, NY 10010

www.tor-forge.com

Tor® is a registered trademark of Tom Doherty Associates, LLC.

Library of Congress Cataloging-in-Publication Data

Lake, Jay.
    Pinion / Jay Lake. — 1st ed.
        p. cm.
    "A Tom Doherty Associates book."
    "A Tor book"—T.p. verso.
    ISBN 978-0-7653-2186-2
    1. Magic—Fiction.   I. Title.
    PS3612.A519P56 2010
    813'.6—dc22

                                        2009040730

First Edition: April 2010

Printed in the United States of America

0 9 8 7 6 5 4 3 2 1

I finally wrote a love story. Submarines, airships and all.

Shannon, this one is for you. So are all the rest.

ACKNOWLEDGMENTS

This book would not have been possible without the wonderful assistance of people too numerous to fully list here. Nonetheless, I shall try, with apologies to whomever I manage to omit from my thank-yous. My deepest gratitude to Ginjer Buchanan, Kelly Buehler and Daniel Spector, Sarah Bryant, Ann Cannon, Todd Christensen, Michael Curry, the Fireside Writers Group, Dr. Daniel Herzig, Ambassador Joseph Lake, Shannon Page, Kris Rusch and Dean Wesley Smith, Ken Scholes, the Scholes twins, the Omaha Beach Party, Amber Eyes and everyone in the blogosphere and the Twitterverse who followed my adventures, answered my questions, and generally kept me entertained through this writing. There are many others I have neglected to name: that omission is my own fault and does not reflect on any of you.

I also want to recognize the Brooklyn Post Office here in Portland, Oregon, as well as the late, lamented Fireside Coffee Lodge and Lowell's Print-Inn for all their help and support. Special thanks go to Jennifer Jackson, Beth Meacham, Deanna Hoak, Melissa Frain and Kyle Avery for making this into a book. Also I want to thank Irene Gallo and Stephan Martiniere for such a wonderful set of series covers as I have been blessed with.

This is the book I wrote between my first bout of cancer and its return. My greatest thanks go to everyone who struggles, and everyone who heals, and most of all, to those who love.

Errors and omissions are entirely my own responsibility.

PINION

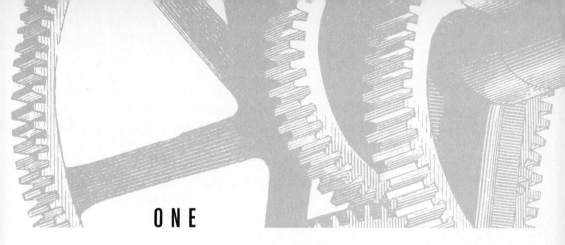

ONE

And I will break the pride of your power; and I will make your heaven as iron, and your earth as brass.

—*Leviticus 26:19*

BOAZ

Red-brown Ethiopian dust blossomed under British artillery shells, furrowing the violently turned earth as if by the plow of God. Overpressure from the explosions buffeted the Brass man like angry fists. The British were standing off to take their vengeance for ships lost and the city of Mogadishu half-burned, one whistling projectile at a time. Fear glistened on the grim faces of the Chinese air sailors who had taken him prisoner long weeks ago.

His kind did not know fear. Fear was an animal emotion, a rush of hot blood driven by squalid monkey unreason. Boaz was heir to an unbroken line of cool precision, the Brass race first created in ancient days by the wisdom of King Solomon and since perpetuated in magnificent perfection.

Or so he told himself as the man Lu Hsu screamed in terror just before a whistling shell dropped into his sheltering hole. Bloody spray erupted laced with rock fragments. Chin Yuen, the surviving petty officer, bawled a Chinese order that Boaz had learned meant "move out."

Boaz once again considered simply walking into the rain of hot steel and lead. Brass were not invulnerable. Solomon's First Seal glowed within his head as with all his fellows, but even it could not remake severed limbs, shattered chest, or tangled clockwork.

He realized Chin Yuen was screaming at him. The little man had much in common with Boaz' closest friend, Angus Threadgill al-Wazir. Those two shared a petty officer's view of human frailty, the idiocies of command and the general uselessness of civilians. *That* came through from Chin Yuen even without a language in common.

The Chinese shouted, his face flushed a dusky rose as his dark eyes glittered. Boaz just stared, wondering what the man was about, until a bullet spalled off his own shoulder with a sound like a flat-toned bell.

Chin Yuen shook his head and raced off bent low, as if incoming fire could distinguish between a man walking tall and a man scuttling.

Boaz decided that the Chinese petty officer was right. This was not a good day to die. The Brass walked after Chin, passing through smoke and fire and boiling dust as if he were the hollow wraith that his heart had become in the absence of Paolina.

Memory is perfection.

To misremember is impossible, in a proper man.

To misthink is impossible, with proper memory.

To act imperfectly is impossible, with proper thinking.

Logic flows in ratios, the magnificent alignment of radii and teeth and the tiniest cuttings of gear trains creating inconceivable precision. Events are captured to be ever available, ever ready.

Until someone reaches into your head and tweaks the crystals. Stores them in the archives of Authority without leaving a record of where the memory has gone. Undoes the mighty power of the Seal and replaces it with monkey unthinking and the wretched errors to which flesh is prone.

Until someone touches you with a bowl of oil and pronounces a name you never knew you could have, then flies away in a cloud of canvas and hydrogen and newborn regret and you are left among shouting madmen who labor like ants at the will of their distant, bloated queen.

Self is a flaw in the patterns of memory, errors in the unbroken chain of reason stretching back through time. Imperfection is unthinkable, literally.

Until you have been broken beyond repair.

Chin Yuen's band of air sailors and marines once more slipped the British trap. They were being driven north, repeatedly forced inland. Their sole blessing was that the Royal Navy could not field sufficient airships to harry them effectively. The fires at Mogadishu had reduced the fleet until reinforcements could arrive.

Only one sailor in the contingent spoke English—Chin Ping, no relation to Chin Yuen. He was small, as most of these Chinese were, his blue quilted uniform torn and patched and smeared with grubby dust until he seemed a soft, mobile part of the landscape. His eyes retained the midnight purity that Boaz had come to associate with these people.

"He ask you," Chin Ping said. *He* was always Chin Yuen. Beyond that, the sailor's grasp of English pronouns was shaky, as if the entire class of words existed only to refer to his commander, or Boaz himself.

The Brass man sat in the shade of a thornbush. The westering sun cast long shadows—his blended with the tree's. The air was still miserably hot for the humans. Dust grated in his joints and scarred his body and sometimes clouded his vision. They were safe enough; no Englishman could approach their rocky highland without being observed long before his arrival.

At least the total lack of water offered little risk to him.

"What does he inquire of me?" Boaz finally responded, speaking to Chin Ping's air of expectancy.

"He ask you find direction."

"Each point of the compass is accounted for." Boaz could scan three-quarters of the circumference of the horizon from where he sat. "Every possible direction."

"Ah . . ." Chin Ping tried again. A few swift, liquid syllables of Chinese spilled from his mouth, with neither the emphasis of a curse nor the resignation of despair. Then, in English: "Path. To big water. Make fire for help."

"The British continue to drive us inland."

Chin Ping nodded vigorously. "Time now, time now."

"A rendezvous."

Boaz stared eastward across the miles toward the sullen glint of the sea. The thread of Earth's orbital track gleamed crisply in the sky. The Wall loomed to the south, rising like a woman's hands to—

Incorrect thought.

Boaz forced himself to stop. Some memories were too difficult. Not painful, for he was no monkey to live on the frothing edge of emotion, but difficult. Paolina had given Boaz to himself, conquering his will like an invading army.

"Tell," Chin Ping was saying. His fingers touched Boaz' forearm, tracing the textured brass greave. "Tell, ah, then have problem no more."

"No more problems," Boaz echoed. He stood, not worrying if the last of the sun would flash bright off his body to catch the eyes of distant watchers. "You have need to reach the sea soon, and avoid the British."

Oddly, something in this high, wasted terrain did stir memories. Africa had its secrets, just as did the Wall. Boaz held the merest fraction of either of those books of knowledge, but his sliver of wisdom was the only sword these lost Chinese could wield to cut their way back to freedom.

Later, there was more labored conversation around a smoldering fire. Chin Ping served as the mouth for two dozen anxious pairs of eyes. They'd cremated seven of their fellows thus far, and a pair of the wounded were not likely to last another day.

"Need tall place," Chin Ping told him. "Tall place close to big water, ah."

"For your signal fire," Boaz said. "At some arranged moment."

Chin Ping nodded vigorously. His shipmates stared like wolves.

"We make for east of north," the Brass intoned, one hand out to point the way. "Past that ridge of rocks we will find a drainage course. We may follow that off these highlands and so approach the sea."

He wasn't sure why he knew this. Another imperfection of memory, surely, for he had never before traveled so far north of the Wall.

Chin Ping translated quietly. Chin Yuen stared across the fire at Boaz. Some of the others spoke softly.

Later they heard the distant cough of airship engines. Boaz couldn't tell the type from the sound, but the unseen vessel passed overhead with a steady grumble. The sentries stirred and watched the clouded darkness, but they raised no alarum.

You will have no secrets of me, Boaz soundlessly told the night. *You who snatched her away from my arms just when I had reached her side once more.*

He didn't know who he hated worse, the Chinese or the British. At least the Chinese were trying to keep him alive, while the British pursued him with fire and sword. For now, he held his own counsel and despised them all.

KITCHENS

Bernard Forthright Kitchens, special clerk to Admiralty, checked himself in the mirror clipped above the chipped basin in his rented room.

His shave was impeccably close. One advantage of having learned the quiet work with a blade was the improvement to this morning ritual that set servants of the Empire apart from the coarser run of men.

Kitchens picked up the straight razor again. Sharp enough to slice muscle down to bone almost unnoticed, as a good blade should be. He worked the edge across his skin, now dry from the earlier shave, to address a few errant whiskers just above his starched collar.

The tug of the metal against his pores was a caress. The danger of such a fine edge near the arteries was a tonic. No hired doxie could approach the passion that a simple length of honed steel inflamed within a thoughtful man.

Closing the razor, he slipped it into the sleeve pocket of his morning coat. The train to Oxfordshire left at 9:07, and he must be aboard or forfeit everything he had worked for. The Queen, the *real* Queen, not that hired actress who stared from the windows of Buckingham Palace, expected him before noon. The ninth Duke of Marlborough protected his royal charge *sans peur* and *sans pitié*.

Kitchens picked up his bowler with the weighted brim and retrieved his umbrella from the stand. As usual, he made a final check before departing. A bed, a clothes press, a small writing desk. The sole luxury was a rack with the adventure magazines that were his quiet vice. Only a destructively thorough search would turn out the room's darker secrets. Fingers would be lost and blood poisoned in the process.

Or so he intended.

Out into the press of the crowd, Kitchens became merely another whistling, anonymous man on the London streets, business on his mind.

With one change to a local line, he arrived at Woodstock well before noon. A tiny English town, unremarkable save for the Cameron Highlanders at every corner. A stranger would have been stopped and not so politely questioned.

Kitchens was expected.

No one asked his name, because no one needed to. He walked briskly along the carriage road leading southwest out of town toward Blenheim Palace. Every one of the Admiralty special clerks knew of this drill, for any of them could be called upon to deliver some report to the Crown in person.

They almost never were, however.

A gentleman did not traffic in rumors, but Kitchens was not a gentleman; he was a *clerk*. Rumors were his stock in trade, under the name of intelligence. As he passed among the grasses fading to autumn, watching the starlings whirl and chirp overhead, he wondered what the truth was of the Queen.

Many were aware of the woman acting out the role of a lifetime in Buckingham Palace, whom those in the highest levels of Government referred to as "the other Mrs. Brown." Too many for Kitchens' taste, but the security of the Crown was not his concern. Not directly.

Some understood that the Queen was in retirement at a country estate. Various locations were bruited about. Kitchens was certain there were more "other Mrs. Browns" in the world.

A very few knew that Her Imperial Majesty had taken up residence at Blenheim, a palace so large that an entire corps of crowned heads could be mislaid within its labyrinthine architecture.

Kitchens knew there must be more beneath even that. He would find out very soon.

CHILDRESS

The submarine *Five Lucky Winds* pitched, even beneath the waves. Captain Leung had been running at snorkel depth until the Indian Ocean storm had come upon them, but the weather was far more dangerous than a black-line squall.

They should submerge, Emily McHenry Childress knew, but there was some problem with their batteries that defied even Leung's efforts at translation into English. Chief al-Wazir was no help. The gruff, improbably named Scotsman was an experienced air sailor, but never an engineer, and knew almost nothing of the ways of the navy of his lifelong enemies. All Childress herself understood of sailing and *les sous-marins* had been learned aboard this tiny, creaking vessel as it carried her out of her old life in New England and into the world of Chinese court politics, divine magic and ancient secrets.

"They'll be taking her down, soon," growled al-Wazir. He and Childress crowded in the tiny wardroom. The only place where the Scotsman could stand upright was the laddered tube leading up to the conning tower, but at least here he could sit against a bench and brace his great legs across the cabin. He cradled the stump of his left wrist against his body, as if he still expected the lost hand to grow back.

Looking away from him for a shameful moment, Childress once more thanked her luck at not getting seasick. A lifetime spent among books had hardly prepared her for such adventures. "Captain Leung needs air for the diesels," she said.

"Not unless they be amphibious." When al-Wazir was nervous, his dialect slipped.

"My friend." Childress forced herself to meet the chief's haunted eyes, ignoring the missing hand and the wounded soul. "This brave ship has carried me halfway around the Northern Earth without mishap."

The hull shivered like a struck gong. They both stared up at the seam joining the wardroom overhead and the starboard bulkhead. As always when the submarine ran deep, water trailed in sweaty profusion down the blackened metal.

Her nose remembered that the ship stank—of fuel and brackish water and unwashed coolies and that vile paste with which the crew polished the brightwork. One grew accustomed to such smells, until they vanished from awareness.

It's the water, Childress thought. *Water makes me think of light and life when I am trapped at the bottom of a steel-jacketed well beneath the desert of the ocean.* At least she was not seeing ice creeping on frost-fingers across the bulkhead, as it had when Leung had caused a ghost to be set upon their political officer Choi, back in the Nipponese port of Sendai.

No more political officers here. *Five Lucky Winds* sailed without a flag, since the girl Paolina Barthes had destroyed an entire flotilla of the Nanyang Fleet to stop the massacre of the submarine's crew. In doing so she had called down the Silent Order's vengeance upon them all. Enemy to Her Imperial Majesty's throne in distant London, traitor to the Son of Heaven in Beijing, the surviving crew were friendless and alone in the stormy waters of the Indian Ocean.

The only purpose remaining to them was Childress' own—stopping the Golden Bridge project, that Chinese effort to cross the Wall using the ancient magics found in Chersonesus Aurea.

"She may be brave, but a smart captain won't be sailing into a storm like this." Al-Wazir's voice had dropped to a rumble that matched the groaning of the hull.

"We're safe from pursuit, I think."

"Aye, till them Silent bastards set a watcher or two upon us. Them as has ways of knowing, ma'am."

He held the right of that. But with secret societies, how could one know?

Timing her movement to the roll of the hull, Childress reached for the chart drawers and tugged out the too-familiar map of the Indian Ocean. Thus far their only course had been to steam north and west, making a furtive landfall at some white-beached islet in the Maldives while end-lessly arguing about where to head next. Water was taken on, fresh fruit and fish, but no answers.

She had a purpose, but no goal yet. Where to lever what strength she had?

Childress stared at the map, feet propped up against the little fold-down table. *Blue pajamas,* she thought. All her life she'd have rather been caught dead than wearing pants, and now she shared a room with this great brute of a man, she clad only in blue silk pajamas.

"There must be more to this ocean than storms," she mused aloud.

"Chinese, coconuts and sharks," al-Wazir offered.

"Chief, your wisdom would challenge even the ancients."

He chuckled. She glanced up again to see an unfamiliar gleam in his eyes.

This man had loved Paolina unreasonably. Childress suspected he mourned the girl more than he mourned his lost left hand.

Childress turned the map in her hands. She had all but memorized the

ports of this ocean, the little picture-words of their Chinese names dancing in her head as she placed them in her *ars memoriae*. Al-Wazir had filled
in a few for her in English: Aden, Mogadishu. Leung had filled in others:
Phu Ket, Penang, Colombo.

A long way from New Haven.

"Chief," Childress asked. "What's this place on the west coast of India?
I cannot tell if it's colored differently, or if that's just a stain on the map."

"On this vessel? They'd have the midshipmen inking a new chart before
they'd leave a soiled one in the drawer." Al-Wazir had acquired a grudging
respect for Chinese seamanship that ran deeply against the grain of all his
years in the Royal Navy airship service.

She let another roll of the hull pass, then slid the chart to him. "Look.
There."

"Aye . . ." He squinted a little while. "And it might be Goa."

"Goa?" The word meant nothing to Childress.

"A city of mad dogs and Portugee."

"Literally? I thought the Empire controlled everything in the western
part of the ocean."

"There's control and then there's control," al-Wazir said. "Some places
follow their own law."

"Like the Indians in America."

"All of 'em wogs," the big man said, already sliding back toward his de-
pression.

Finally, a place to stand, she thought. *And plot our next move.* My *next move.*

PAOLINA

Fleeing her own power, and the greed of men, she'd listened to the angel
tell her of someone she should meet. Paolina had expected to be brought
before a jeweled throne. Or introduced to an ancient sage beneath a withered peach tree.

Not *this*.

The Southern Earth lay beneath her, the curve of the globe quite visible from her dizzying altitude high up along the Wall. Ming was ahead,
trying to find a route around a knob of stone that would force them back
several days if they could not pass it. He was roped to a promising nub in
the outward-leaning rock face, but if he fell, she didn't see how to rescue
him.

The gleam was heavy in her pocket: the new stemwinder she'd built
aboard the dying Chinese airship, when she'd needed to escape the Wall
storm that had threatened their lives. The new one she'd used to take
hundreds, possibly thousands of lives. No matter that she'd saved herself,

the surviving crew of *Five Lucky Winds*, al-Wazir and that strange English librarian Childress. Paolina had sworn off dealing with death after the explosion in Strasbourg, which was as surely her fault as if she'd lit a fuse herself.

Otherwise she could simply *move* them off the Wall.

The last time she had used the gleam to do that, hundreds died in the resulting earthquakes. The world went to great trouble to right itself after such an insult. Which ought to be a clue to any thinking man or woman as to how such magic was intended to be used.

That was to say: *not at all.*

She desperately needed to shed herself of this power, without being destroyed by it.

Ming shouted something. She looked up from her reverie to see him wave. He then began making his slow, patient way back to the anchor point of his rope. Paolina watched carefully, marking the handholds and footholds the sailor used. She was longer of leg and arm than he, but his strength overmatched hers.

Enough, she thought. *When there are no choices, one simply does what must be done.* If there had been anything to learn from the sad, quiet women of Praia Nova in her youngest days, it was that.

Soon enough she was roped and climbing outward. Paolina clung to the rock like a leech, forcing herself into the Wall so the ancient, cruel magic of gravity would not pluck her down untimely. The stone was damp and gritty, far too soft to be trusted. The pain rose quickly in her arms as an acidic burn that gave no quarter. She worked her way along, always gripping with three points while moving the fourth.

Again Ming shouted. Paolina's section of the Wall was tilted forward like a dog trying to shed a troublesome insect.

A bronze blade stabbed into the rock next to her. It barely missed her cheek, would have laid her open to the bone. Paolina turned to see one of winged savages—those flying horrors of which al-Wazir had babbled in his fever dreams aboard *Heaven's Deer.*

It leered at her. The expression contrasted with the empty black eyes and the reek of slaughter. The sword pulled back as wings beat to hold the creature in place, eighty miles above the churning oceans of Southern Earth.

She could let go. She could fall. She could twist in the air, tug the gleam from its leather pouch, set the hands and find some use that would banish this monster and save herself. *And Ming,* Paolina added with hasty guilt. Save herself and Ming.

While perhaps shaking this entire face of the Wall loose with her.

"You are nothing," she told the winged savage, and loosened her grip.

The stone that struck it in the side of the head surprised them both. Paolina fell free, screaming, lost already to unreason before her hand ever found her salvation even as the winged savage spiraled away.

The rope held, slamming her into the rock forty feet below the tied-off knots. Paolina slumped there, lodged against a vertical cleft in the Wall.

Just below her, standing on an undercut pathway, was a man in yellow leather with a tall, narrow cap rounded as a thumb. A sling drooped from his right hand. His left held a feathered staff topped by bright jewels.

Her safety rope tugged. Paolina scrambled for a grip, trying to help Ming pull her up. She nodded at the stranger as he slid away from her view, hidden once more by the overhang.

Finally, palms bloody, feet torn in her ragged shoes, she lay gasping on the flat apron of ground.

"We . . . can go below . . . ," she managed to bite out. "A road . . . near the end . . . of our rope."

Ming smiled, though she did not think he meant it. "Who down there?" he asked in the careful, simple Chinese he used with her.

Paolina tried to shrug. "A man in . . . yellow. He had a sling. He stared at me."

"Maybe not so good to meet down, ah?" Ming tried in English.

She stared up the worthless trail that had led them to this impasse. "Up where we were, you think?"

"Up," he answered in his language. She didn't need a translation to hear his emphasis, his worry, his fear.

I can lay waste to cities and transport ships across oceans, she told herself, limping behind Ming's heels up their backtrail. *Surely I can carry myself down the Wall.* She had to find a way to shed her power, to live for herself. And for Boaz, Paolina admitted.

WANG

Cataloger Wang busied himself among the most recent scrolls to come out of the pit of the library at Chersonesus Aurea, that lost city of the ancients hidden within scattered islands of the Kepulauan Riau near to Singapore. A history almost long enough to rival the Celestial Empire was drowned in swamp water and ancient ghosts. Something of that spoke to his librarian's soul, whispering in the secret language of archivists.

All were loyal to the Son of Heaven; all were loyal to their name and place in the great wheel of society. He could do no less than practice the same loyalty.

There had been a sick, tempting fascination in the foreigner whom the damnable Captain Leung had brought into the heart of Wang's demesne. She was doubly offensive in being both English and female. The devils from the deepest West wore their deceit plain upon their ghost-pale faces.

If only the Han armies had pursued the Romans after the Battle of Sogdiana, the world would be a much more orderly place today.

Wang smiled; it took a librarian to regret something two millennia past while misremembering what he had eaten for breakfast.

The Romans begat their fractious broods of irrelevant barbarians for many centuries, and China forgot what it had barely understood to begin with. Later, the Khans were a greater difficulty, and then the Manchu in their time, before each accepted the eightfold path and became entrapped in golden chains under the banner of heaven. When the English returned, great-grandchildren of the Romans, China had not remembered enough of the old lessons.

Now sorcerers and temptresses stalked like hungry ghosts through the Middle Kingdom, building their nests of lies and taking up residence amid the palace-islands of Phu Ket. Bringing women here under the wing of the nearly rebel Beiyang Navy.

All came back to that Childress.

"Wang."

One of the Kô's clerks stood in the doorway. They did not like to come down to the library, which reeked of mold and the rotting of a thousand tons of paper trapped in the brackish water below, but stayed instead in the partially restored palace up on the ridge of the city, composing poems about the sublime beauty of plum blossoms, or fighting with willow wands, or doing whatever courtiers in an exile such as this found to occupy their time.

"Yes?" Since politeness had been dispensed with, Wang saw no need to observe the proper forms of address. This bright-silked fool might be able to have Wang's head back in Beijing, but here it was the cataloger and his researchers who did what was needful.

"You have been summoned before the Kô; he will speak to you now."

Wang made a show of leisure as he slowly rolled the scroll, securing it with the pale blue ribbon signifying this piece of work had passed his review. He stood, searching idly for the shoes in plain sight by the door.

Shiao, that was the clerk's name. A sorry little climber with a keen instinct for following the shiniest turd. The man's irritation at being made to wait was manifest.

Wang spotted his shoes with exaggerated delight, slipped them on, then bowed to Clerk Shiao. "Would that you had not delayed me so. I shall be merciful and not inform your master of your dilatory ways."

Shiao returned the bow. "We will proceed now, and pray that the Kô has not taken offense at your heedless tardiness."

They walked out single file, soft leather shoes squeaking against the grimy floor. Only a few of the researchers even looked up at the noise. Almost all of them were that very intelligent sort of simpleton who could perform a single task to perfection and otherwise barely walk upright.

Cataloger Wang hated everyone and everything about his sunken island kingdom, except the books themselves. He had a sick premonition that even that pleasure was about to be stricken from him by noble fiat.

It was not so long a walk, for all the knife-edged lack of courtesies between Cataloger Wang and Clerk Shiao. Soon the two of them were at the steps of the Kô's palace, which were being swept clean by a toothless coolie armed with a straw-bundle broom. Doubtless the old man and his implement had been imported all the way from China for the purpose.

Shiao paid no more attention to the coolie than he would have to a broken cart by the side of the road. Out of sheer spite, Wang smiled at the old man. He then followed the clerk up through a set of red lacquer doors also imported from China, and into a darkened hall that smelled of incense, damp silk and ice.

Ice? Wang thought.

Then he was surrounded by the court Mandarins whom he ordinarily avoided. They wore formal robes, layers of red and black and gold and scarlet, each with his flat hat and colored stone of rank. Silent servants replaced Wang's shoes with silk slippers, turned back his cuffs, pressed a strong tea into his hand to clear potential offense from his breath.

This was familiar enough. The Kô took his guests as if he were still in the sacred precincts. Of course, at the Summer Palace, Wang would not have been fit to beg scraps from a kitchen gate. Here at the very edge of the empire he was accorded nearly the dignity of a lesser servant from a foreign court.

With the striking of small bells and a low sweep of incense, he passed through a brocade curtain into the presence of the Kô. Even Clerk Shiao remained behind.

For a man bound by so much ceremony and tradition, the Kô seemed very plain. He had an open, round face, apparently guileless as any single-minded beekeeper. He was short and pudgy, and at least here at Chersonesus Aurea favored plain-sewn changshans that would not have been out of place in a rural teahouse.

He was also a man with a power to deal both life and death at the slightest whim, personal representative of the Son of Heaven here at this most critical footing of the Golden Bridge, that road across the Wall toward China's future. Judging from the languid expression on the Kô's face, something was very wrong.

Though it exceeded protocol, Wang dropped to his knees and kowtowed. His forehead knocked three times against the cracked marble floor, his ample belly pressed against the cold stone. On the third tap, the cataloger closed his eyes a moment in a silent, unseen plea for mercy, then stared cross-eyed at the textured stone beneath his nose.

"Do not be a fool," the Kô said. "You know better."

Cataloger Wang pulled himself to his feet. "Lord," he began, then stopped himself.

"Few things exercise my poor humors more than dealing with fools," the Kô went on. "Perhaps you would care to hazard a guess as to what disturbs my qi this day?"

Wang would rather chop off his thumbs. Still, such a question must be answered. "It is beyond my poor imagining, lord."

"Pity." The Kô turned a porcelain cup within the circle of his fingers. The delicate piece glowed in the pale light filtering from high above. Blue brush strokes peeked around the edges of his grip, each with the fragility of a dying bird. The cup carried the look of centuries about it. "As this concerns your actions of late, I thought you might care to enlighten me, your lord and master, as to why the Dragon Throne has taken an interest in you." Into the heart-freezing pause that followed, the Kô added, "By name."

"My lord," Wang muttered through a tongue thick with portents of disaster.

"Indeed. Your presence has been requested in Phu Ket, by the fastest available means." The Kô leaned forward. "Since the crippling of the Nanyang Fleet by those running dogs whom you aided, this means my own ship must take you from this island with all due speed."

Phu Ket! The island fortresses of the Silent Order stood offshore from that harbor, lording over the secrets of Asia as surely as any palace eunuch with his poisons and his secret whispers. ". . ." Wang could not speak.

"I thought you might tell me why, my friend." The Kô shattered the ancient cup with a clench of his fist. Shards glistening with scarlet drops spun to the floor amid a shower of steaming tea. "No matter, then. I shall not allow myself to be disturbed that a lowly servant has business with the Forbidden City that has been hidden from me."

Wang dropped to his knees again and crawled backward. Splinters of porcelain stung his hands. The Kô's breath was as a dragon's rising from a river bottom.

No more words were said. No more blood was spilled. Cataloger Wang fled, wondering what would be left behind and who would arrange the affairs of the library and the Golden Bridge in his absence and whether he would survive even an hour aboard the Kô's personal yacht.

KITCHENS

He was stopped twice before reaching the great doors of Blenheim Palace. In front of those ugly, pale stone facings he was questioned at length by a man in a dark suit whom no one would mistake for a clerk. Two burly fellows in unmarked British Army kit stood by with pistols in hand, not quite pointing at Kitchens, not quite pointing away from him.

As his umbrella was being carefully disassembled, Kitchens reflected on the stories that just after New Year's of 1901 while in residence at Osborne House, Her Imperial Majesty had suffered a fever of the brain. The details varied, but all of the potentially reliable rumors dated from that winter. The "other Mrs. Brown" had already been playing the role in Buckingham Palace and elsewhere for several years by then.

The suited man started in on Kitchens' shoes. One heel was hollow, though the picks within were not so much dangerous as useful. This man was certainly aware of every trick Kitchens knew.

The Queen, since the winter of 1901, had rarely been seen. Her stand-ins had aged visibly, through the magic of theatre and doubtless a certain amount of brutal coaching. But the quiet whispers in the break rooms of Ripley Building where Admiralty was housed said there was far more afoot.

Kitchens had thought he might be forced to strip, but he was given a handshake instead, which process relieved him of both the razor and the piano wire in his sleeves. It was as smoothly done as any Newgate pickpocket slipping a copper's badge for a lark.

"They'll be returned when you leave," he was told.

If hung in the air. No one Kitchens knew admitted to seeing the Queen since her illness. Surely Lloyd George had done so, but this trip to Blenheim Palace had no recent precedent among the special clerks or the officers whom they served.

"Thank you," Kitchens replied.

A quiet, angry-eyed man in MacGregor tartan appeared at the entrance of the palace. "Come on, then." His voice was a deep burr of sheep and rocky hills.

Kitchens walked with measured pace toward the great, carved doors, aware with every step of the pistols tracking him. No bustle of servants, no hurrying army of maids and men-at-arms—just a palace quiet enough to be a mausoleum, surrounded by force sufficient to hold off an entire jacquerie.

The English queen abided somewhere within the marbled halls, quietly dreaming of distant empire.

The MacGregor led him down long halls shrouded in pale muslin. Blenheim Palace had been sealed up, made over to a box of dust and memories. Twice Kitchens saw dark figures scurrying furtively ahead. At some unknowable midpoint in a corridor, his guide stopped, then turned and gave a calculating stare. "Tell me what you know, clerk."

Kitchens nodded, closing his eyes a moment that he might better listen, sense, and scent. A special clerk's trick, to look away from the world's light in order to see the darkness better.

Air moved in faint currents. Something close by clicked with a complex, irregular rhythm. The temperature was unusually cold, even for the deep interior of a great building. The smells were complex, as well. Ammonia. Vinegar. Blood. A peculiar and faint fleshy stench, like a distant slaughterhouse in summer.

He opened his eyes to meet the MacGregor's mad gaze. "A morgue is nearby. Or possibly a vivisectionist's. There are other explanations, but they make less sense."

"If it's sense you're looking for, lad, you've come to the wrong place." The man hawked and spat on the floor. "Madness is loose here, and I don't have a care for whoever might hear me say that. You're the first to come from London since the New Year's honors." He leaned close. "What makes you so special?"

"Nothing, sir." Kitchens mentally mapped escape routes. "I perform the task I am set to. The Prime Minister has given me this job, and instructed me to appear before Her Imperial Majesty."

The MacGregor began to chuckle, an odd, hollow sound closer to tears than laughter. "Appear before the Queen you shall, then." He turned on his heel and strode to the next set of double doors. Kitchens noticed the polished scuffs on the marble floors beneath the Scotsman's feet. Quite a lot of something heavy had been dragged through here.

The doors were thrown open. The MacGregor waved Kitchens through the thick brocade blocking the view beyond. Kitchens could imagine pistols, swords, snares, pits, snakes—anything in the darkness behind the cloth. What he could smell was more of the corpse odor, leaking out of the room beyond the arras.

He pushed through anyway, afraid for the first time in many years.

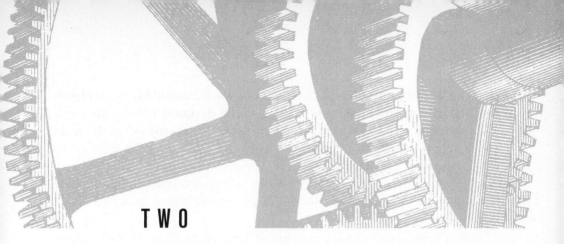

T W O

BOAZ

The Chinese air sailors made their way through a bleached, barren country. Pale rock rose in columns twice the height of a man, each topped with a darker, overhanging capstone. Everything was crusted in a white fuzz that Boaz finally realized was salt. The sun beat down like a molten hammer, warming his brass shell and even the crystals within his head.

Chin Ping walked close behind Boaz.

"I am remembering more," the Brass said aloud, almost unwillingly.

"More, ah?"

"More of matters which properly I should not recall."

"Is echo," Chin Ping responded.

"Echo," Boaz muttered. The Chinese might have the right of it, at that.

He had never been to this place before, not during all the centuries of his life, yet it seemed familiar. As if each step were bringing him closer to a forgotten home.

Yet forgetting was something he could *not* do. Memories could be stolen from him, as Paolina had so painfully proven, but they could not slip away as did the thoughts of men. He could well imagine what the girl would have said to this:

"*Explore; find your way; open what has been closed.*"

Not Paolina's words, for she spoke differently, but surely her meaning.

"Sometimes ghost come," Chin Ping added to Boaz' surprise. "Pass by, leave thought in head."

A ghost of someone he'd never been. Except, of course, all Brass were the same, from the first hammered in the foundry by the wise power of King Solomon himself. Brass were Brass, different in their roles and duties, but one metal, one sword in the hand of an ancient king, united by the Seals glowing in their heads.

Shem, the very word of YHWH.

"I believe that you are correct," Boaz told Chin Ping. "A thought has been left in my mentarium."

They slogged onward over the broken, uneven ground until the columns gave way to sloping dunes netted down by indifferent grass. The ocean sparkled close by.

Chin Yuen shouted orders. Some of the men headed along their back-trail. Others raced forward to scout to the water's edge.

Boaz stood still, soaking in the flood of memory.

A vessel. Ship-fat, square-sterned and slow as any merchanter too proud to run before a pirate.

A storm. Water raised high to strike at an impious, impudent fleet.

A coast. Rock-bound and time-worn, even here in the early days of Creation, anvil for the hammer of the seas.

Somehow the broken-backed fleet did not vanish entirely beneath the angry ocean. Brass and flesh, angel and servant, ox and boy—they dragged themselves up the beach like Noah's rearguard.

Lightning raged among the rocks. Freshwater floods turned the shoreline to sliding muck. Some people died, more did not, as wrack was wrenched ashore to the cost of straining muscles and more than one burst heart.

The great fleet out of Asiongaber was no more. Her people and her ad-miral walked the Abyssinian coast with their eyes still on distant Ophir and the awful majesty of the Wall. A man greater than all the kings of old waited in a jeweled palace back in Jerusalem. A mission spread before them.

Some things could not be carried into darkness' heart. Some things were safer left behind, secured against return. Ships might die, but so long as men sailed on, the mission was never lost.

A cliff. Scarred by sand, hidden among the dunes, an errant bone of the earth exposed to harsh light and the ravages of weather.

A cave. Grave-dank hole, a collapsed tube of softer stone eaten away by the cares of the world and the ceaseless patience of water.

A box. Laid within, marked by runes and seals, ensorcelled with the magic of the divine to hide it from prying eyes.

Safety, the lie of treasure hidden in a place to which no one ever re-turned. Until today.

If he had been made of monkey meat, Boaz would have awoken sweating. As it was, he stood quiet in the moonlight. A fire crackled to itself nearby. Chinese voices chattered softly.

A fire? he thought. *They must deem themselves safe from the British here.*

The men had scavenged driftwood to burn. He could not see the flames, but a glow edged the line of dunes between Boaz and the sea. The men were silhouetted atop a sandy ridge. That was very unlike Chin Yuen, here in the country of his enemies.

Paolina would have suggested some more subtle method of signaling. A fire in a bucket, perhaps, or an arrangement of lenses, to keep them safely hidden until need and opportunity presented.

His mind circled the fear, seeking distractions. Boaz forced his thoughts back toward the . . . dream? *Memory.* Brass did not dream. Not even renegade, flawed Brass such as himself.

Memory.

Of this place. Somewhere nearby was a cave, protected by magic as old as Solomon, as old as the Seal inside Boaz' head. If only Paolina were here to discuss the problem, to think it through in her strange, human way. She would have seen the true meaning of this memory far better than his poor sense of time and self could discern.

Boaz resisted the urge to race toward the cave, wherever it might be. He had no way of knowing—the memory was a fragment of this place, not a map.

He walked carefully into the dunes. There was a cliff to be discovered, and a cave within. The simple logic of geology and place would help him know where to search, for such a rock wall could not be hidden under every slope of sand.

CHILDRESS

After the storm, they held a council session on the conning tower. The place was small as ever, barely room for four to stand together, that space interrupted by the speaking tube and the small metal pilot's wheel. The ocean smelled new, clean, bright. Even the horizons seemed freshly scrubbed. The Wall loomed to their south, a brooding reminder of God's handiwork in the world. Childress fancied she could see a glint of brass at the top.

She would never grow accustomed to the sight, nor ever understand whether the Wall was a prison to trap man upon the Earth, or a stairway meant to open up the heavens.

God's plan was obscure, even to God, or so it seemed. Reverend Chea-
dle back at the church of St. John Horofabricus in New Haven would have
been appalled at the thought.

Childress chuckled as Sun-Wei, the chief engineer, scrambled up the
ladderway. Captain Leung and Chief al-Wazir were already in the crowded
tower.

"Why do you laugh?" Sun-Wei asked, speaking with sufficient care that
she could follow his Chinese.

She worked a moment to construct a coherent reply. "The world is too
large for one woman."

Leung chuckled. "I would have thought to say the world was too small
for even one woman."

"Only some women," al-Wazir said, glancing toward the Wall.

Paolina, thought Childress. "There is much to be done here. The Chinese
effort on their Golden Bridge threatens to take their empire across to the
Southern Earth. I cannot see yet how to stop it, but I will. In any case, we
must take a respite first. *Somewhere*. To that end, tell me more of this Goa."

"The port is . . ." Leung glanced at a paper clipped to his map. "In English you say Old Goa. Goa Velha, the Portuguese call it."

"Portugal is a protectorate of the British Crown," Childress said. "I do
not see how this is of aid to us."

"I dinna know for certain," al-Wazir said slowly. "I never sailed to Goa,
not on any of my ships, but the wet-ears like it well enough. A free
province, that Her Imperial Majesty never took the charter of. It's all card
houses and fancy gi—" He stopped, embarrassed.

"Chief, I believe I understand." Childress kept the gentle amusement
from her voice. "They don't bar the harbors to foreign ships or neutral
flags."

Leung cleared his throat. "Even so, a submarine might be taken amiss.
Your navy does not make use of them, preferring to contend from the air.
There will be no mistaking our origins."

"Then we shall fly another flag," Childress announced.

Both Leung and al-Wazir looked horrified. Sun-Wei just appeared
puzzled.

She stared them down. "Are you concerned with sailing under false
colors? What colors do we sail under today, pray tell me?"

"None," al-Wazir admitted.

She bored on. "We cannot sail under the Chinese flag. I don't imagine
the White Ensign is aboard, and our valiant submarine would deceive no
one even if she did show that English banner. *Quod erat demonstrandum*,
we fly another flag."

"But 'tis wrong," al-Wazir said.

"What flag do you suggest?" Leung asked.

Childress took hold of her temper, which threatened a rare escape. "Do you have any territorial ensigns aboard? A flag of Singapore, or Taiwan?"

Leung barked a series of orders to Sun-Wei, then smiled. "Singapore is my birthplace. Also a former British outpost. It would be appropriate. Sadly, I do not carry it."

"Then I shall design one for us. I know your men can sew."

Al-Wazir grunted. "You're both cracked."

Leung began to plot a course. Al-Wazir stared moodily at the extent of the Wall rising to their south. Childress watched a school of silver fish skimming the wavetops like so many coins and wondered how they would be received in Goa.

Their entrance to the port in no wise resembled *Five Lucky Winds'* homecoming to Tainan. The harbor was different here, merely a great, shallow river mouth. The bar was about two miles wide, offering little shelter from westerly storms. The old Portuguese town perched several miles up the river, not even affording the luxury of an airship tower. That suited Childress' purposes well enough, since it meant no nosy British captains lounging at the rail to remark upon the arrival of a submarine in their waters.

Even if there had been, she and Leung had little choice. The submarine's battery problems continued to elude resolution. This meant she could not long remain submerged below snorkel depth. Airships were very good at killing submarines, Childress had been given to understand—one reason the Royal Navy had never troubled itself with the difficult, dangerous vessels. *Five Lucky Winds'* only safety from attack lay in deep waters, moving quietly far enough below the surface to evade watchful eyes.

As they drew closer, she realized why they saw no towers at Goa Velha. There was barely a town. Just a collection of massive churches atop a hill sloping up from the estuary, surrounded by fields and huts. A half-rotted dock jutted out into the riparian waters, two fishing boats tied alongside.

The greenery of the shore struck her as strange, too. Neither the tropical riot of Chersonesus Aurea, nor the more measured greens of a New England spring, this place was dusky, dusty and dark. The grasses by the roadside were burned a deeper shade than she might have expected. The wind brought unfamiliar scents as well, more resembling Tainan than New Haven.

Leung shouted orders down the speaking tube, slowly conning the submarine in to her mooring.

This was the most dangerous part of their plan. An excitable English officer with artillery to hand could end all their hopes between one breath and the next. For that reason alone, the sleepy isolation of Goa Velha was a welcome sight to Childress.

Even a small town should have food for sale. The river here promised an abundance of water, though she might prefer not to drink the murky stuff.

She would be the Mask Childress here, speaking to whatever bishop or local farmer came to the docks to treat with them.

Their flag snapped overhead, false as it could be. After further argument Childress had sketched out a narrowing quadrangle, the shape of a pennant with the tip cut off. The field was white, hopefully signifying a lack of warlike intent to the English coupled with the Chinese color of mourning. The device on the banner was a simplified gear, square-toothed and hollow, a solid circle set within.

The Earth, Northern and Southern halves united in heraldry as they were not in life. "We sail all oceans," Childress had urged. "Pursuing peace in the world. Let us put the world on our flagstaff and they all may wonder at our coming."

"They'll be wondering at our submarine," al-Wazir had growled.

However the locals chose to read the submarine's banner, they neither fled screaming nor mounted a welcoming party. A handful of fishermen tended the gear aboard their boats, incuriously eyeing the arriving vessel. Farmers working the fields along the shore did not even look up.

Sailors sprang ashore and made the submarine fast to piers of dubious substance. Even Childress could see this would not be a place to tarry. "I doubt we will find fuel here," she said, "nor machined parts. Food, yes."

"Information as well," replied Leung, biting his lip. "Beginning with the knowledge that the Beiyang Navy's charts are inaccurate. Clearly the British have moved whatever port was once here to some other locale."

"And you're complaining now, are ye?" Al-Wazir eyed the skies, looking for airships on the rise. "Better we trot through this little costume play like good kiddies than stride onto Her Imperial Majesty's battlefields not even knowing our lines."

After a few minutes, Childress took herself down to the deck.

"Nothing is here," Bai, one of the ratings, said to her in Chinese.

Childress smiled. "This is England's doorstep," she replied.

She was still dressed in her ship's castoffs. Touched by sun, with her hair pulled into a queue by Lao Mu, she could almost pass for one of the crew within the shapeless blue top and straight-legged trousers.

Bai laid down a plank for her to step ashore. Another agreement: She would go first if there was no obvious course of action, mumble in Chinese at need and listen to what was said in English. If Portuguese was the language here, so much the worse that they did not have Paolina. Childress' face would fool no one, of course, but they counted on the thin hope that the clothes would make her the man she wasn't.

Childress was not above a bit of brazening if it came to that. Something else the woman she had been would barely have understood, but long months of violence and deprivation had changed much within her.

She reached the end of the dock and set foot in India. Nothing in particular happened except that a mule brayed. Childress looked up the hill to see a corpulent man riding down the road. His skin was sun-reddened, and he was dressed in black vestments.

A priest, though whether Portuguese Catholic or good Church of England she could not say. Childress briefly examined her standing with God and decided that nothing had changed of late. The last time she'd knelt to prayer had been inside that Catholic church in Singapore, under the watchful eye of a priest who himself had hailed from somewhere here in India. Where that young man had been handsome in a sort of nut-brown way, even from a distance, this fellow on the mule gave the impression of being resolutely uncomfortable.

For a moment, she was almost overwhelmed with the temptation to beg for mercy, to ask to be released from her durance vile aboard an enemy vessel on the high seas. Childress laughed at herself, her voice pealing silver-bright into the warming air of this Asian morning.

She tossed the thought aside and strode forward to meet the priest, trusting the others to trust her with the task. If she could not speak with a divine after all her years in the Day Missions Library at Yale, then her presence aboard *Five Lucky Winds* was little more than a waste.

WANG

The rakish yacht *Fortunate Conjunction* had not been constructed along traditional lines. The glossy white paint and teakwood decking appeared so very English. The Kô, for all his Confucian propriety, was a man of forward leanings. Very unusual, in the Imperial Court. Wang had come aboard her by the night, along with the water barrels.

Being packed out of the library that had been his entire work this past six years took only a few hours. Once the Kô's mind was fixed on something, everyone on the island hewed to the letter of his intent. One of the senior Mandarins had even come down from the ruined palace to scowl disapprovingly. The readers at their research had barely noticed, but Wang's little covey of archivists and papermakers and bookbinders and clerks had been set to panicked fluttering.

His belongings were down to a small silk roll—much had been discarded, or held against a return that Wang had already come to realize was highly unlikely. His work had been transferred to the offices of Yoo Wing-Chou, his first deputy, and he had secreted the little round statue of some ancient goddess in an inner pocket before lowlier servants came to sweep his chambers clean.

The Kô was erasing Cataloger Wang from the Golden Bridge, as thorough a purge as man could ask for who did not now sleep a head shorter than when he had awoken.

"You've gone and spilled the vinegar, haven't you?" said a man, interrupting the drift of Wang's thoughts.

He was surprised to find a monk next to him at the prow of the ship. The sailors had not threatened the cataloger's life, but neither had they made him welcome. The prow seemed safest, for it had been deserted since they'd cast off with careful soundings of the island's twisted little harbor. Wang had been small, fat and slow as a boy. He knew the trouble that could find an unpopular personage in what someone else had decided was the wrong place.

"I do not know," Wang admitted with uncharacteristic frankness. Another lesson of his youth, as well as of his service of the Dragon Throne: Say as little as possible, for in time someone, somewhere will surely call you to account for your words.

The monk smiled as he rooted about in a leather pouch slung across his saffron robes. "Ah!" he finally announced, and pulled forth a small jade pipe.

A smaller pouch followed. The monk tamped down his smoking mix with a grubby finger, then lit it with a struck match. *Very English,* Wang thought. A long, slow pull on the bowl fired the embers enough to touch the monk's face with orange light.

That was when Wang realized he had been speaking to a woman. Her cheekbones had shown in the flaring light so he could see past the robes, the shorn head, the wind-chapped face.

"You . . . ," he said, then stopped.

"I am a monk, yes." She took another long pull from her pipe. It did not smell of opium, but rather of a sickly sweet herb.

Hemp, of course.

"You are a monk," he said, then closed his mouth. What business of this was his? He was already lost, rushed away from his place in the order of things on the irritated word of a man who could order Wang's death out of sheer, indolent boredom. Surely the Kô knew who was aboard his own ship.

"Unanswered questions are the way the world teaches us our limitations."

"Rude monks are the way the world teaches us humility," Wang countered.

She laughed at that, her voice snatched away by the wind off the ocean. *Fortunate Conjunction* slid swiftly through the night-dark waters among the islands of the Kepulauan Riau.

They were in for a long sail to Phu Ket, he was sure, even at this yacht's speed.

The monk offered Wang her pipe. He shook his head. Neither spirits nor smoke had ever served him well. He treasured the sharpness of his mind, such as it might be, far too much to blunt his intellect with temptation.

Without reason, he was nothing.

"Are you a friend of the Kô?" she asked after a while.

"Have you *met* him?" Wang blurted, then covered his mouth in horror.

"Even the dragon at the gates of Hell has friends. It might have been better to ask if you know the Kô as a man."

"No," said Wang, his voice slowing. He had already betrayed himself several times over to this monk, should she have the ear of power. "I only know him as a dragon at the gates."

She grunted, finished her bowl, and tapped the ashes back into her pouch. Pale fish skimmed away from their bow, fleeing among the sheltering waves. Not so many weeks ago a great storm had risen here. A fleet had been murdered—an incident that might well yet end their mining of the ancient knowledge of Chersonesus Aurea to rebuild the Golden Bridge of the ancients.

"Have courage, little man," the monk said. She brushed fingertips against Wang's cheek. "You are being called, not sent. That is the difference between an ox-cart to Heaven and a chariot to Hell."

PAOLINA

There seemed to be as much upward as downward on *a Murado*. Ascending the northern face of the Wall had not been nearly so difficult. It seemed the wildness of the Southern Earth was matched by the wildness of *a Murado*'s southern face.

"Follow," the angel had said before flying off into the mists. Follow *what*? Paolina began to wish she'd remained in the ruined temple atop the Wall, up against the towering brass of the gear ring. The building had been fascinating and strange, the grounds not yet utterly wild. She and Ming could have stayed a long time, living off the neglected orchards, the rabbits, the old gardens overflowing with feral vegetables in the cool damp.

It would have been for naught, she realized. The whole point in her crossing the Wall was to escape the entanglements of Northern Earth. Too many had died by her hand. She'd made the hardest choices, then found them snatched away.

Try as she might, Paolina could not bring herself once more to the point of being willing to submit to unreason. Simply erasing the knowledge and skill to make another stemwinder was not enough to stop the men of that world from seeking to strip bare her mind, body and soul.

They knew no limits, no more than any man did.

Some were different. Al-Wazir. Perhaps that Chinese captain, Ming's commander who'd sent him away with her.

Boaz, a voice whispered unbidden somewhere deep inside her head.

"He is not a man," she shouted. The words were a lie before ever they left her mouth—if anything was true of her lost Brass, he was definitely a man. Not in the matters of shaving and *pilinhas*. Rather, the shape of him.

Paolina could not set Boaz aside.

KITCHENS

The MacGregor did not follow Kitchens into the abattoir. The clerk stepped alone into a room so underlit as to be almost black. Great, shadowed shapes loomed, while the thumping and the stench were much stronger.

A narrow-bodied man in a black coat and maroon watered silk vest barred Kitchens' way. His monocle gleamed with a faint concentration of light. The man held a top hat in his hand, as if just alighting from a carriage.

"Are you expected?"

"Yes," Kitchens said simply. He wondered how many unexpected visitors anyone in Blenheim Palace received, passing through so many layers of sharp-eyed men and their conceits of secrecy.

"The clerk. From London."

Kitchens touched the brim of his bowler, comforted by the weight of the sharpened pennies sewn within. This man was the first person in Blenheim who'd frightened him. All the others were just duty-in-boots, not much different from Kitchens himself. This fellow had the frightening intensity of someone who truly believed.

"I am Dr. Stewart. Step this way."

He turned, top hat still in hand, and threaded between a pair of massive bellows that creaked in time to the thumping. Past them was a small pool of light where an elderly woman in a fine dress sat picking at a framed cloth with a needle and thread before another great, hulking machine.

Her Imperial Majesty! Kitchens thought with an excited leap of his heart, but he quickly settled. This woman was years too young, for all the gray in her hair, and of a different build.

She rose to her feet at the sound of footsteps, her eyes screwed shut against the glare of the lamp. "I am afraid the Queen is indisposed."

One of the maids of the Queen's chambers, then. That she was here in this strange, reeking place bore frightening implications.

"All is well, Daphne," said Dr. Stewart. "It is only I, and a man from London to see Her Imperial Majesty."

That was when Kitchens realized the maid's eyes were not screwed shut against the glare. Rather, her lids were sewn together, with thick, dark sutures that bristled like a hedgehog's quills.

Then why the lamp? he wondered.

Daphne dropped her chin, folded her hands and stepped aside. Kitchens noted she kept the needle in her fist. A good blow with that between her fingers could be troublesome.

Dr. Stewart stepped into the pool of light, slid aside the sewing frame and addressed himself to a small, gleaming black quadrangle set into the curving bulk next to which Daphne had been seated. "Your Imperial Majesty," he whispered with exaggerated care, enunciating slowly, "the Admiralty clerk is here to see you."

Something low and raspy rumbled in the darkness. The sound carried the crackling hum of a loudspeaker. Stewart cocked his head, listened a moment, and nodded. "Of course, Your Highness."

He stepped back from the little porthole. "The Queen will see you now, Clerk."

Kitchens was afraid again—afraid of the blind maid with the needle in her hand, afraid of this doctor who smelled like a slaughterhouse, afraid of whatever relic of England's monarch rested in the gigantic coffin with the little window.

Nonetheless, fear had been part of his training. He stepped forward with a reflexive bow toward the doctor, fought the urge to kneel, and peered into the gleaming, dark window.

Imagine a woman left to float in saltwater the temperature and composition of the amniotic fluid through which all fetuses swim. Imagine a woman fed through tubes in her throat, tight sewn to leave her mouth free for bubbling speech. Imagine a woman grown large, metamorphosing into a cetacean goddess of bitter vengeance against the land walkers with their hard-toothed splinters and their water-cutting hulls. Imagine a woman alone in the dark with her damaged thoughts, her mentation assisted by a clever array of difference engines feeding their outputs through copper wires drilled carefully into the phrenologically correct places on her shaved and tattooed scalp. Imagine her spirit, fighting the old, old loss of her beloved and the mounting burdens of Empire and the sense that a body can be kept far beyond its time; yet as life always seeks life, so the body seeks to live, even here, even now.

Like the queens of old when ice lay upon all the land and the sun had grown small and forgotten its benison upon the world, she was oracle for her people. Sacrificed in the dark to float on rivers of blood and think the strange thoughts of brass machines.

All of this was apparent to Kitchens as he peered through the little window at the pale, bloated face washed with oily, dark fluid. Eyes vacant as polished opals stared back at him from amid an encircling nest of wires. Fluid bubbled on the pallid lips.

There was no mistaking the lines of that raddled visage: She was still and always Alexandrina Victoria.

"Your Highness," he whispered. "What have they done to you?"

More fluid bubbled from the dead-fleshed lips as a voice boomed and screeched from the loudspeakers. "You are the clerk."

The words, Kitchens noted, did not seem to match the popping of her lips. "I am," he replied. "Unworthy of your attentions."

"War brews," the speakers announced. Again, her lips moved, but not in time to the words. "The Oriental steals a march upon us."

"Yes, Your Highness." Kitchens watched closely, for he was by no means certain what he saw in the tank had anything to do with what he heard.

She rolled slightly in her fluid bed, like a log caught on the tide, until the famous profile came into view—chin, nose, and cheeks. Nothing was familiar about the horror of her scalp.

"You readied the Scotsman we sent before." The one rot-pale eye he could see flickered back and forth. "Follow him and the German. They have become lost to us at this worst of times. Bring our will to them, and their word home."

Kitchens did not ask why he should be the one, for that was the one question no special clerk ever asked. He did not ask why Africa and the Wall, for that was a question to which he already knew the answer. The question he would have voiced, had he possessed the nerve, was to wonder for what purpose the Queen—or the people of her household—had called him here to her bedside. Vatside. His mind failed on the word.

A memorandum would have done this job, without the horror.

"I will go, Your Highness." His words were a whisper, almost a caress.

"The Oriental steals the greatest march upon us. England will fall if we do not stand. You must unlock the secrets. But first . . ." The loudspeakers trailed off in a rumbling hiss. She rolled back to face him, then shrugged. Gelid, pale fat was barely visible rippling beneath the dark fluids. An arm emerged, spastic and slow, slick-sheened as any suet pudding, to touch something below Kitchens' line of vision.

Bolts slid back with an audible clunk. Pressure equalized with a hiss. A section of the tank popped loose. A hatch, Kitchens realized, with the little window square at its center.

Behind him, Daphne whimpered. Dr. Stewart muttered imprecations.

The hatch opened, and the dripping, ancient arm of Empire reached up. Kitchens took the withered hand within his own. The Queen's grip tightened until his fingers were threatened. She held him there, close as a lover, deadly as old murder, for a long ten count before releasing her clutch and slithering safely back into the tank.

The hatch shut a moment later. Bolts clicked home. A pump chittered as pressure was restored.

"She rarely does that," Dr. Stewart said from behind him. "Sometimes we cannot get her to open up even when it is required."

Kitchens turned, realized he had something damp in the palm of the hand that still ached from the Queen's grip. "Why!?"

"Because England needs her," Stewart said.

"The needs of the Empire are the needs of the many," the loudspeaker squawked. The voice sounded ever more alien to Kitchens. He looked at Daphne, who was stabbing herself in the thigh with her needle, right through her dress. He then glanced at Stewart, whose monocle had fogged over.

Kitchens turned back through the dark, reeking room to the curtains, and through the curtains to the hallway where the angry Scotsman stood. Now the clerk understood the MacGregor's fury.

"You've seen for yourself, man." His erstwhile guide's voice was flat steel.

"Yes." They began to retrace their steps through Blenheim Palace. For all his patient training, Kitchens could not hold the next question inside. "How many know?"

"Only one who matters." The MacGregor's words began to tremble. "She knows what they've done to her."

"Stewart? Lloyd George?" The matter of guilt suddenly became of intense interest to him, who had always been far more focused on ends than means.

"Them. And the real masters as well."

Kitchens was not searched again, though his equipment and belongings were restored to him. He was just as glad of it, for he would have fought to death to keep the damp, bloody token the Queen had given him.

GASHANSUNU

The circle in which she spent her hours met now, unquiet as any broken stem. Her city, indifferent power of the Southern Earth, navel of the Shadow World, had made its unease known these past days. Citrine and chartreuse had been called from the sunrise—colors rarely seen—while birds dropped exhausted from the sky, their hearts burst within their jewel-feathered chests.

These colors, these sendings, signified regrets. She wondered whose misdeeds had set the tones of the world to disharmony. The music of the circles sustained all. When one or another lapsed, the tones lapsed with them and everything fell to cacophony.

Baassiia stood centerpost to the meeting, his *wa* hovering closer than was usually the case. Even the Silent World was unquiet, Gashansunu knew.

He was a massive man, their circle caller, dark as a wine-soaked betel nut, with the fire of the sun blazing inside the snake of his chest. There was a tender mercy to his long fingers and the insolent curve of his blade, so that when he approached the heartstone even the sacrifice would cease to protest and instead smile into the vacant arches of death.

"We gather," Baassiia said. His voice echoed with the power of his *wa*, as if he spoke from a well. "We listen. We seek. We find."

"We find," the circle answered. This was not a working, just a consultation, so the ritual was abbreviated to lend comfort and sensibility to those who followed.

Gashansunu regarded Baassiia with the patience of obsidian, though inside she roiled more like hot rock. The center's beauty was not lost on her, for all that the initiates of Westfacing House were supposed to be beyond such worldly concerns. His eyes strayed past her, gaze pausing for the merest moment.

Long enough to meet the flash of her secret smile.

"Who among us has seen testimony from the Silent World?" he asked. His *wa* stirred, moving like spiderwebs on the wind.

No one answered.

"Who among us has read the passing of the birds?"

Ninsunu spoke. A terrible little vixen, that one, Gashansunu thought, and climbing for a sacred seat in the Westfacing House years earlier than was the norm. "I turned three and three of them from inside to out, to read their haruspices."

Baassiia nodded with a slow, brutal power. It was like watching a rock acknowledge a tree. "Did they show you aught of the city's distress?"

"They show another passage of power across the Wall. The impure North sends again what it cannot keep cleanly within its craw."

The center looked around. Eight faces looked back, three and three and three the number of a working. Gashansunu knew Ninsunu to be a terrible little liar, but there was something like truth in her words, even if her tale was concocted.

"Who among us has read the colors?"

This time Gashansunu answered. "The greens are for what grows toward us surely as poisonweed in a usurer's garden ditch. The yellows are the sign of angels, that some foreign god has sent her minions."

"We will not dance again to those tune-callers," Baassiia replied.

They spoke around the circle a while, each mouth adding a word, until the wisdom of the city came from their three threes of lips like song from a pod of merfolk. Though Gashansunu listened until her ears ached, she always heard the individual voices, not their union.

THREE

And it came to pass at the time of the going down of the sun, that Joshua commanded, and they took them down off the trees, and cast them into the cave wherein they had been hid, and laid great stones in the cave's mouth, which remain until this very day. —*Joshua 10:27*

BOAZ

Chin Yuen's beach fire remained a fitful glow in the sky, though Boaz quickly lost sight of the sailors on their dune top. He wished them well of whatever they hoped to call down with their beacon.

If he'd been human, Boaz knew he'd be tired. Brass didn't have muscles, blood, the little furnaces of flesh and bone that drove animals and people forward. The Solomonic Seal in his head was sufficient to power him through a dozen human lifetimes. But even his kind needed to stop for metal to cool, joints to ease, tiny caches of lubricant to seep forth.

Perhaps most importantly, to settle thoughts.

Brass debated why King Solomon had gifted them with a need to rest. Some said it was so their kind could follow the clocks of men and pursue their daily affairs in a conjoined rhythm. Others claimed it was a necessity not to challenge YHWH's plan for the world by creating an unsleeping intelligence, as the Divine had placed no speaking, thinking creature who did not daily retreat to the fields of dream. Even the monsters from high along the wall had their dens and nesting places.

Boaz favored the theory that King Solomon had intended Brass to share in the dreaming of men, that their minds might fall idle and drift across the landscapes of consciousness bereft of direction and intent. From dreams came prophecy, understanding, the very physiognomy of the soul.

Sand was both slick and sharp beneath his feet. Boaz had been formed, as all Brass, with the likeness of muscles in his outer shell, along with the necessary cannulae and outlets for such cables and braces as were required for full articulation. His sense of touch was exquisite, so each step brought a thousand thousand grains into rough contact with his soles. The wind worried at him, such that if he were to be stopped completely for a long while in this place as once before far to the west along the Wall, he would awaken to a dull-scarred casing. Enough sand within his joints without eventual maintenance from the Palace of Authority in Ophir, and in time he would fail.

Without a moon, the night sky was a riot of glory, shedding sufficient light for Boaz to pick his way. The dunes looming around him were darker. These were waves slowed almost to freezing, progressing through their dusty sea over months and years. His sense of imminent recollection was failing again. Those memories so sharp by day had become a kind of dream. The soul he imagined for himself, awoken in him by Paolina, fed by her, sustained by her, seemed a dream as well.

With her now gone to a Chinese prison, that soul was lost to him.

He scuffed at a scattering of gravel. Something of the true shape of the land was visible here, the sea floor atop which the dune waves passed. More gravel wound ahead between two of the sand hills, into a deeper vale of shadow.

The Brass followed.

Air grew colder as he stepped into the shadows. Something electrick crackled on the wind. He felt a slickness of his casing, like dewfall descending. The dune sides seemed steeper here, almost impossibly so.

A cliff rose ahead, a rock face emerging from beneath the sand. His memories stirred once more. Even in the shadows, he could see this was of the same pale stone as they'd passed during the afternoon. The bones of this land, laid down in the six working days of Creation and bared as the world aged into itself in the millennia since.

He approached slowly, uncertain what to expect. Carved lions, perhaps, or the chiseled sigils of a temple. Magical gates gleaming with a deep inner light of their own. What he saw instead was steep rock with a tumbled pile at the bottom, as if a fall had taken place in some earlier era.

But the pile was too well laid. Living on the Wall these past centuries, Boaz was quite familiar with rock falls. They spread out like river deltas, a mix of stones from dust grains to whatever monstrous boulders had been loosed.

These rocks were mostly of a size, and while not close-fitted as a temple wall, they were well stacked. As if built by someone who meant them to stay where they were. A Brass, lifting the heaviest alongside dozens of sweating men stripped to their ragged trousers as they too labored under a merciless sun. A man shouting in the bright light of recall, words half-heard and quarter-familiar. A priest—a Kohanim such as they had not seen upon the Wall in at least a thousand years—chanting from a book. His ancient blessing in memory was so strong that for a moment Boaz thought he heard a voice in the present day.

He blinked away the sight and stared thoughtfully at the boulders.

A Brass can easily move four or five times the weight a very strong man can shift. Though they need to rest, they do not tire in the human sense. Monkey bodies lose vigor over the hours of a day until they are finally claimed by sleep. Not Brass, who can run just as swiftly and lift just as much in the last watch of the night as under the burgeoning light of dawn.

Boaz shook off the dream-phantoms that had dogged him and set to unstacking the boulders. He knew without consideration which to take first and which to take later, for the ordering of this pile was still in his memory. Even the largest were within his ability to lift, further confirming what he already knew about this place.

Laboring, Boaz wondered how often the rocks had been buried beneath sand. Had he come in another season of the wind, he might never have found this.

Very close to dawn he reached a crack in the cliff. Eager to have access, Boaz pushed aside the last of the obscuring rocks.

Sand slid free. This place had definitely been under the dunes. Behind the sand stood a wooden wall, or possibly a door. It was very old, silvered by moonlight and age both, riddled with the tracks of worms, abraded by the insults of time. Boaz ran his fingers over the surface. Clinkered planks, sawn as a slab to fit in this place.

A piece of the hull from one of the ships in Asiongaber's fleet.

His fingers traced the lines on the wood, feeling the textures of ancient seas. Almost three thousand years had passed since the wreck that had founded the Brass nation. All of Ophir's history ran through this doorway, back to Asiongaber and Jerusalem in the bright days when YHWH's people held their kingdom in close-wrought power beneath the hand of their Lord.

As if at the command of his thought, the ancient wood collapsed in a cloud of dust and splinters. Behind Boaz, someone murmured. He turned to see Chin Ping, with half a dozen men and Chin Yuen as well. They all stood in the dark, eyes gleaming, waiting to see what he would do.

This is my history, Boaz thought, but he said nothing to the band of armed enemies crowding close behind him as he stooped to pass within the crack in the cliff and step across the gates of history.

———

Chin Yuen lit a stick of punk. The sputtering flame lit the cave like a distant artillery bombardment.

The space was small, barely more than a wide crack in the cliff. An altar stood before Boaz, three ashlars rough-worked from the native rock then stacked in a table. Dusty threads showed the remains of an altar cloth. A brittle ceramic lamp perched at one edge. In the center lay a bundle wrapped in cracked leather positioned at a slight angle, as if the Kohanim priest had dropped the thing and stepped away too quickly to see that it was properly square.

Another whisper of Chinese behind him, then Chin Ping: "This is place of Brass people?"

"Not precisely," Boaz said absently. He was tired again, in that too-human way, but also shaking with a sense of impending time and the collapse of destiny like a moon tumbling loose from the sky. "But our nation was born here."

His fingers brushed the lamp, which seemed likely to vanish just as the door had done. Somehow it remained intact beneath Boaz' gentlest touch. He picked up one of the surviving threads of the altar cloth. Silver, or gold, woven into a textile that had not survived the years.

Finally, the leather.

The bundle had heft. Boaz cradled it in his arms the way he might have carried a wounded animal. It fit as if folded for the grip of a Brass. All Brass were from the same mold, after all—Boaz himself was the strangest of his race already, thanks to Paolina and her will, but still virtually identical to all of his fellows.

He wished she could be here now. Perhaps there was something she could see in this place, some hint he might miss for carelessness or excitement or distraction or sheer lack of understanding.

With only the glittering gaze of his enemies for witness, Boaz unfolded the leather to discover what secrets might lie within.

WANG

The mate Wu, who had hustled Wang aboard the night before, leaned on the prow. There had been no evidence of the monk this morning, and the cataloger wondered where she was. *Fortunate Conjunction* was small, a dozen *bù* from stem to stern, twenty paces for a man not in a hurry. She rode low as well, the pilothouse her tallest point. She was much tidier and faster than any vessel Wang had ever traveled on.

"Sir," Wang said, offering himself.

Wu spat downwind. Then he turned to face Wang.

The cataloger knew he was pudgy, pale, a man who spent far too much time on a stool. The mate was a man carved to sail the seas. The infelicitious shade of sun-darkened skin that would have branded Wang as a peasant somehow became heroic on Wu, hinting at manly deeds and blood spilled in the righteous service of the Emperor.

Wang did not like blood.

"You were called, not sent," Wu said after a while.

The echo of the monk's words surprised Wang. "So I have been told," he answered cautiously.

"*Fortunate Conjunction* is not a lucky ship."

Those two statements did not converge happily in Wang's mind. He remained silent to see what the mate might offer next.

Wu surrendered first in the staring match, speaking with care. "You are no prisoner to be guarded or beaten or fed on water and rotten rice. Yet you are not free to go—not until you have answered the call."

"This is true." Wang tried to listen past this man's cautious words.

Then, in a rush of speech that reversed Wu's care to nervous rattle, Wu said, "You are also almost like a priest, yes?"

"I am a cataloger, which is a kind of librarian."

"A cataloger?"

"We practice the Rectification of Names among the words of men long dead. If you would seek advice on the best way to thresh millet, one of my kind will have made a list of those scrolls and books that discuss millet and other grains, the practices of agronomy, and the tools by which farmers pursue their daily tasks."

"So you know the proper order of things in the world." The mate leaned close. "Do you understand the hierarchies of Heaven and the Imperial Court and the small places of the Earth?"

"Who does not?" Wang blurted.

"We have a ghost aboard," Wu said, his voice now tinged with bitterness. "This ghost most certainly does not understand what is needful."

"Why not ask the monk?"

The look Wu gave the cataloger scorched him to silence.

An hour later, they climbed up from the bilge hatch. Wu shrugged. "The Kô holds the power of life and death. But even he cannot slay what cannot be brought before him."

Wang was grubby, bruised, bleeding from several small cuts, and now knew more about boats than he had ever intended. The mate had taken him through every *cun* of the boat, handspan by handspan, from the cables controlling the rudder to the little chain locker at the bow.

The only space they had not visited was the Kô's private cabin. The door was sealed with a blob of red wax binding a long red ribbon, and according to Wu it had been shut just so for months.

There was no monk. There was not even any sign of the monk. On a vessel this small, with eleven crew plus Wang, there was little possibility she could have slipped ahead or to the other side of the deck.

"She has been a ghost for how long?" Wang asked.

"Since we last sailed from Hainan to bring the Kô south to Chersonesus Aurea."

Wang puzzled at those words for a moment. "He was aboard with the ghost?"

"Yes, though we never knew him to see it."

"Did you ask?"

Wu gave him another smoldering glare. "Would you ask the Kô if he had seen a ghost?"

Aboard a vessel smaller than his sitting room in Beijing? "No," Wang admitted.

"A *female* ghost," Wu muttered. "Worse even than some distressed ancestor seeking vengeance."

"What would you have me do?"

"Use your powers to banish her from this boat. Or persuade her ashore. Rectify her name so she has no more hold here."

Wang shook his head. "I cannot simply bid her to be away. You do not need a librarian; you need a priest. Or a spiritual pulmonist."

"We had hoped," Wu said. "Captain Shen will not speak to the problem. I believe he fears even saying the words will lend dread power to this haunting."

The cataloger had briefly met Captain Shen at the helm. The man had been uninterested in anything but the course before him.

"Your captain is a creature of the Kô," Wang told the mate. "Freedom of thought is not so well rewarded in his service."

"We are all bound to him," Wu replied. "Like peasants in their field, we are sworn to *Fortunate Conjunction*, and through the boat to the Kô."

"Can you not take another ship should the mood strike you? Form a new crew?"

Wu's grin was terrible, a tight band of gleaming regret. "Not in this life, or the next. Someday we will sail with the Kô into Hell itself." He turned up a pale blue sleeve to show Wang a brand scarred onto the underside of his right forearm. *Chiang jian*, the mark of a rapist. "We are every one of us sentenced to death. That we even breathe today is only at his intercession. That we live to breathe tomorrow is only at his mercy."

"You are all dead men," Wang said, horrified.

The mate leaned close, eyes blazing. "We fear those we have sent to the next world to open the way before us."

Wang sat in the prow all day, the Andaman Sea splitting before the knife edge of *Fortunate Conjunction*'s keel. He contemplated the matter of the missing monk. Wu was convinced she had been a ghost, but then the mate himself was little different—a man in the world past the ordained time of his death. This was not *orderly*. Heaven, the Middle Kingdom and Hell all had their own arrangements, each reflecting the methods of the other like three mirrors in a great temple hall.

One could believe in the hierarchies of the other world without crediting superstitious hauntings. He'd spoken to the monk, watched her smoke a pipe, smelled the pungency of her herbs, heard the flap of her robes in the wind. She was no more a ghost than he. Or in truth, Wu.

Yet Wang and the mate had searched the boat stem to stern. Unless the monk had been very swift and stealthy, she could not have remained undetected.

Except for the obvious, of course. She was hiding in the Kô's cabin. It was the only place they had not searched.

Wang headed below to check the seals on the cabin door. He knew perfectly well how easy it was to forge such a thing. Ribbons were cheap, wax and lead easily worked. A clever man could cut a seal open from the back, with the slit of a knife tip or a quick slip of a razor.

Or a clever woman.

But how had she locked herself in?

With the aid of one of the crew, of course. Those silent, surly men kept secrets the way a cave kept darkness. Someone had slipped the monk in and out of the cabin.

Alone in the small companionway, Wang bent to examine the seal—a large blob of red wax with the impression of a dragon biting its tail, bound to the hatch handle by a twisting wire. He reached behind to explore.

A loop, clipped to a hook. The wire wasn't even joined at the back.

Wu glanced at the ladderway. Sunlight streamed in, but no shadow lurked close by. The other end of the short passage was a storage locker.

He slipped the seal free and pulled open the door.

The room was startling in its simplicity, much unlike the elaborate chambers of the Forbidden City, or even the Kô's quarters back on Chersonesus Aurea. A low, flat bed of black wood with pale *die*—tight-woven straw—for a mattress. Walls lacquered imperial red. A porthole rimmed in brass. A table to match the bed, empty now but clearly intended to host an altar. The smell of old incense, polishing oils, and the musk of damp straw from the *die*.

For the sake of thoroughness, Wang tugged open the closet door. Nothing but dust within, not even spare robes. He bent to look beneath the bed. Only someone folded paper-thin would have hidden there.

Why was the seal broken? Nothing was here to hide.

Wang backed out, frustrated. Where could the monk be? When he straightened from jiggering the seal back into place, he saw Wu staring from the ladderway. The mate just nodded once, then turned away.

A ghost, indeed. At least as ghostly as the rest of this strange crew.

Fortunate Conjunction reached a set of islands just as the day was failing. These were the most unusual formations Wang had ever seen, jutting like limestone thumbs. They resembled the most fanciful scrolls of Guilin. The lower edges overhung the water, as if their bases were being stolen away by the sea.

A rambling building covered the top of the nearest island. Wang realized it was a palace—wings and towers and jutting balconies, *shi* after *shi* of stonework and bamboo stretching farther than the largest Gan River rice farms of his youth in Chiang Hsi Province.

Not a building, a city.

Lights flickered within hundreds of windows. Gongs rang the watches of the evening. But no banners flew, no sigils depended. This fortress ruled itself, answered to no court or emperor, solitary above the porcelain-blue waters of the ocean.

"We are at Phu Ket?" he asked quietly of no one in particular.

One of the sailors glanced up at him, then answered in a thick Annamese accent. "Phu Ket lies east."

He turned that way. Land loomed on the horizon. "But that was my destination."

"Phu Ket is the port of entry, not the destination," said Wu, behind him. "Very few come straight to Phi Phi Leh. Most who do never return." The mate glanced into the waters of the night-darkening sea.

Wang followed his line of sight. Something ominous lay on the pale sand. A ship, the cataloger realized. His eyes roamed across other shadows, reefs of broken hulls and dead men. Captain Shen still stood at the wheel, eyes riveted on the fortress looming in the sky above.

"I am to row you to the dock," Wu added.

"Of course." Wang followed the mate to the rail, where a dinghy waited, a sailor already at the oars.

Wu climbed down the rope ladder. Wang followed. Another sailor tossed a bundle after them that nearly bounced into the ocean. Wang's meager belongings. A second bundle followed; then they pushed off.

Wu sat in the stern of the tiny boat, Wang in the bow. The other sailor rowed amidships, his back to Wang. No one spoke as they pulled across the waters. Dusk vanished in a blaze of stars before they reached a tiny dock at the foot of the overhanging cliffs.

The cataloger stepped cautiously from the dinghy to the ladder, then up to the dock. The sailor shipped the oars and followed Wang. Wu tossed up one bundle, then the other, which the sailor caught. He turned, looked at Wu, and winked.

The monk.

Of course, Wang thought, struck with amazement. Where else to hide but among the crew?

"Good luck," Wu said, then rowed away as if the woman had never existed.

She shucked out of her roughspun uniform. Wang turned away, embarrassed, once he realized what he was seeing. Moments later, she tapped him on the shoulder. The saffron robes were back, taken from the second bundle.

"I believe you are expected," the monk told him.

"Above?" Wang peered up at the rickety wooden stairs affixed to the side of the island cliffs. Hundreds of steps. Impossibly high. They made his head ache.

"The journey of a thousand steps begins with a single climb."

Wang couldn't think of a suitable response, so he picked up his bundle and began the endless trudge.

KITCHENS

Amberson, another of the special clerks, met Kitchens on his return to Paddington Station that evening. Quiet sympathy rode in the other man's eyes.

The two of them exchanged no words as they boarded a private carriage for the trip back to the Ripley Building. The enclosure reeked of someone else's cologne, and the smell of polished boots. Amberson handed Kitchens a blue leather folder. Most confidential, Crown privilege.

Kitchens ignored the rush of London outside the glass of his conveyance as he slit the pair of black ribbons binding shut the folder and looked within.

The typed note was unsigned. Kitchens didn't recognize the face from any particular typing machine. He didn't need to. The hand of Lloyd George touched everything he'd seen and felt this day.

You now understand the deepest secrets of the Empire. She has spoken. Go to Africa and find al-Wazir. Make the future ours.

Nothing more. No instructions, no vouchers, no orders. No plan. Kitchens had always been trained to work within a plan.

Worse, he had never before left England's shores. Rarely ventured beyond London, in truth. Africa! A mix of thrill and terror surged within him, and he ruthlessly suppressed it.

Turning to face his colleague, the clerk asked, "Were you briefed on any details? This is remarkably laconic."

Amberson frowned. "Not such as you'd find useful. HIMS *Notus* awaits you at the Dover towers."

"*Notus?*" Kitchens stared at Amberson. "I thought her captain and crew were being debriefed." He paused. "At length."

That was a polite way of saying that Captain Sayeed of HIMS *Notus* had been in a special interrogation unit at Pentonville prison these past weeks, his men held in isolation at Gosport's brigs. All for their involvement with Ottweill, and the girl-wizard from the Wall.

"*Notus.*" Amberson looked haunted. "She's to be used, and her captain and crew. You'll have warrants for their necks, Kitchens. Admiral's Mast has been held in secret. There'll never be a question asked if they don't come back."

Kitchens shivered despite himself. "And if I fail to return?"

"You will return."

"Of course." He still had the Queen's soggy gift concealed close about his person, untouched so far out of a mix of awe and fear. Her Imperial Majesty taking an interest in him personally had not been anything like he might have hoped. "I am ready whenever Admiralty wishes me to depart."

"The crew will be in place within two days." Amberson drew a deep breath. "Your funds and the supporting papers can be drawn tomorrow. There is one other order, given to me verbally."

"That order would be?" Kitchens asked carefully.

"You are to communicate with no one, speak no words, write no letters, save to me. Not until *Notus* departs with you safely aboard." He looked very uncomfortable. "I have been advised to place you in a quiet room in the cellars of the Ripley Building. This was not an order itself, merely a suggestion."

Kitchens could see the clutch of the Queen's dead hand in this matter. "Where does the Prime Minister stand in all this?"

"As far away as possible," Amberson replied, staring out the rippled glass of the carriage's window.

PAOLINA

By the time the two of them passed down out of the heights of the world and over a broadening coast that could not in truth be too far south of Mogadishu, weeks had passed. They had ridden with caravans twice, stopped for a brief while in a city made entirely of glass and silk, and once slept in a field of nodding purple flowers tall as a ship mast that gave Paolina strange dreams of teeth for days after.

Now she stood above a rising stretch of hills, backed by jungle and, farther west, a mountain that rose up almost to her current level of the Wall. Africa lay once more beneath her feet. The distant mountain spilled away from *a Murado* as if part of the fabric of Creation had rent. She'd never seen such a thing.

Her conviction that they had passed onward in the direction intended by the angel atop the Wall was beginning to flag. She'd run so hard, but she was starting to realize she did not understand her destination. "Where do we go now?" she asked Ming.

The Chinese had taken advantage of the halt to scout for mushrooms in the damp shadows of the boulder field that dropped away to their immediate left. He looked up from behind a lichenous rock. "Down, ah?"

"But where? We were supposed to meet someone."

"Long time back." He shrugged, his face suddenly expressive. "Long time forward. Who to say?"

She answered him in Chinese. "Time to walk some more."

Paolina intended to set her course for the top of the curious mountain, the point where its slope met the vastness of the wall. Surely some agency watched the Southern Earth from that vantage point.

As they walked she continued to puzzle over what she saw and what it meant for the making of the world. In cross-section *a Murado* was much wider at the base than at the top. Otherwise they would have climbed up and down like flies on a brick course. Each little ledge, each boulder field and waterfall and forest and narrow clinging city added to the extent of the Wall's base until eventually it merged into the land and sea below.

It had also become clear to Paolina, walking at such great heights, that the Wall was in some fundamental sense an insult to the shape of the

Earth. Though it was right and natural that the world be divided into Northern and Southern halves—clearly that was God's design—why did the African coast on each side seem to line up? As if the Wall had been set down atop the shape of the land. Likewise the oceans were aligned on each side.

Did the landforms pass beneath? Did the seas flow from one side to the other? The air did not, except for the bit at the top. She could not see that weather in the Northern Earth could have a connection to weather in the Southern Earth.

It was as if a draughtsman had prepared a chart, then slashed a great line across the middle. God could not possibly have been mistaken when He had created the world six thousand years earlier. His plan must mean something she had not yet managed to discern.

That the system of the world *could* be discerned was never a doubt to Paolina. That she was the one to discern it was no more of a question. The how of the thing was a challenge, meat to the gnawing teeth of her mind.

As for the why, who could comprehend the mind of God? Such priests as she had known did not encourage any trust to be placed in them. Ming's people clearly had a different view altogether of the arrangements of Heaven and Earth, though Ming was difficult to draw forth on the matter.

The Southern Earth, with its absence of any evidence of man, at least as seen from these rocky, difficult heights, did make her doubt whether Adam had in fact been the true purpose of Creation, or just another animal in the Garden.

A heretic thought encroached: What would the world be if some great cat, or an ambling bear, had taken the Forbidden Fruit?

CHILDRESS

Up close the priest appeared even more uncomfortable than from a distance. He was not so fat as Childress had first thought, but rather wore vestments billowing about him as if he had once been grossly overweight and somehow since managed to forget the existence of tailors. The skin of his face hung down his neck like the jowls of a bulldog, testament to what he had lost. He was burnt red by the sun, his thinning hair orange to match, but even through it all there was a gentle humor in his pale eyes.

The priest's mule was as wretched as he. The man pulled his mount to a halt, then asked in English, "Who is this come calling?" His soft voice contained a trace of some European accent Childress could not place.

"My clothes belie my path in life, Father," Childress answered in measured tones. She pulled the spirit of the Mask Poinsard around her, shedding the dead woman's duchess-arrogance but keeping close grip on the confidence, the power, the purpose.

"No one would doubt that, Mistress . . . ?"

The question hung in the air as if the fate of nations depended on her answering it. Which in a sense was true. "You may call me Mask." Her right hand flickered in a birdlike gesture.

His eyes widened in recognition, but he returned no signal, instead saying, "I am Father Francis, of the Archdiocese of Goa. Please allow me to tender my apologies for our poor welcome, but we were not expecting an invasion of the fleet of Erehwon, peopled by charming villainesses such as yourself."

"I charm no one." Childress admitted some of the talking-to-students tartness back into her voice. "I merely speak of what I see before me."

"A far too uncommon failing," observed Father Francis.

"What I see before me seems to be a man who has been gravely ill."

The priest nodded, a frown easing onto his sun-drenched face.

Childress continued. "One not sympathetic to the flight of the white bird. A follower of the Silent Order, perhaps."

She did not mean to twit the man, but there was little point in failing to declare themselves openly at the outset. Not here, not now, where guile counted for little and clarity weighed much in the balance.

Father Francis shifted in the saddle. The mule snuffled mournfully. "Though you and your ship full of vile miscreants see things differently, I say a pox on both your houses. God left us His word and His world. There is no need for further interference from spiritual parvenus."

"I am a librarian, Father." She smiled at him. "I have spent my life among priests at their training. I am quite sick of interference from spiritual parvenus myself."

"Oh, my poor child." Though his words were heavy-hearted, the smile had returned to the priest's face. "Did yon vessel of wrath liberate you from such bondage?"

His words brought old regrets to mind. She took hold of those emotions before continuing. "In a manner of speaking, yes. I am here today seeking aid and counsel."

"You've certainly come to the wrong place, then." He nodded at *Five Lucky Winds*. "If your crew is not set to storm the beaches in a body, perhaps you would take a morning tea with me?"

"I would be delighted." Childress turned and gave the agreed-upon signal for her personal safety, then favored the priest with another smile. "Lead onward, Father."

Childress sat in a wicker chair on a tiled porch, a small rattan table between her and Father Francis. An Indian boy had laid out the tea service,
along with slices of fruits she didn't recognize, glistening wedges of pastel
flesh. The ceiling was high above them, and in another place might have
hosted a fan. Here they were merely hot.

A cathedral loomed close behind this rectory, its location implied but
not explicit from where she sat. No other priests had been visible on her
walk upward with Father Francis, but then there were few other people
of any calling here. The porch was large but empty, innocent of furniture
except for their little setting. An errant breeze carried the scent of distant
jungle, and a spice she could not name.

Goa Velha was a pleasant place. She wondered where everyone had
gone.

Her host fussed with a pitcher of musky cream that she had already
declined. After he had adjusted the color of his tea to his liking, he tipped
in a bit of grainy brown sugar. That was followed by a bright smile directed
at Childress. She could see the handsome young man he had once been in
the gleam of his eyes and the lines of his face beneath the sagging envelope
of skin.

"The Portuguese moved the capital to Panjim after the plague of 1843,"
Father Francis said. "Your map must be very old."

Not just a priest, but a thinking man, Childress realized. Even though
he was probably an adversary, she found herself delighted. "It was not my
map," she offered, to see what else he might reveal in the vacancies of that
truth.

"Next I suppose you will tell me your face did not launch a thousand
of those underwater ships, either." His expression over the rim of his cup
was downright mischievous.

"I should hardly think so." She met him smile for smile. "All faces are
masks. All Masks have faces."

"Mmm." He set his cup down, speared a slice of dewy pink fruit with a
tiny silver fork. "What does a good Anglican heretic such as yourself want
in my poor parish? You come armed with a warship, and fly a flag of fic-
tional intent, unless there has been some new empire aborning whose cries
have not reached my ears."

"I come armed with nothing but my wits. That is not my warship down
in the harbor." Even as she said the words, Childress realized they were
the closest thing to a lie. *Five Lucky Winds* did fly *her* flag, and they sailed

the course she had suggested. Their future in all likelihood hung on her ability to play the part of Mask that she had assumed so reluctantly on first being taken violently aboard that vessel.

"What do your wits tell you?"

"That my map is old."

They both laughed. The priest let silence stretch a while, content to invite Childress to fill it.

Being the supplicant, she did. "We search for a neutral port; seeking fuel, food and fresh water. Access to a foundry or a machine shop would not go amiss, though our troubles there are not too serious." *Yet.* There would never again be a warehouse full of parts and ship mechanics awaiting *Five Lucky Winds,* as in the ship's former home port of Tainan.

"We come directly to the heart of your matter," the priest replied. "Few harbors here in the western Indian Ocean would admit a vessel such as yours. You have chosen well, poor map or no." Another sip of tea. "I am certain the children of God in my parish will be pleased to sell you melons and dried fish and bushels of whatever they have in surplus."

Childress heard the slap of sandals outside as some unseen listener raced away with the good tidings. "Thank you, Father. That is most welcome news."

"Mmm. As for fuel and machinery, unless you can burn palm oil and repair your ship with wooden batons, I am afraid we will not do you much good here."

Something unsaid hung at the edge of his voice. Something she would have to be clever enough to ask.

Some willing treason he cannot simply volunteer, she thought.

"We will deal fairly with the folk of your parish," Childress said slowly, bargaining by the syllable. "I respect the delicate nature of your position." A shot into the darkness of this man's purpose.

Another long, slow sip of tea as his eyes hardened. "I should imagine someone bereft of the protection of any crown might well comprehend such things."

Crown. This place was a sovereign neverland, if she understood the political arrangements. Childress tried to think like Admiral Shang, like William of Ghent, like all those persons of high purpose and obscure intent she had encountered along this journey. "Loyalties can be stripped away in the passages of power."

Father Francis' weight shifted. "What does your banner signify?"

"That there is one world under the gears of God," she said softly. Her own words surprised her.

"One world, many flags. You know our history here?"

Childress nodded. "Under Portuguese rule for quite some time, though you are no Lusitanian. Now the British Empire holds sway through its client monarch in Lisbon, yes?"

"Yes. For most people there is no change. They follow an ox through a paddy, or pull golden perch from the river. The colors of the flag are little more than another flower blooming on a narrow wooden stalk. But for some there is grave difference. . . ." He ran a fingertip around the rim of his cup. "I am here because I am dying."

"I had thought you to be a much bigger man not so long ago, Father."

"To be sure. Soon I will take my leave of you, to deposit even more of myself in a stinking hole. I am not so healthy as I look." He grinned, but quiet despair loomed behind the crooked, brown-stained teeth. "I hold a secret, librarian-who-is-a-Mask. In other times I would have wished a bloody plague on you and the Silent Ones both, but these are my last days. You come asking; I will give you my gift."

She felt balanced between potential and horror. "I should thank you for your legacy."

"Perhaps." He ate another slice of fruit, slowly chewing as a trickle of palest green ran down the stubble of his chin. Then: "There is a fort up the coast. I will give you a chart. Pirates once ranged there, not so long ago, for the same reason you have come—Goa is a place with little law and less care than most. Those bandit sailors are departed, impressed aboard Her Imperial Majesty's ships or returned to their fields and farms, but some of what you need may yet be found."

"Pirates?" She almost laughed, but this man was serious as the disease that ate him from within. "Surely their treasures are defended; surely the British keep watch to see who comes looking for more."

"Surely enough, but with Chinese submarines cruising these waters, who has time to watch an old cave cluttered with rusting parts and leaking fuel barrels?" He reached into his vestments and pulled out a long, beaded rosary from which hung not a cross but a key. "You will need this."

"Will you come?" she asked.

He shook his head. "Even the ride down to your ship was almost too much for me."

"Why do this at all?"

"Word came." His voice was growing threadbare. "You were to be stopped. The birds said this; the Silent Ones said this. But the Royal Navy is not rumbling. Anyone who can stir the hidden powers of the world while leaving the lions at the gate asleep is a truly worthy troublemaker."

She took the key, and a little leather map he handed her. She stepped around the wicker table and kissed his sweating forehead. "I have no blessing to bestow," Childress said, "but my thanks are yours."

"One world, under the gears of God." The imp was back in his eyes for a moment. "Make it so?"

"We shall try."

As Childress walked down the steps of the rectory, Father Francis called after her. "I used to be a priest, you know. In truth."

She turned and gave him a long look.

He was grinning full now, as if this were his last, best joke. "Before I took the black flag and rode the high seas, I was one of God's sworn men. The Archbishop was kind enough to let me come home again at the last."

"Bless you, Father, for you have sinned," she replied, and walked away through the searing tropical morning to the sound of his thinning laughter.

GASHANSUNU

Baassiia came to her in the Hour of the Pod. Gashansunu meditated in the house of her second spirit, a small room near the top of a tower in the Spider Wheel of the city. Being Baassiia, he flew to see her.

As if raw power could impress anyone who had spent time in the Silent World.

She let her *wa* speak for her, in the Silent tongue: YOU DISTURB.

"It is not needless," Baassiia said, answering with his mouth.

ALL IS NEEDLESS WHEN NOTHING IS NEEDFUL.

The big man knew better than to argue circularities with another sorcerer's *wa*. He stepped from air to stone and settled next to her, so they both faced out across the Great Sunset Water.

Gashansunu ignored him a while. This was her right, in meditation, and also her spite at him for coming unbidden into this place. He might have the body of a god, and the bed manners to match, but this man had no claim on her outside the working circle. He was not even a hierarch in her branch of the Westfacing House.

He was just a big, beautiful and worried man.

In time the Hour of the Pod passed. The blood flowers in the plaza below sighed as they released their holds into the air. A dog barked thrice before subsiding into the bubbling whimper of sacrifice. The air changed as the Silent World passed from one state to another, much as water might become mist.

"What brings you here?" she finally asked.

He had been sitting still as an idol, master of his fear, but her words awoke him as if they were a sacrifice of their own. "This disharmony in the order of the world."

"We performed a working," Gashansunu said mildly.

"In which we learned precisely nothing." His voice was thick, freighted.

So like a man, she thought. *Craving certainty when the only thing to do is wait to see what time brings to your hearth as it passes by.* "There was nothing to learn. Yet."

"The city has had a message from the Bone People."

Those words fell heavy. Two years earlier, a sky-kite of the Bone People had been stolen from the city's docks by a party of animals led by a suet-skinned stranger, kin to another pale man chained to the Pillar of Restitution for his crimes. There had been much more to that episode—there always was—but the Nightslaying House had held the axle that moon, and the later troubles had largely stayed within their towers.

She never heard the good gossip. The rest of the Earth, both Southern and Northern, was filled with people who were little more than talking animals, speaking words like sharp barks without the nuance or subtlety of a sorcerer of the city. Their doings were ordinarily beneath notice.

"What message?" she asked.

His reply was too prompt. "They fear a return of the prior madness. Another gleam has passed across the Wall." A pause, though from the stillness in Baassiia's breath, he was not done. "Your name has been sent up from the Bone Coast."

"They do not know me," she said, shocked.

Now grim amusement tinged his voice. "Tell that to their eyeless oracles."

"Whose regrets are driving the signs and portents?"

Baassiia looked out across the circles of the city at the sullen waters beyond. He did not meet her eye, or speak directly to her, though Gashansunu could feel his *wa* circling, whispering, crying. "The world, we think, speaking through the city. All turns—all is round—but a fragment has been plucked as a man might snatch a hair from the hide of a lion. The lion weeps for the tuft in its tail."

"This gleam comes for me." Intuition, yes, but also common sense. The Bone People were not so free with words, for they understood all too well the binding power in the naming of a thing. They would not have called her out without good cause.

"Borne on yellow wings," Baassiia replied. "Hence the nature of our portents."

"I shall arm myself, lest the gods smile."

He turned to face her now, the spirits of the moment sloughing away to leave only naked longing and the private regrets of the body. "I fear for you. Lie with me, that I might remember you better if you do not return."

Gashansunu slipped her hand under his kirtle and was comforted by the lengthy firmness she encountered there. "It would be disrespectful to do so in this house," she answered with a sly lilt in her voice. "Let us go to a place of your choosing, that you may dissuade me from my own regrets."

He stood and stepped out into the air, smiling as he fell. Wasteful of power but filled with lust, she followed.

Besides, Baassiia was always a great one for speaking softly when at the breast, once he'd spent himself. She might learn more there than ever from sitting with him in the quiet of a holy house.

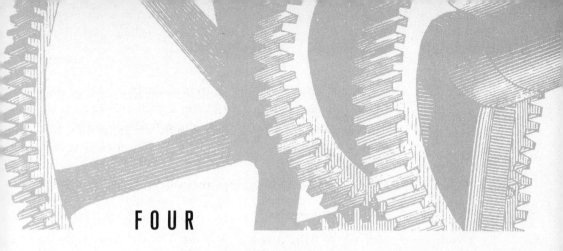

FOUR

Behold, I have created the smith that bloweth the coals in the fire, and that bringeth forth an instrument for his work; and I have created the waster to destroy. —*Isaiah 54:16*

BOAZ

Wind rustled within the newly exposed cave. Dust stirred as if someone invisible walked through. His fingers—strong, precise brass pincers that could safely pluck an ant from a pane of glass, or just as easily crush a man's throat—picked at the lip of the leather wrapped tight about its contents.

Nothing should persist so long, Boaz thought. *Everything passes from dust to dust, stopping at life along the way.* The leather obeyed his misgivings, cracking to pieces as he unfolded it. Flakes fluttered to the sand floor.

He tugged further, peeling the skin back in a vanishing layer until he was forced to turn the packet over in his hand. Additional leather was exposed beneath, this a bit more robust. The back came off in chunks much as the front had; then he turned it again.

The next round of wrapping broke off in larger sheets, sloughing away at his gentlest tug. Thus it went, seven times around, each turn a bit less brittle, more pliable than the one before, until finally he reached leather that was almost supple. Boaz wondered what it smelled of, for he could feel oils against his fingertips.

The Kohanim who had wrapped this packet had expected it to stand the test of years. Possibly the test of eternity.

Time stood exposed, three millennia naked in the span of minutes. The sheets of destroyed leather were a blizzard of centuries.

"My people began here," he said.

"All people begin somewhere," Chin Ping replied softly.

Taking that as his sign, Boaz stripped open the final layer.

Within was a small book, bound with strips of flat wood secured by blue and white threading. Also a smaller bag of worn cloth, containing something flat and heavy. Boaz dreaded what that might be.

He set the bag down upon the altar stone along with the ruins of the leather wrapping, and turned his attention first to the book. The boards were pressed fiber made solid with glue, bound along the right side. He faintly traced the cover while wondering if this, too, would collapse to raddled dust.

History refused to claim its own, however. The book remained resolutely solid. He teased it open.

Words.

Words in the Hebrew of King Solomon's court. Written in a crabbed hand with faded, pale ink that spoke of privation and disaster even as the text made golden promises concerning the magnificence of the reader, the poor estate of the writer, and the hidden powers of distant thrones.

"What say?" Chin Ping asked.

"It is a . . ." Boaz reached for the appropriate term. "It is a formula. In the style of heralds of the Temple. A method of introducing a difficult topic while minimizing offense."

Chin Yuen muttered in low, rapid Chinese. Then, Chin Ping said, "Please to tell what topic of difficulty is."

"I do not yet know," Boaz said simply. He turned the pages, skimming. A description of Solomon's court, written by someone who was *there*. The sailing of the fleet from Asiongaber. Storms upon the ocean. Their casting ashore on the margins of Africa. A council upon the beach, the priest speaking for himself within the text for the first time, the admiral on his deathbed, the first Brass prophesying. An agreement to conceal certain knowledge lest it be lost to savages or misfortune as they journeyed on-ward.

As well as the knowledge itself . . .

He stopped, hands trembling. *The making of a Seal.*

In all the days of Ophir's history, there had only been six kinds of the Seals of Solomon. One powered every Brass who had ever lived. Another had raised the buildings of the city and set the bounds of the city's empire during the centuries of its greatness. A third had coursed fire through the Spears and other Sealed weapons with which Brass had gone conquering. A fourth powered the cars that shuttled deep within the clattering depths of the Wall. A fifth brought weather down from the skies and banished it again. The sixth and last was said to have opened the ways from Earth to the dreaming mind of YHWH, though even with their fabled memories, no Brass today was certain what that had signified.

But no one had ever had the making of a new Seal. Over time, through error and mischance—and once, sheer, raw evil—the making of Seals had been lost, until only one survived: the Third Seal that powered their weapons and allowed them to craft Spears anew. New Brass could only be made with an existing First Seal taken from one who had been slain or otherwise given up his life. Every century fewer of them remained. Should they ever lose the art of placing the ancient Seals into new forged bodies, their line would dwindle until none were left except as armored scrap.

This book spoke of *creating* a Seal. The purifications, the prayers, the summonings, the meaning of each twist and turn and fleck in the pattern. On and on it went for pages, diagrams and details and lists of materials. Boaz' eyes passed close over each of the ancient, brittle sheets.

In his hands he held the knowledge to renew the power of Ophir, bring more Brass marching bright-limbed into the sunlight of this world.

Reverently he set the book down and took up the small bag. The fibers of the cloth shed in his hand as he tried to open it, until he held a round, heavy stone limned by a cloud of dust.

He turned it over.

A Seal, recto, in opposition to the blank, bone-smooth verso. Boaz traced it with his fingers, not quite touching the surface. The design was wrong, flawed somehow. Instinct deep as his own construction told him this.

Then he realized it was inverted. This was a master blank from which Seals could be made. As for the design . . .

The Sixth Seal.

The Seal that carried words from the mortal world to YHWH's very ear. YHWH, who had been absent from His own Creation these thousands of years, only His killer angels and wretched monkey-priests serving as proxy for His terrible, awful presence.

Overcome, Boaz dropped to his knees just as Chin Yuen snatched the book from the table. With a wordless roar, the Brass jumped once more to his feet. The sailors scattered, a few screaming in fear, as Boaz erupted from the cave mouth in pursuit of his patrimony.

He scrambled up a dune, blood and blue silk rags wrapped around his raging arms. Someone close by was firing a weapon, but wherever the bullets went, they had no effect on Boaz. His vision was narrowed to a single line of focus, pursuing the Chinese petty officer as an arrow pursues a target.

The man ran as if his heels were ablaze. Another sailor stumbled. Boaz snapped his spine with one step, smashed his head with the next, continued racing for the book.

At the crest he lost his footing and began to slide down the other side. Ropes dangled from the lightening sky, sailors already scrambling up them.

Chin Yuen ran toward the Chinese airship that wallowed too close to the earth.

Boaz increased his pace, knowing he was overspending irreplaceable lubricant. He raced to overtake the thief before the man could gain the safety of the ropes and be lifted away from this place bearing *his* book. *Ophir's* book.

More bullets. This time Boaz felt the shock in the armor of his chest. He looked up to see rifles bristling from the foredeck of the airship. Ahead of him, Chin Yuen had gained the ropes. Chin Ping stood below his superior, guarding the line. The translator stared at Boaz with a stricken expression.

I am sorry, he seemed to say. *We have stolen the heart of your magic. Your people's renewal will never come now.*

Boaz reached Chin Ping, fist ready to smash the man's teeth out through his lower back. The translator's mouth crinkled into a small smile that gave Boaz pause. Chin Ping grasped the trailing line and was lifted bodily into the air as the Chinese vessel bobbed on the morning breeze.

Boaz looked upward, marking the lean, hawkish shape and mottled colors of his enemy. Three British airships of familiar design closed out of the east, dawn's glare behind them.

The wind rose from off the water. The Chinese captain would have to run inland before catching enough of the gage to beat back toward his own precincts.

Boaz spun about to race away from the ocean. He had brought down an airship before, with help only from al-Wazir and a single, unreliable weapon. He could do it again.

The Chinese flyer passed overhead, engines straining to gain speed ahead of the wind. The British were visibly closing. They must have maneuvered for hours over the night-dark waters of the Indian Ocean to achieve this precise advantage.

Boaz ran into the valley beyond. The Chinese strained to gain altitude, passing out of his sight line over the lip of the glittering white cliff.

That would defeat him if he did not find a way around.

Something whooshed overhead. He looked up in time to see the trail from a rocket. The Chinese had fired on their enemies.

Guns barked in unison, bow chasers from the pursuers. Boaz raced madly along the cliff to the next rise in the sand, trying to gain sufficient altitude to see rather than merely hear the battle.

The Chinese airship could *not* go down. Not until he had recovered the book!

A pair of rockets were answered immediately by gunfire.

He felt more than heard the explosion that followed. Dust danced on the sand dunes as a second sun flared in the east. Boaz slipped, sliding on his face several handspans before he could recover. He scrambled up again as a denser barrage passed overhead.

They were in the fight for real now.

He finally topped the cliff to see the Chinese airship wallowing southward. One engine was aflame. Back to the east a column of black smoke marked the crash of the destroyed British airship along the coast. A lucky hit to the gasbag had sent dozens to their graves, but eased the odds a little.

Not enough.

With a damaged engine, the Chinese airship could not maneuver through her turn. The British closed fast, decks bristling with screaming riflemen who fired in ragged volleys. Boaz raced for the site where his erstwhile captors must once again come to ground.

Enemy ordnance caught up with the fleeing Chinese long before Boaz did. Her other engine flared and she loafed into a short, sharp dive. The vessel recovered, but several men fell from her decks in the process. She was dead in the air. In seconds she would be slain there.

Not the hydrogen, Boaz thought with something between a summoning and a prayer. Whatever angels were listening failed to heed him, for another round of missiles opened rents in the aft section of the gasbag.

Closing in to the kill, the British poured their fire into the stricken airship. When the flames came, they moved very quickly indeed.

He finally stopped running and watched the history and future of his people fall burning to the ground.

Somewhere in that moment Boaz was surprised to find that he still carried the Sixth Seal.

Already the British were quartering for survivors, shooting downward indiscriminately. He moved off as quickly as he dared, though not in the enraged rush of before, keeping to the cover of the thin thornwoods until he could escape the threat of murder and the death of hope.

CHILDRESS

They cruised offshore, waiting for the afternoon's low tide. Leung had explained that there was no point in making an approach to shore in anything but the slackest water—the vessel bore far too much risk of grounding if they mistook the depth.

When the captain judged the moment right, he and Childress climbed to the conning tower. Al-Wazir turned his team out on the foredeck, ready with greased rifles, grapnels and pry bars. In their motley of uniforms and gear and duck fat smeared across exposed skin, she thought they looked more like train robbers than sailors preparing to assault a port.

The key still hung around her neck, for none of them were certain of the priest's intent. The task might be as simple as opening a door, in which case al-Wazir would send a man for it.

Or they might face something more obscure, that would call upon Childress' knowledge of divine tradition and her assumed powers as a Mask. In which case, al-Wazir would come back for her.

They closed on the shore. A man at the bow took soundings with a lead line. Childress reviewed the map—a dogleg approach waited past the haystack rocks just ahead, if the symbols were to be believed.

It didn't look like an accessible port. It didn't look like anything but rocks rising out of the water. She wondered if Father Francis had sent them to their deaths, *Five Lucky Winds* trapped aground until a British patrol happened upon them and shelled or bombed them into bloody shards.

The man on the lead line called out excitedly. Childress followed the line of his finger. What had seemed like a solid wall was really two rocks close together, a narrow passage opening between them.

"I wish I still had a boat," Leung said. Paolina had taken theirs, off the coast of Sumatra. "I'd have the men row her in."

"Tow the vessel?" Childress asked, surprised.

"It can be done." He smiled. "Slowly. Very slowly." He called directions down the speaking tube, shouting adjustments moment by moment. The hull ground against rock once—a slow scrape, not a rending tear—as they made the turn. *Tight, so very tight,* Childress thought. Though Leung winced, no one seemed too alarmed. Then they slid into shadow, a narrow cave opening up beneath the headland, walls slimed white with guano, the sea sloshing lazily among the shadows beyond.

Al-Wazir shouted and dove overboard. His men followed him, swimming into darkness as Leung shouted for all stop.

They had located a port, perhaps. If they were lucky and strong. She looked back behind them, but saw only rock hemming them in. Like life itself, gates shut as they were passed. The only way was forward.

Ahead of them, a voice shouted, indistinctly at first, then al-Wazir roaring. A shot rang. Leung's face flushed, but they held their ground. The submarine could not advance until the landing party cleared the way.

One of the sailors emerged from shadows, head bobbing in the water. He gave the signal for *Five Lucky Winds* to proceed. As the submarine eased forward into darkness, Childress thought she heard laughter from the cave.

Passing into shadow, a man with a lantern could be dimly spied in the glow of his flame. A few shapes clustered alongside, someone arguing in Chinese, al-Wazir grumbling like a railroad train in a very deep tunnel.

With much shouting and casting of lines, *Five Lucky Winds* warped into a berth alongside a stone quay. The cave was far bigger than it had seemed from outside, the hidden inlet large enough for the submarine to have made a complete turn.

Safe enough for the hull, past the bottleneck of the entrance.

As her eyes grew accustomed to the light, she saw that there were three berths within the cavern, arrayed in a semicircle along the eastern boundary. Roofless buildings stood beyond. Everything was covered with rime and dust and guano.

Father Francis had not lied. This place *had* been left untended for some time. She touched the key around her neck and wondered what portal or spell or lock it was intended to open.

Al-Wazir clomped onto the foredeck and approached the conning tower. "All clear," he growled.

"What was the shot?" Leung asked.

More laughter from the shore.

"Just opening the way." He stared up, eyes gleaming in the deep shadow of the cave. "Sir."

Leung looked at the dripping sailors now standing with fixed grins on the dock. In Chinese, he asked, "What took place?"

"He shot a . . ."

Childress didn't catch the word. "What?"

The captain began laughing. He tried English. "He shot a, the word is . . ."

"Seal, Mask," al-Wazir said from below. "I shot a seal."

"Why?"

Muttering: "Because I thought it was attacking me."

She was torn between the general hilarity and a rush of sympathy for the poor beast. "Well, don't do it again."

"No, ma'am. Permission to patrol the shoreline?"

Leung was now studying his speaking tube, trying very hard to remake his face with the proper aura of command seriousness.

"Go forth, Chief," Childress said.

As evening dimmed the entrance, al-Wazir and his men explored seven buildings, a series of caches and a tunnel blocked by an ironwork gate wide enough to admit a cart.

The mystery of the key was solved, at least.

Not much in the way of expendable supplies was present, but the cave boasted a fair stock of those things sufficiently durable to have withstood a decade of neglect—cables, scrap steel, deck plating. They located two freshwater seeps, each leading to a slimed pool that in turn drained into the little hidden bay. Water barrels were dry or foul, ropes rotted nests of rat-gnawed straw, food lockers long since reduced to dust.

They had a secure tie-up, some basic materials and, most miraculous of all, a small machine shop with a forge. The belts transmitting motive power from the little steam engine to the lathes and drills were rotting in place, but that would not be so difficult to repair.

What they needed was coal for the forge and steam engine, diesel fuel for the submarine, and whatever copper wiring and electrickal valves might be required to repair the ongoing trouble with the batteries.

Childress, al-Wazir and Leung studied the gate, along with Sun-Wei the engineer. They had an electrick torch taken from the submarine's equipment lockers. Its flickering yellow light swept back and forth across the wrought iron.

"This does not discourage spies," Childress observed, turning to look back into the cave. Running lights glowed on the mast and forestaff of *Five Lucky Winds*, while the men had lit a fire on the small shingle beach that sent shadows capering across the dome of the roof. "One can see much of the cavern from this point."

Childress slipped her key into the lock. She turned it, forcing the iron against the weight of rust and years, until it squealed. Something clicked loudly and the gate popped loose.

"Who's first up the passage?" she asked.

"Not you," said Leung and al-Wazir in unison. The two men eyed one another as Childress laughed.

Al-Wazir was back in twenty minutes, grinning. "It comes out in a shambling go-down filled with festival carts and huge monstrous heads of toothy red gods."

"Did you look outside?" Childress asked.

"Of course." His grin grew wider. "A stand of them palm trees, and some fields beyond. A town down the road a bit, I think from the glow. Likely that proper port we knew was north of Goa Velha."

"Panjim," Childress said. "In the morning you and I shall go into town to bargain for fuel and supplies, and see if there are any electrickal mechanics to be found."

Leung opened his mouth and closed it again. She took his arm. "You and your men are too conspicuous, dear. I am afraid I shall be forced to wear my dress once more."

"Don't get caught," Leung said.

"You will need to ensure that I am in funds," Childress replied. "I will need to seed my entrance into Panjim. No one will take me for a great English lady, so money must needs do."

The words were braver than she felt. Whatever trouble she fell into, only she could get herself out of it. On her own, as she had been that morning in Velha Goa, marching into the heart of the enemy.

When did the Queen's dominions become that seat of darkness for me? Childress was surprised at her own thought.

KITCHENS

He stared up at HIMS *Notus* berthed at her tower, where three ranks of masts rose on this side of the harbor. The disgraced vessel rode in splendid isolation. The airship was in quarantine, well separated from the others at the massive Dover aerodrome.

A bored sergeant attended Kitchens. Thin and dark like a Welshman, with eyes the liquid brown of a roach's wing, the sergeant was dressed in the blue woolens of the aerial service, but his rank was British army.

"Sergeant Penstock, I'd care to see aboard her before the crew is returned here."

"Field commander says that lot won't be let back out of the stockade until they're all transferred in." A dire glee at the fate of Imperial malefactors filled the sergeant's voice. "Fine thing you're doing, sir, giving them such a chance to make amends."

Kitchens thought of the sheaf of death warrants in the locked attaché case he carried. Traveling to Dover with Amberson, he'd still not been able to examine the Queen's token. Kitchens pushed the reflections aside and mounted the stairs leading upward to his future home.

He had always harbored a horror of flight. Being so far from safe, safe ground made his gut twitch. While training as a special clerk, he'd barely passed the roof-running and bridge-diving exercises. Here, so far above the soil on a tower that only swayed and creaked a bit, he felt a touch of the panic that pursued him in dreams.

Notus hung stolidly, sufficiently large to provide the illusion of stability. The platform at the top of the tower was mounted on a turntable, ensuring the airship stayed facing into the wind at all times. Pumps kept her gasbag at neutral buoyancy, but she still appeared a bit sad and wrinkled. He crossed a wooden bridge to her deck, for the first time in his life aboard an airship. A completely deserted one at that.

The vessel seemed empty even of rats, though he seriously doubted that could be true. Deck gear sat in place, but not square and polished. The air of abandonment was peculiar.

"Ain't been nobody aboard but the maintenance detail," Penstock announced from behind Kitchens. "Out here on the third line, no one can get close without half the aerodrome knowing."

"The crew is in for a long, slow march, I should think," Kitchens said absently. He mounted to the poop, where the helm stood.

These ships were relics, he knew, built in a fashion that had been obsolete on the water these fifty years and more. Everything crossing the waves under a naval ensign these days was iron-built with great turbine engines and long, smooth guns that could bark a shell to the horizon. In the sky, where weight efficiency was paramount, they invested metal only in the engines, while using the experience of older times to build a light, sturdy hull out of a mix of woods. The result was as if Admiral Nelson's fleet had taken to the air, slung beneath the long, gray sausages of balloons.

He touched the polished brass of her wheel. Chains through the spokes locked it down. The engine telegraph and the binnacle stood adjacent. The captain conned his ship from an open deck, much as they had a hundred years earlier.

Only now they flew, dying in the air instead of on the water. Taking a deep breath, Kitchens looked to the rail. His knees almost gave way at the sight of the ground two hundred perilous feet below.

How would he manage at cruising altitude? These vessels passed two miles in the air and more, depending on wind and weather and the needs of their mission.

He dragged himself step by step to the rail. Penstock trailed behind, silent now. Kitchens did not care for what the man thought, but he did care what the man might say in some written report to Admiralty.

Gripping the rail so tight his fingernails ached, Kitchens leaned forward and looked at the next rows of masts, the neatly mowed green below, the hills beyond where the town spilled toward the aerodrome. A knot of figures at the rail of another airship along the distant row of masts stared back at him.

Well, Kitchens thought, Notus *probably has something of a reputation as a ghost ship by now.*

He wondered if he would soon become a ghost clerk.

PAOLINA

A bowl of cliffs rose to surround them as they walked down off the Wall. The path descended into a snowy mountaintop crater that held a strange building, though it resembled a gargantuan termite mound more than any of the buildings of Europe. How the builders had buttressed its rising masses, Paolina could not say. She caught glimpses of long, tawny vistas of grassland leading away south and east and west from the foot of this mountain.

Soon enough those distant, open plains were blocked by crumbling, rotten rock. Banners began to sprout alongside the path. Tall poles bent slightly with their own weight bore the bundled tails of animals, wrapped strips of bright-printed cloth, or sprays of colored ropes knotted in particular fashions.

In front of the termite palace they were met by a tall, dark-skinned man dressed in linens and a spotted animal skin. He carried a drum and favored Paolina with a bright smile before speaking with vigorous intent in some language she did not know.

She strained for comprehension, then answered in English: "I do not understand you." Would she have to use the gleam for speech? The stemwinder was so dangerous. She'd seen the bodies in the water just before she and Ming had fled to the Wall.

She wished mightily for Boaz to be with her on this adventure. Ming was cheerful enough, and quite capable, but also strangely deferential. Boaz would have been thoughtful and wise. The Brass had always known what to do.

Paolina took the stemwinder in hand before she tried greeting the man in Portuguese, then Chinese.

At the last, he launched into a rapid patter of speech in that language. Ming answered. Paolina caught perhaps two words in ten as the two exchanged first courtesies, then introductions, then expressions of mutual goodwill. She shivered in the wind.

"Wait," said their guide in Chinese. He put up a hand. "Let us go within." He spoke much more slowly now, for Ming had explained that Paolina had only a little of the language. "Feast, then talk."

She slipped the gleam back into its pouch among her skirts. Paolina was both relieved and disappointed not to use it. Surely one woman's ability to talk did not weigh so much on the mechanisms of the world as did tons of submarine trapped amid of a Wall storm.

As they mounted a winding, irregular flight of stairs, she turned to face the Wall. She had a moment of illusion, as if the soaring mass before her were in fact the surface of the Earth, and she an insect crawling up a wall of some other Creation, ready to tumble into the cliffs below.

The corridors within were just as organically shaped as the exterior. The dried-mud walls were covered with white and ochre and golden paintings that ran for dozens of feet, spiraling in on themselves and opening to starbursts. The patterns were beautiful, though they plucked at her eye in a manner that Paolina found both curious and fascinating.

Their guide, whom Ming whispered was named Seven Trees, led them unerringly to a large, rounded chamber. A feast was being spread there by a quiet group of men and women coming and going from a series of other passageways. All were tall and dark as Seven Trees.

Eight mats were arrayed in a circle. Each was a different color—one a maroon so dark as to be almost brown, another a gray-green, a third dusty tan, and so on.

Bowls and gourds stood on each mat. They were different from place to place, one presenting mashed fruits and vegetables, their smells mixing together in a medley of salt and starch. Another mat was covered with rich, dark stews that were almost bloody in their scent. A third held leafy greens and long, narrow slices of glistening roots.

The mix of odors made her stomach growl. She and Ming had eaten well enough while passing along the Wall, but their diet would never have been confused with plenty, or even variety.

Seven Trees spread his hands. "Eat," he said in Chinese. "And we will know."

Ming stepped into the center of the circle of mats, then paused to look back at Paolina. "What is your care?" he asked in English. His brown eyes darted to one side, indicating their host.

"I am not certain," she admitted in the same language. "Ask him what he means by 'we will know.'"

Ming looked to Seven Trees. His Chinese was more slow and careful now, so that Paolina could follow some of the conversation.

"What is it you will know when we eat?"

Seven Trees bowed slightly. "What the . . . signifies." She'd missed several words there.

Apparently so had Ming. "Who is this which signifies?"

"Those who come," Seven Trees said. "The Wall sends ambassadors at times. You. Furthermore, you do not always understand your own purposes. This feast is intended to . . ." Again she lost the sense of the words.

The Chinese glanced back at Paolina again. "They tell fortunes by the foods we choose," he said in English.

She glanced down at the mats. Were some of these dishes drugged? Poisonous? A ritual meal was a far different thing from a welcoming banquet.

The tall man smiled. "All the ambassadors of the Wall have been welcomed here. Including the . . . when they come down from the heavens."

A missing word.

"Where are they now?" Ming asked.

Seven Trees shrugged. "Some have moved on. Some stay to join us. Some leave their bodies behind."

Paolina froze at that last. "The food is a test," she said, also in Chinese.

"Of course." Seven Trees looked surprised. "How else would we know you were bearing rectitude?"

"We will not choose from among *poisons*." That last word was in English, for she did not know the Chinese.

Their guide drew his fur close around him and frowned. Paolina's hand once more reached for the stemwinder. The sailor dropped his shoulders and let his feet slide a bit farther apart.

"You will eat." A stillness hung in Seven Trees' voice, low and threatening. "You will eat, and we will know you by your choices."

She pulled the winding knurl out to the fourth detent. Paolina had become something of an expert on focusing her will.

Bringing down the ceiling was not an option. For one thing, an entire building rose skyward above them. Everyone would be crushed. Nor did she want to stop Seven Trees' heart. Yet if she simply moved herself and Ming away from here, she risked another earthquake like the catastrophe she had caused back in Sumatra by calling *Five Lucky Winds* to her aid.

"We are not ambassadors," she told Seven Trees. "We are travelers who would be upon our way now, without delay."

"You will choose, then eat; then we will see who you are."

Men stepped from the various passageways. At least a dozen, wrapped in cloths of various patterns and colors, each carrying a long spear with a diamond-shaped black iron blade.

Ming gave Paolina a hard, wordless look. His meaning was clear enough. *Do something. I cannot fight them all.* She had defeated an entire navy. Stepping out of this danger was well within her means.

She had sworn not to use this power. She had been willing to accept oblivion of the spirit to send it away from the world. She had fled here to the Southern Earth to escape the threats of venal, grasping men who would take it from her.

Now she was to be made a pawn again by her own fear.

Paolina felt her anger rising. *Men*, it always came to *men*. Boaz had been different, Ming was quite decent, but these people in their termite palace atop their frozen mountain were no better than the *doms* of Praia Nova who had made her childhood such a lengthy misery.

With anger grew resolve. With resolve grew intent. The warriors stepped closer, their spears at the ready.

"Ming," she said. He took her arm. She closed her eyes and thought hard on the angel who had met them atop *a Murado*.

Where had he meant to send us?

She opened her mouth to say something else, but the breath was snatched from her in a whirl of dust and the long, terrified scream of a grown man in pain.

WANG

He followed the monk upward. Clearly the woman had been hiding among the sailors aboard *Fortunate Conjunction*, had worn their cotton blue uniform, head shaven as most of the crew kept themselves.

Wu, the mate, must have known. Perhaps not Captain Shen, who seemed lost in his own head. It had been obvious to Wang that Wu ran the boat. As for the monk, she was . . . what? A ghost in truth?

Perhaps all the Kô's crew were madmen.

Wang certainly felt like such an unfortunate. The stairs were slippery with dewfall. Tiny, secretive plants grew in the gaps between treads and frame, the places where the rails twisted. Mosses flowed from the side of the cliff.

Below him, *Fortunate Conjunction* was already a pale blur in the deepening gloom as it steamed away. Wang had never thought he would miss Chersonesus Aurea—it had been worse even than Hainan—but he was sorry to see the boat depart without him. The waters so clear and glassy by day now seemed a dark curdle ready to swallow the vessel whole.

He turned his attention upward. His thighs shivered. Tight bands clutched his chest. He turned to sit upon a landing and was surprised to find his breathing harsh and loud.

The monk called down from two turns above him. "The climb will only grow more difficult if you let your body take too long a rest."

"I cannot go on." Was this stupid island a mile high? Could no one build their secret headquarters amid a simple meadow?

"The upward road always leads to Heaven."

"Enough with your monkish blather," shouted Wang.

Laughter echoed, accompanied by the continued tap of footsteps.

Wang realized if he let her get too far ahead, she'd be long gone when he reached the top. Strange as she was, the monk was Wang's only friend in this mess.

His only friend at all. He might have liked that dangerous English-woman who'd come to his library not so long ago, but for the fact that she was English and a woman. She'd had sense, and a good eye.

The cataloger heaved himself to his aching feet. The monk had been correct. His first few steps were leaden. His body did not want to go on. Yet what choice did he have? The future lay above him, the past below. He had been called, not sent.

The upward road might lead to Heaven, but right now it led to a jelly in his legs and a burning in his mouth.

Wang did not at first understand that he had reached the top. The night was not so dark, even with the Wall looming black-line on the southern horizon. Stars quarreled high above. The moon would soon rise. The world seemed strangely filled with light. Or maybe that was just his head.

When he arrived at a landing much larger than normal, he set about looking for more steps. What he encountered instead was a row of hibiscus redolent with night-blooming scent. Turning, nearly stumbling with the motion, Wang saw another row nearby. He turned again, consumed with the inertia of the movement, to face a very large doorway gleaming with dark lacquer and studded with brass nubs. This entrance was set within a very traditional gate much as he might expect to find in any palace of the Imperial Court.

The monk waited on the stone step before the gateway, puffing on her little pipe.

"I could have climbed up and down twice in the time it took you, fat man." She extended her hand, offering him a smoke.

"No," Wang gasped. "Am . . . am I expected?"

"Do you think the eyes of this fortress miss any of what takes place in their own waters?"

He sprawled beside her on the step. "I think there are more eyes in Heaven and Earth than ever I'd dreamt of."

"You are one thousand, two hundred and seven steps closer to Heaven now." She smiled through the wreath of her smoke.

"I was called, not sent." That was fast becoming his mantra.

"I came because I am curious," the monk replied.

Wang sat breathing very hard for a few minutes. His head hung between his knees, his back bent and lungs tired. Finally he looked up.

Her smoke still trailed in the air, but the monk had vanished. The hibiscus shivered, possibly with the wind.

The cataloger had not heard the gate creak open. He turned anyway to look. No gaping darkness. No inviting lantern light. No rush of incense.

Everything under Heaven has a name, he thought. *But how to describe this monk, who disappears like morning mist yet is solid as Grass Mountain?*

His abused legs nearly buckled as he stood. Wang found no bell pull, no gong, no waiting servant. He raised his fingers to knock, but the door swung open as if at his thought.

A pale man dressed in patterned gray, strangely featured like a Mongolian, stood within. He stared at Wang with speculation. "You have come. I would bid you welcome, but that would be a lie." His Chinese had a very northern accent, as if he'd learn from a Manchurian. "You may call me Dunkerjav."

The librarian. "I am Cataloger Wang. I was called for."

"Of course you were." The pale man continued to block the doorway. "Beware your idle tongue while here, and shut your ears against those words not meant for you. This is a Silent house, but it is not a quiet house."

Bowing again, Wang murmured a polite acknowledgment. Then he followed the Mongolian inside, passing from star-bright night into musty shadow.

The island house of the Silent Order was as much of a warren as any Imperial Palace. Hallways opened onto more hallways; high walks crossed over lower chambers filled with grunting, shouting monks or copy desks vacant in night's dimness. Some areas were illuminated by flickering electrick lamps; others shone with the warm, buttery glow of kerosene. Still more lay dark—fallow fields awaiting the plow of light.

After passing through a vestibule crowded with wicker armor and ancient, useless swords, they arrived at a great room. Three levels of balconies were visible below them. The floor held a great, round map of the Northern Earth, atop which three lithe men walked in black slippers.

The map-walkers positioned small markers, then moved others about, in response to instructions pointed or shouted by men standing at the bottom of the deep room. A whole crowd surrounded the map—men and women of many races.

Wang felt a freezing stab of fear. He'd always understood the Silent Order to be beyond the boundaries of nationhood, but its aspiration of an orderly, controlled world had seemed so Chinese. Here he saw a project even the Dragon Throne might not have dared.

The Englishwoman Childress had been something else entirely—a Mask of the white birds, wicked and foreign and dedicated to chaos and disorder. But these people . . . They did not honor rank or precedence— he could tell by the way they stood admixed and unthinking. How did each of them know who he *was*, where he *belonged*?

The Mongolian watched from close by. "This is our best approximation of the order of the world. Oracles and difference engines both work along-side, considering word that is brought from half a thousand spies and har-bor masters and simple folk who value what we do."

"I am a librarian, in service of the Imperial Court," Wang began.

"No. You are the man who has unearthed the Golden Bridge. You are also the man who has let the most dangerous Feathered Mask in genera-tions slip our nets and walk free."

"So what would you of me here?"

A snort. The Mongolian appeared almost sympathetic. "We will de-scend, and you will be told everything there is to tell you. Then you will sail into the world and find this Feathered Mask and the traitors with her aboard *Five Lucky Winds*."

"Why me? I am needed on the Golden Bridge, as you said yourself."

"You are the only one of us to whom she has spoken. You will be able to approach her in trust, far more than any of our other operatives can hope to do."

"Then what? Strike her down in anger?"

"Bring her home." A fever lay upon the Mongolian's eyes. He seemed as if he would spring to wild action at any moment.

Wang wondered at this madness and why anyone would think him part of it.

CHILDRESS

The Mask Childress strode into the town of Panjim with her hulking ser-vant trailing behind her. She wore a tattered, high-necked black dress like armor beneath a helm of tightly wound pepper-gray hair. Not even bullets could pierce such dignity.

The servant was a one-handed brute of a man, with thinning orange hair and skin that had seen far too many seasons in the sun. He carried a strongbox of Eastern design underneath each arm.

The Mask was dangerous in that subtle way that prompted dogs and beggars to turn aside. All one had to do was look to her confidence to see that she was a projection of a far greater power. The street people of Pan-jim, like street people everywhere, understood the implicit threat.

At least that was what Childress hoped. She walked with purpose. She had al-Wazir—a man who would literally fight tigers. The beggars scuttled away, but in truth more likely from his looming glare than anything in her.

They were intent on finding a chandler if possible, otherwise a hardware store. She knew nothing of Indian towns, but any place that had been run by the Portuguese, then the British, should have a sensible mercantile district.

The town was designed in a European manner. Stone and brick facades lined the central streets, a cathedral square at the middle. A small, fractious palace glowered on a hill behind the church, as if resenting the imposition of the soaring cross that speared the sky between it and the ocean. As she walked Childress noted the profusion of Portuguese names on the storefronts, but also a mix of British and Indian names.

She had expected more people, somehow, but then they had chosen an out-of-the-way port with purpose.

Children dark as soaking walnut shells ran screeching in the streets. Like children everywhere, they played cock-a-hoop, kick the can, kitten-in-a-bag.

Laborers clad only in pale, grubby loincloths bent beneath great baskets of fluttering chickens or bundled greens. Servants and younger daughters of households walked with jars, bags, packages; each wore bright wraps drawn over one shoulder. Some had a red dot placed on their foreheads. Men, too, in a variety of fashions from a pair who could have been Boston bankers to hurrying fellows in long, straight robes fronted by lines of buttons.

Finally, her eyes roved across a scattering of British soldiers under a banyan tree. The lads rested, cupping cigarettes and looking at nothing in particular, but Childress noted that al-Wazir kept his eyes averted. Despite her fantasy of walking cloaked in the power of her stolen office, Childress knew that none of these people would pay her any mind.

"I am doubly glad we did not bring Captain Leung," she said quietly to al-Wazir. "Those men would have taken note."

"And I doubt that," the big Scotsman growled. "Not so long as he dressed the part. Did you not note the Chinee businesses down these side streets? I marked an herbalist, two apothecaries and a tailor just now. If we brought him some of the local linens and a pair of them sandals all these wogs wear, he would look as if he were born here."

Childress was unaccountably delighted at the thought. "You may have just solved our delivery problem, my friend."

The day, though young, was already as hot as she had ever experienced back in New Haven. She halted at a pushcart where a man hawked chilled fruit and shaved ice. "How much?" she asked, pointing to some fresh mango.

He leered up at her, his mouth twisted from some punch thrown fifty or sixty years earlier. "Ten annas for the pretty lady."

"Angus," Childress said in her speaking-to-students voice.

This was an important test. *Five Lucky Winds* carried Chinese Imperial scrip, of course, that would be dangerous here. Gold as well, for emergencies. This they had brought some of in al-Wazir's strongboxes. But of local money they'd had none, until Bai had stumbled over a sack of loose base metal coins in the ship cave. Quite clearly those had been struck in the Portuguese days of Goa.

They needed to know if the coins would cause comment. No one aboard the submarine had the least idea how long ago the currency might have changed, or if the British had bothered to take the old specie out of circulation.

Gold was fine if you wanted to buy two thousand barrels of diesel fuel, but it would hardly purchase eggplant in the market.

Al-Wazir shifted both strongboxes to his handless arm, then dug into a pocket to produce a handful of small-denomination *réis*. He offered them to the vendor, who raised his eyebrows in disdain, then picked out four of the coins. "Sell the family silver," he muttered as he handed her a small paper cone with mango over ice chips.

Childress turned away without thanking him—*for that is how the Mask Poinsard would behave,* she thought, with a small regret from the dead woman whose role she had taken on—and sampled the fruit as she walked. The pale flesh had a pleasant tang.

"Hope you're enjoying it, milady," al-Wazir grumbled behind her.

She laughed, morbid memories fleeing in the face of a sunlit tropical morning. A tinge of confidence seeped in. "Let us try these Chinese streets. If any businesses there speak the language of our friends, they can perhaps hide in plain sight, and all of this effort will be eased."

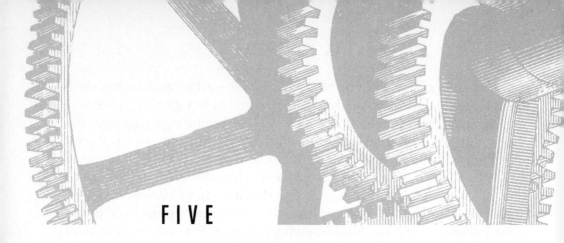

FIVE

The ships of Tarshish did sing of thee in thy market: and thou wast replenished, and made very glorious in the midst of the seas.

—Ezekiel 27:25

BOAZ

He finally rested that afternoon in a wind-hollowed cave on a sandstone height affording him a view of the distant sea and the deaths that lay close by its shore.

Mourning was not something Brass did. Especially not for humans. *Except for Paolina,* a stray thought suggested, but he pushed that idea away. She was not dead, so how could he mourn her? So long as she continued living somewhere, a spark inside his head, Boaz could carry on even though he would never hear from her again.

If he were to mourn anything, it would be the loss of the ancient book. Boaz had scanned the Davidic Kohanim's secrets too quickly to reproduce it with accuracy. Even what notes he could make might revitalize the life of Ophir and the Brass, if he were to reach home and catch the attention of Authority before being erased as a renegade.

That had happened to him once before, for reasons he still did not understand. Or more to the point, recall. Paolina had demonstrated to him how wide the gap in his memory yawned.

Boaz would need to write out what he could before reaching Ophir, so the knowledge would not be lost completely.

Faint fingers of smoke marked the locations of both lost airships. Boaz wondered if Chin Ping had survived, or any of those strange, violent little men. The lion-and-the-unicorn had finally gone to open war with the Imperial dragon.

Boaz wondered how he should feel about that. These flatwater kingdoms were their own affair. Any denizen of the Wall understood this as a first principle. YHWH's purposes, inscrutable as they were within the effulgent cloak of the divine, were different in the rising lands than down below. The Creator had provided His children on the Wall with endless variety, while peopling the rest of the world with a greedy, squabbling monkey sameness.

Though he had known a few fine folk, Boaz was weary of human beings and their discontents.

Setting that thought aside, the Brass looked over the die still clutched in his hands. If this truly was the Sixth Seal, it could change all. The kings and prophets of old had spoken with YHWH as one might seek out a wise man in the market. The Lord was not so inscrutable to them.

Such wisdom as He had left behind in Creation for His thinking children to accumulate had worn thin. The fires on the horizon were proof of that. Likewise conspiracies and treachery among the Brass of Ophir. The world was indeed running down, as free will replaced thoughtful obedience to the divine plan like a widening stain in water.

Carefully, he opened a compartment in his belly. Boaz wrapped the Sixth Seal in a bundle of leaves he'd harvested as he walked, then snugged it within. Closing his belly again, he felt the thing within like a cancer, an unaccustomed weight that would bend his body out of alignment. *As it already bent his thoughts.*

That stray voice again.

"My thoughts are my own," Boaz told the horizon. He settled into the torpid rest that was his approximation of sleep and waited for nightfall.

By daybreak Boaz was much higher up along the Wall. He'd reached a familiar country of stunted trees and low, flowing aprons of scree. He examined the small miracles that were the flowers flickering in the breeze. They grew in tenuous clumps among the heaped rocks that flowed in still, silent rivers down the face of the Wall, brave colors like tiny standards in the green armies of some forgotten war.

Each of them has been made by YHWH, he thought. Every blossom, every petal, every stem represented another page in the book of Creation.

He sat down to stare a while at a blossom. The outer part of the petals was an almost delirious blue. It shaded to a pale subtle color toward the center before becoming a white cup around the delicate structures that lay at the flower's middle. Those were curling up, their season passing, the flower's beauty flowing back to the mind of YHWH.

Boaz sat up in the fading light of dusk. He had been kneeling in the rock field since that morning, staring at flowers and overflowing with the thoughts of the Creator as He set every bit and piece of the world into place.

This was literally incomprehensible. No one could encompass the infinite possibility inherent in a single plant, let alone all the complex majesty of the earth and sky.

Why are you thinking on this? His inner voice again. He recognized it now. The oil-spot chrism on his forehead burned slightly.

The voice arose from his memories of Paolina and al-Wazir. From his sense of what it might mean to be human. From his sense of his own recent ensoulment.

This was the voice of self-doubt, of monkey unreason, the voice of mistake and creative inspiration.

Logic only comes in the light of illogic. Otherwise the universe exists without purpose. Does a rock know logic? Does the sun?

A different thought: YHWH would not have it so. He reached, trembling, for the portal in his belly where the Sixth Seal was hidden. It was changing him, bringing him closer to YHWH, so close that the infinite attention of a Creator God could overtake Boaz in a clump of flowers and trap him as thoroughly as the erasures of Authority in Ophir had trapped Boaz at the Armory of Westmost Repose.

He shuddered and clawed at his belly, but could not seem to open the access port. For the first time in his centuries of life, Boaz' own fingers, his own body, refused to obey his conscious intent.

"Paolina," he cried out. "Please, help me." *Dear one.*

Boaz sat trembling a while, then finally rose to climb away from the marvelous, tempting flowers under the cover of darkness.

Just as there was war between empires to the east of him, inside Boaz' head there was war between the empires of reason and faith—hardwired, blindered faith that left no room for doubt, because there was a speaking tube in his center that admitted the words of YHWH.

"I had not meant to come this way," he gasped, and continued walking upward, westward, away from Paolina and everything he'd come to care about.

Once he was on the Ophir road, even this decayed, rubbled end of it, Boaz made much better time. This was the highway of his people, which he had passed along recently enough in the company of al-Wazir.

Like much of the Wall, this area was deserted. Evidence of prior settlement abounded—a staircase cut into a rock shoulder that connected nothing to nothing; a tributary road leading away from the main highway to an empty meadow; blocks of worked stone in a little cascade of rubble alongside his path.

Staving off the competing voices in his head, Boaz wondered anew what had befallen the life and cultures of the Wall. Ophir was a shadow of its former greatness. An empire once stretching along the Wall from the shores of the Indian Ocean all across the waist of Africa and well into the Atlantic was now little more than an aggressive city. Their days of building great highways and trading around the entire Wall through the car system were a thousand years in the past.

Why? Had YHWH planned for His Creation to grow, and prosper, then tumble back into chaos?

The world was almost six thousand years old. That was incontrovertible fact, the moment of Creation well established by both the inerrant recordkeeping of the Bible and verified by the astronomer-horologists in David's court who had worked out the epicycles and rhythms of the heavens in order to count backward to the original setting that YHWH had established before He put His worlds into motion. Denying the literal truth of Creation was as demonstrably erroneous as denying gravity. Water ran downhill, no matter what one's private faith might argue otherwise.

That the world had been running down for at least a thousand years was likewise incontrovertible. The flatwater kingdoms had prospered in their strange monkey ways, but nothing Boaz knew of along the Wall had maintained its former greatness.

Boaz wondered if the world had reached its peak. What if the coming of the last prophet, Yeshua bin-Joseph, had been the zenith of Creation? The world had existed for four thousand years before His birth. Perhaps the long, slow decline of the civilizations of the Wall was nothing more than Creation returning to the unsprung chaos from which the Lord had first assembled it.

Boaz regretted that he'd pulled that idea from the stream of his thoughts. Yet it held the eerie fascination of the inevitable. Such inexorable symmetry, if it in fact existed, could not be denied.

He quickened his pace. If this insight was true, if the world was in fact already entering its senescence, then the future was inevitable. That, of course, had been implied since the moment of the first words of Creation. But at the least, the Brass of Ophir could make ready for the end, spread the word and employ their collective immortality to watch and wait.

You are a fool, said the human voice within his head. *You make much of nothing, and would take away the only thing that makes us free in the face of the overwhelming might of God's will.*

"Choice?" he asked aloud, his voice sending a startled hyrax scuttling from a rock.

Hope, replied Paolina and al-Wazir in unison.

GASHANSUNU

The sun that night appeared to spiral twice before it touched the horizon, much as a bird might do on approaching the nest with a predator in sight. The earth's lifeline flared with the setting, but night came as swiftly as ever it did in this place.

Gashansunu stood in ibex pose atop the First Ring of the city, looking across the jetty. Her dalliance with Baassiia had been more than pleasant—the man really did understand the secret pathways of a woman's need—but his breast-talk afterward had been of his own fears for the city, and the wrath of the Bone People.

She did not believe so much in the wrath of the Bone People. They had their own relationship with the world, seeing it as a fixed point in the universe about which both space and time revolved. She had heard they claimed every moment was the same to them, but clearly that was not so. Why else would they bother to travel to the city, to elsewhere in the Southern Earth as they were known to do with their powerful, silent airships?

Evening settled over the Great Sunset Water. She consulted with her *wa* on the meaning of the sun's strange passing, but even the Silent World had no special wisdom this day.

SOMETIMES LIGHT IS MERELY LIGHT, she was told.

Yet the world moved strangely. Not so much as it had done two years earlier, when the combined might of all the houses in the city had been required to hold off the boiling walls of water thrown up by the shakings of the world. Even the greatest of old mages dwelling amid the Poison Ring at the center of the city, their bodies wrapped in beaten silver with jewels excrescing from their skin, had been disturbed by that.

The pale stranger had come then, who had inflamed the Bone People with his daring theft, and fled as more of the wave-storms arrived. She wondered anew what he had done, whether he had been cause or solution to the violence that had racked the land and sea then.

Now the world moved strangely, but on a different path. Not so much the vulgar shaking of the body of things, but ripples spreading in the earthsoul. The Silent World.

Discontent was afoot. Some part was aimed at her city.

Gashansunu took the implicit advice of her *wa* and ignored the strangeness at the setting of the sun. Everything in the world was a sign. That was the First Lesson. But not every sign was a signifier. That was the Last Lesson, which she hoped to understand someday before she walked out of her body for good to join her *wa* in the Silent World.

She set out looking for first a bath—to take the crackling, slightly rotten scent of sex off of her body—then food. Tonight Gashansunu thought she could fancy some fish. If she ate it with the right sauces, the dreams that followed might open some of the ways.

Something was happening. Soon enough she would know what. Once she knew what, she would know whom. Once she knew whom, she would know how. Once she knew how, well, if some change was needed, such a thing could be wrought.

If only Baassiia had not been so useless. As a man, he was brilliantly good. As a circle caller, well, he was only a man.

KITCHENS

The next morning, the crew of HIMS *Notus* marched in ragged file across the green of the landing field, then assembled at parade before the base of the tower. Guards surrounded them, rifles at the ready. A few minutes later Sergeant Penstock climbed the stairs, followed by a compact, sallow man sporting a bloody eye and a pronounced limp.

"Harrow, Chief Petty Officer, reporting, sir," the man muttered.

Kitchens studied the newcomer. He appeared miserable, and not just from whatever recent violence had taken him. "Are the commissioned officers with you, Mr. Harrow?"

"They's all sitting in barracks. Says they won't set foot out the door without Captain Sayeed."

Penstock nodded. "Sort of a work stoppage, you might say."

"Well, I don't suppose it's my problem until they arrive on the deck," Kitchens replied. A bald-faced lie, of course. *Notus* would be the most unhappy ship in the history of the Royal Navy. What had Admiralty been thinking to treat these men so?

Well, he knew the answer to that. Government and Admiralty both were mortally afraid of whatever magic the girl had brought aboard the airship; she had used it first to destroy a pursuing Chinese vessel, then later to bomb Strasbourg. That the men might be somehow enslaved to the girl, or simply contaminated with whatever spirit had moved her, was a real fear.

Kitchens looked the petty officer up and down. "Are your men ready to sail, once their officers come aboard?"

Harrow made a show of examining the deck, the gasbag sagging overhead, the general state of affairs on the airship. "Sir, it will take at least a day to get her ready to move, assuming we don't find nothing that's unairworthy enough to require a maintenance takedown. Where would we be sailing to?"

"Back to the West African station, Chief, to set right what was done wrong."

"Ain't us that brought the bitch aboard, sir," Harrow said bitterly. "Begging your grace for my speaking too freely, but I ain't got a lot of patience left. Ain't us what took down the *Shirley Cheese*. Ain't us what decided to haul her into Strasbourg."

"A ship's crew is as one man," Kitchens replied softly. He didn't believe that himself, thought that collective guilt was arrant nonsense, but with such a power loose in the world as these men had touched, no one was taking chances.

Harrow met his eye. "You ever wear a uniform, sir?"

Kitchens touched the dark lapel of his suit coat. "Only this one, Chief. But it exacts its own price."

"Maybe that coat does. But you'll never understand us." He drew himself up and offered a formal salute. "Permission to bring my men aboard, sir? I'd like to have them begin preparing the ship for the air."

"Permission granted," Kitchens replied.

Penstock gave Harrow a long, suspicious look, then headed back over the plank to make his way down the tower stairs. Kitchens waited in silence as the clomp of feet began echoing upward.

Once aboard, the crew set about preparing HIMS *Notus* for sailing. Kitchens made no attempt to address the men. Public speaking was something his training had neglected.

Faced with his gaggle of men, Harrow had come to life. Gone was the somber, depressed affect with which he had addressed Kitchens. Instead the chief practically attacked his crew—berating them, shouting down their work, handing out discipline like sweetmeats on Easter morning. Harrow was everywhere on the deck, harassing the divisional petty officers, liberally putting his boot into the common seamen, and in general making a very noisy nuisance of himself.

"Mr. Harrow," Kitchens said as the chief rushed past a few minutes later with a curse flying. "A word with you, please."

Harrow ceased his pursuit of an errant tool and the hapless sailor who carried it to step close to Kitchens. His voice was very soft, pitched too low for overhearing. "Sir?"

"How dangerous is this crew right now? To themselves and others?"

"We's ten minutes from a mutiny," Harrow said bluntly, still keeping his voice low and soft. "First wrong word comes out, first man who falls upon you, it will all be over. I could not be less surprised should it happen. Whoever in Admiralty gave you to this ship did you no favors, sir, for you've got your hand in the hornet's nest, pure and plain to see."

Despite himself, Kitchens felt a tinge of exasperation. "I am not their enemy, Mr. Harrow." In memory, the Queen bobbed in her bloody tank, face fish-white and drowning-fat. Who was the foe now? The Chinese had not done that to England.

"Begging your pardon, sir, but you *is* the enemy. Any man in a civvie suit who comes from Admiralty will be that to them, for the rest of their lives." He paused, obviously considering his next words. "Sir, should Captain Sayeed or any number of his officers take an idea to do so, *Notus* won't never be coming back to England's shores. Some mutinies start at the top. You might want to go back down them tower stairs and find another place to berth."

"Thank you, Mr. Harrow, but I expect that I shall persevere."

The chief grunted, then strode off without waiting to be dismissed.

Kitchens realized the man had a very good point. Without order and discipline, it wasn't that the sailors might simply run riot, as Kitchens had already foreseen. The entire ship could break loose, a mutiny from foredeck to officers' cabins.

A mutiny that would have only a single victim in hand the day it took place. He did not want to imagine the crew's reaction to the death warrants that lay within his case.

The captain and his officers came aboard the next day without significant ceremony. Sayeed was a dark man, precise in his carriage and bearing. The captain appeared unscathed by his recent incarceration. The seven officers with him had not fared so well, sharing as they did an assortment of split lips, blood-filled eyes, and bandaged hands.

Kitchens hoped one of the latter was not the ship's chiurgeon.

Crew stared at their officers. Officers stared at their crew. No one spoke, no bosun's pipes shrilling, no welcome or orders. Just silence punctuated by the cries of wheeling gulls.

A seaman thumped his mop against the deck once, twice, three times. Another stamped his foot to pick up the rhythm. Within moments the entire crew was pounding out . . . what? A welcome? A salute? The opening act of Harrow's predicted mutiny?

Sayeed rubbed his hands together, gave Kitchens a long, slow look that smoldered like a match-lit fuse, then began speaking. The crew fell silent.

". . . have order on this ship." The captain's voice was quiet, almost quavering. "We fly the Queen's flag; we will behave like the Queen's men." He
drew a deep, shuddering breath.

Kitchens had the impression that Sayeed intended to shout, but what
followed was no louder.

"Return to your posts. Prepare to cast off within the hour."

Notus' master turned away from the sudden scurry and made his way
toward the poop, trailed by the limping, battered officers. Harrow caught
up to them, a look of vast relief just leaving the petty officer's face.

Kitchens braced for what would come next.

PAOLINA

They stumbled, shaking. Dust whirled in an angry, stinging cloud. Paolina
blinked away the grit as Ming cursed softly.

He did not scream, she thought with a guilty sense of relief.

Around them, the world had changed utterly. She'd meant to leave the
termite palace, but she hadn't known her destination. They could have gone
anywhere. Here it was green.

Green.

The rotting, brilliant, blazing viridian of a true tropical jungle. The lungs
at the waist of the world. Broad-leafed and dripping and very, very silent.

This reminded her of the land outside of Ottweill's camp. A horrible
thought struck Paolina: *Had she taken them north of the Wall?*

A quick glance upward told her nothing. They were in a cleared space.
Great, ramified boles rose high over them to meet in an intertwined canopy
that glowed ethereally with the light of the hidden sun. She had no view of
a Murado or the angle of the daystar by which to judge her apparent latitude.

Ropy vines larger than her thigh connected the trees in all directions.
Those vines were wrapped in yet more growth: teeming orchids with their
bright, bobbing flowers; sprays of bromeliad; mats of chartreuse moss; little
curling opportunistic plants filling the spaces between all.

In the airy green cathedral a profusion of butterflies moved, as though
the flowers themselves had detached from their seats and gone hunting
for mates. Flashes of color, some larger than her hand, flitted in aimless
circles driven by the dim priorities of insect intelligence.

Paolina lowered her gaze to Ming. He was brushing dust from his road-
worn blues and frowning. Behind him a spiderweb strung between two of
the great trunks held a slender beauty with an hourglass body and trembling legs that could have spanned Paolina's face. She took half a step back
from that sight, and turned again.

The cleared space had no path leading out. An old deadfall, a void in the rising riot of life that claimed this place. Broad-leafed plants the color of the deepest shadows nodded as if in sleep, shedding huge drops of water with each cycle of movement to make tiny rainfall onto the deep furze that had already claimed the feet of the two travelers.

Then the noise came back. Whatever shock their arrival had introduced to this place was dying away. If there had been an earthquake as a result of her using the stemwinder, it was not here. Something high up hooted once, twice, then crashed away in great leaping arcs completely unseen. Her ears painted the motion as clearly as her eyes would have. A chittering arose, blending into a cycling hum that opened up a whole vista of other noises: animal, insect, bird, wind, water.

And the smell. Rank rot of water standing in old tree trunks, the cloying sweetness of the flowers, the peculiar musk of monkeys high in the canopy, the strange edge that any close mass of green-growing things had, like the ozone prickle before the coming of the storm. The scents were a tapestry of their own, weaving a story just as compelling as the sights and sounds of the place, and just as overwhelming even if she closed her eyes and covered her ears.

"This is horrible," Ming finally said.

"Do you really think so?" she asked softly.

"Yes." He turned in place, making the same assessment she had just conducted, except that his eye as always would be scanning for threats, for opportunities, for dangers that might claim them unawares.

"Ah," said Ming, and stepped toward one of the banyans encircling them. He reached into the shadows of the braided mass of the trunk and pulled out a feather.

It was a yard long, pale as an albino's skin.

"The angel," Paolina blurted, her heart flooding with relief. She was not so used to following blindly. "It has left us a sign."

"Or a very big bird." Ming handed her the feather.

She took the pinion by the quill at the base and turned it over in her hand. Big as this was, it seemed like a sword to her, though it weighed a tiny fraction of what a weapon would. The spine was hollow, just as a bird's feather. The vanes gleamed with little rainbows as tiny irregularities in the barbs caught at the light and plucked beauty unlikely from it.

She realized the feather was blood-warm. "We go that way," she told Ming, pointing at the banyan from which he had retrieved the feather. "We are close."

He looked at the dense growth beyond and shrugged. "I have no . . . ," he said, using a word she didn't know. At her puzzled look, Ming added, "I do not have a knife large enough."

If the feather had in truth been a sword, they could have cut a path with it. Without a machete, they would have to push through as if they lived here, rather than coming as invaders.

That seemed humble enough, somehow. The jungle would be pitiless, as was its nature, but approaching in humility was better than being cloaked in false pride.

Humility. Boaz would have been humble.

She pushed thoughts of the Brass out of her mind and followed Ming into the depths of the forest.

They soon located a trail. Narrow as the path was, she was relieved to stand upright without being wrapped by clinging fingers of green and brown. "A game trail?" she asked.

Ming glanced at her, apparently unsure of her meaning.

"Did animals make this?" Paolina clarified in Chinese. "I think not."

He grunted. "Persons. Or big animals."

She held the feather at arm's length, using it like a pointer. Left, then right. Right, then left. After three tries, Paolina decided that the right caused the feather to tremble more. Judging by the angle of the sun, that was mostly a westward path.

"There," she said. "We will go west."

Before long they came to a rise, a shallow crest of stone emerging from the sea of muck and soil and life that covered the world's hardnesses in this place.

They crested the ridge to find a monkey standing on the path. The creature was almost the height of Paolina's shoulder, and straight-backed. It also wore a grubby loincloth and carried a spear.

Not a monkey, then. Not exactly. Also not threatening. Just blocking their way and staring at them.

Ming shot her a swift glance. Paolina nodded and whispered, "I will do this." She stepped around the Chinese to stand before the monkey. There she spread her arms as if welcoming, to show no weapon but the trembling feather still clutched tight. She smiled, careful not to bare her teeth.

"Friends," she said softly in Portuguese, the language of her birth. "Travelers." She repeated herself in Chinese and English, showing the angel's feather as if it were a token. All three tongues seemed stupidly unlikely in this place.

The monkey-person's liquid brown eyes stared back at her. "Welcome," it said in perfectly good English. "We have been expecting you."

WANG

He did not ask for a tour of the room-of-the-world, and the Mongolian did not offer. Wang would have loved to see how they arranged their information. Knowing a thing held small purpose, if the fact of that knowledge was not itself a known thing. Otherwise people continually reinvented that which had been previously perfected, repeating old errors and ramifying them. This was the whole point of indexing.

The emperor had commanded a bridge be made over the Wall in the manner of the ancients. Even the rudest savage may discover some useful thing not known before. His job had been to coordinate the savants who studied the chaos salvaged from the flooded library, to find those pieces of lost wisdom and assemble them into the hermetic structure that was the true Golden Bridge. Not a thing of stone or altitude, but a pathway of knowledge.

Any good Confucian could understand this. Not so much the disorderly English with their engineer-god and their obsession over the workings of the world.

Now this Mongolian, speaking for the Silent Order, wanted him to walk into the heart of the lion's empire and fetch home a woman of power and the warship on which she traveled. An officer had been brought to command Wang to volunteer.

"Cataloger Wang?" he asked. Lieutenant Hsu was a serious man in a Nanyang Navy uniform. Wang did not believe the rank pips for a moment. Hsu was far too forceful and articulate to be a junior staffer. "Surely your mother did not name you Cataloger?"

The librarian felt chastened in the face of authority. "Wang Bao Wu."

"Hmm. Well, *Cataloger*, the English devils killed over four thousand officers and men."

They were in a large room with slate walls that slid back and forth on tracks. A water tank occupied the center of the floor. Color-coded ship models floated in a desultory array.

Wang had been led through a detailed description of the pursuit of *Five Lucky Winds* after it left Chersonesus Aurea. He was pleased to see that these people recognized the responsibility of the Kô and his Mandarins in allowing the vessel first to dock, then later depart.

That meant Wang's head was perhaps a bit safer. After all, the sum total of his crimes was the mere revelation of state secrets concerning the Golden Bridge to the English Mask.

Hsu wrote out a ship list on one of the slate boards, name after name, while narrating their types and fate. "Three airships, all hands lost, and two of the vessels unrecoverable due to their eventual unguided landings. One heavy cruiser, all hands lost, vessel recovered. Four destroyers, all hands lost, two vessels sank due to mutual collision. Three troop transports, all hands lost, one vessel run aground. The imperial yacht *Divine Jade*, two princes of the imperial family lost, five senior Mandarins of the Imperial Court lost, all hands lost, vessel lost at sea." His chalk piece scratched on a while after he fell silent. Then he said, "We may also add the airship *Heaven's Deer*, lost with all hands during a Wall storm, and the Iron Bamboo submarine *Five Lucky Winds*, suborned and lost to mutiny."

Wang was appalled. "Did they even take casualties?"

"They murdered approximately fifteen of their own crew," Hsu said, so quickly and smoothly that Wang wondered what the officer was concealing—he could not imagine Childress ordering the deaths of men in her service. Or, indeed, her pursuers.

"H-how did our men die?" Wang asked. *Your men.*

"With no mark upon them," Dunkerjav said before Hsu could answer.

Wang nodded. Childress had warned about terrors from across the Wall. "I can see why there has been no effort to send another force after *Five Lucky Winds*."

"We would just lose more men and ships," Hsu said.

Besides, thought Wang, *you are the Silent Order, and navies of China do not belong to you. Not directly.*

Dunkerjav spoke again. "This is why you are here. You have had more dealings with this English Mask than anyone else. One man, aware of the dangers, can be smarter than a thousand guns."

"I take your point," Wang said. "But I do not see where it leads us. Presume I somehow find this woman and her submarine. Imagine they welcome me to their table without striking me down. How should I hope to convince her and *Five Lucky Winds* to return to these waters?"

"The crew are Chinese," Hsu replied. "They will heed the will of their emperor. Find this Captain Leung, and convince him that a pardon awaits if he and his men can return with the English Mask. Alive, for preference, but at least her corpse that we might know she is dead." He paced close to Wang. "This woman threatens China's very existence."

"She is a white bird, as well." Wang's voice was as thoughtful as his racing mind. "It could be the death of your Silent Order."

The faux lieutenant exchanged glances with Dunkerjav. The Mongolian nodded slightly, then spoke to Wang's question. "We ensure the order of Heaven is reflected here on Earth. The plan of the spirit world for the physical world is as real as the brasswork in the sky. If the Masks, with their individual heresies, should gain ascendance, there will be chaos. The reign of Heaven could be threatened."

Wang stirred at that. He burned incense in the temples much as anyone did, but as a thinking man he had never taken the celestial hierarchies literally. Or even seriously. "Are you saying they are demons out of Hell?"

"They could be. How would you set about slaying four thousand men without leaving a mark on them?"

If the white birds were demons, the Silent Order would have realized that centuries earlier. A weapon was feared here, not some pyrotechnic magic out of a gong-clashing opera. "Captain Leung will not likely heed my appeal to his loyalties."

Hsu smiled. "You will find a way."

"How will I locate her?"

Hsu's smile broadened into a grin. "*Five Lucky Winds* has laid in for repairs. The Silent Order has word of precisely where."

Perversely, Wang wished the ship and crew well, hoping for their escape from wherever the dire magics of the Mask Childress and the vengeance of the Silent Order led them.

CHILDRESS

Everything seemed take several times longer than she thought it possibly could. No matter what they did, three other things were required to happen first. This effect was recursive, so each of these begat in turn another handful of needed tasks.

She was no closer to dealing with the Golden Bridge, as they sat here.

"Aye, and it is the way of ships," al-Wazir told her. "All the more so a submarine such as our vessel, for she is made like a puzzle box that must leak neither water nor air."

She considered that before replying. "Whereas an oceangoing vessel can be open at the top. An airship is required to be sealed nowhere but the hydrogen cells themselves, and is actively discouraged from carrying armor or pressure plating by the nature of her missions and the situation within her most natural environment."

"Each of them has their own challenges, ma'am."

Which, Childress realized, probably did not require removing much of the upper deck one bolt and weld at a time to reach the battery arrays and engine compartment aft. Right now *Five Lucky Winds* resembled a fish gutted from the spine down. She rode oddly high in the water due to blown ballast tanks and a strong desire on the part of Leung and his crew not to have a tidal surge slosh the salt sea into the delicate compartments.

Childress and al-Wazir sat on cut-down barrels in front of a rickety table on which a messy, unending game of mah-jongg was laid out. The players changed in a rotation opaque to her, and the game was only idle during the midwatches of the day when all hands were either sleeping, on guard or working on repairs to their ship.

If the British caught them now, there would be no point in fighting. *Five Lucky Winds* was as vulnerable as an aether-addled boxer laid out on the operating table. Should his opponent enter the room with bare knuckles and bloody intent, the match was over before it began. Likewise their position.

"How progresses the work, Chief?" Leung was tight-lipped, a bit unusually so for him—something that in turn stirred Childress' fears.

"It depends on that fellow from Bombay. He's the electrickal johnnie, and he knows what can be purchased here in India and what must be made up to order, or bought at salvage."

"Does electrickal gear go to salvage?" Childress' curiosity was piqued.

"Wrecks get stripped." The big man shrugged. "Equipment gets replaced that can be easily refitted or broken down to useful parts. And theft. Never forget theft, ma'am. The quartermaster's friend." Regret seeped into al-Wazir's voice. "Her Imperial Majesty's services are full of it."

"Chief," she began. Childress changed her mind, stopped, and tried anew. She would have taken his hand had it been within reach, though the impulse seemed disloyal to Captain Leung. "Threadgill. I cannot say if you have done the right thing here. All I know is that your loyalty to Paolina, and your willingness to aid an old woman in her need, speak very well of the state of your soul and the quality of your intentions."

"The girl never was more than a river-soaked kitten," he mused, still sad and distant in his tone, "who could either save the world or destroy it." He gave Childress a long, slow look. "I only knew her a double handful of days, ever. Six in Ottweill's camp when she first came to us alongside John Brass, who was the strangest man I ever met. Then five more from Mogadishu to *Heaven's Deer* to *Five Lucky Winds*, afore she was away up the Wall with that Ming fellow.

"In that time, ma'am, she won more loyalty from me than forty years with the Queen's shilling in my pocket had bought. Aye, I shall never be proud that she led me to betray my oaths, but the world needed her safe more than it needed me to follow my orders."

"When did you betray your oaths, Chief?" Childress knew part of the story. "You sent her to England aboard one of Her Imperial Majesty's airships. That was rightly done. Since you came into the east on wings of storm, you have been scrambling only to survive and to ensure the lives of those around you. We have fired no shots at a British ensign." *Yet*, she thought. "Your loyalty to the Crown should not be in question, even now."

The big man seemed close to tears, a strange expression on his craggy, weatherworn features. Childress saw a gaping need for comfort, but had no way to fill it. "I hae forsworn myself by abandoning Dr. Ottweill's expedition without ever returning with relief. I hae since taken service with a Chinese vessel, ma'am." His voice caught in his throat as he sank deeper into the rough, burred Scots of his youth. "I hae sat here four days in an English port and nae whispered a word to any of the wogs nor held a chaffer with one of them sergeants walking the streets of Panjim. I hae made nae attempt to seize command of *Five Lucky Winds*, or escape myself to friendly forces. I hae not rescued you, an English lady, from your vile fate in yon hands. Any of 'at would hae me before a court-martial, or belike an Admiralty board of inquiry."

What to say? This was like talking to a divinity student at exam week, when the doom of a semester's worth of unread texts descended on the final hours standing between him and a ruinous mark in a key class.

"Threadgill, I cannot shrive you. I am merely one of Her Imperial Majesty's subjects, neither an officer of her Royal Navy, nor a judge in her courts. But I am also a Mask of standing." To her surprise, Childress believed that last. "I am heir to the power and writ of the Mask Poinsard, and someday the Feathered Masks of *avebianco* in their halls at Valetta will answer to me for the crimes they have committed. When I am successful in that, I will in turn address the insults of the Silent Order to the progress of the human spirit and the orderly continuance of the world for both Imperial thrones."

She leaned forward to touch his shoulder, almost brushing the mahjongg tiles from their careful, scattered towers. "You have done well, making goodly choices that may have literally saved the world. Whatever an admiral says to you at a later moment in your life will be forever outweighed in the eyes of both man and God by the good you did for that poor girl."

"It is to those admirals that I answer, ma'am, neither to man or to God. I have lain hard by an English port for days, and discharged none of my sworn duties."

Childress sighed. "I speak from no man, and God does not listen to me. But I will not stop believing that you have done well and good by both England as a whole and by those whom you have met and aided along the way."

His smile, a rare enough commodity of late, quirked at her. "Thank you, ma'am."

A Chinese sailor dashed up to them. "An airship is outside," he shouted in his own language. "I was to tell you."

"We'll go look," growled al-Wazir. Childress quickly followed him to the tunnel mouth. The chief grabbed a carbine from the guards there as he hurried into the rising darkness with her not far behind his heels.

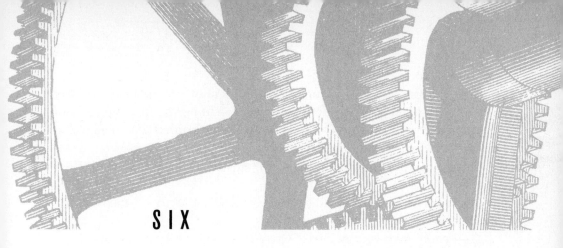

SIX

BOAZ

Early in his sixth morning on the road, an airship of unfamiliar design cruised past at a fairly high altitude. A Royal Navy scout? Dawn colored the hull pink. Boaz could spot no standards flying.

An hour further into that day, the small airship returned from the west. This time it sailed more slowly at a lower altitude. The vessel moved in a quartering pattern, suggesting the captain searched for something.

Him.

Boaz considered going to ground to wait this out, but realized that if the British truly wished to find him they would so long as he kept to the road. Better to meet them head on, hear them out, and if possible convince them of his own mission to Ophir.

Ottweill must be on their minds. Perhaps Boaz could use his time in the doctor's work camp along the wall to be persuasive.

He stopped in the middle of the road and waved his arms to signal the approaching airship.

The aerial fast packet HIMS *Erinyes* was commanded by a Lieutenant Ostrander, a brown-haired boy with brown eyes and brown teeth, sprouting stray hairs from his chin and speaking in a voice that cracked every sentence. At the moment, he focused his very serious attention on Boaz.

"Colonel Pinter wants you back in Mogadishu."

They stood on the deck of the airship, which was slung very close to the gasbag and thus forced the vessel's overtall commander to slouch. Al-Wazir would have been scandalized.

The Brass had come aboard in brief, shouted negotiations, and now watched Africa and the Wall turn as the ship's pilot attempted to head her into the wind, keep station here where they had picked Boaz up and not move her in any direction—three contradictory orders Lieutenant Ostrander had issued in quick succession.

From the expressions of the crew, all had not settled well aboard HIMS *Erinyes*.

"I cannot travel to Mogadishu," Boaz said patiently. "I have critical business farther west along the Wall."

"I—I could take you by force." Ostrander's voice was uncertain.

"You could make the attempt, but you would not hold me long." Boaz turned to look at the bosun, a compact, red-faced man with hair the bluish black of a soldier's best-polished boots, suspicions burning in his eyes. He grasped a Webley service revolver cocked and ready. "Your men know what it is to fight Brass. I expect they've been out to the tunnel camp, or heard stories. I am aboard as your friend, not your enemy."

Ostrander almost shivered as he continued to stare intently at Boaz. "I am under orders."

"As am I," the Brass lied. He would hardly admit his destination of Ophir to this pup. "You brought me onto this vessel under your word we would engage in negotiations. If you arrest me, I *will* tear your ship apart. If you release me, I will continue on my way west. Or . . ." He did his best to sound sly. "If you carry me westward, once I reach Dr. Ottweill's encampment, you can seek new orders and we can renegotiate."

"A word with you, sir," said the bosun to his commander, keeping his hard eyes on Boaz.

Ostrander held up a hand in protest. "No, no, Mr. McCurdy. I shall work through this myself." He stepped away from Boaz and paced aftward to stare at the vista of the Wall swinging by, far too close.

"How long has he been in command?" Boaz quietly asked the bosun.

Something akin to relief darted across McCurdy's face. "Since last night, John Brass."

"Too many promotions, too quickly." He'd heard al-Wazir say that.

"There's a war for you." The bosun uncocked his revolver and slid the weapon back into its holster. "Ain't you the fellow who brought the Chinee to Mogadishu?"

"I came out of the west with Chief Petty Officer al-Wazir of the Royal Navy. He was taken by the Chinese during the raid on your city."

"Ain't my city," muttered McCurdy.

"As may be. In any case, too many were lost in that action."

Lieutenant Ostrander stalked back toward them, head bent forward like some wading bird. "If I convey you to Ottweill, will you return to Mogadishu with me afterward?"

He's struck at the bait. Al-Wazir in a similar situation would have just thrown a Brass invader overboard, or possibly brazed him into irons and restrained him with an anchor chain upon the open deck.

"Let us sail westward and see what orders wait," Boaz replied, which was no answer whatsoever. From McCurdy's expression, the bosun understood that perfectly well.

"Very well," Lieutenant Ostrander said. "Set a course to the west," he called out. "The port at Ayacalong on the West African station."

HIMS *Erinyes* was a faster ship than Boaz was accustomed to. He measured their progress by observing the apparent passage of features along the Wall. That first afternoon, Ostrander had gone below to do whatever commanders did alone in their cabins. The midshipman had the deck.

Bosun McCurdy seemed to have inherited charge of the Brass interloper. The man's attitude had shifted from suspicion to resignation. Boaz missed the easy camaraderie he'd shared with al-Wazir.

"Sure you do not somehow imagine that I shall murder all the crew in their bunks?" he asked McCurdy as the two of them stood at the rail, gaping upward at the immensity of the Wall.

The bosun snorted. "You had the right of it, John Brass. I been on the Wall at the camp, running courier when Lieutenant Mafwyn had *Erinyes*. We heard all about your lot, how you was unstoppable forces of nature and the like. Your kind can take a bullet, spit it out and shove it up a man's arse without breaking stride. If you were of a mind to pull herself out of the sky"—he patted the rail with his free hand—"there ain't so much none of us could do for it unless we wrassled you overboard before you tore all our arms off."

"Then why did you bring me aboard?"

His head tilted, signaling somewhere over his shoulder. "Lieutenant had orders. Looking for a Brass what left the Chinese fight along the Abyssinian coast. No one was sure what they saw, but your footprints was in their beach camp, and word is some of them chinkers got took prisoner and sang."

Boaz wondered who might have survived among the men he had known. "Orders were to bring me in?"

The bosun shrugged. "Not rightly certain. But the lieutenant here, he's the talkingest fellow I ever served under. I don't believe he'd pinch the crap off own his butt if there was someone around to ask about it first. He wanted to talk; you wanted to talk. Me, I'd have shot you down where you stood, sawed your arms and legs off, and brought you back to Mogadishu in five separate barrels."

"That would probably prove an effective deterrent," Boaz admitted. "Your honesty is refreshing."

"Not my decision. First thing that wet-eared pup Ostrander did once he come aboard was pull me aside and explain the chain of command. Me, in Her Imperial Majesty's Royal Navy, boy and man, these past thirty-two years."

::*This man does not render the proper piety to his superiors.*::

With a tinge of panic, Boaz realized the Sixth Seal stirred in his belly.

"I am well enough pleased with the current state of affairs," he told McCurdy, trying to change the subject before the voice of the Seal grew stronger. He did not want to slip into lost time again. "How fares the fight against the Chinese?"

"Hah." The bosun gave Boaz a sidelong glare. "Likely I'm consorting with the enemy to even speak of that with you."

"Do I seem Chinese?"

"No. But you was with them, before."

"Taken prisoner," Boaz reminded him.

"Aye. You being a fellow who can snap mainstays with the strength of his bare arms." McCurdy reached over and rapped Boaz just above the elbow. A hollow thunk echoed.

::*disrespect*::

"I prefer you not do such things," the Brass said quietly.

People touch each other all the time, said the human voice inside his head, that blend of Paolina and al-Wazir. *That is how they remember each of them is people.* The damage was done, though, as the bosun's face closed and he turned away.

"Ships burning." After a moment McCurdy spoke, to Boaz' surprise. "The chinkers shelled Kismayo. Not enough of either of us around for a fight like this to go on long. Not until someone sends a lot more ships and men."

Or an army comes along the face of the Wall to put you both down. Boaz was relieved to find that was an Ophir thought, something of his own past and people. Whatever he could see of them, in truth. Not one of the new voices he continued to hear.

More and more he was coming to appreciate the complexity of the human mind, monkey meat being made to think in imperfect channels, not like the crystal arrays and Sealed precision of a Brass brain.

Still, his belly was strangely warm.

"I am certain it will work as you hope," he told McCurdy. "Dr. Ottweill is poised to discover great secrets."

"Ottweill?" The bosun snorted. "He's gone so deep down his own rabbit hole ain't nobody knows for sure he's ever coming out."

"They are truly lost?" Boaz could not decide whether that was good news or ill.

"Why would a John Brass like you be thinking the lieutenant set a course for Ayacalong instead of the Wall camp?"

Their conversation drifted into silence after that, while the little airship beat her way west, ungainly and pregnant with destiny.

As shadows slipped deeper into night, Boaz settled down along the rail for his sort of rest. McCurdy squatted close to him after a few minutes.

"John Brass," the bosun whispered.

Boaz blinked away muzzy visions of Paolina in a jungle somewhere. "Yes?"

"Ostrander, he's not such a bad sort. The middie's all right as well, but he truly is just a lad and needs someone to mind his nappies. Our lieutenant, though, he was a supply officer in the depot at Mogadishu before the Chinese raid. His wife and baby died in the fires, and the colonel gave him *Erinyes* because there weren't nobody else to take the ship. But I think . . ."

In the following silence, Boaz held his tongue. Treachery stirred. The bosun seethed with a dire need to confide about something that frightened him.

Finally, McCurdy completed his thought. "I think he doesn't sleep, because all he sees behind his eyes is flames. That will make any man mad, rightly smartly so."

"What is it that you believe I might do?" Boaz asked.

"Nothing." For the first time, Boaz understood the bleakness that had been lurking in McCurdy's voice all day. "You're the enemy. But what you might *not* do is this; you might not break the poor man."

The bosun feared for his ship, of course. Boaz tried to reassure him. "It is my ambition to better the world, not worsen it. I see no difficulty in applying that philosophy to Lieutenant Ostrander."

The bosun lightly brushed Boaz' shoulder with his fingertips. *Monkey touch*, Boaz thought—the voice of his own mind, though he could hear approval echoing deeper within. "Yes," McCurdy said, "and if you was an Englishman I might even be trusting in you."

"I shall endeavor not to disappoint."

KITCHENS

The airship HIMS *Notus* headed south and east out of Dover. The English Channel slid by quickly enough; then they passed over the farming country of Normandy. Kitchens watched their progress from the navigator's station on the poop deck, a folding chart table open before him. He'd clipped a length of foolscap there onto which he periodically made coded notes in a tiny, precise sequence of dots that in truth signified nothing whatsoever.

Captain Sayeed finally stepped away from the helm to approach Kitchens. The special clerk made a point of covering his notes to keep them from the officer's view.

"Would you prefer to give me my orders here on the open deck," Sayeed asked, "or should we repair below?"

Kitchens knew he would have to stay far ahead of this man, so best to keep the lead open as wide as possible. "We are proceeding according to a sailing plan delivered by Admiralty into your care. Our destination is known. I am merely here to observe."

"And report, as well." Sayeed frowned. "I know what you carry in your papers. Admiral Towle was quite careful to inform me how critical your good opinion is to the continued health of my men and my ship."

"For my part," Kitchens said, speaking the words he'd so carefully considered, "I do not believe your ship and crew were well served. You least of all. There has been panic over the secret societies. This fear has been turned on *Notus*."

"You have surely seen my dossier." The captain's stare was unblinking. "They would not have set you on this deck without knowing of my affiliation with the Silent Order."

If Sayeed was not worried, he would not be, but this subject was rarely spoken of in open company. "Yes," he said simply. "That is not my concern. I am charged with aiding Dr. Ottweill and the tunnel project. You and your ship may be redeemed from suspicion through exemplary service in pursuit of my mission."

"Hmm." Sayeed looked decidedly unimpressed. "Mr. Kitchens, perhaps you are familiar with the circumstances of my birth?"

"Beirut, 1869," the dark clerk responded promptly. "Of Arab parents, under Ottoman rule, taken to England as a small boy after the Battle of Acre and raised in fosterage."

"My skin is an unfortunate hue, and my name condemns me as a wog." Bitterness laced the captain's voice. "I have never been redeemed from suspicion before this, Mr. Pale Man with the Very English Name. No more so will I be now."

"If you have labored under suspicion all your life," Kitchens asked, leaving his scripted words behind in pursuit of this opening, "why did you become involved in the Silent Order?"

"I rather imagine for the same reason you wear that dark suit and little round hat, and carry those papers under your arm." Sayeed quirked a secretive smile. "Because I believe the world can be a better place for all men. This path seemed wisest to me."

"Does it still seem wise to you?"

The captain had no answer for that as his face hardened and he turned away.

Kitchens stood with Simpkins the navigator as the charts were laid out. "Should we meet no adverse weather, twelve days and nights under three-quarter power to make our port," the officer said.

"With a stop for fuel and ballast in Marseilles or Algiers?"

Simpkins met his gaze. Only one of the navigator's green eyes was visible—the other was swollen shut beneath a crusted purple bruise. "We can make the whole run without tendering, but there are no facilities at Ayacalong. If we arrive low we should be forced to beat back up the coast to the new station at Cotonou. And sir . . . no sane airman will be over the deep desert without as much gas, fuel and water aboard as he can possibly manage."

"Would full power trim our air time?"

"Certainly. But we'll use her fuel twice as fast. Oil is heavy stuff, and *Notus* does not carry so much of it as you might like to think. You could be walking back from the Bight of Benin."

"Not many men have made that trip unassisted," Kitchens said, thinking of al-Wazir.

Later, in his own small cabin, Kitchens considered Ottweill's mission, and what *Notus* would likely find amid the savage wonders of the wall. It was not so difficult to build a case that any country wishing to spread its dominion across the Northern Earth was ruled by men as mad as hatters. The awful majesty of Queen Victoria in her sad decline was enough to convince Kitchens that the Wall held no monopoly on the breaking of the human mind and the shattering of the human spirit.

With that thought, he reached for the little case in which the Queen's bloody paper had been deposited.

It is not about imagination, Kitchens thought. All of this—empires, the Wall, England's endless bickering with China—all of it was about fear.

The paper had long since dried. He should have unfolded it before the bloody goo had set up to a stiffening dye. Since then, there had been no appropriate moment. Kitchens had not been ready.

He feared whatever message the Queen had given him. He feared what she would ask him to do. He feared turning back to England's shore and setting his neck before the blade for a command from a madwoman floating in a tank. He feared refusing the lawful order of his sovereign. He feared declining the dying hope of a monarch beloved across half of the Northern Earth.

Kitchens indulged himself sufficiently to wish that the paper had never come into his hand. A choice not presented could not be refused.

He placed it now on the tiny table unlatched from the cabin wall. A folded scrap, about the size of a postage stamp. The original had been kraft paper rather than the fine stationery of a royal palace, or even the decent writing paper of a gentleman in a hurry. Something a servant might use to keep a laundry list. Something a woman might secret away, whose every movement was constrained by mechanism and close observation.

At a practiced flick of the wrist, the razor fell out of his sleeve into his hand. Kitchens thumbed open the blade without looking at it. It would be hair-sharp and silver-bright. His blades always were. The note was stained a cranberry color, mottled with blood and fluid, crusted into a papier-mâché square.

He used the tip of the razor to lift the free edge of the small, folded piece. Little purpose in tugging with blunt, clumsy fingers. The paper made a popping noise, then flopped into a rectangle.

To his surprise, it did not break at the spine of the little joint now revealed.

A bit more work with the blade tip split the crust on the next set of open edges. He was patient as a man mixing explosives.

The ship rocked with some shift in the winds. Kitchens set the open razor down on the table, one finger pressed to the handle to keep it from sliding away in the event the deck canted. The engines growled more loudly for a brief moment, then settled down to their usual thrum.

After a few minutes of quiet, he resumed his surgeries.

WANG

The monk led him back down the long steps, through the darkness. "You have yourself a thoroughly modern quest," she called to Wang over her shoulder.

"I am relieved to know that I have not fallen into some ancient *xiákè* epic."

"Not to be so lucky. I am afraid your epic is likely to be short and brutal. Are you familiar with any weapons?"

His breath came so much easier on the way down, though his knees complained. "Only personnel and requisition forms, ma'am."

That drew a laugh. "With which one may lay waste to armies from the comfort of one's own desk, to be certain. Surely you have cut your own brushes?"

"Any man knows how to use a small blade," Wang said defensively.

"A small blade is all that most men have," she replied. "No matter."

After a moment, he asked, "That is everything?"

"You were expecting mystic revelations?"

"I was expecting . . . more . . ."

She laughed again. "You hunt a Mask of great power and ferocious reputation. Your only weapons are your words."

"Followed by some watcher in force, I am certain," he grumbled, then paused his descent in dawning horror as he realized just who his watcher would be.

"*Quis custodiet ipsos custodes?*"

It took Wang a moment to realize the monk had spoken to him in Latin. He did not take her meaning, but she seemed quite pleased.

"I believe you have a boat waiting for you down below," she added.

PAOLINA

Following their guide, she and Ming descended into the village. The settlement was scattered along the riverbank as far as Paolina could see in both directions before the dark, overhanging shadows of the jungle obscured her view.

Open walls were formed by pillars and posts that leaned at odd angles. Roofs were a haphazard mass of reeds, flowers and dangling leaves. No doorway was particularly square.

Familiar habits of thought reasserted themselves. She noted that the architecture conformed to the demands of this junglescape. Rain would not fall directly on most of these houses, but rather filter through the upper layers of the trees. This place was so warm that the inhabitants should never need sealed windows. The materials were harvested by gathering, rather than by gangs of men with axes, so the surrounding tropical forest remained almost unchanged.

"The home of the Correct People," their guide said with a shy smile.

Her folk were everywhere. Many lounged, but somehow even then they had a quality of coiled motion. Many more carried fruit, speared fish, splashed in the river, whittled—all the business of a tropical settlement, but with a curious and refreshing quality of *play* about it.

Ming nodded to the right. Paolina looked up to see a much larger structure lodged in the trees. This one resembled a European building. Gabled roofs overhung balconies and porches. A Correct Person in a wrap of pale cloth gazed solemnly down at the travelers. She seemed the only sober-mannered individual in the whole village.

Paolina raised a hand in greeting. Her gesture was returned with a quiet, patient nod before the Correct Person stepped back into the shadows of the enormous house.

"Who lives up there?" she asked their guide.

Without even glancing toward the house, the woman said, "Kalker will explain all."

Who is Kalker? Paolina held her tongue.

They descended into an amphitheater set along the riverbank. A net of vines overhung the space. Rows of seats had been made from stones or split logs.

"Kalker will meet you here," the guide said. "This is a special place, built up to honor our . . . Well, that is his story."

Paolina smiled. "What is your name, that I might be more properly grateful later?"

"Arawu," the Correct Person said shyly. She added something in a sibilant, hissing tongue. Then: "I go."

Ming bowed from the waist. Arawu giggled and trotted back up to the top of the amphitheater before vanishing into the jungle.

"What now?" the sailor asked in Chinese.

"We wait," she said in the same language. Switching to English: "I think this is the place the angel meant for us to come."

Enjoying a sense of accomplishment—whatever she had been pursuing since crossing the Wall was at hand—Paolina examined the feather. The pinion was ragged from their passage through the jungle. As she walked through their village, the Correct People had stared at that feather even more than they had stared at her.

She tried to imagine a bird-mad jungle monster cruising low above the treetops. These folk did not live as though they feared death from the air. They did not live as though they feared much.

Paolina wondered what Boaz would have made of this place. Ming was a fine traveling companion—respectful, protective, thoughtful—but even though they'd been together for the better part of a month, Paolina could not call it friendship.

Nothing like what she and Boaz had developed upon *a Murado*. The Brass man was by turns intriguing, infuriating, disrespectful, even strange; but always there had been an innocence about him.

Even Ming with his endless Oriental patience and calm politesse was a man. A man to step in front of her, to pick up a weapon at need, to make an urgent decision and issue peremptory demands.

Her inner self-honesty interrupted that thought: *Had Boaz not done so, in carrying you down the Wall against your will?*

That had been different. Paolina knew this, surely as she knew the span of her own hands. Different because it was Boaz, and he was special to her, lovely in her eyes? Or different because he was not human?

Could she love a Correct Person?

Ming tapped her arm again. She followed his gaze.

An elderly man of the Correct People hobbled down the bowl of the amphitheater toward them. His fur was silvered, his face deeply lined, and he walked with a short, twisted cane. A few heads bobbed briefly behind him, others taking a look, but they withdrew as soon as her eyes lit upon them. This one had to be Kalker.

Paolina stood. "Welcome, sir."

Shuffling, Kalker peered up at her. His eyes were crusted with rheum, though a strong spirit glowed within them. He then examined Ming, tapping the Chinese sailor's knee once, very gently, with the stick. Finally he turned his attention back to Paolina.

"You have a feather." His English carried the strange, sibilant accent of these people's speech, which made Paolina wonder how Arawu had come to speak the language so well.

She held the angel's feather out. Kalker took it, turned it over in his hand once, then handed it back. "Messengers from the Northern Earth," he said, his voice freighted with authority. "We have our own Creation here. The Wall keeps the Garden safe, as your people would explain it."

"How do your people explain it?" she asked, intrigued.

He smiled, an easy grin filled with age-blunted teeth. "The Correct People do not explain. We experience. Every day is the morning of the world; every night is its ending. Only you Northerners require time to flow like a river from a hidden spring to a dark and distant ocean."

She sat. It felt rude, but so did towering over him. This way they could speak eye-to-eye. "Is it you whom I was sent to meet?"

"No." Kalker laughed, wheezing. "Like one of your God's angels, I am only a messenger. A prophet lives among us, who was sent forth and brought back again. He will never again leave this place, but you are the first to come to him." The Correct Person grew more thoughtful. "The last as well, I hope."

He looked at Ming. "What manner of man are you?"

"I am a sailor of the Middle Kingdom," Ming responded in Chinese.

"Hmm." Kalker closed his eyes a moment, then said in English, "Welcome to our village."

"Does this place have a name?" Paolina asked.

"Does it need one?"

She had no real answer for that, so she let the silence unfold. Kalker seemed happy to join in, until his head cocked at a distant hooting. "Ah, we are ready. Please do come."

He turned and walked slowly up the log steps. Paolina followed, trailed by Ming.

Out on the path, the Correct People had gathered. Many carried fruit or flowers, as if going toward an offertory. Others clutched children, or held hands with their friends. Faces were smiling and proud, not fearful or tense, she noted. Ming walked so close behind her that he almost stepped on her heels.

Paolina was unsurprised to find they approached the almost-European house. Kalker led them to a ladder that had been carved into one of the great tree trunks supporting the structure. He stepped aside as the solemn woman of the Correct People awaited them there.

"I am Arellya," she said, also in English. "Are you ready to climb?"

"Of course." Paolina was intensely curious to meet their prophet.

"I will follow last," Ming told her softly in Chinese.

Paolina clasped the gnarled wood of the rung at her eye level. It was rough and mossy. She felt tiny flowers crushed beneath her grip. She climbed into deepening shadow. The ascent was easy enough, though surrounded as they were by the mass of Correct People, it carried the taste of ritual.

At the top, she pulled herself onto a porch. A wide doorway led inward. Thin curtains stirred in the breeze. A man sat within—no, a thin-shouldered boy of her own people, barely grown to man-height. He was only a silhouette to her.

Not waiting for Ming, she stepped inside. The boy looked up, his face visible now in the shadowed interior. He had been comely enough once, dark haired and pale eyed, but the ravages of pain and ill use had set lines upon him prematurely.

"Welcome." His voice was accented like an Englishman's, but with the trace of another country. "I have been making a clock." Without getting up, he pointed her to a chair across from his worktable. Ming sidled over with her and took a place at her shoulder.

The prophet leaned forward, still seated. "I am Hethor Jacques. Tell me, what mischief has God set upon the world this time?"

GASHANSUNU

The way of dreaming opened with a pallid crocodile swimming as in deep, rushing water. Its body twitched like an armored eel. The great legs snapped back and forth, propelling the beast forward. She rode along beside it, much as her *wa* rode along beside her, watching in the sun-bright depths of the beast's gold-flecked eyes.

The waters opened before her like clouds, and Gashansunu understood the crocodile had not been sounding the pelagic depths but the argosy of stars, never sighting land, for its eyes had always been trained on the heavens. This was a hunter of souls, an eater of spirits, and the medium where it pursued its sport was the Silent World.

Using the Precepts of Dreaming, she stepped away. The crocodile grew smaller, then smaller still, then tiny, until it became a pale silverfish swimming against a current, a tiny chip of fire in the eyes. Gashansunu reached out and crushed it between her fingers. The swift searing of her flesh she accepted, for in truth it was only a pinprick.

When she opened her hand to inspect the damage she saw that a tiny tattoo had been placed where the crocodile had died. The mark was a map of the skies, the ring-of-Earth with the ring-of-Moon both encircling the sun. She stared at the markings until they grew to overwhelm her vision; then she stepped through them into the space between the stars where the great beast had swum. Kicking, she found her own momentum, settling into the easy, purposeful rhythm.

After a while, she realized that her *wa* was pacing her, close and nervous. Ahead, the stars parted to reveal a great waterfall. An entire ocean cascaded from beyond the skies, but her *wa* retreated from her, growing smaller and smaller against the gigantic raindrops until two great, ridged pincers came to crush her life.

She awoke sweating.

Her hand ached.

Gashansunu again used the Precepts of Dreaming, this time to determine if she was in fact awake, or somewhere within another layer of the Silent World.

This time she was in fact herself. Outside, a sunrise stippled with the gelid colors of fruit threatened the world with what was to come next.

The meaning of the dream was obvious enough. She was being drawn into a self-consuming circle. Gashansunu and her *wa* would need to see past the traps that were coming and find their way to reconciling the regrets of the world.

She rose, pulled on a kilt of muslin with a tooled belt, and a beaded vest to bind her breasts and cover her back. She gathered her satchels— one for promise, one for fear and one for the practical filth that was the body itself.

Down the long, winding stairs cut into this tower and off to find Baassiia or one of the other circle callers from Westfacing House.

Gashansunu knew from the angle of the dreaming crocodile's circling that she was being drawn to the inland east. Almost the direction of the hold of the pale wizard, though that one was now thought to have been lost some time ago.

Birds followed overhead as she paced the dawn streets. Though Gashansunu did not take note, the morning mists swirled in her wake with a hot agitation that brought them puddled to the ground behind her.

She would tell Baassiia about her dream. Whatever troubled the world was out there. Gashansunu would find it, and set things to right.

CHILDRESS

They peered out the window of the festival warehouse. The fields beyond were empty even of cattle. The road to Panjim was deserted. Engines droned close by, but they saw nothing.

Al-Wazir stood by the door, four sailors with him. He had an ear cocked as well.

"Can you tell anything by the sounds, Chief?" she asked in a stage whisper.

He looked pained. "If I were out in the open, ma'am, probably." His voice was normal, though. "'Tis muffled by the walls of this wretched building. I dare not look until I know. No point in showing me remaining hand."

One of the sailors looked at her. "I can try to reach the top from within," he said in Chinese.

Childress nodded. "Go, then."

The chief watched him head back through the warehouse, hunting for a ladder. "Now you order my men around."

"*Our* men." She forced a smile.

"Only one captain on a ship, ma'am."

"He is below in the dark with his vessel."

Chinese hissed from above, too rapidly for Childress to follow. Fong, one of the other sailors, looked back and forth between her and al-Wazir— one, twice, three times—then gave up and addressed her.

"It is of the Middle Kingdom. Lu does not recognize which fleet, but in these waters that should be the Nanyang Navy."

A *Chinese* airship? Over Goa? "He says it's one of theirs," she told the chief.

"They don't operate here," al-Wazir said shortly. "Not in the ordinary run of things. Too damned dangerous for them along the Hindoo coast, pardon my language, ma'am."

"They operate here now." Childress returned to peering out the window as the engine noise grew in pitch.

"It turns," whispered Fong. "Lu says another approaches from the west."

Far more likely they are both sub hunting in these waters than that they have the temerity to attack British India, she thought.

Then two ships passed into her line of sight, making for Panjim. Definitely of Chinese lines. They trailed long banners of black silk. Someone out there rode to war on wings of cloud.

The chief eased the door open and watched from shadow. "Damn my eyes, they're making a bombing run."

"Who would bomb Panjim?" she asked.

"Someone who wishes to show the Royal Navy how overstretched British forces are." Al-Wazir almost choked with laughter. "Every ship on the East African station could be here and altogether they would not even begin to cover such a coastline. John Chinaman is calling England's bluff."

Childress joined him at the door. Smoke already billowed up from the town. She could hear the crackle of gunfire, but no answering airships rose to the defense.

Death was the same whatever guise it came in. Childress had learned that from Anneke, aboard the *Mute Swan* all those months ago. Part of another woman's lifetime, some unreal drama for which she had once held a scripted role.

"The British will answer," she said. "This is war, not a skirmish or test or reconnaissance. It will not be waved away at a table by drunken diplomats."

"To what gain?" al-Wazir asked quietly.

"Have you yet met a Chinese who would trust us?"

"N-no," he replied. "And nae without reason."

"Whatever they hope to draw out, it will come with a swift sword." Childress turned to the sailors. "Find the captain and tell him we will be receiving no more supplies from our friends in the town for the foresee-able future."

She had a cold, sick feeling that the order of the world had come to an end in this bombing. "I shall be the Mask," she told no one in particular. "The Mask shall set this foolish game to rights."

"Good luck, ma'am," al-Wazir growled. "All of us, we'll need it."

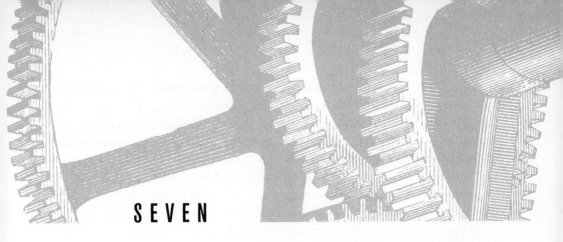

SEVEN

And, behold, six men came from the way of the higher gate, which lieth toward the north, and every man a slaughter weapon in his hand; and one man among them was clothed with linen, with a writer's inkhorn by his side: and they went in, and stood beside the brasen altar.

—*Ezekiel 9:2*

BOAZ

HIMS *Erinyes* approached the drilling camp at the base of the Wall at dead slow, through a thick, blood-warm fog off the Bight of Benin. Lieutenant Ostrander stood by the helmsman, his eyes fever-bright. The vessel's lone midshipman was forward with a small party of sharpshooters, while the bosun waited in the waist with a handful of men prepared to descend to scout.

Dusk would be soon upon them, though at the moment the world was a uniform, impenetrable gray. The bow watch murmured a warning. Ostrander adjusted the engine telegraph. Their propellers feathered, then reversed, halting the nearly imperceptible progress of *Erinyes*.

Moments later the engines coughed to silence. They hung still, listening to the wet, dead air of the world.

"There," McCurdy whispered, pointing downward.

Boaz leaned over the rail to follow the line of his arm. A thinning of the fog revealed a darker surface below—amorphous, textured, vaguely brown.

"It is the field of fire that they cleared before the stockade," the Brass said with a sudden recognition. "We are almost exactly over the encampment, within a few hundred yards."

"I recall it," the bosun said shortly.

They listened harder, straining to hear sounds of fighting, work, men at bivouac—whatever might be gleaned from below. The world remained obstinately silent. Strangely so.

::*they have been struck down*:: the voice of the Sixth Seal whispered in his head. ::*As men who raise themselves too high before God will be.*::

He placed a hand on his closed belly and wondered if he might burn this thing out. The Seal was too important to lose, especially after the destruction of the ancient book. But the Seal spoke without reason or compassion or even good sense.

Except that they *had* been struck down in this place. Boaz had fought in that battle against his own kind.

"*Ariadne* come here, not long after the big fight." McCurdy's voice was quiet and thoughtful. "She said they was building their camp within the Wall itself. Outside was only sentries and hunters and traps for John Brass."

"My city and its Sealed armies. We Brass are not so many, and prefer to fight with weapons in the hands of others."

"Everyone stands against England now. *Ariadne*, she was kilt by the Chinee this week past. If you was up on the coast where they fought, reckon you saw her die."

"I suppose I did, Bosun McCurdy." Boaz stared down at the turned soil, willing the fog to lift before the day faded. "But I am no Chinese airman bent on your destruction. Even in my own city of Brass, I am accounted a rebel and traitor. I will not pretend to a love of England or your queen, but we share our enemies."

Besides which, he thought, *al-Wazir and Paolina stand closer to England's banner than any other.*

Ostrander shouted out, "Can you make your way down to the soil of Hell, oh chief of dreams?"

The bosun shook his head very slightly before calling out, "Aye aye, sir. Party can go over the side if you'll give me another fifty feet less of altitude."

"I'll not be venting our laughing gas this merry night!" Ostrander giggled. He then rang for the engines, intending to force them lower.

"What will happen when he unravels completely?" Boaz asked.

"Middie Longoria will assume command." McCurdy's tone was unconvinced.

The deck pitched too steeply as Ostrander shouted at the helmsman. HIMS *Erinyes* clawed her way downward.

Boaz followed McCurdy and four of the ship's men down the ropes and into the ruins of the encampment. Little had changed within. Battle wrack was still spread in mounds about the compound. Boaz had received his chrism and his name within one of those smashed tents. That thought moved him to sadness, but not so much as the shattered Brass staring blindly up from the mud. Their faces were already covered with verdigris and a rapidly advancing mold. Boaz turned away from their accusing gazes. So many Seals lost on this field of battle. Elsewhere, skeletal, rotting winged savages lay with their breastbone keels sticking up in the air.

There was no pretense of order, except for the path winding inward from the gate area.

"This is what *Ariadne* found?" Boaz asked McCurdy. "And she reported the camp still at work?"

"Don't see no English dead, do you, John Brass? The good doctor strike you as the kind of man to care for his enemies?"

"I should not think he would be."

Even through the fog, Boaz could see the great broken hulk of a tunneling machine. Work sheds had been repaired. A coal tip spilled free, where they must come back up the tunnel for resupply.

Finally they came to an enormous metal door, riveted from armor plate obviously scavenged from the ravaged machine. View ports and gun slits had been crudely cut into its face. McCurdy approached nose-to-nose with a hatch sized for a small man to pass through. He banged on the door with the butt of his pistol. "Open up, in the name of the Queen!"

A gun barrel poked out of one of the slits. "We've already sent for the doctor. I'll thank you to be quiet afore he arrives." More gun barrels appeared as the metal door sprouted violence in steel bristles.

Boaz realized he'd been feeling something through his feet for a while. Somewhere deep inside this tunnel before him, the mad Dr. Ottweill's great machine was still chewing its way ever deeper into the Wall. When he reached the spinning brass at the Wall's heart, the good doctor was going to be quite surprised.

Boaz smiled. Ophir was close—he was almost home—but the fate of this expedition was worth learning.

::*they violate Creation*:: said the Seal.

They follow their curiosity, proclaimed the human voices within.

Silence, Boaz told them all. *I want to know what happens next.*

WANG

When the cataloger and the monk descended the one thousand, two hundred and seven steps to bring them farther from Heaven, *Fortunate Conjunction* awaited them out on the water in the earliest glimmering of dawn.

"I thought she had sailed away," Wang said.

"No one anchors here," the monk replied. "They only pass through, then wait at sea for further signals."

"Surely there is a better anchorage, an easier landing."

"Of course." The monk sounded surprised. "But not for the likes of you."

Wu rowed to meet them. He obviously knew the way. Wang waited, fascinated to see if the monk would now behave as if she were a person of substance in the Silent Order.

She simply dropped to the bench behind Wu, then waited for Wang to scramble down. The mate nodded at Wang, ignored the monk, and began rowing them back toward the yacht.

The cataloger studied Wu, who projected a practiced indifference. "Are you carrying me west to India?"

"We will carry you wherever the need bears. You travel under their mandate." Wu pointed with his chin toward the temple-fortress.

"Surely the Kô would like his boat back."

"That may be the case. But Captain Shen has his orders, and I have mine."

"What about—," Wang began. A sharp look from the monk cut him off. She smiled at his confused silence.

"We are a ship of ghosts," Wu said. "Who counts ghosts?"

Other ghosts. Wang did not put that thought to voice.

Fortunate Conjunction was different. Her pennants had changed to complement the European lines of her hull. So had her sailors, who now wore canvas and dungarees instead of rough-spun cotton and padded silk. One of them painted English words across the facing of her pilothouse, large enough to be read from a distance.

Good Change, it read.

"Perhaps you mean *Good Chance*?" he asked in that language, but the sailor ignored him.

"There are Chinese all around the Indian Ocean," Wu said. The monk had once again disappeared. Wang had been watching the crew carefully, but had failed to catch her eye beneath one of their stubbled scalps.

"Chinese are everywhere on the Northern Earth," he answered.

"I do not know. I have never seen the Atlantic or the barbarous lands that line its shores." Wu was expansive this morning.

As he probably should be, Wang realized. This onward journey meant farther distance from the threats of the Kô.

Wu explained. "We are the boat of a wealthy merchant out of Serendip. You are his man, sent to carry precious documents. With a British flag on our staff and the lines of this hull, no one will question us."

"An excellent stroke of luck for us that I speak English." Even so, the flaw in that plan was obvious to Wang. "Unless an airship of the Emperor's should happen upon us and take practice at his targeting."

"They are busy with one another in the sky of late, and take little interest in a small civilian vessel."

"Who fights?" Wang asked, suddenly concerned. The Middle Kingdom had already lost one fleet to sorcery.

"The Nanyang Navy and the British, over the African and Indian coasts."

"How did this foolishness begin?"

"I do not know."

Wang let it drop. This mission called for a cleverness that he did not possess and was unsure how to bring to bear. He wished once more, mightily, that he was back in his library. The Golden Bridge he understood. These sailors, not so much.

KITCHENS

The bloody note broke on the third unfolding, but cleanly. It now lay flat on the desk. He set the snapped pieces close together. The staining was visible in squares of varying intensity of carmine, a quilt of red and pink patches. The Queen's script—Kitchens was certain this was Her Imperial Majesty's own hand—was in pencil. Her letters were rushed, crabbed, and difficult to read, though he could see evidence of the graceful copperplate script she must have once employed.

Had she written it while floating in the dark? Her hands at least must have been out of the tank, Kitchens realized, with access to someplace flat enough to press a pencil against. That wretched lady-in-waiting, Daphne, would have brought the Queen anything, certainly.

Reluctantly he focused on the subject of the note. His eyes scanned the drunkard-walk handwriting, both reading the words and searching for hidden meanings.

Nothing Kitchens saw in the Queen's message lessened his fears.

The problem presented by the Queen's words was twofold. If they were false, then a conspiracy was afoot that aimed to make Kitchens its patsy in a monstrous crime. If the words were true, then he held a terrible order from his sovereign that aimed to make Kitchens her accomplice in a monstrous crime.

He could see no answer that made sense. No action, no deed, no report to which a wise man would want to have his name appended.

He looked at the carmine-stained rectangle once more. Spidery, quavering handwriting. Bloody residue crusting the paper. The memory of Daphne, the Queen's maid, with her eyes sewn shut.

The words accused:

Remake what has been undone.
Break my throne.
Help me finish dying.

How could any man stand silent in the face of such a plea from his monarch? What could any man do?

He understood none of it, except her plea for death. Regicide was not a path he had ever thought to follow. But her bubbling face would not recede from his mind's eye, no matter how he tried to banish the Queen from his thoughts.

PAOLINA

"You were sent?" Hethor asked. A patient kindness dwelt in his voice.

He is so young, she thought. *And so* old *at the same time.* "I encountered an angel atop the Wall, who told me I should meet you." *And so lent purpose to my flight.*

The chiaroscuro interior of Hethor's house lent an unreality to the conversation, as if they were shadow people in a shadow world. The windows revealed the bright places beyond, but inside was a microcosm of dream.

Hethor nodded, then turned his attention to Ming. "And you, sir?"

Ming shrugged. Paolina answered for him. "A Chinese sailor, from the ship that rescued me when my airship crashed on the Indian Ocean."

"Nothing surprises me anymore." Hethor turned some intricate wooden part over in his hands, shifting his weight in his chair. Paolina realized with sympathetic horror that this young Englishman had no legs below his knees. He looked up at her, caught her eye. "Yes. I traded my feet for more wisdom than a young man should have. Now I am confined to this place, where that hard-won learning cannot put anyone else in danger." Even in the shadows of this room, his smile was troubled. "You are the first to come to me."

"I did not know you," she replied. "I still do not."

"Do you recall two years ago, when the world was shaking so hard that waves swept the shores clean in many places?"

Paolina nodded. Her village's small fishing fleet had been destroyed in those cataclysms, which in a sense was what had led to her departure from Praia Nova. "The mechanisms of the world were out of true. Time was slipping."

"You know!" Hethor seemed surprised. "No one understood. And I am the one who repaired the order of the world."

The enormity of the statement took her aback. That a boy—he could

not be but a year or three older than she—was able to affect the clockwork
of God's creation should have been unthinkable.

Except for the plain truth. He was an English boy living deep in the jungle
south of the Wall, where no Englishman of any age had business being. He
was watched by angels, surrounded by a village of worshipful warriors.

More to the point, she was *here*, improbably so.

"Everything has purpose," Paolina said quietly.

Hethor seemed to follow the unspoken line of her thoughts. "I have
spent much time on exactly that question. My education is reasonable,
my experience in matters of the divine extraordinary, but otherwise I am
as plain a person as anyone." He set his carved plaything down with a
gentle thunk upon his worktable. "All of Creation is a clock. Each piece
turns in its own measure as inexorably as the gear trains of a timepiece,
and for much the same reason. Just as clock parts do not strike out on
their own, do not seek an independent destiny or freedom of action, how
is it that we subjects of God's creation can imagine ourselves free to do
what we will? Our roles and destinies must be as foreordained as that of
any mainspring or escapement."

"That cannot be true." Her response was reflexive, an impulse born
deep within her. "I lift my hand. . . ." She raised her left in a fist. "I drop
my hand. That is my volition, and the world turns just the same whether
I move or not."

"A clock advances just the same whether a jeweled movement is in
light or shadow," Hethor replied. "Dust falling from the pendulum does
not affect its swing."

Paolina was drawn deeper into the argument. "We are not dust."

"Of course we are." His tone was surprised. "Does the Bible not say so?
From dust and ashes we are made, to dust and ashes we return."

"You have clearly never attended a birthing," Paolina said, perhaps
more sharply than she intended. "Dust, yes, but mostly we are made from
blood and flesh. I have never seen ashes arrive with a newborn."

"It is only metaphor. In any case, the debate is irresolvable. If all is
foreordained, then the argument is as well, and likewise its outcome. If
we are blessed with free will, then the argument has no outcome because
we would never come to true agreement."

Arellya brought three steaming mugs: crude and slightly misshapen bits
of ceramic. "Forgive me," she said, "but we have never found a tea that
Hethor craves. This is a brew of roots and flowers that you may enjoy."

Paolina took the offered mug and clutched it beneath her nose. Though
the day outside was jungle-hot, and even the shadows here within Hethor's

house almost blood-warm, the heat seemed like a gift to her hands. The scent was oddly musty, like leaves left in a puddle too long, with a cloying undertone. Flowers? She sipped cautiously.

Definitely not tea, which she had come to enjoy while sailing aboard *Star of Gambia*. But not so bad.

Beside her, Ming slurped, then glanced sidelong. In Chinese, "It is better than no tea at all."

"I apologize that we do not possess the finer things of English life here," Hethor said. "Or, for that matter, of the Chinese court. What we do have is fruit in tragic abundance, a wonderful assortment of curious meats, and an endless supply of overwarm days and pleasant nights."

Arellya stood beside him now. She clasped Hethor's free hand. The way they leaned into one another just ever so slightly told Paolina that these two were lovers. Hethor, not a large man by English standards, was still twice the size of this woman of the Correct People. Paolina wondered how strange this might be for them.

Yet you long for Brass Boaz, who is far stranger to you than these two are to one another.

After taking a long sip at his mug, Hethor stared solemnly at Paolina. His eyes glinted in the shadows of the room. "What do you seek here in the Southern Earth?"

"Safety." Her answer surprised Paolina. *Purpose. What of Boaz?*

"This is a safe enough place," Hethor replied. "If you are careful of spiders and don't mind snakes and crocodiles, and avoid bad water, and don't sleep on the ground at night, and remember which fungus will kill you just by your breathing too close. Do you hope for a place of refuge?"

Paolina glanced at Ming. His face was bland, impassive.

"I seek a place where my own . . ." *Power* seemed like a wrong word. ". . . wisdom, I suppose, will not bring me more trouble."

Hethor set down his mug. "May I inquire as to the nature of this wisdom?" He put up a hand. "Only what you wish to tell me."

"The angel seemed to believe I should seek you out." That sounded weak, even to Paolina.

"Do not place too much faith in the counsel of angels. They do their best in the absence of God."

"That is a very odd thing to say."

He did not answer, instead just staring mildly at her until Paolina realized she should respond somehow. She stared down at the draggled feather in her hand. "I—I do not consort with angels."

"Of course you do," Hethor said. "If one sent you here to visit me."

"Only the once!" She could feel herself blushing and was grateful for the shadows in this room. "I will tell you what befell me, but first I will show you." She was so very tired of the burden of her knowledge. Paolina plucked the stemwinder from its pouch within her skirts and handed it to Hethor. This one had none of the elegance of her first effort. It was crude, battered, cracked, worn, and never so beautiful to begin with—a brass roundel like a short, fat pipe section, the necessary movements stuffed within. She wished she still had the finer one destroyed by the Silent Order, but this clockmaker would know her work even from the crude approximations she'd been forced to aboard *Heaven's Deer*.

He turned the bulky thing over in his hands a few times, then set to examining the face. After a few minutes he asked, "May I open the casing?"

"P-please." Paolina was surprised to be so nervous.

Hethor turned to his worktable and selected a slender tool. Very carefully he prised her stemwinder apart. He spent a long time studying the interior without touching anything, his eyesight apparently untroubled by the dim light of this workroom. Eventually he began probing within with a deft touch. Finally he looked back her.

"You built this." A statement, not a question.

"Yes." Paolina was oddly afraid of what Hethor might say next.

"Can others make use of it?"

"Yes. My first one was . . . captured and misused. The Silent Order destroyed part of a city and killed many people in doing so."

"Hmm." Carefully, he shut the casing again. "You have done something very important."

That was not what she had expected to hear. Questions. Castigation, almost certainly. Even bafflement, if this young man was not everything he appeared to be. But not praise. "How so?"

"I have certain abilities. They were given to me, or perhaps awoken, through divine agency. The world was running down. Gabriel needed a key to rewind it. He chose me."

"Why?"

"He never told me." Hethor sounded wistful. "Even now I would be a journeyman at Master Bodean's clockworks in New Haven if the angel had not come to me in need. Instead I am here, with hard-won wisdom and a few strange powers. *But . . .*" A warning finger. "I can speak to you of how this world works, and you might even understand me. What I cannot do is grant you the least iota of my powers. That would be like giving you the color of my eyes or the timbre of my voice. It cannot be done.

"On the other hand, *you* have built a mechanism that draws on the hidden order of the world to express similar power. Much as a clockmaker might sell a watch to a man who would never otherwise recall the time, you can build this, give it to someone else, then build another. There will only ever be one of my powers, but there can be as many of your powers as you care to expend the time and effort to create."

"This is the safety I search for," she said earnestly. "Freedom from the men who would have me build more of these, who would have me teach them how to build more, so that each person could have the might of a sorcerer."

"I have known a sorcerer or two," Hethor told her. "Their might comes with the wisdom of years. You are the only young sorcerer I have ever met."

"I am not a sorcerer!"

He turned the stemwinder in his hands. "With this, you are." Hethor reached out to give the device back to Paolina. "The people here would call this a gleam."

"I am familiar with the term," she replied, very glad to have the stemwinder's solid weight once more in her hand. "I was told of another gleam that passed two years ago. Was that your crossing to the Southern Earth?"

"Perhaps. But even if I am a gleam, I am a gleam like the seven Great Relics of Christ. I am a distinct thing, not repeatable. Each gleam in history has been unique. Like the difference between a rug woven by the hands of children and a cheap throw woven on a power loom. You have created a way to repeat the miracle." His voice dropped, hurried toward the next words in his excitement. "Think what this means for the possibility of true free will."

"That every man would rewrite the world to suit his purposes?" Paolina was horrified. "This would be chaos. Precisely what I fled the Northern Earth to avoid."

"Have you avoided it here?" Hethor's voice was shrewd now, thoughtful. "Did you progress across the Southern Earth to my jungle village without the aid of this gleam?"

"N-no . . . ," Paolina admitted slowly. "We were forced to use the stemwinder to escape imprisonment, or possibly a worse fate, atop a great mountain to the east of here."

"What have you gained by coming here? You could not put the thing down. Believe me, there are those in the Southern Earth who will know its use, just as there are those upon the Wall who knew of my passing."

She felt a shuddering wave of desperation. Ming touched her shoulder softly. Paolina glanced into his eyes to see a sad warmth there. She looked back at Hethor. "I wanted to stop running. I had hoped to erase the knowledge from me, tear it from my mind and heart, and go back to being a simple girl."

"Were you ever a simple girl? Besides, you cannot erase knowledge from the world. In time, it might be forgotten or overlooked, but once men know a thing can be done, they will find a way to do it again." His voice thickened with passion. "You have taken the magic of Creation out of the realm of the divine and placed it into the realm of the mechanical. In doing that, you have stolen free will from the dreaming mind of God and brought it to the hands of man."

"I do not want this power!"

"You cannot set it aside. The Southern Earth is no more safe than the Northern Earth. You will just be used by different powers here, if you do not assert yourself."

"Show me how to control it." Paolina hated the desperation in her voice.

"Would that I could." Hethor seemed sad. "William of Ghent might have been able to, but he is lost to us now." He paused. "I slew him. Twice."

"You do not seem a killer."

"You do not seem a destroyer of cities. Neither of us travels on a chariot of skulls or wields a flaming sword. Those are symbols of another age. We are of the age of steam and iron, progress stamped out in metal and sold by the pence in the marketplace. We are of the time when man's ability to remake the world around him has risen to intersect with God's original craftsmanship. Hence your stemwinder."

"Then what will I do with it?" she whispered. "How will I control this demon I have unleashed?"

"You will do as everyone confronted with overwhelming fate has done since the beginning of history." He shifted again, then reached for Arellya's hand. From behind his shoulder, she took it. Paolina could see the love that passed between them like an electrick current. "I cannot help you, but I know some who may. There is a city along the ocean shore south of the mouth of this river. They practice strange and terrible sorceries there, and I once stole something of value from them after they murdered a friend of mine. They are capricious and dangerous. But they have immerse experience and understanding, and I think it may be true that several of the Great Relics have lain safely in their hands since Joseph of Arimethea crossed the Wall nineteen centuries ago.

"These people honor no passports, nor letters of safe conduct. But if you carry your power openly, they will take note of you." His voice was soft, sad. "This is the best I can offer you. My place here is safe and quiet, but the world will find you in time. Possibly these same sorcerers, for they cannot have failed to notice your use of the gleam here in the Southern Earth. Or those who would pursue you across the Wall will make their own way here."

Paolina had wild thoughts of throwing the stemwinder in the river, smashing it to bits and hurling the shards into a bonfire, feeding the thing still ticking to a crocodile. But unless she smashed herself in the process, the problem would still exist. That was the choice she had tried—and failed—to make off the coast of Sumatra aboard *Five Lucky Winds*.

"Life always seeks life," she said. "I will go to this city, because I would rather control this than be controlled by it."

His voice was solemn. "If you succeed, and this power comes more widely and peacefully into the hands of men, you will have been the first since the Brass Christ to revise the bargain of God's Creation. My advice to you now is to heed the counsel of your own heart over the honeyed words of angels or men."

"Thank you." Paolina sipped at her musky tea, which had grown cool as they talked. "I have but one request of you and your house."

"Ask it," Hethor said. Humor was returning to his voice and to the set of his eyes.

"I would have something to eat before I set out."

He laughed at her then, and she laughed with him. Even Ming could not help snorting.

Arellya went out on the balcony and called down in the hissing speech of her kind. A great cheer arose from below where before there had only been the noisy, fractured silence of the jungle. She turned back. "At sundown, we will feast. For now, would you like some fruit?"

CHILDRESS

Leung's crew labored around the clock to finish the repairs to *Five Lucky Winds*. Panjim burned fitfully from the bombings, but the Chinese were long gone. The British, however, were not.

She and al-Wazir took the submarine's new launch—a reconditioned dory salvaged from the cavern—out of the hidden harbor and rowed down the coast. "I do not want to appear from the landward side," she'd told the chief and the captain. "They will wonder all the more where I came from along that road of fields, where no Englishwoman has business being."

"We can tell some tale of a vessel overset on the high seas if need be," al-Wazir grumbled. "Wear that black dress of yours that looks like you've been swimming in it."

Childress was glad she'd been able to find more clothes in Panjim before such things became impossible. The black dress had been on her back when she left New Haven so long ago, and was good now for little more than disguise.

He rowed them south, well outside the surf line, heading for the town's little harbor. The left-hand oar was strapped to his forearm in a rig that appeared hideously uncomfortable, and he shipped the oars and rested far more often than he obviously would have preferred, but they made progress.

She was unhappy at leaving their hidden safety, but even more unhappy at a lack of information. The Chinese living in Panjim would either be hiding behind the walls of their houses, or shot for spies and traitors. If the British discovered that some of the Chinatown merchants possessed Middle Kingdom scrip from *Five Lucky Winds'* strongbox, that would only make matters worse.

They needed to know. Who was hunting whom, and why. As the only Europeans aboard the submarine, it fell to Childress and al-Wazir to do the scouting.

"My greatest fear here," she told al-Wazir as he pulled again at the oars, "is that some well-intentioned officer or bureaucrat will attempt to remove us for our own good."

"You try telling our story to any Queen's officer," he growled. "See what response you'll be getting."

He rowed on, while Childress wished she knew some way to ease his fears—and her own, for that matter, for her concern was with what they would find in Panjim.

GASHANSUNU

"The Bone People have sent a message," Baassiia told her.

They met now in the Plaza of Inordinate Desire. A wizened tasseomancer with teeth black as his brew served them coffee in shallow bowls of silver beaten over the upper curve of a child's skull. Gashansunu stirred cardamom and honey into hers, seeking the comfort of the inner sight that combination was said to bring.

Not that she had great need for revelation from a shallow cup. Her *wa* was clear enough on the meaning of the disturbances in the Silent World. The very sky above the city had shouted its distress.

She tapped her spoon dry and set it on the tiled tabletop. A pattern of flowers was glazed into the ceramics, the trumpet of each vine in turn consuming the stem of the next, so they were an endless circle of blossoming and devouring.

The tasseomancer was a member of the Many Petals House. Many Petals had not had serious dispute with Westfacing House in at least a generation. Though if someone *had* wanted to poison her, the oily, bitter brew would have been an excellent mask for any number of herbal assaults.

Not this moon, luckily. That would have been one more complication. Death was a marked inconvenience at its best.

"What message?" Gashansunu finally asked.

"They inquire if we will trap the gleam that has come across the Wall."

Persons from across the Wall had been a difficult subject since the theft of the Bone People's airship two years ago.

"Trap? We know nothing of the gleam yet, save that the city regrets its coming, and that the Southern Earth will probably regret its passage."

Baassiia looked at his bowl for a time. His brown eyes were filled with an air of destiny. Gashansunu knew this only meant that the circle caller was stalling.

"You are lost in this matter, are you not?" she asked him.

He pursed his lips, then glanced down into his coffee. "I am afraid that counsel has not come to me yet from the Silent World."

"Well it has come to *me*." She leaned forward. "I dreamt of a great crocodile, calling me east as it swam in ever smaller circles, dragging the waters down with it."

"Is that your dreaming, or your ambition?"

"I am not Ninsunu to wriggle my oiled body before the circle callers in a ploy for advancement."

"I thank you for that," he said. "But if you follow the monster into the depths of dreaming and leave the walls of the city, who will come back?"

NO ONE, whispered her *wa*. OR THE ENTIRE WORLD.

"I follow what the signs tell me," Gashansunu said primly. "The Bone People know the gleam is near. The world tells us its regrets through the dreaming of the city. My own inner sight sees the journey under way. I would not be of the city if I did not follow this."

Later she walked the circled ways of the city by silvered moonlight. The *wa* of the dead roamed in darkness, dangerous to anyone not warded by their own *wa*, but even cloaked in safety Gashansunu could see the shadows full of teeth, smell the stale blood.

They were a violent lot, those left behind when the greater spirit moved on. They were also the wardens of the city, invisible and invincible, at least until a certain gleam had walked among them two years ago.

Each ring was laid outside the ring before it to make an ever-widening circle around the beating heart at the center beneath the Pillar of Restitution. In time the city would birth another ring. The houses of the sorcerers would sing praises to this happening, then cautiously move into the still-glistening streets to rip the drying cauls from the buildings and find what spirit gifts might lie within. Someday the city might circle the Southern Earth, given an uninterrupted span of years.

The city preyed on the unwary, but no one preyed upon it. Gashansunu and her kind knew themselves as fish on a reef or fleas on a dog. Their power was as a swimmer before the ocean wave that was the city.

She walked the smooth streets, passed darkened doorways hosting a thousand glistening eyes with no mouths. Gashansunu tolerated the murmuring worry of her *wa* and wondered what or who in the Northern Earth was sending such gleams across the Wall. Twice in a pair of years. Her people had not seen the like since the days of simony and miracles nearly two millennia earlier.

Soon enough she reached the gate, massive and brutal like the legs of the strongest slave, and stepped from the true world of the city into the illusions of jungle and water and bitter scent blown from the ocean.

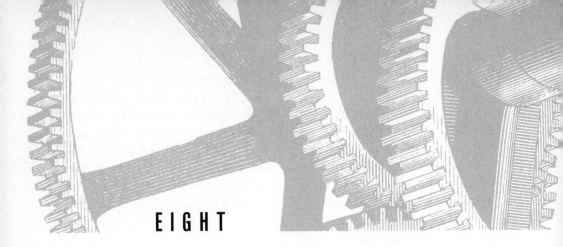

EIGHT

My name is Legion, for we are Many.   —*Mark 5:9*

BOAZ

Eventually the doorway groaned open. Dr. Ottweill stepped out. The man's white coat was stained gray-black. His hair streamed wild as any eremite prophet's. His face was seamed and pocked and blistered. Fever flickered in his eyes.

"You I am before knowing, Brass traitor man." Ottweill glared at Mc-Curdy and his handful of crew. "Here is the miserable relief that wretched al-Wazir sends?"

"Sir, I don't know al-Wazir," the bosun replied. "I am Bosun McCurdy of HIMS *Erinyes*, here to find how you is doing and bring dire news."

Ottweill seemed displeased. "An officer for me they do not dispatch."

"Lieutenant Ostrander is aboard the airship, sir," McCurdy said doggedly. "With his compliments, he sent us down to scout out while he kept a sky watch. I am charged to find you, and inform you that the Empire has gone to war with the Chinese. You should be wary of new attacks."

The doctor laughed. "New attacks? We are not finished being wary of the old attacks! Our dead we have not all yet buried. My men live underground like black moles. Coal we hoard. Ourselves we hide from the sky. Most of all we dig, dig, dig, boring Her Imperial Majesty's tunnel ever deeper into the Wall. Are you carrying out all your duties, man!?" He finished with his nose inches from McCurdy's face, spittle running down his chin.

McCurdy gulped. "Sir, I can't say, sir. I am only here to advise you to send a signal to Mogadishu should the Chinese encroach."

"Now a telegraph line across to the east from here you have laid?"

The bosun gave up. "Sir, no sir."

This man, after all, had overmastered even al-Wazir, and McCurdy was no al-Wazir. "Doctor," Boaz said, interrupting.

Ottweill spat. "You. Machine. Sooner my borer should talk."

"Perhaps it shall someday. But you will swiftly meet with trouble if you have not already. I sent word before that the Wall is hollow. Beware when you break through the rock into those inner spaces."

The doctor's voice almost screeched. "What does a machine know?"

"What does a man who has lived along the Wall for centuries know? I have passed within by secret ways. Can you say the same?"

McCurdy gave Boaz a look that might have been grateful.

"Och," snarled Ottweill. "You have nothing for me. Come back when that worthless chief sends you at the head of an army."

"Sir, thank you, sir," said McCurdy.

The doctor stepped through his little postern gate, then paused to look back at Boaz. "Brass man. When through I break, what will I find?"

"Wonders," Boaz said. "The machineries of Creation laid bare. Spinning walls of brass that will rip your borer from its wheels with all the force of an entire world in motion. What you will not find is a walkway to the Southern Earth."

::*he will find the price of his pride*:: echoed the voice of the Sixth Seal. Boaz touched his belly as if to silence it.

"Bah." Ottweill slammed the door. The gun slits rattled shut.

In moments, Boaz was alone with McCurdy and his men.

"I reckon that could have been worse," the bosun finally said.

Now was time for him to leave and head for Ophir. He was almost home. "I shall head back to the stockade and see what of the sky can be glimpsed from there."

"Shaw, de Koonig, make a camp right here before the door," McCurdy ordered. "A small fire and cook up some of them oats. I'm going with John Brass here to have another look."

It will not be so easy as walking away, Boaz thought. He did not want to fight this McCurdy, who reminded him too much of al-Wazir. Men of a type, cast from whatever mold the Royal Navy had for petty officers, much as Ophir cast its Brass sons from molds almost as old as time itself.

They gained the top of the stockade. Africa was nothing more than a few arm spans of swirling gray overlaid with shadows. The Wall loomed behind, massive as another world.

"Where is your airship, Bosun McCurdy?"

"If I knew that, I'd be a happier man," the bosun replied. "Lieutenant Ostrander might have decided to fly her to the moon."

"Your midshipman is no force, you said."

"Not to stand against a commander, he's not." McCurdy sounded sad now. Nothing so resolute as al-Wazir would have been. "As for you, John Brass, 'tis now that you'll climb over the fence and carry your tales home?"

"I am afraid I should be leaving," Boaz admitted. "Though they will not like to see me there, for Ophir names me traitor. I have a tale to recount that they will not want to hear." The Sixth Seal stirred within his belly, its desires and anger all too divine, but most unfortunate for the man he had become.

KITCHENS

His first glimpse of the Wall came with the dawn of their seventh day of travel. The bow lookout shouted the warning as night still lay firmly on the Northern Earth. Kitchens had stood close forward and stared intently, but his untrained eye took some time to catch the solid line of darkness now marking the southern horizon.

The Wall had consumed the ambitions of more than one empire, spat them out again as bloody bones. Israel at her height under the kings of old tried to conquer it. So had the Romans, once, or so legend ran. Now England would scale the divine precipices and claim this awful place for her very own.

The Wall had devoured men, too; good, bad and indifferent. Kitchens was familiar with the reports concerning the fate of Gordon's 1900 expedition. HIMS *Bassett* likewise lost in the same efforts, one Angus Threadgill al-Wazir the sole survivor. He had sent al-Wazir back to the Wall in company with the mad and maddening Dr. Lothar Ottweill. Though it had been mere months since that expedition set out, they were already presumed lost by pessimists at Admiralty and Whitehall.

"My job," Kitchens whispered to the distant, uncaring Wall, "is to be an optimist."

"Different once you've seen it, yes?"

Kitchens started. He was most unaccustomed to being surprised.

Sayeed stood just behind Kitchens' shoulder. The captain smiled, a lean and predatory expression.

"Yes, Captain, it is a . . . presence, I should think to say."

"When we draw close, you will feel that presence like a fist wrapped around your heart." Sayeed stepped to the rail, standing close to Kitchens. "Admiralty is using me and my ship because we are already stained beyond redemption. No captain would have *Notus* now. She is unlucky in a way that few would accept under their command."

Kitchens swallowed a smile. "I shouldn't know the superstitions of line officers."

"What about the superstitions of clerks? You place an uncommon faith in paper."

For a brief, panicked moment, Kitchens thought that Sayeed somehow knew of the note from the Queen that remained below in his quarters. Had the captain been snooping? Then he realized Sayeed could not mean something so specific, so personal and secret.

"It is not faith we have in papers," Kitchens said. "Papers are just the lifeblood circulating from one vital organ to another. Everything else vital to the interest of the Crown—funds, directives, reports—travels by the medium of those papers."

"Yes, yes, I know. Every war ever fought was won on paper long before the trumpets faded over the empty, bloody fields. But consider this." Sayeed actually *poked* Kitchens in the side with a finger. "One may walk away from paper, at a high enough cost. One cannot walk away from the point of a sword. Sometimes a man has to stand and fight."

"Is this a declaration of mutiny?"

"Far from such." Sayeed matched Kitchens' quiet tone. "I swore my oath twenty-six years ago. I will be loyal until the moment you have me hanged."

Which was demonstrably untrue, Kitchens knew, for the man had taken the destructive female genius to his secret masters in Strasbourg rather than bringing her to London as he was duty-bound to have done.

Sayeed continued. "Who in Admiralty knows you to be aboard *Notus*? Who there understands why? You are being used as much as I and my crew and this poor vessel." He patted the rail as if it were a dog. "Papers have been drawn up to end your life as surely as mine. They are spending you along with us to see what may be gained by one last, wild throw."

The same thoughts had occurred to Kitchens. The countervailing argument, one that he would never voice to Captain Sayeed, was the fact of the Queen's personal interest. She had summoned him to her royal presence. Surely she had also set him on this path.

"Since we are being so boldly direct with one another," Kitchens said, "why did you take the girl to Strasbourg? I fail to see how you could not recognize that act as fatal to your service in the Royal Navy. You say you are the Queen's man to the gallows, yet you abandoned your oath to her in that single act."

"Why is it that you imagine an act in the service of the Silent Order is not an act in service of the Queen?"

———

By the next day the Wall was much clearer. He could spot cliffs and bays and plateaus; spy the weather moving across on the plane of the vertical. Soon half the sky would be blocked.

Below them, the dense jungle was riven with watercourses. The rough, endless green of the roof of the forest was speckled with the flight of birds over the treetops. The Bight of Benin loomed to the south, separating West Africa from the foot of the Wall like a moat.

"Airship ho!" shouted the bow watch.

Every sailor not immediately engaged in some vital task rushed to the rail. In moments Harrow was haranguing them back to their posts. "Don't you be gagging away from me now, you little bastards! If that ship is an enemy, we're already dead. To stations, to stations, damn all your eyes."

Kitchens made his way forward. Captain Sayeed joined him there a moment later, along with two other officers and the chief of the gunnery division.

"There," said Grantland, the gunner. "Five points off the starboard bow. She's got several thousand feet on us."

They all looked east and south in the indicated direction, eyes above *Notus'* current altitude. A small airship, one of the Cumaean-class couriers, Kitchens thought. He looked past her, toward the Wall. "There's two more chasing her," he exclaimed.

"Chinese," Sayeed confirmed. "Beta-class cruisers. We would overmatch one of them in a straight fight. But not two working in formation."

Kitchens thought the odds plainly unfavorable. The little airship could presumably climb higher and fly faster, but she wasn't built to circle and fight alongside *Notus*. "What, then?"

"Break out the signal flags in the red chest," Sayeed ordered. "I shall be at the helm."

The little knot of men vanished with sudden purpose, all but Harrow, who stayed a moment longer to look at Kitchens with sad eyes. The chief shook his head once, then went off to harangue the deck division.

The Wall was so close, but Kitchens realized he had just lost what little control he might have held over *Notus*.

WANG

Good Change sailed the west coast of India flying a large British ensign. Wang understood that should the Royal Navy happen on the truth of the matter, the boat and all aboard her would be summarily dealt with.

Captain Shen had adopted a white coat and cap that appeared more English in style and stayed at the wheel almost constantly. Wang was unsure when the man slept. The rest of the crew were silent and sullen as ever, only the mate Wu talking to Wang beyond the most perfunctory remarks. He had not seen the monk since they had reboarded.

Wang finally found a quiet moment with Wu in the galley. Privacy was rare enough aboard *Good Change*. The mate was brewing tea and did not seem overwhelmed with responsibility. "I must ask you some questions," the cataloger said. "I should hope for some clear answers, as my mission from our masters depends on this."

"My master is the Kô," Wu said, but his voice was not combative. "Your service is unclear to me."

"I am loyal to the Dragon Throne." Wang wondered how he had been put on the defensive so rapidly. "As are you, in that you serve the Kô while he serves the Emperor."

Wu grunted, pouring out his tea.

"Who is this monk?"

The mate looked over the rim of his teacup. "What monk?"

"The woman from the rowboat. Who took me in to the fortress of the Silent Order, and rode back out to the boat with us."

Wu shook his head. "You are mistaken. Women are unlucky aboard a ship."

"I do not understand this game," growled Wang. "She appears and disappears like the wind. She is nowhere when I search. I know she must be hiding among the crew, but there are only eleven of you, and none of you have her face above your collar."

"Some ghosts are transient," Wu offered.

"Not aboard a vessel this small!"

"Perhaps you should dwell on the nature of death a while. A speculation that can hardly fail to profit you."

The mate pushed past Wang, leaving him alone in the galley with his frustrations and the rock-solid certainty that Wu knew perfectly well what was going on. The Golden Bridge slipped ever farther away, and with it eroded his habits of obedience. He was unsure what would replace that in his heart.

The boat cruised slowly past a ragged coast. They'd twice spotted airships in the distance. Few settlements were visible along this stretch, and those they did espy were tumbledown shacks with ragged docks kneeling into the water.

The monk stepped up beside him at the rail.

"How do you do that?" he asked listlessly.

"It is not so difficult to disappear," she told him. "Being able to reappear without being noticed first is a more challenging art."

"I can fall overboard and disappear. Reappearing would be another matter."

"You can see patterns of meaning in ancient texts that are no more than the walking of ants across a leaf to me. Is that miraculous?"

"No. Just training and practice. It is my place to know how to do this."

"So it is with me. Just training and practice. It is *my* place to know how to do this."

Wang was frustrated. "But what of your *methods*?"

"What of your methods for reading ancient Indonesian scrolls?" She fumbled some leaves into her pipe, then lit it.

"There is no purpose in arguing with you," he grumbled.

"You preserve me from boredom."

That wasn't worthy of a response, Wang decided, trying to think like this very difficult woman. He took another conversational tack. "I assume your mystical reappearance indicates we are about to experience something of significance."

"Of course. Why would I wish to stand at the rail and watch a thousand *li* of empty sea slide by?"

"I have wondered much the same thing," Wang admitted.

"Then you have already set foot on the path of wisdom." She sounded delighted. "Now, however, we are nearly at the Goan port of Panjim. The Englishwoman hides there, or did so as recently as a week past. There has been much trouble in the skies, so the situation may have changed."

"I am to walk among the angry dogs of their foreign queen and ask questions about the whereabouts of one of their own kind? A man of the Middle Kingdom will not be so welcome within the walls of Panjim."

"The British do not wall their cities so much," she replied absently, then took a long, slow drag on her pipe.

"I am not British."

"Neither am I." Smoke curled from her nostrils, giving her an uncomfortable resemblance to classical paintings of the *lung* dragons. "Being invisible is a great asset when one walks among one's enemies."

"I am no more invisible than I am English," said Wang.

"We'll have to see what may be done about that." Another long drag. "Pity you didn't join me in the *guang* as a child. There is much we could have learned together." This time she grinned, somehow disarming and maddening in the same moment.

Much like women everywhere, Wang reflected. One reason he had never taken a wife, and likely never would.

PAOLINA

She embraced her regrets as evening folded itself into night. Though she was barely come to her womanhood, life had already overwhelmed Paolina with experience, so that those things that most pained her seemed also to be her oldest friends.

At least that's how it looked from the bottom of a wooden bowl of papaya wine. Sweet, sticky, yellow as a bee's back, the drink tickled her throat and set her mind wandering in ways she did not usually indulge.

Is this liberation of thought what the fidalgos *of Praia Nova craved so about* bagaceira? She could see the attraction, but also the difficulty.

Kalker came to sit beside them. Paolina could not remember if she had spoken to him earlier this evening. The whirling insects and the dancing fire seemed to have taken her outside time. Boats on the river guarded the edge of events from her sense of passage, so she was secure in this circle, alone endlessly, always talking to Kalker, always listening to Ming, no difference between one moment and the infinity of the next.

". . . will go by boat," the old Correct Person was saying. "Safe on the river, most likely."

Paolina focused on that. "What about the crocodiles?"

"They are great monsters with teeth to drag you under, but they are as much children of the water road as the eels and fishes and waterbirds. In any case, I believe the world wants you to pass on. That is a powerful force to keep you safe and propel you forward."

"Gleam. The crocodiles can see my gleam." She wondered in that moment where Karindira of the troglodyte women was. Did her kind have cities on this side of the Wall?

"The world wants. *He* is sending you where you are needed. Your way will be sped."

In Paolina's experience, her way was never sped. Quite the opposite. "The world does not want me," she announced. "I have proven myself evil beyond measure."

"The world does not judge, woman of the Northern people. It merely exists. What we do within the world is our business, between us and the Creator. You bear a gleam."

"That excuses nothing," she shouted, throwing her board of food aside.

Ming touched her arm, seeking perhaps to calm her, but Paolina would have none of it. She took a deep draught from her wine bowl and tried to gather her thoughts in a more seemly array.

Kalker spoke in a low, soft voice. "There is no excuse. There is only re-sponsibility. Do not think your soul is freed from accounting for your deeds. At the same time, this poor accounting does not release you from your obligations to the world, to life itself. You may do evil one day and still serve the order of the Creation the next."

"My evil was in building the gleam." She recalled the words of Hethor, of Childress and al-Wazir aboard *Five Lucky Winds*. "Even more so, my evil was in showing that the stemwinder could exist in the first place. That a thing has been done once is more than enough reason for it to be done again, as far too many see the world."

Kalker shook his head. "Do you imagine you are the first to unleash a force upon the world? God Himself put the snake in the Garden, at the beginning of all things. Men have built fires that could burn cities."

"You live in a jungle." Her voice was too loud again. "What do you know of cities!?"

"I know that I am a simple person who thinks on things," the old Cor-rect Person replied. "I know that my own children have gone far away into the world, with only one of them returning. I know that a prophet lives among us who is terrified that we will notice he is only a frightened boy not finished sidling into manhood. I know many things beyond the bounds of my village. Is it not the same for you?"

"The bounds of my village were scribed by small, frightened minds," Paolina muttered. "They made walls higher than *a Murado* itself to hide be-hind, and boxed their women ever smaller to enlarge themselves within their cage."

"Then perhaps it is your work in this life to reduce the cages and open the boxes."

"It is my work in this life to kill people with the things I make of my hands." The excellent meat had turned to paste in Paolina's mouth, and the wine seemed sour in its bowl.

Kalker stroked the side of her face. "You are already finding a way, one you cannot yet see."

She began to weep in the firelight, hating herself for the shameful weak-ness but unable to stop. In that moment, Paolina realized she'd known her path all along. It was time for her to find her way back to Boaz.

GASHANSUNU

Wrapped in power stolen from the lives of the animals of the jungle, she followed her *wa* along spirit paths through the Silent World. This was rarely done within the city, for fear of the ghosts crowding the shadows like teeth in the mouth of a needlefish. In any case, the Silent World was so dense inside the circles that the distance was almost always greater from one point to another than simple walking could manage. Hours to pass from one house to the next, for example.

Outside the walls, the Silent World was largely attenuated, so that a few steps might cover a mile. Knots and snarls and tangles existed, of course—sites of old battle, or the working of great magics in the past, or some irruption of the earth and its chthonic streams of power. With alertness and a clever *wa*, one could avoid such distractions. Gashansunu's *wa* was very clever indeed. To her mind, one of the very best.

Also, away from the glittering abyss of the city, the spark of a gleam was much more visible.

She walked the miles of jungle with as much effect as the passing of a breeze. Snakes stirred in their humid sleep deep within the hollow boles of fat-bellied trees, their slim, silver-threaded minds intruding in the Silent World more strongly than most meat animals could manage. Bright birds fled shrieking like scattered jewels from the passing chill of Gashansunu's *wa*. Great crocodiles louche and hungry in their river bottoms stirred mud as they dug deeper.

The outer world spun beneath her feet. The Silent World stayed stable as always.

In time, her *wa* told Gashansunu to stay her journey. She stepped from the Silent World onto a crumbling black knob of rock rising above a rich, damp swampland. Buffalo cropped amid grasses shoulder-high on their great bodies. A young bull watching for predators looked up to meet Gashansunu's eye. She sent her *wa* to bid him rest easy, and so he did.

She swept a small ledge clear and sat upon it, her gaze to the west as required by the practices of her house. This was not foolishness or suicide—they could look any direction prudence, safety or convenience demanded—but when at rest the Westfacing House lived up to their name.

West was where the sun went as he fled the precincts of the heavens. West was where the boundless ocean rose up to meet the shore. West was the home of the leviathans of the deep, birthing-source of the savages of the air.

Gashansunu's people knew better, of course. The sun fled nowhere, for in truth the Southern Earth turned its face away. Likewise the ocean was just as bounded as the land, its borders reversed as a tunic pulled inside out. As for the leviathans, they lived in all the waters of the world.

But just because a thing was true in the outer world it did not change other truths of the Silent World. The Silent World prospered on a diet of symbols and a dialect of journeying shadows. In the Silent World, the sun did flee, to die and be reborn each day. The ocean was boundless as the waters of the amnion that cradled each new baby on its journey from the infinite possibility of the egg to the fatal limitations of the human.

It was not difficult to argue that the Bone People were more practical than the sorcerers of the city. While they lived in an isolation of the mind and spirit that made her own kinsmen seem like fish in a school, the Bone People also built devices for measuring the heavens and the Earth, and machines for transporting those devices according to their purposes. Some of their constructions were mysterious to the point of nonsense. Certain houses of the city averred that even their great walls here had originally been raised by the Bone People.

Yet here, atop her knoll, her head full of notions of the world, Gashansunu wondered far more at their kindred nature than at their differences. Would the Bone People have sent someone after this gleam? Or did they do so already, in seeking to have her dispatched?

She did not call her *wa* back for questioning just then. It had wandered since the matter of the buffalo. Gashansunu knew from long experience that if her *wa* foresaw danger, she was best advised to listen to its words and not delay it in its purposes. Whatever had pushed them out of the Silent World was nearby.

That thought in turn drew her eyes skyward. She had expected perhaps an airship of the Bone People, but only a solitary flier speckled the deepening blue. It was strangely shaped, either one of those treacherous Northern angels or one of the good, honest winged savages of her own Southern Earth.

It circled over her once. Gashansunu flexed her spirit to reach up toward it, until her hands could almost brush the flier's leathery wings. It stared, eyes like hooded lamps, and moved on. She pulled her body back down to the rock far below. Such an exercise of power was profligate, even transgressive, but outside the city she *could* flex herself without fear of censure.

In time, her *wa* returned. It bore no message save that of its presence. *We carry on,* she said.

Without answering, her *wa* took her into the Silent World once more. Something flared in the distance, closer to the base of the Wall.

The gleam? She honed in on the beacon and quickened her pace.

KITCHENS

The maneuvering that unfolded struck him as very strange. Had he been the captain of the fast-packet airship, he would have closed in on *Notus* seeking protection under the larger ship's guns. While the two Chinese ships could almost certainly defeat *Notus* and the Cumaean-class vessel together, their fight would have gone from a long chase followed by an easy kill to a short, hard contest. The enemy were far from their own supply lines here and could probably not chance the need for serious repair.

Instead the little English airship clawed for more altitude, fleeing both the Chinese pursuers and the possibility of intervention from *Notus*. Sayeed, meanwhile, closed on the Chinese airships while his bosun and the deck idlers shifted signal banners with the avid intensity of cardsharps just before the closing bell.

The Chinese were signaling back.

Either a Silent Order game was afoot, or every bit of treachery suspected in *Notus* and her crew was turning out to be doubly true. Kitchens wondered which was more frightening. Then he wondered how soon it would be before he was cast over the rail.

Executions aboard an airship would be brutally simple to effect.

The Chinese vessels broke off their pursuit to begin a slow pass around *Notus*. Not a circle of trust, Kitchens realized, for the manouevre kept their guns trained on the British; but definitely a discussion. The smaller airship continued to make good its escape. He watched in silence as Sayeed conferred with his signals officer, checking through a small leatherbound volume, then squinting at the Chinese flags.

Somehow they had gone from the blood scent of battle to the aerial equivalent of a bureaucratic conference.

To Kitchens' surprise, Sayeed turned to him. "Mr. Kitchens, might we have a word, sir?"

The two men weren't fifteen feet apart, but this was as if he'd been invited to pass through a gate that had earlier been slammed shut. "I await your pleasure, Captain."

Sayeed stepped close, the leather book still in his hand. "Your fellow clerks did not search this ship so well." He tilted it toward Kitchens. "This is a code book. I am confessing treason to even admit this, but the matter at hand is greater than even the question of my guilt or innocence."

Kitchens kept his voice measured. "Which would be what, Captain?"

"This is no frontier skirmish of the air. We chase one another about the borders of the Wall quite regularly." Sayeed grimaced, the expression strange on his elegant face and quite at odds with his cultured voice. "A sport, you might well say, with certain understandings passing between captains on both sides."

"This would not be a surprise to Admiralty." Though so far as Kitchens was aware, the high command did not suspect the full degree of complicity implied by Sayeed. Was the entire West African station corrupted? That the captain was even telling him this now strongly suggested Kitchens would not survive to make a report to London.

"Most of these . . . understandings . . . happen in the smaller ports, where ships may call side by side without engaging in hostilities. Some few of us take a more active role." The navigator slipped Sayeed a paper that the captain read without showing it to Kitchens. He continued. "Suffice to say your fears of secret societies are well enough grounded. The senior captain yonder is a member of the Silent Order, as you know I am. He judged it more urgent to communicate with me in that capacity than to engage us."

Kitchens chose his words with care. "It is not so often that you come to open warfare here anyway, as I recall."

"No, not so often. But it is so now." Sayeed tapped the book in his hand. "The British Empire is at war with the Middle Kingdom, though London may not yet be fully informed. Thanks to the girl Paolina, *Notus* brought down *Shi Hsi-Chi* during our last journey north from the Wall. I am told by Captain Huang there that our forces destroyed another airship on routine reconnaissance over the middle of the African extents of the Wall. That was in turn followed by a Chinese raid at Mogadishu resulting in the loss of vessels on both sides. This has escalated to full-scale fighting involving the East and West African stations as well as the Indian Ocean station. Their orders are to destroy all British assets."

"Why do they talk to us? And why are you telling me all this?"

"Because I believe the world can be a better place," Sayeed said bluntly. "The Silent Order works for many things, but our objectives do not include warfare between the two greatest empires on the Northern Earth. Such a contest could not be won, and would only cost far more lives and treasure than any man could stomach, for scant return. If London were properly apprised of the full situation rather than reacting to attacks piecemeal, wiser heads might prevail."

The last round of open fighting between the two empires had led to the Chinese conquest of Singapore, and the dramatic unseating of British influence in Asia east of the Irrawaddy River. Calcutta was a city permanently on the edge of siege, everything between it and the Irrawaddy in dispute.

"Does Captain Huang speak for the Chinese throne?" Kitchens asked icily.

"No more than I speak for Whitehall, sir." Sayeed returned his tone. "Would you prefer we commence hostilities? They have the advantage of us in numbers."

Kitchens bit off the first replies that leapt to mind. "My part in this is presumably to guarantee your safe conduct should we return to England posthaste with this news. Is this not so?"

"Yes."

"Then suggest to Captain Huang that we have an urgent mission not of direct military interest. If we are able to pursue it unmolested over the next few days, I will work to enable your return to England without legal jeopardy."

Sayeed's divided loyalties were on the point of the knife now. Kitchens did not imagine that either of the great secret societies—the Silent Order or the *avebianco*—sought widespread conflict. Fighting at the edges, continued instability, the constant bickering of nation-states: those were the stuff of leverage, expansion and opportunity. If cities burned, no one's interests would be served.

Sayeed once more barked out flag codes from his secret book. Kitchens would have given much to see the contents of the volume. What one chose to encode was far more significant than how one chose to encode it. A look at the standard signals would speak a great deal about the tactics of the Silent Order.

After a few moments, the Chinese airships broke off and headed toward the African interior.

"I told them I will keep station for thirty minutes," Sayeed said to Kitchens. "Then we will resume our flight. We are half a day from Ayacalong, and the work camp is a few minutes beyond that. We have twenty-four hours there; then we must head back toward England. Huang cannot divert his own men and ships for longer, and he cannot guarantee that another captain with ambitions may not close-haul down the Wall hunting British prey."

"Why are the sailors silent on this?" asked Kitchens. "Theirs and ours? Surely the docksides know that enemy captains consort."

Sayeed gave him a strange look. "You were never under arms. Enemy captains have always consorted. More than one battle has been won in advance by sheer common sense. This open signaling is a more rare thing, as it is usual to meet in some low tavern where few will overhear. In any event, when has anyone ever listened to the tales of common seamen? Except for other common seamen, of course."

After their thirty minutes had passed, *Notus* began to beat southward. Fingering the razor in his sleeve, Kitchens could still see the Chinese ships above the eastern horizon, but they had dwindled to textured ovals in the sky. If he simply challenged Sayeed, it would accomplish nothing. The crew would not take his orders in any case. He could not fight them all.

Instead, Kitchens watched abaft, to see if the little airship would swing round once again.

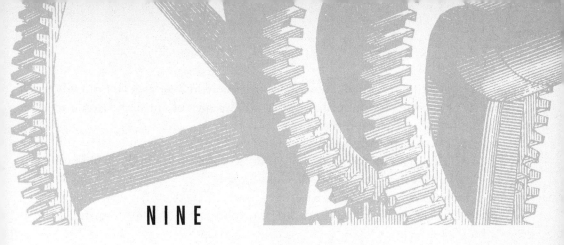

N I N E

He tunnels through the rock; his eyes see all its treasures. —*Job 28:10*

BOAZ

Midday brought a clearing of the fog and no sign of *Erinyes*. Though he had become eager to depart, especially before the strange and irrational Lieutenant Ostrander made another appearance, Boaz stuck by McCurdy. The Brass recognized enough of al-Wazir in the bosun to stir his own conscience. He was certain that if he left this place without seeing to the bosun and his men, there would be no survivors.

Well played, the mixed voice of Paolina and al-Wazir told him. The Seal just grumbled, a magic-laced cursing below comprehension.

He wondered if this was what humans felt in their heads, with their complex minds and contradictory ideas. Brass were certainty itself. Unwavering, unchanging, confirmed in their thinking. People had too many voices—if you knew them well enough, you could read it in their faces, hear it in their words. The monkey was never far from the surface, but below that were other, darker elements. YHWH had played a cosmic joke on His most beloved children, reproducing all of Creation within their heads.

Very few humans had the singleness of purpose that characterized all Brass. Well, all Brass other than himself. The most focused human he had met yet in his life was Dr. Ottweill, who was manifestly abnormal.

McCurdy certainly exhibited a divided mind now. He and Boaz continued their watch from atop the damaged stockade, though his men had left their defensive position hard by the Wall and spread out through the compound to pick over the wreckage for salvage, or so Boaz presumed. With the fog lifted, their sense of imminent danger had mitigated considerably.

The bosun was far from relieved by that. He tapped his fingers on the splintered wood, stared at the uncaring sky, studied the jungle below with the distant glint of the Mitémélé River at the port of Ayacalong.

"Under ordinary circumstances, Ostrander would be relieved of command," McCurdy announced at one point, apropos of nothing. "Doing so under fire is far more serious."

"Are you under fire now?"

McCurdy made no answer, but continued to fret at length. A bit later he asked, "Is it the Wall that makes us all mad?"

Boaz could offer no answer to that.

Several hours into the afternoon, he spotted an airship descending. "Chief, look, *Erinyes*."

"No," said McCurdy almost immediately. "That's not a Cumaean-class gasbag. Looks more like one of the cruisers. Something along the lines of a Boxer-class. Or maybe an Artemis." He squinted. "One of Her Imperial Majesty's, to be sure. The Chinee run a different trim entirely."

Boaz was not keen at the possibility of being taken on the ground by yet another crew. "I believe this is where my involvement should be terminated," he told McCurdy. "Before they make their landfall."

The bosun gave Boaz a sidelong look. "You going over the back fence now, John Brass?"

"The front stockade, I should think."

McCurdy stared upward at the approaching airship. "Do you see *Erinyes* following behind her, much higher up? My little chicken has flown to the protection of an eagle."

The appearance of the smaller vessel in no wise changed Boaz' calculus. "All the same, you and your men will have that eagle to see you safely back to Mogadishu. With luck they may carry an officer who can be spared to properly command your own ship." He nodded and slipped over the front wall of the stockade. When he hit the ground, Boaz looked up to see McCurdy on the rampart with his pistol drawn, but not pointed downward.

"John Brass," the bosun said, hardly breathing. "Look you now."

Boaz looked. Birds circled the incoming airship, a great flock of them. *No,* he corrected himself. *Not birds. Winged savages.*

McCurdy barked orders. "All hands to the stockade! Deploy rifles! I want sky watches above and behind us, with eyes right and left. De Koonig, you've got west. Shaw, east. Margolies, our backs. These bastards can drop on you like a stone from heaven!"

Boaz hesitated. If he sprinted, the sailors were unlikely to do him harm. They could scarcely give pursuit now.

But the winged savages disturbed the voices inside his head. The Seal continued to mutter, while the others gibbered with frightened anger.

He could not hope to defeat a whole flight of the decadent angels, but he could stand against them far better than even well-prepared humans were able to.

Guns cracked high in the sky as sailors shrieked. The winged savages spiraled around their target like sparrows on a falcon.

Erinyes closed faster, trying to catch up to the battle. Boaz could not say whether that was valor, madness or both. The larger ship circled, as though bringing her broadside to bear would somehow aid in repelling the flying enemies.

"Stand against them," he said in a quiet voice. "Stand them down. They respect no life, not even their own, but if the price is too high, they will back away."

He turned and scrambled to regain his place on the stockade next to McCurdy.

The airship trailed smoke as she approached. Winged savages continued to swarm. "Keep sighted in," the bosun ordered, "but don't fire except on my command." Boaz held McCurdy's pistol, their near conflict already forgotten. "That's *Notus* maybe, or *Aeolus*," the petty officer said. "Regulars on the West African station."

Erinyes was closing from behind, unheeded by the larger ship's harassers. The stricken airship yawed suddenly, causing the winged savages to scatter. As they circled, she righted herself and opened up with her waist guns.

A party of the fliers broke off and dove in a sweeping arc, obviously intending to circle in ambush.

"Rifles fire!" shouted McCurdy.

This was extreme range even for a stationary target, but his volley had the intended effect of distracting the attack run. The winged savages' formation broke up. They circled and turned their attention to the stockade.

"We's in for it now," quavered one of the men.

"Stand to," McCurdy snapped. "We've got help coming down from the clouds. Our own boys and the tommies on that big bess."

The large airship took advantage of the respite to issue mass fire from the rail as well as another volley from the waist guns. The rest of their attackers broke off to move into an attack from *Erinyes*.

"She's dumped too much hydrogen," muttered McCurdy. "Airship shouldn't ought to dive that fast. We'll not have nearly enough ceiling later on."

Aeronautics went by the wayside as winged savages descended on the stockade. Boaz stood, allowing himself to be prominently seen, and bellowed in Adamic, *"Heu!"*

Away, a command more properly used for dogs and demons.

Two broke off. Five more continued their dive, flying into the fire from McCurdy's little party. Boaz held back his pistol until the last possible moment, then put a round directly into the face of a winged savage with raw blue-black tattoos across its cheeks and shoulders.

His victim screeched, windmilling as it lost control to smash into the stockade wall just below Boaz' feet. Another pair flew past, bronze swords bloody, while the last two tumbled broken to the ground within the wall.

He looked frantically around. De Koonig was down, bleeding and crying, while another man—Margolies?—was missing his head entirely.

"Form back up," shouted McCurdy. "Reload right smart! Help is coming now; we only have to live long enough to bring 'em in!"

The big airship was decidedly wallowing now, *Erinyes* circling her like a distressed mother starling. The winged savages had swung out in a wider arc and were overflying both vessels. They dove once more, seeking another opening for their attack.

When the volley opened up from behind the stockade—Ottweill's men shooting over the head of McCurdy and his party—even Boaz was shocked. Though not so shocked as the winged savages who tumbled ragged and broken from the afternoon sky.

CHILDRESS

The docks were not busy with refugees, which surprised her. Several fishing boats were in, which also seemed odd for a midday. "Where is everyone?" she asked al-Wazir. "I would have expected more hulls."

"Nae. Who would put to sea where any airship that happens by could bomb you to the bottom without a second thought? There's all of India to disappear into just over those hills." He maneuvered them close to a pier. "I am sorry to be asking this, but could you please secure us with yon line?"

Childress hopped up, grabbed the bow line, and climbed the ladder to tie the boat in place. Al-Wazir shipped his oars, then tossed her the stern line. Moments later they were both on the dock.

A squad of soldiers waited at the landward end. Childress had hoped to slip into the town unnoticed, but tensions were too high. She squared her shoulders and marched toward them, marshalling a convincing tale of being lost at sea.

"Ma'am, I am going to have to ask your business?" The squad's leader was a boy so young he still shaved his pimples. His voice cracked with uncertainty. His fellows were no older than he. When did the children come to work in the world, she wondered?

"I am an Englishwoman, a librarian going about her lawful concerns," Childress replied with the full force of decades at Yale.

This time his voice positively squeaked. "Th-that would be up to Lieutenant Roche to decide."

She leaned forward, forcing the boy's discomfort ever higher. "And *who* is Lieutenant Roche?"

"H-he's the officer interrogating everyone who doesn't h-have papers to live in Panjim."

Her reply was interrupted by a piercing whistle. Childress looked up as a larger squad of soldiers rushed past her, marching so fast they might as well have been running. She turned to watch them race down the water-front . . . for what?

A white motor yacht pulling up to the dock. It flew a British ensign. Nonetheless rifles were being pointed amid a great commotion and a man's toneless shouting.

"*That* is Lieutenant Roche," said the boy.

Childress allowed her voice a grim satisfaction that she in no wise felt. Still, one must play the part. "Then we shall go see what he is about."

WANG

It wasn't much of a harbor, footing what wasn't much of a town. Wu leaned into Wang. "This is the place," he said urgently. "You will go ashore and persuade them of our intentions."

"What intentions?" Wang protested, watching as a covey of red-coated soldiers flooded the dock ahead of them, looking most unfriendly. "Our tale is as thin as the scum on last night's rice water. Why do we put in here, now, when the navies are out in force?"

"Because this is the place," Wu said, his patience obviously strained.

"Do you *see* a submarine tied up there?"

"It could be hiding."

Wang snorted, not bothering to conceal his amused contempt. "In which case these British will not know either."

"Our task is to bring you to this place so you can rein in the English demoness. Your task is to determine how this should be done."

The Silent Order are idiots, the cataloger thought. To send him here on so thin a thread. The more he knew of them, the less worthy they seemed of his loyalty. He wanted to go home, wherever that might be now. "I expect we'll all be dead within the hour."

Wu shrugged. "Then we'll sleep easier tonight."

Where *was* that damned monk? He had a vision of her sprinting light-footed across the ocean waves to perform some damnable trickery under the noses of the English to ferret out the missing submarine and her mutineers.

Everything about this mission stank.

The boat slid to the dock. A line of English soldiers stared down at Wang. Their weapons were unslung, but not quite aimed.

"Greetings!" he shouted as cheerfully and artlessly as he could manage.

An English officer glared at him. "My good sir. You either have more gall than Julius Caesar himself, or you are the most foolish man alive."

"We sail for Prince Jallah of Serendip." Wang tried to smile. "I am his confidential secretary. We have put in for news of battles, and to report sighting of submarine vessel surely belonging to enemy navy." He was rather proud of that last touch.

The officer frowned. "Have you an Englishman aboard with whom I might speak?"

"To my sorrow, no. Prince Jallah trusts only his Chinese servants with his moneys and his papers. English are for laws, Chinese are for counting, we say in shadow of his throne." Somewhat to his own surprise, Wang was enjoying this conversation.

"Hmm." The officer frowned, craned his neck to look at the crew of *Good Change*. "You have any weapons aboard that vessel, lad? We're at war with the Chinese, you know."

Wang bowed again, allowed some of his true nervousness to seep into his voice. "War between thrones is not war between every white man and every yellow man. No weapons, good sir. No contraband. Just papers for commerce, heading to Bombay. We call in here, to see what news of war!"

"Your airships are a bloody nuisance, that's what news of the war. What of this submarine you've reported?"

"Offshore, twenty knots south," Wang replied promptly. He was hoping for some confirmation of the presence of *Five Lucky Winds* in these waters.

The crowd of local fishermen and wharf coolies split with a mutter as another group of British soldiers pushed through, led by an Englishwoman and a flame-haired giant. Not *an* Englishwoman, Wang realized. *The* Englishwoman.

Five Lucky Winds was here somewhere, for even now he faced the demoness Mask Childress. For her part she looked at him once, twice, then opened her mouth before shutting it quite firmly with a quick shake of her head.

PAOLINA

The stemwinder was warm in her hand. She could not recall the last time she had used the device with calculated intent rather than a rush of panic. Never for this one, she realized.

Head still aching from the wine, she sat on one of the benches of the amphitheater. Ming was up and about this morning. Three rocks lay on the wood beside her—one the size of a small toad, one the size of her fist, and one flat and jagged piece that could have served for a dinner plate.

She caressed the stemwinder. Her old one had been built into a case of Enkidu metal, filled with English clockwork, salvaged parts and bits of her own making—all that work performed from inside an impromptu prison while in the depths of a desperate fugue. It had possessed a certain elegance. This one looked like something brazed together under threat of violence.

It had the four hands and the multipurpose stem of the old stemwinder. One hand measured the time that beat at the heart of everything, one measured the beating of her own heart, one measured the turning of the earth, and one measured whatever she set it to.

She was concerned with that final hand now, though all four were connected in ways she might never understand.

Paolina carefully tugged the stem out to the last setting. Something within the gleam resisted a bit too much—it had been knocked about terribly in her journey since the crash of *Heaven's Deer*—but did not snap free. A frisson of dread overcame her. In this position, the device was as dangerous as any grenado or smoking pistol.

She began to adjust the fourth hand, watching it swing blindly across the blank dial. Paolina closed her eyes and visualized the smallest of her rocks, letting the hand home in on the gleaming speckles of mica, the bird's egg shape, the comfortable hand-conforming size of the thing.

A familiar state of attunement overtook Paolina in a subtle change. Like an ocean with no shore, it rose. She could feel the rock, sense all the tiny resonances deep within it as God's clockwork structure of the universe was replicated at so tiny a scale the human eye would never witness it.

Quod est superius est sicut quod est inferius.

As above, so below.

Everything rested on everything else, clouds moving within clouds, a mesh of gearing and bearings that stretched the width of creation. She studied the bit of the world that the stemwinder was tuned to now, saw how it knew its position, changed the stone's motion so that the position became uncertain, then set it back into place *elsewhere.*

Something sizzled and stung at her right hand. Paolina was jolted back into wakefulness. She shook her arm, hoping to drive off whatever insect had landed there, before realizing that a dozen splinters were embedded in the skin of her hand and wrist, more caught in the sleeve of her ragged dress.

A smoldering little dish-shaped crater was scalloped into the wooden bench where the smallest rock had been. The rock sat serenely in the middle of the beaten-down clay that served this amphitheater as a stage.

Paolina was both impressed and disappointed. Impressed because she had no idea whether she could summon so much precision again. Disappointed because even the very small task of moving such a modest rock a modest distance had produced a modest disaster. Paolina sighed and studied the next rock, wondering how far away she should position herself to attempt the experiment once more.

Further efforts with the three rocks of varying weight, and distance of projection, proved that the sending was not harmful to the rocks themselves. Of course, under uncontrolled circumstances she'd pulled *Five Lucky Winds* several hundred nautical miles without apparent incident to vessel or crew. Likewise when she had sent Ming and herself into this jungle from the mountaintop fortress at the base of the Wall.

The amount of damage created at the origination point of the sending did not vary much. She wasn't sending any of them far enough to evaluate the effects of distance. Paolina knew all too well what the effect had been of transposing *Five Lucky Winds.*

She wondered what caused the violence of departure. Was it like thunder, an effect that naturally attended the presence of lightning, and just as uncontrollable? Or was there some aspect of the relative motion and position for which she had not yet learned to compensate?

"It can be done."

Startled, Paolina looked up. Hethor stood at the top of the amphitheater, pegs strapped to his shortened legs and a crutch under each arm. Arellya steadied the young prophet with a hand on his elbow.

"I—," she began, then stopped. Hethor was no *fidalgo* come to refuse her simply because he didn't understand what she was about. Nor was he an English stooge wrapped up in their conspiracies. He was the one person in the world who could truly understand both her purposes and her methods. "I seek to control this better," she said, apology for the aborted lie hanging heavy in her voice.

"There is much I cannot tell you." He made his way down the steps. Each rap of the crutches on the ground wrenched a shuddering breath from Hethor. "But I may be able to help you."

Paolina waited until he reached her level and took a seat on a bench undamaged by her experiments. Hethor laid one crutch aside, but continued to lean against the other. Behind him now, Arellya shook her head sharply at Paolina.

Don't what? the girl thought. Don't talk to him. Don't tire him out. Don't ignore him. She was leaving soon, and would likely never come back to this village by the jungle river not so far from the shadow of the Wall. She would hear him out, and say what needed to be said.

"I thank you for the kind offer of the boat," she told him. "But I think that is not my way. I wish to follow my heart back to the Northern Earth."

A smile quirked across Hethor's face. "You do not still think your salvation lies in flight?"

"No." Paolina looked down at her stemwinder. "You were right in what you said yesterday. This thing is done. The box has been opened, and troubles loosed upon the world. I can follow along through disasters and troubles unnumbered, or I can try to lead, and perhaps direct the energies I have unleashed."

"You can *choose*." She heard the urgency in his voice, sensed some intense longing he would not or could not put into words. Hethor continued. "When you reach into the fabric of the world to move that rock, you change fate. You introduce a free decision into the preordained system of the world."

"But it is no different than if I grasp the rock in my hand and cast it into the river." Paolina paused. "No, I tell a lie. When I move the rock by hand, I am a part of the world acting on another part of the world. When I use the stemwinder to move the rock, I am changing the position and alignment of gears that turn at all levels inside the world."

"Precisely." Hethor seemed pleased with her. "This is where you and I are different. I was sent out to pursue the slipping of the Earth, and aided along my way by angels and other guides. My path was chosen for me, and even paved bright in advance of my steps upon it. *Your* path is being made by you."

"You were part of the destiny of the world," Paolina said slowly. "Much as the Brass Christ was. But you say I am stepping outside that destiny to act in my own interests."

"In the interests of everyone, I think." Hethor glanced to the north, where the Wall loomed close but hidden from them by the canopy of jungle over the rim of the amphitheater. "I have begun to believe that God meant us to rebel, meant us to step outside His plan and make our own way in the world. That is one way to read the tale of the Garden of Eden. Those ancient Jewish priests who wrote our Bible were afraid of what had been done in Adamic times. They sought the shelter of God's laws, as a terrier might seek the safety of a kennel when confronted with the opportunity of an endless, open street."

Hethor's words grew inside Paolina like a storm tide. "The snake was our savior?" she asked.

"Where is he now? You can read the book of Job, or Isaiah—God had an Adversary. Where did Lucifer, son of the morning, go to when he fell from Heaven?"

"He was punished." The voice of Fra Bellico echoing from the years of Paolina's childhood. "Hidden from the grace of God."

Eagerness infused Hethor's voice. "If Creation had been formed with an Adversary to Heaven, if man had been given the true choice of contrary action, rather than the muttering dissent we see under a clockwork sky, imagine how different the world might be."

"You believe the stemwinder opens the door to contrary action?"

"To everything good and evil." He pointed at the device half-forgotten in her hand. "With that, you can change the order of the world at a thought, in a way that armies of slaves could never do should they shift every stone and brick that makes up the Wall. You can alter Creation."

Paolina turned it over in her hand, looking at the scratched casing, the scars and dings and stains that had accumulated. The gleam seemed like such a small thing to be a lever to shift the weight of all destiny.

"I . . . have not thought of it this way."

"Why should you?" he asked. "Some things were not made to be questioned. If God had meant to challenge us to find His path, He would not have autographed the sky in brass. That is as a clear a signpost as any that we are to follow, not to lead."

Paolina considered that. "Yet He made us with the capacity to question."

"You have crossed the Wall. You have feasted here among the Correct People. How many thinking races have you met, or seen evidence of? Surely they all have the capacity to question." Hethor glanced over his shoulder at Arellya, who nodded sadly. He turned back to Paolina. "Consider that every one of those might be a separate Creation, a separate play at the table."

"What was He looking for?" she asked.

"That." Hethor pointed to the gleam. "He was looking for someone to stand before Him as an equal. Think on this, if I might be right. Lucifer failed. The men of Adamic times fled from the true meaning of the Garden. The Brass Christ tried to awaken us—read His words with this in mind, you will see what I mean—but the habit of obedience is too strong within all of God's creatures."

"I—I must consider your thinking," Paolina said. Her heart twisted. "I hold little brief for the machinery of faith, have never met a priest who was not corrupted by his own fleshly desires, whatever his mouth might say. Even so, there is a distress in your words that troubles me."

"I do not dissent," he told her quietly. "God is undeniable and everywhere. I simply believe there can be more to a human being than submission to the will of the world."

"Even here in the Southern Earth you worry about submission?"

"No, no." Hethor reached for Arellya to pull her close. "I have made my place, my little paradise amid the jungle. But that does not change the world. At most, it changes me. You and your gleam can reweave everything."

"What the British and the secret societies fear so much," she replied.

"Precisely." He seemed exhausted, as if propounding his theories of free will and divine intent had worn too much away. "I came here to tell you something else."

"Which would be what?"

"That it is possible to relocate without leaving ruin behind."

"How?" Paolina asked eagerly.

"I do not know for certain. The powers I have were granted as a blessing, a miracle in the technical sense of the term. But the archangel Gabriel took me to the moon, then here to the heart of the forest, without leaving destruction in our wake. I know it can be done. My thought is that the angel sent the energy somewhere else, so the push in one direction was matched by an opposing push in the other."

That idea corresponded so perfectly with Paolina's observations on the nature of the physical world that she could almost hear the click as it slid home inside her head.

KITCHENS

He crouched in the waist of the ship, clutching a naval carbine. Plainly all the crew from Captain Sayeed down to the rawest cabin boy were terrified of the consequences of the winged savages gaining a foothold on the deck.

These creatures were no Barbary pirates from such ha'penny dreadfuls as *Airships Ahoy!!!* and *Electrick Adventure Fortnightly* that were the closest thing he had to a vice. He'd read al-Wazir's reports of fighting them aboard *Bassett*, had seen the accounts of the increasing number of encounters along the Wall in the two years since the failure of the Gordon Expedition of 1900.

Nothing gave a hint to the shrieking terror that was these false, leathery angels sweeping along the deck with their bronze swords glinting. They were bloody-mouthed horrors with tattooed skins and blank eyes, and they rammed time and again into *Notus*.

Harrow had men on both rails, with a small party in the bow. The greatest danger was from the sides, where the winged savages could readily gain purchase. Sayeed and his officers defended themselves on the poop, while a party from the gas division had gone atop the bag to reinforce the navigator's rest.

The fight was a game of stoop and shriek and wait. The flyers closed, attacked briefly, then circled off high and away like falcons before returning. The waist guns had opened time and again, the ship bucking as they barked roughly into the empty air, but they were almost useless. Their shells and bombards were meant to bring down other ships, not man-size targets on the wing. The volleys of the sailors under Harrow were somewhat better, but right now Kitchens was bitterly regretting the absence of *Notus'* company of marines.

With every pass, the winged savages took a loss or two. With every pass, *Notus* took three or four. A man down here with his eyes clawed out, another there shrieking as his heart's blood pulsed from the ragged wound where his arm had been ripped free. The lucky ones died as they were struck. The rest crawled and wailed on the deck, begging an indifferent God or the harried chiurgeon for something, anything to restore them.

Gunsmoke filled the ship until his eyes ran with choking sobs. The stench of blood stole his breath. The attackers had their own special foetor, a reek like all the rotting horses of Hell's cavalry released to the charge in one shambling herd.

This was not his sort of fight. Kitchens could kill a man two dozen ways in the dark. He could sight in a rifle from a frightful distance with a steady enough hand to choose which eye he might take out. He knew arts of *gong fu* and blade and poison and unsubtle trap.

Even so, the face-to-face brawls of common soldiers and drunken street boys were as foreign to him as the court magics of William of Ghent and his ilk, as alien as the prayers of Christian ecstatics dancing with brass rods through their tendons before the cathedrals at Westminster and Canterbury. He would willingly fight and die for England, for his queen, for his honor.

Just not like *this*.

Over the rail, Africa was much closer than he recalled, as if *Notus* were heading toward a hard landing. Smoke billowed. The Wall loomed ahead at a drunken angle, a second, stone sky that would swallow them all.

Not while he still lived.

Kitchens shook off the moment of vertigo and fired his carbine, a three count after the ragged volley released by the survivors along his rail. Turning to anticipate where the winged savages would reappear, he saw the smaller airship closing in. For a strange, long moment, Kitchens thought the other captain was firing on *Notus*, but he realized the chasers in her bow were aiming at a lower angle.

A volley rose from the ground. Something out of his line of sight squawked in pained surprise. A cheer rose from the other rail. *Notus'* waist guns spoke one more time.

Then silence.

It was the silence of straining engines, crackling flames, whimpering men passing the door of death, creaking lines, groaning planks, spent cartridges dropping metal-dull to the deck, the sighing of three dozen survivors realizing they might live to see another sunset. It was the silence of whistling pipes, Harrow shouting orders in a voice so hoarse he could have been calling from beyond the grave, a bell tolling from the poop, a signal gun firing, flags flapping as they were dropped overboard on a weighted line to communicate . . . what?

Ottweill's camp huddled against the Wall, stockade blocking the entrance to a recessed bay. Where he had expected a bustling city of industry below was a ruin, though. The wooden wall stood, but with obvious damage. The tents and equipment behind it were just so much shattered wrack. A small group of men were formed up on the walkway of the stockade, protecting a polished idol—no, a Brass, who was among them. A much larger group was arrayed in a loose rank behind them, rifles at the ready.

Rescue from the ground, then, sufficient confusion and firepower to drive away the winged savages. Ottweill's men, but he was unsure who the Brass was. Prisoner? Spy? Decoy?

The smaller airship hovered much closer now, seeming almost to shiver as it kept pace with *Notus*. His vessel was definitely in serious difficulty, with a list to her deck and the unsubtle panic of a shipboard fire seizing the crew.

"Captain's compliments, sir," said a vaguely familiar-looking boy at his elbow. "We're putting everybody over the side who ain't working the fire or keeping the ship in the air. For your safety. There's a line aft."

"No," Kitchens responded unthinking. "I have government papers below, and I am responsible for this ship." *The Queen's note to him.*

"Sir," the boy insisted. "If the fire gets into the gasbag, there won't be no more ship, not no more you either upon 'er. Captain says you go over the side, yourself by name."

Kitchens briefly weighed the possibility that this was a ruse meant to take advantage of the fighting and strip him away from the airship. If Sayeed meant to mutiny, there were far simpler ways to accomplish that end. He looked over at the poop, to catch the captain looking back at him.

Sayeed nodded once, then stabbed his index finger downward. His lips moved, and though the sound did not carry above the din of the deck, Kitchens could read the words well enough. "Go to ground, man. If we live, we shall fight this out."

Nothing in his cabin mattered if the ship exploded or crashed in flames. It did him no good to die alongside the dispatches and death warrants. In that moment, Kitchens let go of something important about his life's work, in favor of something important about his life.

He suffered himself to be led to the line. *Notus* was keeping station now, perhaps two hundred feet over the cleared, muddy expanse in front of Ottweill's stockade. Down below, a dispute was emerging between those who held the ramparts and the far more numerous and better-armed party behind them.

Perhaps he could avert yet another disaster in the making.

"Into the harness, sir," said the boy earnestly. "You must be going now."

Far beneath his feet a handful of sailors secured the other end of an arrangement of ropes. Kitchens was strapped to a set of tackle with a brake lever.

"Hold on to this!" An older man tapped the brake, part of his scalp torn and hanging in a flap over one ear. Kitchens was fascinated by the bloody gleam of his skull showing through. "We've got a static line," he shouted, "but if we dip, it will take you right into the soil. Ride the brake!"

Screaming out the last of his fear, Kitchens fell into the African afternoon while bells clanged out the dangers facing the airship he was so rapidly leaving behind.

GASHANSUNU

The Silent World flared. She paused in her walking to hearken with senses that had never touched a sight or sound in the Shadow World. Her *wa* scuttled with nervous energy, something she had not before seen it do.

The gleam was being used. Whoever carried it reached into the Silent World with blind, questing fingers. Brief, sharp irruptions marked where damage was being done to the warp and weft that made up this most real of places.

At least the invader was out where the spirits were thin and the world not so filled with memories. She could all too easily imagine what effect such experimentation would have within the city. Gashansunu sharpened her perceptions.

There could not be two of these in the Southern Earth at this time. Her goal was close. The gleam, whoever carried it, whatever they represented. The regrets of this world and the fears of the Shadowed next.

She resumed her pace and walked quickly into the direction from which the violence had emanated.

Rivers have power, even in the Silent World. They carry such a weight of memory from the soil on their banks and amid their water meadows that while the texture of the world might be thin all around them, a river course serves to concentrate it. They are bright lines on an empty map, veins for the power of the land to run within, barriers and highways both, depending on the intentions of the traveler. Gashansunu came to a river pregnant with the sluggish thoughts of a wide, vacant land. She was close, so very close to the gleam, but it had stopped detonating amid the echoing interstices.

She would have to drop back to the Shadow World where the majority of her life lay and look in the usual, everyday ways. Her *wa* would range wide, scouting for her, but now was the time to lay down the mantle of this place.

The danger of stepping so far and long in the Silent World was the feeling she had now, the sense that there was no need to take up once more the burdens of the body. Ensouled and empowered, right here Gashansunu was everything she would ever need to be, possessed everything she might ever desire. The hollow shell of the Shadow World was so *base*, so mundane, so *imperfected*.

This risk was well known to any adept of the houses of the city. Gashansunu closed off temptation and willed herself back to the Shadow World before the questions could take any deeper root in her spirit. The meatbellows of her lungs coughed back to life as the coursing of blood in her veins woke her up from the dream of walking.

Waking, she was in a deep jungle, the plants and trees subtly different from those of the coastline around the city.

Waking, she stood on a little bank of mud near a riverside path.

Waking, she was wrapped in heat like chains, subject already to the investigations of a dozen birds, a score of scavengers, hundreds of insects.

Gashansunu took all their tiny soul-fragments in a single sweep of her will and stepped away from the falling, silent bodies that marked her entry into this place. Voices muttered ahead. She pushed through the path, beneath a broad, glossy-leafed branch, and into the edge of a clearing.

Three of the Correct People stared at her in vivid, comical alarm. Beyond, a pair of pallid folk, by their coloration from the Northern Earth, sat talking with another Correct Person behind them.

Her eyes were drawn to the hand of one of the pale people.

The gleam.

Gashansunu called in her *wa* to take the measure of these folk, their intentions, even their barbaric tongue should converse be necessary.

The male Northerner looked up at her. Crippled or unfinished, he bore no alarm at all, just a curious smile. The female turned, gleam still clasped in her hand, and opened her mouth to shout.

The sorceress raised her fingers to still them. Much to her amazement, she found that she could not. Her *wa* flapped in panic, folding into a mist that sought to swirl hidden behind her.

Who *were* these people? For the first time in her life, Gashansunu wondered if she had made a potentially fatal error.

TEN

Then came in the magicians, the astrologers, the Chaldeans, and the soothsayers: and I told the dream before them; but they did not make known unto me the interpretation thereof.

—*Daniel 4:7*

BOAZ

McCurdy continued to argue with Ottweill's men. The bosun's tone was desperate, as he obviously longed to be in the skies doing something, *anything* besides standing here in disputation. The doctor himself was not present, admittedly a blessing, but the gloomy little man in charge was uninterested in McCurdy's pleas.

"I do not care what your captain says, you're to lay down your arms and be coming with us," the interloper said. "I'll not be telling you this again." The forest of rifle barrels around his head aimed toward the stockade. "Be bringing John Brass with you."

"I am in Her Imperial Majesty's service—," McCurdy began.

Boaz whispered into the momentary silence of the bosun's indrawn breath, "Jump off the stockade."

The man paused, glanced at Boaz, then said, "Shore party down the back side, *now*."

They jumped, tumbled, fell as a ragged round of firing whistled overhead in response. *Not an ordered volley, then,* Boaz thought as he caught his balance ankle-deep in mud, *just overexcited tunnel rats.* The human voices in his head agreed, saying, *That won't matter so much if we're dead.*

"To the ropes," shouted the bosun.

They scrambled away from the stockade before the defenders could gain the rampart and start shooting again at fatally close range. De Koonig had injured his leg, and was being helped along by Pratt and Shaw. All ran toward the knot of sailors escaping from the burning airship.

"Chief," Boaz said, loping beside McCurdy. "It is not so wise to race toward a burning reservoir of hydrogen."

"British tars, my Brass," McCurdy gasped. "Our safety is in their numbers."

Indistinct shouting erupted behind them. Ahead, two of the sailors manning the lifeline caught a descending third who screamed all the way down. The rest turned to face McCurdy's party, most armed with short knives or improvised weapons.

The bosun declared himself before fresh violence could erupt. "Bosun George McCurdy of *Erinyes*, circling up yonder. The fort behind is held by English civvies who have conceived us as enemies."

"Leading Seaman Patrice," replied one of the sailors. "Of *Notus* above." They both looked up at the smoke billowing from the listing airship. "She's in distress, sir," he added unnecessarily.

"Keep bringing them down," McCurdy told him. "My lads, face the stockade, weapons ready. Mr. Patrice, any sailors you can spare will be of great assistance."

"What about the hydrogen?" Boaz asked.

McCurdy and Patrice both stared at him. The seaman wasn't surprised to see the Brass, which was logical enough as *Notus* had put in at Ottweill's camp when Boaz was first there.

Someone bellowed above. They all glanced up to see a series of objects falling. "Clear," shouted Patrice. His men scattered as a small rain of chests, books and cloth smashed into the churned mud.

The screaming man staggered to Boaz. The Brass realized this was no sailor. He was bloody, begrimed and had a look of shocked panic in his eyes, but still bore a certain spare elegance. Even his draggled, ruined suit displayed a former glory under the rents and stains.

"Who the blazes are you?" the newcomer demanded in a voice ragged with panic.

The rescue party was re-forming around them to bring more men down from the stricken ship. Two of the naval ratings scooped up what had been thrown overboard. A few sailors joined McCurdy's men in forming a defensive perimeter to face the hostiles on the stockade. *Erinyes* continued to circle above, her helplessness apparent even from the fracas on the ground.

"I am Boaz of the Brass folk. I am no subject of your Queen's, but I claim friendship with Angus Threadgill al-Wazir of your Royal Navy." ::*you owe them no loyalty*:: rumbled the Sixth Seal in his gut. The al-Wazir–Paolina voice protested that.

The civilian had drawn breath to continue the argument, but he stopped cold at that statement. "You know al-Wazir?"

Something small smacked into the ground between them. "Yes."

"We will speak, later." He looked up the hill. "Are those English guns being pointed at us?"

"I should think so," Boaz replied. "Your men inside the Wall have taken a great dislike to visitors."

"Ottweill survives!"

"The mad doctor? Unfortunately, yes. I have tried to convince him that his project is fruitless, for the Wall is not a solid thing to be dug through, but rather a shield to contain billions of tons of spinning brass required to balance the Earth and tune its rotation."

"We will *definitely* speak later."

Boaz turned his attention to helping organize the defense. The new-comer began to aid the cleanup in the descending tangle of codebooks, ship's logs and other materials. More men came down the line, some bear-ing navigational instruments or similar valuables.

A grubby little man with three freshly missing fingers landed after a few minutes. "Sayeed is taking her back up for risk of a gasbag burn-off. 'Ware a ballast dump."

The rescue lines were cast away. One last heave from above sent a scat-tering of small objects to the ground. Then *Notus* dumped her ballast tanks, drenching the lot of them with fouled water. Boaz was just as glad in that moment that he had not been created with a sense of smell.

The airship shot upward, trailing smoke and a last spray of water. *Erinyes* widened her circle, moving away from her stricken sister.

McCurdy woke to his task and began shouting again. "Eyes on the stock-ade. Won't do us good to stare up if the doctor's men are going to shoot us down like dogs on a chain."

A sallow man who'd been among the last down the lines sent scouts down to the lower edge of the open, muddy firing field to look for possible refuges. Every second man was told off to stand ready for attack from the stockade, armed with such weapons as could be mustered from the ragged group.

Bells clanged above. *Notus* drifted badly to the port now, and the smoke had grown denser. Then the forward portion of her gasbag erupted in a pale, almost invisible explosion that was more felt than heard by those on the ground. Her bow dropped precipitously, sending men to fall screaming through the afternoon sky.

The midsection of the gasbag blew next. *Notus'* hull broke at that, the fore shearing away to tumble in a further spray of bodies. It landed in the trees at the east edge of their clearing, perhaps half a mile away. The aft still clung to her stays and the mizzenmast that connected her to the re-mains of the burning gasbag.

Those last cells did not blow. The remains of *Notus* spiraled in slowly, drifting toward the Wall so that her final flight ended against a rock outcropping several miles distant.

Soaking wet, bloody, injured, the surviving crew stared into the eastern distance as the smoke rose above the scattered ruins of their airship. The sallow man who'd been giving orders to the crew of *Notus* looked at the gentleman in the suit. "Mr. Kitchens? What should we do?"

Erinyes beat low above, circling now, her engines straining.

"Do not put Lieutenant Ostrander in charge," Boaz said. He could only imagine what the unstable young officer might order.

Kitchens looked to Boaz and McCurdy. "Who's Ostrander? Commanding above?"

"Master of *Erinyes*, sir," the bosun said reluctantly.

"A difficult man at his best," Boaz added, to a grateful look from McCurdy.

"My warrants do not extend to his vessel," Kitchens said somewhat mysteriously. "I have no standing with those on the captain's list."

"Meaning what?" Boaz asked.

Kitchens gave him a slow look. "It means that unless someone from *Notus*' command made it down, the man in charge up there is the senior surviving naval officer on this field of battle. Harrow here, and your chief from *Erinyes*, are each loyal to their ship and master, but Harrow's captain is now presumably dead, while your Lieutenant Ostrander appears unfit for duty."

McCurdy made a small noise, as if he'd thought to protest, then swallowed his pride along with his words.

"You are all fools," Boaz declared. "How your throne came to rule half the flatwater kingdoms of Northern Earth is beyond me." He pointed at Kitchens. "*You* are in charge of these men, for there is no one else to do the deed. *I* will aid you until affairs have settled a bit; then I am off on my own mission. Now let us find our way out of this killing field."

The sailors followed their scouts downhill in a large, fractious party while *Erinyes* circled low to keep the men on the stockade otherwise occupied. When they gained the safety of the trees, McCurdy and Harrow called for a camp to be made. Boaz stole a quiet moment with the man Kitchens at the edge of a tangle of lianas.

"I am Boaz of the Brass," he said, introducing himself with a bit more of the formality these English were said to prefer. "I am not accounted an enemy of your people, though the doctor's men upon the stockade will tell you differently."

Kitchens took Boaz' offered hand. "I am Bernard Kitchens, clerk in the

Special Section of the Admiralty, on extremely detached duty. We have much to discuss, though this is not the time."

"I think not," Boaz answered. He studied the English clerk carefully. The man had a fevered gleam in his eye, but seemed in possession of his senses, to the degree that any human ever was.

::*this is not our mission*:: the Seal grumbled.::*our purpose lies elsewhere*::

I am not your servant, Boaz thought. The voice was loudest when the world was quiet, and quiet when the world was loud. The Brass touched the man's sleeve. "You come dressed differently than all of them, ready to kill but regretting it. You are no soldier nor sailor nor working man. What are you doing down here along the Wall?"

"Looking for Ottweill, and al-Wazir."

The Brass did not mince his next words. "Ottweill I have seen just this morning at the diggings. Al-Wazir was taken by the Chinese in Mogadishu a month ago and must surely be dead."

"Then I have failed him," Kitchens said. "It was I who sent him back to the Wall, to see to Ottweill's safety."

"You are the spymaster?"

"No, no. I arranged his training and transmitted his orders. The true purpose was ordered from much higher up."

Purpose, Boaz thought. *Everything was down to purpose.* The will of man, walking freely in the world of God. "Well, for my part," the Brass said, "I am very sorry to see the chief at an end."

"Dozens more men met their end today," Kitchens replied. "It is not even nightfall yet. I should see to a parley with those fools upon the stockade, so we Englishmen do not all kill one another and save the Wall from so much trouble." Gathering up his much-abused attaché case, the clerk strode away into the viridian shadows of the forest.

Boaz looked up at the smoke still drifting in the sky and wondered if *Erinyes* would ever come to ground, or remain aloft until Lieutenant Ostrander was but a skeleton at her helm.

KITCHENS

The stockade stood above him. In another place it might have loomed, great tropical hardwood logs trimmed to points at the top in order to provide firing rests between each pair, their faces scarred and splintered from prior battles. Here the Wall behind it left the stockade with little more dignity than a child's toy.

A handful of men stared down at him, rifles sloping nearly into aiming. "You h'aint no h'officer," said a twitching fellow.

"I am from Admiralty," Kitchens said, clutching his salvaged attaché case and wishing his suit retained any scraps of dignity. "Here on a mission from the First Sea Lord and the Prime Minister's office." Which, while not strictly true, was more impressive than confessing to being a clerk. "I am to ascertain Dr. Ottweill's safety and whether the tunneling crew needs further assistance."

"You're 'aving me on, right?" Setting down his rifle, the man on the stockade began to laugh—helpless, hysterical, *angry*. "You walks out of a burning h'airship, you looks to be the dog's breakfast, and you comes here where we been hiding h'inside the Wall like mice in a rectory, and you h'asks if we needs 'elp."

"Must be government," said one of the other men darkly. "No one else could be so stupid."

"I shall speak to Dr. Ottweill now," Kitchens said sternly.

"Oh . . ." More giggling. "I h'expect you shall."

A rope slithered over the side. Unlike most clerks in the city of London, Kitchens knew how to climb it, even with an attaché case under his arm.

He was escorted rapidly through the wreckage of the compound in the afternoon's failing light. Shattered Brass, corpses of the winged savages, an entire supply train's worth of quartermaster gear and provisions—all lay strewn about fields of clutter. The only order was in the large piles of tailings that stood close by the face of the Wall—rock spoil, sand and other material from the tunneling.

A substantial metal barrier glowered over the tunnel entrance. It had been bolted together from bits of hull plating, boiler shells and other less obvious components. Someone watched from inside, for a postern door creaked open as they approached. Kitchens allowed himself to be hustled into the darkness beyond.

An oil lamp flickered, casting buttery shadows against the impenetrable darkness of the tunnel beyond. Two sets of tracks lay at his feet. A standard gauge ran within the embrace of the wider, special gauge of the boring machines. He hadn't seen the rails outside. Either they'd been torn up by the attackers, or salvaged by the defenders.

Two dozen men faced him packed wall-to-wall, pistols and knives in hand. They shared the heavy breathing and glittering eyes of a pack. Hunted, not hunting. His interviewer from outside waved off the other guards.

"Too much to tell 'ere, but there's a big passel of tars 'iding in the woods h'out there what should draw h'off h'any h'interest what comes h'our way tonight. Reg'lar guard, h'I should think."

"I got duty," muttered a large man black as a clinker. He was not African, Kitchens saw, merely grubby beyond measure with coal dust. "Who's the fish?"

"Fellow from London, come to see the doctor about h'our little problems."

That provoked another round of desperate laughter.

"The doctor is in," muttered someone else.

Flicking another lamp into life, the entire outside party and most of the door wards headed deeper into the tunnel. They swirled Kitchens into their midst, not quite taking him prisoner, yet giving him no choice but to move along under their control. A pack of dark demons returning to their labors somewhere in the depths of hell.

Where else would I go?

CHILDRESS

Cataloger Wang! The Golden Bridge had come to her!

What on the Northern Earth was the man doing *here*, in Goa? She'd last seen him ensconced in frustrated arrogance amid the flooded library of Chersonesus Aurea. It seemed no more likely that he'd leave his books than it would for al-Wazir to walk to the moon.

The lieutenant—Roche?—turned to her. "You are acquainted with this man?"

"Yes." Childress could feel al-Wazir close by at her shoulder, knew the big man was straining to ask something of his own.

Lieutenant Roche's voice grew cold. "Why should that be?"

"She works for my master," Wang said.

"You said you was a librarian," the squad leader muttered.

"I am." Childress drew up to her full five feet, one inch.

Wang smiled. "My master employs librarians and archivists."

"You were both on your way to Bombay?" The lieutenant sounded more incredulous than suspicious.

Maybe we shall find our way out of here after all, Childress thought. But what was Wang *doing* here?

Following her, of course. That latter idea had frightening but unsurprising implications.

"My journey would be eased by this man's aid," she announced.

"I would be pleased to take her aboard *Good Change*," Wang said with a broad smile. "We shall convey her to Bombay."

"Bloody great coincidence, if you ask me," muttered Lieutenant Roche.

"Gentlemen, I am distressed, and travel-weary, and much separated from my belongings. If Mr. Wang and his master's boat are free to carry me to Bombay, then I would be just as pleased to leave with him. Your fine soldiers may return to their bounden duty of defending this poor town."

She took a calculated risk here, using Wang and his purposes to escape the attentions of the British Army. Childress looked up over her shoulder at al-Wazir. The chief would follow her lead until they had time to confer.

Lieutenant Roche chewed on her statement a bit. "Madam, I find that you are free to go." The lieutenant turned to Wang. "It is your great luck that this good Englishwoman knows you, and can attest to your character and purposes."

Wang bowed, his smile a rictus now. "She is always a friend to my master."

"Come, Angus," Childress said to al-Wazir. "Let us be aboard. Wang, my good man, please have your fellows take my launch in tow."

A shaven coolie on the docks pushed out of the crowd to help with the small boat before Wang could even order his men off of *Good Change*. The Chinese librarian started visibly at the sight, then focused his attention once more on Childress. "Please to come this way," he said.

Almost breathing in her ear, and surely he had to bend down to do so, al-Wazir growled, "Are you sure about what you're doing, Mask?"

"Of course not," she whispered. "But boarding a boat with a man I know has to be better than being interrogated here. Our story will not stand in a light breeze."

They climbed down the slime-covered wooden ladder onto the deck of the trim white yacht. The entire crew seemed to be Chinese, Childress noted.

"Welcome aboard," Wang said. There was something both genuine and sad about his smile.

PAOLINA

The woman who stepped out of the jungle along one of the Correct People's paths was very strange in appearance. Over six feet tall, thin as a boy, with skin the color of burnished teak, and her long face was regal, almost mannish. She wore swirling robes of deep burgundy, brown and maroon, layered so that Paolina's eye slid from any real sense of the lines of the clothing. The newcomer's wrists were covered in copper bracelets almost to the point of being armored by them. Her neck was crowded with similar decoration. White dots spread across her face, and a cowrie shell had been affixed to the outside corner of each eye, so she appeared to see in several directions at once.

The woman's hand flashed up in a swift movement. Paolina shouted a protest. Hethor said something soft in the same instant, lost to her under the sound of her own voice. Whatever the stranger was expecting did not happen, for she looked baffled a moment, then very disappointed.

"Step easy," Hethor told her. "We are among friends." He followed that with words in a hissing language very unlike the speech of the Correct People.

The woman replied in the same language, her black eyes flashing, then approached Paolina. Hethor said something else in that hissing speech. The stranger looked quite surprised, her attention turning to him. Her next words were in English: "What is your House?"

"I do not hold to a House as you do," Hethor responded, "nor do the others of my people."

"I am of no House but my own," Paolina added.

"I am Gashansunu of Westfacing House, in the city," she told them. "We compass all the wisdoms of the Southern Earth, from the ways of the Great Sunset Water to the colors of the morning sky. You are come among the Silent World as something new."

Clearly her people fancied themselves great magicians.

Hethor answered for them both. "We are from the Northern Earth, where the wisdoms are different. If you come as a friend, we are friends. If you come as an unfriend, then we beg you in all goodwill to swiftly take your leave of us."

Gashansunu considered Hethor's words before replying. "The Shadow World is tinged with regret. There are flares in the Silent World. You bear a bright treasure that should either be cloaked or laid to rest. I am sent to be neither friend nor unfriend, but to settle the worlds back to their accustomed balance."

"Then we have no conflict here," Paolina said. "This man has abided in the Southern Earth these last two years without bringing trouble. I only pass through this place as I return northward. Soon your worlds will reclaim their balance."

"May I inspect your gleam?" Gashansunu asked.

The stemwinder was still clutched in Paolina's hand. This was not a request she had any inclination to grant. "I am sorry, but the gleam stays with me. It must be so."

"There are those artifacts I would not share even with my closest lovers," Gashansunu said, in an obvious effort to be polite.

In English, Paolina thought. She looked at Hethor with speculation. What transformation had he laid upon this alien woman? Hethor appeared pleased, in point of fact, rather than threatened by this woman's presence.

This was not her place, the safety of the Correct People not her responsibility. She wished to apply Hethor's thought about displacing the force of travel. Using the stemwinder under Gashansunu's unblinking gaze did not appeal.

"I would have time alone with my pursuits," Paolina announced.

Hethor smiled. "Then I shall invite our guest to my house to sip at the freshest juices and speak of the Southern Earth."

Paolina glanced up at Ming, tilting her chin to indicate that he should go with Hethor. Ming would tell her later what he could of the woman's behavior, and warn Paolina if Gashansunu were to seek to quietly return to the amphitheater.

Watching Hethor slowly ascend even the shallow slope of this place was painful. Arellya walked close by his side, but all the other Correct People watched Gashansunu as a flock of birds might study a snake.

The foreign sorceress calmly stared back at them, then followed to the top in less than a dozen swift, easy strides.

Moments later Paolina was alone with her rocks, and the endless cycling whir of the jungle.

The action suggested by Hethor involved sending her target in one direction, while displacing a ghost of it, in effect, in the other. The simplest way she could think to explain this to herself was as if a thing could be heading in two directions at once, and only resolve its location upon arrival.

The wooden benches were still disturbed when she sent rocks across the river, but now instead of splinters and smoke she was rewarded with a hollow thump followed by a burst of dust.

Everything that turned, turned against something else. Every wheel had an axle. Every gear had a mate. The world moved in *pairs*, in *sets*. Nothing spun or rolled or shifted on its own. A human being walking set a foot against the ground to push off again. The attraction and repulsion between the two—twinned forces of gravity and musculature—combined to produce a motion in which all was balanced.

This she'd understood for years. That the same principles should apply to actions taken in the hidden worlds too small, or too large, to be comprehended through normal means, well, that was obvious now that Hethor had shown her the way. The stemwinder was truly only a tool for reaching into those other places where the reflections of the everyday world grew small, and decomposed into their respective parts.

Like taking a lever to a rock.

This was translocation. Or perhaps erasure and re-creation. Which led her to wonder if the rocks, once moved, were the same rocks they had been before.

The question was meaningless. All aboard *Five Lucky Winds* had moved without becoming different people. Likewise she and Ming, fleeing that mountaintop to these jungles at the waist of the world. If she had been erased and re-created, the copy was sufficiently perfect as to be identical to the original.

This was good enough for her purposes.

The stemwinder still clutched close, she put herself to the greatest test of all. She set the fourth hand to the rhythms of her own body, looked at the collection of spinning, whirling bits that made her up, and visualized herself in the shadowed workroom where she'd first met the young English sage.

What if it did not work?

"Better that I know now," Paolina said to the uncaring insects and the thoughtless river.

Push *here*; push *there*; leave the centerpoint without stress or undue force applied against it. The concept was not so hard to understand.

Paolina took a deep breath and sent herself forth.

WANG

Captain Shen shouted for the boat to cast off. The Englishwoman and her giant servant stood by the rail. The man had only one hand, the left arm ending in a stump covered by a leather brace.

The cataloger was very doubtful of exerting any of his will upon that formidable woman.

The monk scrambled over the aft rail, still dressed as a dockside coolie. She slid close, speaking out of the corner of her mouth around her little jade pipe. "Tread lightly in these waters. We will be watched."

"Thank you," Wang said. "I should never have thought of that."

"You push back instead of bending away." She sounded delighted. "You are transforming from bamboo into a tiger, my friend. Bamboo merely survives. Tigers rule."

"I rule nothing, except the inside of a library that I will almost certainly never see again."

The Kô's yacht steamed slowly out of Panjim's harbor. Wang called up to Shen, "Set a course to the north."

The Englishwoman turned at that and added, "Stay close to the coast."

By all the demons of Hell, he had forgotten she spoke Chinese. "What am I to do with the Mask?"

"Take lessons?" the monk asked impishly.

Wang slapped his right hand against his left palm and made to answer, but once more she was gone, leaving him with only his irritation and a cloud of foul-smelling smoke.

He stepped forward to greet his guests.

"Cataloger Wang," Childress said in English, "this is my man Angus." She added in Chinese, "He does not speak your language, and so will be very suspicious at all times. This is his duty. Do not be alarmed."

"Welcome aboard *Good Change*, madam." In English. Wang bowed. "As well to you, Angus." He stumbled a bit over the unfamiliar name.

She nodded. "My thanks. We nearly experienced an unfortunate situation just now in Panjim."

"The world is in an unfortunate situation. Our empires seem to have found themselves at war."

"Ain't no finding to it," al-Wazir rumbled. "Your lot brought the fight to us in East Africa."

Wang realized the servant was far larger than anyone else on the boat. Childress might seize *Good Change* on the strength of this man alone.

"I should not pretend to know how the war came about," Wang said carefully. "Only that we seek to avoid making it worse."

"By flying a false flag?" Childress' tone was gentle, even curious. "Here you are sailing under a British ensign and speaking much better English than you pretended when you received me back at Chersonesus Aurea."

"You were a woman." Wang realized as soon as the words left his mouth that he had stated himself poorly.

"I still *am* a woman."

He had already lost what little face he had. Directness in the European manner was all that remained. "You are a woman who overmastered a submarine of the Beiyang Navy, then unleashed a terrible fate upon an entire fleet of the Nanyang Navy to the death of thousands. You are no longer simply a woman, you are a power to be reckoned with."

Her expression grew very pained. These British were weak, their lies written in the set of their eyes and the flush of their cheeks. "It may all be true, Cataloger Wang, though certainly not so simple as you seem to believe. Yet I am still a Mask of the *avebianco*. I am a power to be reckoned with, even here among your men." She leaned close. "If you truly believe I suborned *Five Lucky Winds*, why do you risk me aboard your vessel now?"

"Because he is a fool," said the monk, now in her saffron robes.

Wang was quite surprised she spoke English. Angus was quite surprised at her appearance next to the Mask. His remaining fist clenched as his face flushed.

Only Childress did not seem to notice anything unusual. She turned to the monk and said with exaggerated politeness, "All men are born fools. A lucky few are unmade."

"Ah." The monk scooped another bowl of smoking herbs from her pouch. "But I am no man, any more than you are, Mask."

The words burst out of Wang without him even realizing they were coming. "Why did they bother to send me here if you can do everything and speak all tongues!"

Instead of answering, she struck a match against the deck, lit her pipe, then flipped the smoldering stick overboard. "That should be simple enough to understand." Smoke streamed from the monk's nostrils. "Even you must know by now how few people can see me. Being invisible is difficult. One is never served in roadside inns; rude fellows on ox-carts are always running one down; none grant me the respect of my station and calling."

"You are hardly invisible to me," Childress told the monk. Her man Angus reached out and fingered a trailing edge of the monk's robe, as if testing it.

"You are a Mask. Less is hidden from you with each moment that passes. Someday you will be able to see into the heart of the world without hindrance." She laughed. "Should you be lucky enough to live so long."

"You're a clown," Angus said in that thick, slow voice. "A mountebank. Some Chinee thief set here by this man Wang to confuse us until we make a mistake we cannot undo."

"I believe you passed that point long ago, devil man." The monk tapped out her pipe. "Would you spar with me, that I might prove how real I am?"

"Nae, I'll not hit such as a one as you."

"Religious? I can be a sailor. Female? I can appear as a man. Chinese? Well, some things sustain no further perfection."

Wang was glad to see the monk talking someone else in circles for a change, instead of harassing him.

"No matter," Angus said, his voice trailing off. He looked helplessly to the Mask Childress.

She gave Wang a long slow stare, then briefly returned her attention to the monk, who now shifted from foot to foot as if she intended to dance. "I believe we have learned enough. I'll thank you to put us both over the side in our boat now."

"I cannot do that," Wang said, while the monk replied, "Certainly!"

KITCHENS

A rough fellow sidled up to him during the slow walk down the tunnel. Kitchens noted the shifty cast of his eyes, the scar on his neck, the edges of some sailor's tattoo swirling above the grubby, frayed line of his collar.

"Lizer Williams," the man mumbled. "Been to Singapore three times, once were a snake agent on the Indian Ocean station."

"Bernard Kitchens, of London, special clerk to the Admiralty. Never left England before this voyage."

"I know you dark clerks." Lizer's voice did not improve with further conversation. "Me daddy was on the old Singapore runs out of Calcutta, when the cotton trade was good, afore the Chinee took Admiral Wellesley in the Battle of the Straits. I seen the city oncet as a boy, oncet as a young man on a spice trader, and last afore I shipped back to England."

"You worked with Admiralty?" Kitchens strained to keep the distaste from his voice.

"Not as such, no . . ." Lizer dissolved into incoherence for a moment before finding his voice again. "There's them snakes off the Wall, you knows. Come down mostly among the Chinee, but they gots their people in our patch too."

"Snakes?" He had all but dismissed this man as mad already. Yet in the shadow of the Wall, madness seemed to be not only expected but perhaps requisite.

"What come from the high temples and slide through the world. Like how you can't see a snake in a field until after too late?"

"Hmm." Though he suspected he would soon regret asking the question, Kitchens had to try. "In that case, what is a 'snake agent'?"

"One like yourself, begging your pardon, guv. What walks through the fields unseen until your teeth is planted in a man's leg and he's got no time left to live."

The fascinating conversation was interrupted by a sentry challenge from just ahead. Kitchens was pulled away from Lizer Williams by the fellow who'd brought him through the iron wall at the entrance.

"Don't you be listening to old Lizer," the man said. "He's cracked as a chocolate teapot. Good enough tamper, God knows, and that's a rare breed what still has all their fingers about them, but too many blasts done bled out what's left of his wits long since." After a pause for breath: "You sure and certain you wants to be down here, airship man?"

Kitchens steeled his reserve. "If the good Dr. Ottweill cannot come to me, then perforce I must come to the doctor."

He was led last through another metal barrier. Beyond was noise. The grinding screech of the boring machine invaded Kitchens' thoughts with the inevitability of a terminal disease. The sound seemed to shape his eyes, so he peered as if through water.

This space was much wider than the tunnel, and lit like the waiting rooms of Judgment Day. Spitting candles, oil lamps, electricks glowing in a few places, powered by some distant generator—together, all shed a fitful, moody light.

The ceiling rose higher than Kitchens could see, the narrowing angle of the walls disappearing into shadow. Closer to the floor it had been widened into something resembling a London tube station, including even the pillars. An ordinary steam locomotive sat cold on a siding—a 2–2 switcher from Boulton & Watt. A number of railroad wagons were scattered about in short trains, flatbeds as well as a few pieces of more complex trackage equipment.

All else was supplies and men. If Hieronymus Bosch had painted warehouses, he might have rendered this scene. Supplies were stacked between the railroad wagons—great piles of sleepers and rails, acres of canvas salvaged from the tent city that should have stood outside in the encampment, glistening water barrels ranging from kegs to gigantic tuns that had to come down the rails on wheels of their own, piles of scrap iron, coal, spikes, tools.

And men everywhere. Peering from tents. Sitting on little dosses. Tangled in blankets underneath hulking iron machines. In folded sheaths of canvas affixed to the rising walls. On rough ledges higher above. Perched atop the railroad wagons.

Here the damned awaited a special ironbound eternity, digging their way into a great, endless hole.

The noise punctuated it all, defined the space, hollowed out the ears and minds of men. Kitchens wondered how many of these navvies were already deaf. Those not yet ear-blind would become so far too soon.

He looked back at the barrier. Weapons were stacked and racked there—carbines, rifles, pistols, grenadoes, sharpened iron bars, caltrops—awaiting some attack down the tunnel or an alert to rush to the surface and defend yet again. The fighting must have been awful, Kitchens realized, to make living in this howling, dark den preferable to defending their camp above.

What did they eat? How was the water brought down? Ottweill's men surely were forced to sally constantly. Calculating the cost of a meal in lives lost would render any band of brothers grim as Papist saints.

The guide cupped his hands and shouted in Kitchens' ear. "You will wait for the doctor in his office."

That turned out to be a shack atop a flatbed railroad wagon. The space around overflowed with papers sticking out of boxes, dropping from shelves, in loose shoals. Two boys sat idle among the pale drifts, but hopped to attention and a feigned busyness at the approach of Kitchens and his escort.

The man stabbed a finger at the shack. Kitchens nodded, climbed up onto the flatcar, and tugged open the door.

Within was blessedly cool and relatively quiet. The windows had been boarded up, the walls lined with sheaves of paper nailed into place. It cut down the noise, Kitchens realized, making this a place where a man might sit and think with some profit, as opposed to merely having his head constantly ringing like a struck bell.

The most prominent feature of the office was a blackboard on which two tallies were kept. One listed the progress of the tunneling project, indicating that they had penetrated 3,861 yards in the seventy-four days since digging began. The other tally showed what Kitchens quickly realized must be a list of the dead.

He studied it. The hand was obviously Ottweill's: precise, Germanic, clean as if it had flowed from a printer's plate.

My men: 142

Other men of the Queen: 97

———————————————

Brass: 38

~~Angels:~~ 29

Evil men: 702

Beneath that:

We are losing.

"There stands a tragedy in one act," Kitchens breathed, "by its presents to be known to all men."

He laid down his attaché case, pulled up one of the hard, wooden chairs in the office and sat down to wait for the return of the master of this unlikely, self-made hell. There was much in the way of files and notes with which an enterprising clerk of an investigative frame of mind might busy himself.

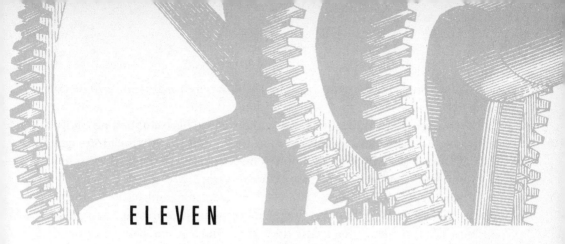

ELEVEN

If I make my bed in hell, behold, thou art there.

—*Psalm 139:8*

BOAZ

That night *Erinyes* hid somewhere in the sky. *Notus* continued to burn fitfully in the distance, but her surviving crew couldn't muster the courage for trekking through the enemy dark to inspect the scattered wreckage. Boaz was in conference with Bosun McCurdy and McCurdy's counterpart from the lost airship, a man named Harrow who seemed overwhelmed to the point of breaking.

"We are done for now," Harrow muttered after they'd spent some time going round the logistics of encampment and defense. "Your little scow won't haul my men back to England."

"'Tis not *my* little scow," McCurdy said darkly. "Lieutenant Ostrander has command, and I reckon he is fast becoming one with the birds."

Boaz knew he should just walk away, resume his quest to take the Sixth Seal to Ophir. His loyalty to al-Wazir kept him here, hoping to find a way to deliver these men to safety.

Moreover, what would Paolina say if he abandoned the sailors to their fates? She had no love for the British, but she still held life dear in her heart. Invaders to the Wall these people might be, but they were still people. Just like her.

"You will likely not see help from Dr. Ottweill," Boaz offered. "He is as mad as you claim your Lieutenant Ostrander to be, and is in critical need of supply and support himself." He turned to McCurdy. "If *Erinyes* returns, will you set the midshipman to take command? She must go to Mogadishu for help."

"Cotonou on the Benin coast would be a sight closer," Harrow said. "But there's no airships based there. Just a brace of towers and some supplies, with a company of marines to guard them."

"Could you ferry men and equipment from here to Cotonou in several swift passages?"

"Aye," said McCurdy. "How many could survive here, left behind? With them beyond the stockade wall so unfriendly, and them winged savages tearing at us from the air, and whatever lives by night in these jungles, too few men would vanish like corbies before a storm."

"I have been north of here, along the coast," Boaz said. "The harbor is on the Mitémélé River. Beyond that is nothing but swamp and foetor. You could march the men down to the river, cross on rafts, and camp on one of the islands there until *Erinyes* either brought help or carried out the crew in measured groups. We would be away from the Wall, and perhaps safer from at least some of the attacks that will surely come our way."

Attacks instigated by his own people, Boaz knew. Both McCurdy and Harrow were surely aware of that source of their dangers, though at the moment they were more concerned with the treachery in Ottweill's camp, along with the loss of their entire leadership.

" 'T'will go far the better for us if my airship does return soon," McCurdy said quietly. "I'll not lead a mutiny against Ostrander, though."

Harrow protested. "He flies like a swallow from the nest, flitting back and away again. Such an officer is at best battle-shy, which is no good thing. Beyond that, he does not seem to have much sense. Not from what you tell me."

"The man is stricken," Boaz said. The voices of Paolina and al-Wazir within him agreed, and offered another point, that he echoed. "Bosun McCurdy will not speak against his own commander, and rightly so by the rules of the Royal Navy." He paused. "Chief, if I relieve Lieutenant Ostrander, will you be able to con *Erinyes*?"

"Ye cannae—," McCurdy began, then subsided into silence.

"This would be mutiny for one of us," Harrow said. "For you, it would be an act of war against the British Crown."

"Better to die here in the jungles while a man bereft of his wits birds it about overhead?" Boaz' disgust mounted again. Even the Sixth Seal was attending now—the topic of madness attracted it. Mutterings in Adamic and Hebrew rose within his thoughts like smoke. Imprecations, doubts, fears. "I can walk away. This is my people's place, these lands where I have spent my life. You would die for rules and pride."

Harrow gave McCurdy a long look in the dark. "Duty does rule us."

"Did duty bring down *Notus*?" Boaz asked.

"Politics killed the ship," the bosun replied. "Those winged savages held the sword point, but it was politics what set the deed in motion."

"That man Kitchens."

"Him, too. He is part of the problem. Our captain . . ." He paused. "Well, I'll not speak against the dead, nor against my own commander."

Boaz leaned close. "Who commands you now?"

"Lieutenant Ostrander, who flits about the sky like a bat on a summer night. He is the surviving officer on the scene."

The human voices in him were practically shouting. "There is a gift," Boaz said, choosing his words with care. Here was a moment when his debts came due. "This gift was given me in that encampment beyond the stockade by a girl of your race, and a petty officer of your navy. They made me my own man, relieving me of the obligation of obedience, only to replace it with the burden of free will. You, now, are detached from your laws and rules. You are likely faced with choosing between obedience and survival. I cannot make that decision for you, but I can and will freely aid you in carrying it out, from loyalty to those who loved me enough to set me free."

Harrow snorted. "There's not a petty officer born who doesn't know how to walk wide circles around a lawful order so the captain gets what he really needs instead of what he thinks he wants. But to throw off authority entirely, that is a different matter."

Boaz understood throwing off Authority, far too well. "Then if *Erinyes* returns with the dawn, or before then, I shall treat with your commander. I have dealt with troublesome airships before."

McCurdy spoke up. "I'll nae stand in your way, but I shan't raise a hand to aid you, neither. Even this much I do is treason."

"Do not say that word," Harrow whispered sharply. "Let it be enough that our friend and ally John Brass has a plan." He gave Boaz a sidelong look. "Not that you are much of either one to my knowledge, but you are here helping us instead of out in the woods making death lists."

"He's no bad man." McCurdy subsided into a sullen silence.

Boaz took his leave of the conference and set to walking the perimeter of their temporary camp. He could add no more to what had already been said, and if the conversation continued, McCurdy might crab away from his acquiescence.

GASHANSUNU

Her *wa* gibbered. It was terrified of this Hethor, in a way she had never seen anyone's *wa* react before. The darknesses within his house were as knotted with irruptions into the Silent World as any corner back in the city might ever be. He seemed to have filled the very air around him with shimmering spirits, unquiet sendings, and an armor of power such as she'd never seen. He held a *wa* half the size of the Earth, though he didn't even seem to notice.

"You are a prophet," she said, the conclusion leaping unbidden to her lips in the words of his barbarous yawp.

"No." Hethor eased into a chair woven of vine whips around a frame of wood that still reeked of life. "I foretell no futures. But you are right in that I have been touched by God."

"A god." Gashansunu shook off the warning of her *wa* that this man might himself be such a one. "The world manifests in many faces."

"There is only one," he told her gently.

"Have you seen that one?"

"No. But I have spoken with His messenger angels. I have held His words in my hand. He has directed my steps, beyond the point of unreason."

"That is not divinity." She turned her hand just so and plucked a shred from the Silent World that glittered in her grasp here in the Shadow World. "That is a fever on the brain."

Hethor ignored the scrap in her fingers. She watched an intensity deepen his face. "He is everywhere," the young man protested. "The sky shouts of His handiwork, the Earth is transparently His creation."

"I created this just now." She rolled the gleaming flash around in her hand. "Pulled it from the Silent World. Does that make me a god?"

"No, it makes you an adept. A sorceress." He shifted his weight. "We know of your city here, and were soon to send you the woman you met by the river. She is in need of wise counsel."

"Counsel she cannot find from your ever-present God?"

"He is silent in the moment," Hethor admitted.

"You prefer her to hear words from someone who moves in the world, rather than take the advice of an absent God."

"He is not absent; He is present in all of us."

Gashansunu laughed. "You should hear yourself. You point to a rock, a tree, the brass in the sky, and say, because the world *is*, I believe this thing must be true. The world *is*, strange prophet, but that is enough. It is its own creation, the border between the Silent World and the Shadow World the fire burning at its heart."

"I could say the same to you," he countered. "You point to a vision of the spiritual realm, and say you believe this thing must be true."

"Ah. But I can visit my realm, show it to you even, should you have eyes enough to see it."

Hethor fell silent, frowning, then said, "We spar to little point. Will you aid Paolina?"

Gashansunu followed his change in topic. "Aid her in what pursuit? I am come to find the cause of the world's passing regrets. She is it. Should I abet the distress?"

"She would have your wise counsel on the best application of her power, and the best control."

Another laugh. "I have sat in meditation in Westfacing House for six decades now. I am still accounted a young woman among my people, newly come to the Silent World and unready for full responsibility, lacking the powers of a circle caller or a house priest. I have honored a bond with my *wa* almost that entire time. This is the only reason I have left the city—I am not yet too pregnant with power to stir from the wards of our circles. All these years I have put toward fully grasping the channels of my power, and you would have me advise some half-grown chit of a girl in the course of an afternoon?"

"Yes," he said simply, then raised a hand to forestall her reply. "Consider this: If you do not, she will go with no advice whatsoever. I have told her what I can, but I myself am a barely grown boy, and my power did not come to me through study, but rather through the interference of the Divine that you so assiduously deny. God made me His instrument, but the mechanisms of that miracle will likely be ever opaque to me. You made yourself an instrument, and so understand the path to power in a way that I never shall. An hour or a day of your time will profit her far more than a season with me."

"You followed the path of faith to your power," Gashansunu said, picking her words with the thread of her thought. "You would have her pursue the path of reason."

"It is not so easy as that. But you may be close enough. I never had so much faith, but neither did I deny it. Like Paul and the Damascene conversion, God came to me in His need, rather than me seeking Him.

"Paolina might have been a Rational Humanist had she been raised in a decent school. Reason is her path, but her faith burns her like a lantern wick. You can see it in her denial, in her rebellion. She would be adversary to God Himself if she could find a stick large enough to beat Him with. I do not think she knows this, though."

Gashansunu studied Hethor, trying to see past the frightening curdles of power eddying about him. The world spun within this boy, she could see that.

Her *wa* spoke:

HE IS THE ONE WHO HAD PASSED THROUGH THE CITY.

HE HAS GONE DEEP INTO THE HEART OF ALL THINGS TO REMAKE AN ERROR.

"Four of the seven Great Relics abide within the city," she told him. "One we are certain is lost. Two more are elsewhere, unknown and unknowable to the eyes of my people. In the centuries after those came over the Wall, gleams have passed through the world time and again, but nothing so touched by power. Before now. What the girl Paolina carries in her hand flares in the Silent World like nothing since those days."

As opposed to you, young prophet, she thought, *who gather shadows to yourself and hide from distant eyes.* Gashansunu realized that meeting Hethor might ultimately be a far more important event than the discovery of the girl with the gleam.

"All the more reason you should help her learn to hold it." Hethor leaned forward, the Correct Person at his side grasping at his arm. "Those Great Relics of the past? They were unitary, each in their way—touched by God or your Silent World or whatever you may choose to call it. Like my power, not to be repeated, but simply as they are. There will never be more than one Cup, never be more than one Spear. This stemwinder of hers . . . It is different. It can be *built.* Made and remade, until an army of men might march wielding them in hand, each a sorcerer more powerful than even your circle callers or house priests."

Hethor shook his head. "You say it takes many decades to grow a sorcerer to power? All she needs is a workshop, some good tools and a little bit of time."

How could she not have seen this!? The world's distress was suddenly far more clear. This was not just another gleam, another power loose upon the land. Gashansunu realized that the girl brought with her a whole new path to power, one that would utterly upset the balance of Creation.

"Why have you not had her killed?" she asked, unthinking.

"Why *would* you have her killed?" he responded, angry at her words. "Once a thing can be done, it will be done again. She at least may have the means to control it, with your counsel."

The Silent World flashed, a ripple passing through Hethor's house so that the walls wavered and the very air grew a set of night-black eyes for a brief, uncertain moment. Paolina stood between them, shedding light and looking quite pleased.

"I think I've got it," she said.

CHILDRESS

The two Chinese stared at one another. Wang looked shocked; the monk appeared smug. *There has been an argument the cataloger didn't realize he was losing,* she thought, and bit back a laugh.

The Goan coast slid past off the starboard rail. Their headland was already in view. She did not fancy taking *Good Change* into the hidden harbor. Wang was an enemy. There was no other reason for him to be here.

She knew how the Mask Poinsard would have handled this monk, though. "Who are you, that you have the power to give orders here?"

"She is no one," Wang almost snarled. "A monk with no name, who holds no respect for the proper order of things under Heaven."

"I am found out." The monk grinned and bowed, flowed out of the movement into a kick that passed within hairs of al-Wazir's chin.

The chief swept a block with his good hand, but she was already beyond his grasp, leaping to the aft rail to take up the line that towed their boat.

"Come," the monk shouted, "if you would be overboard." She dropped out of sight.

Childress stepped to the rail. Her launch bobbed in the churn of *Good Change*'s twin screws. There was no sign of the monk.

"Where did she go?"

"A question that often troubles me," Wang replied. "I have come to accept I will likely never know the answer."

A much taller Chinese stepped to the rail and grasped Childress' arm. She stared up at the sailor. "Release me," she told him in Mandarin, "or it will go very poorly for you."

He grinned, tightening his grip. "You speak like an English cow. You will come below."

"Wu . . . ," Wang began.

"Don't be a greater fool than you must," the sailor told him.

Childress nodded at al-Wazir, who struck Wu in the back of the head with his remaining fist. More sailors shouted as they poured out of a hatch.

"Over the side," Wang urged.

"Why?" she asked, already climbing the rail.

"Because I believe that idiotic monk." He yanked at the line in an effort to bring the launch closer.

Childress summoned her courage and leapt away from the stern. She hit hard, cracking her shins smartly enough to moan with the pain, but dragged herself to the rear of the boat.

Al-Wazir landed with a heavy thump a moment later, and they spun away from the wake of *Good Change*. The yacht was already turning. The chief took up the oars as best he could and began to gamely row toward shore.

It will be over in moments, Childress thought. *Either we will be run down, or they will force us back aboard at gunpoint.*

But *Good Change* circled out to the west and steamed away. She saw Wang being beaten at the aft rail by a knot of sailors. Through the windows of the pilothouse, she thought she spied a flash of saffron.

The monk, setting them free.

———

They slipped into the dank, guano-smelling darkness of the sea cave. Torches and electrics strung from the submarine showed the upper plates being restored as her engine compartment hatches were resealed.

"We go into the waters once more," she told al-Wazir.

"Where bound, Mask? Me, I have errands in Africa. A Brass man needs helping, and a mad doctor besides."

"If you wish to be left there, it can be done," she said with a serene confidence. Her purposes had been made clear by Wang's arrival in Goa, as if the scales had dropped from her eyes. God, answering her prayers with a burst of inspiration?

The only counterweight to the Silent Order was the white birds, so to the white birds she must go in her full estate as a Mask.

"I am bound for Europe," Childress told al-Wazir. "And the halls of the *avebianco*. I will finish the mission of the Mask Poinsard, and take her place in their councils, to stem the Golden Bridge and the Silent Order."

"How will you do that?" He shipped the oars as they glided to the stone pier. A Chinese sailor called down a greeting.

"First, Suez." She smiled into the darkness. "We will find our way beyond that. England if we must, or at least the *avebianco* redoubt at Valetta, in Malta."

Al-Wazir busied himself making them fast, then helped Childress up the ladder. The sharp whiff of his fight was still clear enough to stir the hairs on her neck. His male essence made her mindful of Captain Leung. To her surprise, Childress found no shame in that thought.

"Mayhap I'll come with you," the Scotsman growled. For a brief, strange moment she took him to mean that he, too, longed for the captain. "See this duty through before I resume my own."

"Chief, voyaging with you has been no duty so far. A privilege, rather." Childress touched his cheek. "Now go to attend to your shore party while I report to Captain Leung."

"Aye, Mask. And you be having a care for that heart of yours." He winked, then walked away into the deeper shadows of the cave.

I fool no one, she thought, and realized she did not mind. Behind her, the launch splashed against the pier. Childress turned to look. The little hull rocked in the water, but no one was there.

PAOLINA

The woman Gashansunu took her back to the amphitheater by moonlight that evening. The day had been quiet, though Gashansunu and Hethor seemed to have been arguing. Ming shadowed her all through the afternoon, very nervous about the sorceress and taking no trouble to conceal his dislike.

Paolina did not find the woman so terribly difficult or strange enough to fear. She was different, and powerful, but this was just as true of Hethor. Or, admittedly, Paolina herself.

Now they stood amid the textured noises of evening. The screeching of the jungled daylight had subsided, but the insect hum was louder. Frogs gave voice in a rhythmic echo that seemed to reach beyond the horizon. Larger things splashed in the river, moving against the slow, greasy waters. Something of great size boomed a lament in the distance.

"This is not my place," Gashansunu said. "I do not have the meditations for open jungle. The Silent World is curdled here, gathered around your Hethor as if he were a spindle with which to wind it."

Something in her tone, even through the magic of Hethor's speech spell, made it clear that she despised her own words.

"I would use your tongue," Paolina told her, "if I could. I imagine we might discuss your Silent World much more effectively."

"It does not matter. I am come to heal the cause of the world's regrets. You and Hethor have both showed me much of what that may be, and how it should be addressed."

"Now I am here." She was conscious of Ming watching from an upper bench of the amphitheater, Hethor's Arellya beside him. The English boy had pled fatigue hours ago and retired.

"We begin at night because when the sun has turned away from the world, some powers wane while others wax."

Paolina understood a constraint when she heard one. "You mean to say that there are fewer considerations in your practice of magic."

"Precisely." Grudging approval hung in Gashansunu's voice. "One might sing among a crowd of one's neighbors; one might sing alone on a rooftop; one might listen to the music of the world. None of those are wrong; none of those are better. But each weighs differently, carries different meanings, makes different demands."

"What do we sing on this rooftop?" Paolina did not yet see where this was going.

"I will show you the Silent World from within," Gashansunu answered. "This will almost certainly aid you in understanding how your gleam may be used and misused."

"When I use the gleam, I see the world as made of, well, levels. Gear trains made of up myriad smaller gear trains. It shows me the inner nature of things."

"You witness an imperfect image of the Silent World," Gashansunu replied. "There are layers. As above, so below, all the way down."

"What lies at the bottom?"

"One can measure a circle beginning from anywhere. What lies at the end?"

"So . . . there is no bottom?"

Gashansunu made a strained noise. "If you were to pursue it deeply enough, you would come back out the top. But not all levels are the same. The Silent World is the true world. People live in the Shadow World, which is a reflection of the Silent World. Or better considered as a projection of it. That which is perfected in the Silent World can been seen here in imperfect copies of the world, of people, of purposes and intents."

Paolina had to ask the obvious question. "If the Silent World is perfected, why do you abide in this world?"

"Because I am imperfect," Gashansunu responded promptly. "I have studied decades to enter the Silent World, but I am not welcome there, however much my spirit might cry out for it. Not welcome *yet*, in any case."

Paolina was glad to note that pride was not a sin confined to the people of Northern Earth. "How will you show me this Silent World?"

"Watch," Gashansunu ordered. "Do not leave my side."

She looped a braided silver cord on Paolina's wrist, then passed it around her own. They stood facing, close enough to touch had there been a need. Gashansunu closed her eyes and began to hum. Something curled around the foreign sorceress, not quite tangible, not quite visible, but right on the edge of perception.

This is magic, Paolina thought. *True magic, before my eyes.*

She blinked, and was somewhere else.

The landscape was no different, yet it was.

That thought did not make sense. Even so, it seemed profoundly true.

Ming glowed. So did Arellya. Gashansunu was far brighter, but cloaked at the same time. Paolina looked at her own hands. Light leaked from within, streaming through the pores of her skin.

The presence around Gashansunu was far more distinct now—a twin, but insubstantial even here. A Gashansunu-copy that was as dark as she was light, also cloaked.

Animals stirred the substance of the Silent World with their bright, rapid passing. The slow dreams of trees left far more deliberate ripples, while the memory of the rocks and soil beneath her feet moved at a pace even more leisurely than that of the tide.

Everything lived, here.

She looked skyward. The Earth's brass track showed as a pinpoint of light drawn out from horizon to horizon. The great, crushing weight of the planet upon the orbital ring must paint it with a smear of all the lives both fast and slow that passed upon the two halves of the Earth.

A sense of thoughtfulness tingled at Paolina, an idea calling for attention. *All is metaphor.* Her lips moved and bubbled, but no sound issued. *The gears and mechanics I see when I dip into the fabric of the world are truly no different than what this Gashansunu sees here.*

You are correct, the other woman thought. *But some metaphors are more accurate. You see the brass in the sky and think the world must be brass all the way down. Is a tree made of leaves all the way down to its roots?*

Paolina objected. *You cannot explain metaphor with more metaphor. That is a cheat.*

Why?

She was not sure how to answer that.

Try this, Gashansunu urged. *Step across the river.*

Matching her spirit-guide pace for pace, Paolina found her foot reaching the far bank—fifty yards, at least—without a strain. They looked back at the glowing lights of life on the shore they had just left behind.

Paolina noted that the dark copy of Gashansunu had not come with them. *Where is your shadow?*

My shadow? Gashansunu seemed surprised. *I am the shadow. The* wa *is my true soul.*

That fit with Gashansunu's view of the world.

Stepping across the river with the stemwinder would have been just as possible. The process was different. Paolina would have pushed backward as much as she had pushed forward, knowing what Hethor had suggested to her today. She and Gashansunu had done just that, stepping over the river while their heels dug into the opposite bank, just as any footfall on a sunlit path might do.

Perhaps the processes were not so different. Was it all metaphor? Was God a metaphor for the boundary between the worlds, for the tension that drove Creation like a spring in a clock?

She hoped so. Paolina had already more than her fill of the needs and deeds of men. In some ways, God was nothing more than the largest, most selfish man in history. Certainly the God of Fra Bellico had been, back in Praia Nova.

Could the world have created itself, and man then made God by way of explanation?

The stemwinder was heavy in her free hand. Paolina slid it from her skirts to study in the strange lightless shadows. The gleam didn't actually gleam—the opposite, in fact. Its ordinariness was aggressive. A shout of solidity in this place of vapors.

I should not use that here.

Paolina heard a note of fear in Gashansunu's voice. *Why?*

Would you build a fire inside a fire?

Metaphors! *I wish to step back,* she thought defiantly.

Then we step together.

Ignoring her guide, Paolina tugged the stem to the fourth stop. She tried to find Gashansunu's heart, the rhythm that drove this woman, but there was nothing. As if she were searching for words in empty air.

Across the river, though, the other Gashansunu was very real. Paolina located her even from this distance, as easy to read as a storm. She set the fourth hand to the rhythm of Gashansunu's *wa*.

The woman stiffened. *We go now.*

Dragged, Paolina was forced to step across the river again. She put her mind to going forward only, not pushing back with her other foot, deliberately re-creating her earlier efforts at translocation with the gleam.

Something flared behind them, and with that they were back in the Shadow World.

"Do not ever do that!" shouted Gashansunu.

Across the river a pair of trees toppled into the water. Mud and clay rained down.

"Impressive," said Ming from his perch above. "You grow ever more dangerous."

No one but Paolina understood his Chinese. She grimaced, then turned to Gashansunu, her pride wounded by the woman's rebuke. That was something a man would have done to her. "Is this how you step across the miles?" The fourth hand swung wildly as Paolina focused on herself. "I will show you an easier way!" She pushed off, sending herself across the river to stand on one of the fallen logs.

"Here!" Paolina shouted across the moonlit river, then sent herself back. Something cracked, and she turned to see the log collapse, split open. "And *here*," she told Gashansunu up close. "As well as to the moon, should I desire."

Arellya and Ming were both on their feet, scrambling the few steps down to the two women.

"We know you have power," Gashansunu said quietly. "The question is how you use it, and whether that will upset the balance of the world too much."

Paolina was breathing hard. The world seemed to click around her, Gashansunu's *wa* almost visible in the moonlight.

"I would prefer not to be ruled by pride," she admitted, ashamed of her own actions. "Or foolishness."

Ming touched her arm as if to pull her back from an edge. Arellya stood at her other side. Gashansunu just stared, the woman's eyes onyx in the moonlight.

"You must learn, then, like a child who has discovered her strength but not the limits of her temper. If I could have you sit in one of the houses of our city for a score of seasons, that might be a beginning."

Paolina felt a stab of temptation at that thought, but she needed to return to Northern Earth, to find Boaz, to see al-Wazir again. Even, she realized for the first time since leaving the miserable place, to return to Praia Nova and help the girls and women trapped there under the dead weight of centuries of male privilege.

All of that must be done in a way that protected the stemwinder, kept her whole, and prevented the demise of everything she might hold dear.

"I am not a weapon," she told Gashansunu, remembering her words before the Chinese fleet off Sumatra.

The sorceress unloosed the cord. "If I knew a method to awaken the *wa* to which you belong, I would do so."

"Come sleep," Ming urged. "We have a good camp on the ridge above."

Paolina knew she must think on what was to be learned from Gashansunu's Silent World. It would never be so simple, of course, but some very important things had happened tonight. "Will I be able to learn to make those steps?" she asked.

Impassive, Gashansunu looked pointedly at the stemwinder in Paolina's hand. "You already know."

The unspoken words *far too much* hung between them.

"My thanks." Paolina suffered herself to be led from the amphitheater.

WANG

His mouth was filled with blood.

He tried to open his eyes and failed. Blinking didn't seem to help. Blindfold?

The noises of a ship at sea surrounded him. Slap of waves against the hull, creaking of the deck, a murmured order. He was aboard *Good Change*. As opposed to having passed over to the judges of the dead.

This time he managed to spit. It didn't go very far, probably down his

chest, but he could breathe easier. A bell clanged; someone shouted; then
everything fell quiet again.

Eventually Wu brought him light. Of course it had been a blindfold, Wang
realized, as the first mate peeled away a length of silk. His head must have
been addled earlier.

The other man squatted in front of Wang. The cataloger realized he
was tied to a chair. "Traitor." Wu's tone was perfunctory, carrying none of
the weight the word called for.

"I betrayed nothing." *Is that true?*

"Our prize was in hand. You let her go, then commandeered the boat."

"What!?" He was shocked. "I stood at the aft rail and watched the shore
as Captain Shen took us out to sea. How is that commandeering anything?" Wang was also amazed that his mouth worked so well. He seemed
to have all the teeth he'd woken up with that morning, though his tongue
was swollen.

Wu's eyes slid away, as if something important were happening elsewhere, then back to Wang. "You forced the wheel, and intimidated the
captain."

"Nothing intimidates the captain except the Kô." Wang could not keep
the anger from his voice. "Certainly not a fat little man from the libraries."

"Nonetheless," Wu replied, "this is what happened."

"I . . . I know we are not friends." The cataloger searched for the words
he needed. "But neither are we enemies. You are the only one of the
crew who will speak to me beyond the most basic of necessities."

"Ghosts."

Was the mate's tone encouraging? Wang tried to follow Wu's lead.
"You are not ghosts. You are men under a spell of law. Your names have
not been rectified, and your place is lost. But your hearts beat, your lungs
draw air, and you bleed when cut. I am no different, except that my place
is separate from your vessel and your oaths to the Kô'."

"*You* are not a ghost," Wu said with a faint smile.

"No. I am not. Neither are you. There is only one true ghost on this
ship—the monk. She passes through like morning mist. I know you have
seen her. The monk influenced our captain, and somehow we set out to
sea."

The mate rocked slightly forward on his heels. "Suppose you were
captain of a vessel owned by a close relative of the Emperor. Suppose your
life was forfeit to the owner's merest whim, as you were already sentenced
to death for a crime beyond forgiveness. Suppose you were sent on a mis-

sion of utmost importance, with a foolish little man who cannot be relied upon for decent tea in the mornings, let alone to fulfill the purpose of your voyage. Suppose you were in fact set upon by a ghost, who forced your prize from your hands at the moment of success.

"Now, do you imagine this close relative of the Emperor, a man known for his hard-headed ways and intolerance of failure, will entertain a wild tale of ghosts in the wheelhouse and confusions of navigation that would not be made by the smallest of children? Or do you suppose this close relative of the Emperor would be more receptive to a tale of treachery and foolishness on the part of a certain fat little man from the libraries, already known to be cowardly?

"Consider if you were Captain Shen, which tale you would bear back to your master?"

"If I am so cowardly," Wang asked quietly, "how is it that I managed to overcome both the captain of this motor yacht and hold off her entire crew sufficiently long for a one-handed man to row himself and our quarry to safety?"

"The tale needs a bit of work," Wu admitted. "How lucky that we face a long sea voyage. Captain Shen will have a boat full of witnesses when he reports to the Kô."

"Do we return in defeat now?"

"Of course not." The mate seemed surprised. "We continue searching for *Five Lucky Winds*. Should we find the submarine, we will set our fat little man from the libraries to speak to her English mistress. Should we fail to find the submarine, well, we have our culprit in hand already."

Wang had to admit there was a certain brutal elegance to the situation. In truth, it changed little about his predicament. "How will you find the submarine if she has already slipped our grasp?"

"That is the job of our librarian." Wu's smile was predatory. "You are a man of education. You shall determine where Captain Leung is most likely to take his vessel next. We will follow that course as far as we may dare."

Wang saw his opening now. "I am to determine this while strapped to a chair, bruised and beaten? You cannot make me both the scapegoat prisoner and the expedition's navigator. Choose one role, and I will fill it."

"Which would you prefer?"

"Show me to your maps."

KITCHENS

He dug through the papers until he located Ottweill's logbook. That described the catastrophic events of the earliest days of their presence and the subsequent attack that had broken the encampment.

What he did not find was any mention of Angus Threadgill al-Wazir. As if the big Scotsman had never existed. The reports from *Notus* had certainly accounted for him here, speaking to Captain Sayeed and organizing the camp's defenses. Yet sometime in the eight weeks since the unfortunate airship had departed the digging camp and the fatal day of its return, al-Wazir had vanished not only from the site, but was also seemingly expunged from the records.

Kitchens went back through the expedition's logs, looking specifically at the time of *Notus'* visit. The paper had been scraped in places and over-written, he realized.

Ottweill had edited both al-Wazir and Boaz right out of his history. Now Kitchens wished he'd spent more time speaking with the Brass.

The door of the little cabin thumped open. Ottweill stood there, covered in gray rock dust except for pale patches where he'd worn a mask and goggles. "The Queen's auditors have come to my little project, I see," he announced in his imperious voice. "Please, yourself to make comfortable among my belongings and confidential papers."

"I believe I already have," Kitchens said mildly. He knew better than to be drawn into a serious dispute with this man.

"The whiskey you have stolen yet? You would drink me dry, I am sure."

"No, thank you. I prefer not to partake when I am working."

Ottweill stared at him a few moments too long. "Always working I am. If I did not partake then, when would I?"

The doctor was combative as usual, but Kitchens swiftly realized this was not directed at him personally. "They are dying, my men," Ottweill said.

"I reviewed your tally."

"We are safer here, inside the depths, but one by one madness will take them. Already many I cannot force outside to hunt and raid."

Kitchens leaned forward. "Where is al-Wazir?"

"Pah." The doctor waved his free hand in dismissal. "He is run off. Cowardly fool. Afraid, too afraid."

Al-Wazir was many things, some not necessarily good, but a coward was not among them. "His name is not in your expedition logs."

"You have been reading my logs?" Ottweill purpled even in the flickering lights of the cabin.

"Of course I did," Kitchens said forcefully, trying to interrupt the doctor's tantrum. "I am here to look over the progress of your expedition. Where else should I look but the logs? Interestingly, I find no mention of the man charged with ensuring your safety."

"Such a job he did, too!" Ottweill settled back into his chair and stared at the dregs of his whiskey. His voice dropped off. "I am not so certain now."

This does not sound like the doctor, Kitchens thought. "Of what?"

"I have been told a thing. A thing that I did not believe."

"What is that?"

The doctor met his eye. "I will show you, if you are brave enough."

They rode a handcart deeper into the tunnel, past the camp. Ottweill pumped the mechanism to keep them moving, the gears within the cart emitting an echoing squeak-squeal. After a moment's thought, Kitchens realized this served at least in part to announce the arrival of the cart, assuming more sentries ahead.

Noise from the boring machine was practically a solid thing this close. Dust hung in the air, as if the ceiling of this section of tunnel were continually vibrating. He smelled scorched oil, hot rock, and the sweat of men.

Soon enough the walls vanished into another wider opening. There were no lights here, either, but locomotives and railroad wagons bulked vaguely in the gleam of Ottweill's lantern. He stopped pumping and allowed the handcart to glide to a halt.

Ottweill gestured with his lantern, a complex signal obviously prearranged. They stood their ground, waiting. No door opened. Kitchens wondered why.

Then the noise faded. It did not stop so much as step down from the roar of a metal hurricane to the grind of wounded stone, then to the clash of very heavy iron on the move, then the shriek of steam being released, and finally to a crumbling silence that very much put Kitchens in mind of the first few moments of a rockslide just before an entire mountain face descended to the valley below.

Ottweill turned to him and said something. His ears were ringing far too loudly to understand the doctor's intention, but Kitchens nodded anyway. No point in a dense-voiced shouting match over how they would pass through into the diggings beyond.

The doctor stepped to the gate set within the armored wall. It swung open before him, courtesy of the hidden watchers. Kitchens followed into a whole new kind of hell.

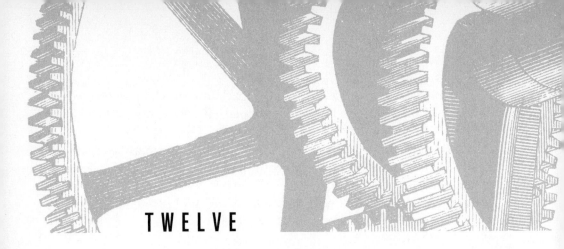

TWELVE

Set me as a Seal upon thine heart, as a Seal upon thine arm: for love is strong as death; jealousy is cruel as the grave: the coals thereof are coals of fire, which hath a most vehement flame.
—*Song of Solomon 8:6*

BOAZ

McCurdy approached Boaz where he had been resting. "Can you walk back to the clearing? The doctor's men are at the stockade once more, and *Erinyes* is circling again. I believe that Lieutenant Ostrander means to land her at our signal, but I'd feel better if you was there."

"She's your ship, Chief," Boaz replied. "You have the man Harrow to stand by you with wise counsel."

"He's all right, but he's no particular friend. Besides, you know the lieutenant at least a little. Harrow's a proper fellow, will look to Ostrander's rank and not to his deeds."

Despite himself, Boaz was intrigued. "Do you mean to relieve him of command?"

McCurdy's discomfort was written large on his face. "Without *Erinyes*, we are trapped here. With the war on against the Chinee, there may not be another patrol for some time. When it shows, it might *be* John Chinaman. We'd not stand against that. Little food, little equipment, and those mad tunnel rats at our back."

"Let the man Kitchens make work of this."

"Mr. Kitchens has gone down the tunnel, and he ain't come back up, begging your pardon." McCurdy's discomfort turned almost to pain. "You're a foreigner, and an enemy besides, and not even human, but I needs someone who can think like an officer. I'll likely hang for this as it is, and consorting with you is no improvement, but I cannot throw down the skipper on my own."

They slogged back up the slope toward the rest of the stranded sailors.

Boaz stared at *Erinyes*, wondering how long before the winged savages attacked again. Two of McCurdy's men moved out in the open with a set of
rough-made semaphores—leaves woven together on sticks. They made a
series of signals in a code Boaz knew nothing of. After a few moments,
the airship dropped a line of colored flags.

"She comes down," said Harrow, standing with them.

"This is going to be a sorry business," McCurdy added. "Even if Midshipman Longoria takes our part."

Erinyes was slow descending, forcing herself down with her motors.
She'd need to take on water ballast if possible, but there was no way to
pump. He wondered how much of her fuel Lieutenant Ostrander had
burned away in his soaring about of the past day or so.

Ain't your problem, laddie, growled the voice of al-Wazir deep within.

In time she cast down her lines. Stranded airmen from both vessels
raced to secure them and warp her close. Boaz lent his solid strength to
the effort as the airship was tethered to a soaring mahogany at the edge of
the clearing. Another set of lines came over the side—knotted rope for
climbing, and a more complicated sling for lifting.

Someone peered over the rail to shout down. Midshipman Longoria,
Boaz realized from the piping voice. "Bosun McCurdy, please come aboard."
A note of panic hung in the young man's voice, discernible even over the
sputter of the engines.

McCurdy swarmed up the rope like a drowning man who could not
wait to escape the waves. Boaz followed at a swift pace of his own. If the
bosun would have him be officerial, officerial he would be.

GASHANSUNU

She entered the Silent World without moving, simply to sit among the
twisted shadows and dark casts of power surrounding the Northern prophet
in his abode. Her *wa* was still agitated, but not so much as before. It flitted
about like a moon moth on a particularly difficult night.

The view here was so very different than in the city. This Hethor was not
crowded by the shades of powers past, as everything was at home. Rather,
his bulwarks stemmed from within and around him. That he saw these as
the handiwork of his god was understandable, she realized. He possessed
only that lens for viewing the world.

Correct People left their own fierce currents here. Small, like animals,
but bright, like people. The house priests had long ago recognized the little
tribesmen as being at some half-state between the kingdoms of beasts and
men, living reminders of an experiment by the world before it settled on
the true shape of what was to come. The Wall teemed with miracles and

wonders, some of them far out of time with the limits of the world. The Correct People had simply come down to live in the jungles, rather than work out their lives among the mists and crags above.

Gashansunu attended most carefully to Paolina. The girl had lessoned frighteningly well. Hethor seemed to think the device in her hand mattered most, but Gashansunu was more concerned with the spirit that burned inside. The sorceress slept now in a hammock in the Shadow World that also served to elevate her here in the Silent World.

The house priests and circle callers and sorcerers of her city were complex, difficult women and men. Those who had spent decades accumulating wisdom tended to be layered so deeply that their core was beyond finding. Paolina was the opposite—nothing *but* core. The girl practically burned with righteous anger at the state of the world, while her power wrapped tight around her.

This did not make her easier to read. In fact, the opposite. But it did lend Paolina an air of inevitability diametric to the subtle indirections of the powers in the city.

Now she dreamed, Gashansunu saw. Ripples of whatever lover or child she had left behind in the Northern Earth seemed to possess her.

This girl would go back to her side of the Wall, and quite soon. Gashansunu was pleased to have caught up with her first. Much about Paolina fascinated her.

I would follow her, Gashansunu told her *wa. To see how she spills her power.*
YOU ARE BOTH BETTER HERE, was the counsel she received in return.

Gashansunu understood this perfectly well. She could likely not restrain Paolina. Besides, the girl's appeal was powerful. Like the draw to touch the flame, a sweet spark in her head that made no sense and did not suit the purposes of her life.

She will not be kept, and I will not let her wander unattended until we grasp the extents of her power.

Her *wa* muttered, then retreated some distance to sulk in the safety of darkness.

CHILDRESS

They cruised the open ocean. "We will cover almost fourteen hundred nautical miles to the Gulf of Aden." Leung's voice startled her, rising over the slap of waves and the mutter of the screws plowing water aft. "A bit less than sixty hours if we stay awash, but we must submerge by day, which cuts our speed considerably."

"More than three days?"

"Perhaps dawn of the fourth." His fingers entwined more closely with hers. "Have you considered how you will talk us past the British patrols at Bab el Mandeb? I should expect to make our way into the Gulf unchallenged, with a little luck, but the passage into the Red Sea is utterly controlled. No vessel in any of the Celestial Emperor's navies has made that transit, except under armed escort with a diplomatic flag."

"Captain," she told him. "We have a diplomatic flag. Our standard of the whole Earth. I am a Mask, and can claim to be an ambassador of sorts. When we sail into the Gulf of Aden, we will do so with all banners flying and the crew turned out on deck, as when we reached Tainan. We will look for the first British ship we can find. We will approach and negotiate. From there, on to Malta or deeper into the British Empire as circumstances suggest."

"Hardly subtle, Miss Childress."

"Embassies rarely are subtle, my friend." She clutched his hand within the warmth of both of hers. "Ambassadors themselves almost always are."

PAOLINA

Morning brought bright sunlight, overripe papayas, and a time for acting on her decisions. *Boaz,* she thought. Paolina knew she'd never be safe, no matter how far she fled, so she might as well be where she wanted to be. Right now she stood on Hethor's balcony looking down on an oh-so-accidental crowd of Correct People.

Arellya stepped out beside her.

"What are they waiting for?" Paolina asked.

"A miracle. A legend. A show." The Correct Person leaned close. "My people find life amusing, but complex deeds wrought by strange folk are particularly entertaining. Anyone might drop a load of taro roots on their neighbor's foot in error, but a truly magnificent mistake requires truly magnificent effort."

"I am . . . er, flattered."

"You will choose well," Arellya assured her. "The world does not hang on this moment, or indeed any moment, but still you will choose well."

"Is that true?" Their eyes met. "Did Hethor not come to such a moment, in his journey south? I recall the great shakings of the earth. The waves they brought killed cities, and drowned much of the African coast."

"Hethor followed a fire I could not see," Arellya answered quietly. "I took a strong band of our young males and went with him. Only he gained the center of all things, though I was taken there against my will. He fought an adversary there, then set himself to loving my life more than his own. A gift, from his heart to his God."

"If he had not been present?"

"Someone else would have gone down." The woman shrugged. "Or the earth would have shaken ever harder until we all fell away like fleas from a flying fox. There was no single moment when the world would have ended as a result of either his presence or his absence."

Paolina understood the argument, but it bothered her. "Choice must enter into the matter."

"What is there to choose? We are born into the world; we live a while; we pass on. What matter if one chooses the left path or the right, the red flower or the blue? The world remains the same."

"If one chose to dam a river, and a great lake grew while the lands below thirsted, that would be a choice that changed the world."

Arellya smiled. "Remember who I abide with. He is the world's worst tease for such conundrums. I should answer you thusly: In time the rains will swell the lake so badly that the dam will break. The breaking will destroy the stream for many miles and days, but half a generation later the land will have reclaimed its own, the dam builder will be long drowned, and the world will once more be the same."

"Would everything have been the same if no one had gone down where Hethor did, and repaired the mainspring of the world?"

"Maybe not." Her smile broadened to a grin. "But I do not worry about consistency of argument."

Paolina returned her smile with a laugh. "You would make a terrible priest. They are obsessed with consistency."

"Why thank you." Arellya gestured to the fruit staining Paolina's hand. "Now you should eat, so that your head might be clear. I have the idea that you are traveling a great distance today."

"I would go around the world," Paolina said, "to find Boaz. He is the only man I truly trust."

"Then he is there, waiting for you, somewhere on the measure of the Earth."

Ming pulled Paolina aside as she returned to the shaded darkness of the house. "Are you going to take us back over the Wall?" he asked in Chinese. Fear darted across his face.

"In one large step," she replied. "Would you walk instead?"

"I am no . . . , but I fear that."

She lost his word, but the context was clear enough. "It is a lengthy journey. I can send you home more quickly."

"Where? *Five Lucky Winds?* I do not know how you would find her."

"Not the ship. Unless that is your desire. Do you have a wife awaiting you somewhere?"

Ming stared at his feet for a moment, then back at her. "A wife, no. But I have someone. In Oluanpi."

"Would you like to go to her? I think I can send you."

The sailor blushed violently and turned away.

What did I say? Paolina wondered.

The strange sorceress Gashansunu stood with Hethor. They shared the uncomfortable expression of people who would rather be doing something else. Paolina addressed the woman.

"I thank you for the time you spent teaching me. You showed me things I had not understood about the stemwinder. I plan to go now, walk north and pass across the Wall."

"You will take me with you." Something in Gashansunu's voice was different today. Had Hethor altered his spell? "You are not safe for yourself or those around you. Not until you understand the Silent World far better."

Hethor cleared his throat. "She has the right of it, Miss Barthes. There is much to understand, especially if you will be stepping across the Wall in one go. Not a guide, as you know the way, but surely an advisor."

Paolina continued. "So I would go. I would send Ming to the true home of his heart as my thanks for his guidance all this time. At Boaz' side, I would think what to do next. It will not include giving the stemwinder to the English or their lackeys in the secret societies."

"Do not judge so harshly." Hethor's voice was gentle, sad. "Even the worst of villains are generally trying to do right by their own lights. That has been a hard lesson for me. Pause before you take action, accept Gashansunu's direction on how best to set your feet upon your own path, and you may succeed."

"I shall." First she must know *how*, of course.

Once more they stood in sunlight. Paolina was very aware of her *place*— the firmness of the pounded clay beneath her too-worn boots; the heavy, moist air wrapping her like the breath of the river; the heat so strong it seemed to be a physical presence; the tropical brightness of the day that flooded her eyes red even with lids shut tight. Every insect drone, every distant splash, every scent of green and growing and water and muck called out to her.

She held the ragged remains of the angel's feather in one hand and the stemwinder in the other.

This is where I begin, Paolina thought. *I have once before gone where I have not been, but I was being called by the angel.*

Opening her eyes, she spoke. "I do not know the place where Ming's heart dwells. The closest I have seen is a beach on the Sumatran coast." Then, to him in Chinese, "Would you go back to the island where we first met?"

"No," he said. "I would go to Oluanpi, or anywhere in Taiwan."

Paolina looked to Gashansunu. "Is it possible for me to send him someplace I have never been?"

The sorceress glanced at Ming. "Difficult. Not impossible, but difficult. Can you begin by going someplace you have visited before?"

Where she wanted to be was at Boaz' side, but she had no idea where the Brass man was. Or in truth, if he even still lived. "I could take us to Mogadishu," she said. "The British and the Chinese were fighting when last I was there. It would not be safe for Ming."

"We left a boat along the foot of the Wall," Ming said in Chinese again, having followed her English. "If we must go back to where we have landed together, I can begin from there."

"Then I could pass on to Africa, and the question of Boaz," she answered.

"What did he say?" asked Gashansunu.

"We will go to the Northern Earth, to the point along the Wall where Ming and I left our boat when we first journeyed south."

The sorceress frowned. "How well do you recall that place?"

Paolina considered the question. They had drawn up in a shallow bay, bounded at the west by a great knee of rock that had weathered into crumbling fragments but still loomed high. The east end of the bay had been a mudflat with scattered trees. Some pilings in the water recalled a time when men—or someone, as this *was* the Wall, after all—had made a settlement, but Paolina had seen no other evidence of habitation. The beach was mud and sand. She had helped Ming draw the boat up and conceal it in a thick stand of bushes bearing pale, waxy berries. There they had startled a colony of pale blue butterflies each the size of her hand.

What had the Wall looked like? Impossibly high, a stone border to Heaven, but she could not recall details. Even the particular path they'd set out upon wasn't coming to mind, though it must not have been especially strange or she would recollect. They'd pushed through the trees a while, until they located a game trail leading up to the top of the crumbling knee.

She vividly remembered the view from up there, looking north toward distant islands dotting the bottle-green waters. The beach had seemed much prettier from above than up close among the algae stink and the rotting bits of broken crabs.

"I can see it well enough, I think," Paolina said. "Though I cannot know if our boat is still there for Ming to make use of." How *had* she come here, when they'd left the dangerous feast at the mountaintop behind? What if an angel stood now on the streets of London, or the mountains of the moon? Could she step from one place to the other so easily?

"We walk the Silent World," Gashansunu said, "in order to know where we are going. I could return home between one breath and the next, for I know my city and especially the rooms of Westfacing House as well as I know my own hands and feet. So it is with you, if you know the place well."

"What if I go wrong? Will I be close?"

"The Silent World is larger than the Shadow World. You could go to a place that has no shadow-side, and be forlorn within the quiet darkness."

Paolina knew where she was going, though. She could recall many places very well. Her little cabin aboard *Star of Guinea*. The cathedral square in Strasbourg. The deck of *Notus*. Praia Nova, *madre deus*; but pity the *doms* if she ever returned to them with her power in hand.

Paolina turned away that thought and the rush of anger that came with it. She wished she knew where Boaz was so she could head straight to him.

It was not that the Brass was made of wisdom. Rather, they had come to understand one another in a quiet way. She wished mightily she had not left him behind at the work camp along the Wall. That was where she would begin her search, once she had seen Ming safely on his way. She could find Ophir from there, if he was no longer among the railroad men and tunnel rats. The Brass would not care about her gleam; their powers were their own, and mysterious besides.

From Ophir, if Boaz was not there on the streets or in those horrid halls of correction from which Paolina had rescued him once before, she would follow her heart.

"I know my course," she announced. "Ming, we shall take you to the boat. Then I will go where my desires dictate."

"Then do as we did last night," Gashansunu said. "Wrap his wrist close by yours. Take your gleam and set it as you did when you stepped into the tree house. Then simply walk to the place of your memories. So long as you know where you are going, you will arrive."

"If I push backward far enough and hard enough, I will not leave ruins or a shaking earth behind me."

Gashansunu handed her the braided silver cord. Paolina looped it from her wrist to Ming's, then grasped his hand. With her other, she cupped the stemwinder, using thumb and forefinger to adjust the stem until she'd identified the correct resonance.

She remembered a beach, towering clouds, the Wall bigger than any country could encompass, the ocean warm and wide, piers in the water, the plash of little waves, sunlight, warmth, and a small boat pitching up onto the land.

They stepped, pushing off carefully to set the force of the journey harmlessly far away.

KITCHENS

He'd thought the chamber of the encampment to be dusty, but in here the dust was an element all its own. It *was* the air, as if the rock had grown just thin enough to pass through without giving up its essential nature. Kitchens covered his mouth with his handkerchief.

His nose told him this was ground-up Wall, but also coal and other things.

Shapes of men and equipment moved by lantern light and electrick glow, looming silhouettes defined by the blurring dust. The noise had not yet died away from his ears, and it seemed to wrap all of those around him with a mailed fist, even in its absence.

The settling, heavy silence was already taking the dust to the floor. The boring machine had ceased its labors, though a chuffing signified continued readiness. Without that dread tip slashing into the fabric of the Wall, the air had a chance to reclaim itself.

". . . a side tunnel," Ottweill said, shouting.

His hearing had returned! Kitchens nodded as if he'd understood all along.

"Come down the main passage and I will show you."

They took a lantern from one of the waiting men—the crew in here wore goggles and masks, Kitchens noted.

Ottweill was right. Another cavern had been opened, and the tracks ran straight across the floor with a branching switch to the left. Lights in the settling dust showed where the borer had stopped in its work to drive a lateral tunnel.

Why?

They stepped along the rails for another hundred feet or so. Ottweill stopped partway along the shaft. "Look here you will," he said, and directed the lantern's lens high on the wall.

A series of metal rods protruded just slightly from the stone, sheared off with the extraction of their surrounding rock. The lantern light swung to the far side of the tunnel, where a matching series was visible.

"This was not seen at first," Ottweill said. "Until our dig we were forced to discontinue, and backward we looked."

The doctor seemed as calm and collected as Kitchens had ever known him to be. In England, he had been positively rabid, spitting and howling. Here at the Wall, the project focused his obsession and his energy. Everything Ottweill cared about was concentrated into one point at the face of this tunnel.

They walked another hundred feet. Electrick lights had been strung here on spikes driven into the tunnel wall, but they were dark now. Kitchens glanced backward to see the small, fitful constellation of lanterns by the door where the digging crew and the door guards were taking an unexpected break.

No one had made a move to follow their leader down this tunnel.

He fingered his ragged sleeve, where the razor still lurked.

"Listen now," Ottweill said, shuttering his lantern.

Kitchens' ears still rang as if they had been boxed, but he closed his eyes, opened his mouth and tried to take in what sound he could from the surrounds. It took him a moment to realize what the doctor was speaking of. Not so much a sound as a vibration, as from the largest pipe in a cathedral organ. Something the bones knew more than the ears did, that stirred the hair on his neck and arms. Deep, rhythmic, and very fast.

Not just fast, he realized. Complex.

"What is it?"

Ottweill opened the lantern shutter again.

The cutting face *gleamed*. Rock had been peeled away in a widening cone from a wall of brass that itself had been shaved down at the contact point of the borer's great drill. Metal parings and iron fragments were scattered around the stubbed end of the rails.

"Here the drill shattered," Ottweill said. "We have many replacements, for we expect damage from even normal operations. But this is not geology." He spat. "This is something else."

Kitchens could barely speak. "The scaffolding of Creation." The tunnel would not go through the Wall; that much was obvious. Whatever else might become true here, the project had ended. Southern Earth would remain mysterious and inaccessible for another generation. If the Chinese and their Golden Bridge project crossed over first, the British Empire was lost.

Awe, and defeat. He felt punctured. His entire errand from Lloyd George and the Queen had come to naught. What remained, but Her Imperial Majesty's fateful letter?

"We drive a lateral shaft now," Ottweill said. "We will turn south again at a distance and see if this structure continues. Good news I do not expect."

"Will you open up this brass?" Kitchens asked.

"That I have been considering. You hear the noise. Behind there something moves. Something very large. It is without doubt that we have touched part of the machinery of the Earth. What God made when our world He built. I am a proud man, Mr. Kitchens. This is my virtue, not my flaw, for without pride, I would have accomplished far less. But I do not think even my pride is sufficient to overturn the handiwork of God."

"We don't want to overturn it; we just want to pass through it."

"Attend," Ottweill hissed. "Great masses move beyond that brass. Counterweights to balance the rotation of the world, perhaps. Shall we cut into a machine that has been running for six thousand years and weighs a thousand billion tons? Sooner the mice in the Frauenkirke would bring down the towers, and all the rest of Dresden besides."

Kitchens cast about for ideas. This could not be the end of the project. If the Chinese reached the Southern Earth first, they would have all the resources of that alleged paradise at their disposal. There would be no front in the ongoing little wars. It would be the world, with England's mortal enemy backed by the riches of an entire second world.

"How do we get through?" he asked. "Surely there are maintenance accesses?"

Ottweill's voice turned bitter. "Does God do maintenance? Is He not perfect, that His Creation should also be perfect? I think you know that I am not a man whom to anything surrenders. I will not cease trying to break through the Wall. Even so, confronted by this brass and whatever lies behind it, no hope of success I can promise."

"What is next?"

The doctor shrugged. "A railroad to the top, with a tunnel to be cut through the footings of the gear, perhaps. Or a sky full of airships to pass over in well-escorted safety. An elevator. The Wall defends itself. Any of those will cost far more than even my ridiculous tunnel. What is the will of the Queen?"

That question struck a cold blade into the doubt already flooding Kitchens' heart. He *knew* the will of the Queen.

Remake what has been undone.
Break my throne.
Help me finish dying.

Had she somehow been undone by this cutting? Her life could not be hostage to something as mundane as a tunnel.

"Doctor," Kitchens said slowly. "I would ask you a thing you will not wish to answer. For the sake of the Queen, and indeed, the future of all of Europe and her discontents, I would beg you to think through this."

"What, a fortune teller you are now?"

"No. Just a man who pursues his monarch's will. Loyal and foolish both, no doubt." He paused, gathering both his courage and his thoughts. "Here are my questions: Are you a member of one of the secret societies? Is this digging at the behest of the white birds or the Silent Order, either one?"

WANG

His head continued to ache. He was sure it would do so for days. Wang's ribs were dreadfully painful, and he did not move so well. Whatever loyalty he'd held to his mission had melted in the face of Wu's betrayals.

The cataloger did enjoy a quiet morning in the little galley with charts spread out across the table. *Good Change* rode with her sea anchor, the Goan coast barely more than a dark line on the eastern horizon. *Five Lucky Winds* could pass submerged within a hundred *bù* and they would never know.

The mate had been kind enough to mark their current position. Wang noted that he'd latched the galley door from the outside.

"Where would I go?" he asked the Indian Ocean.

Leung had few choices. His life and ship were forfeit after the murders of the Nanyang Fleet's task force off the Sumatran coast. Heading south and east around Cape Comorin toward the eastern Indian Ocean and the Andaman Sea was right out. Airship patrols would be frequent. Fliers were quite good at spotting submarines. Even Wang knew this.

From Goa, *Five Lucky Winds* might sail south and west to the Maldives, but Wang could not imagine any purpose to that. What would they do there?

Due west toward the Arabian Sea would force them south to Mogadishu, or up into the Gulf of Aden. If the Mask Childress had simply meant to reach the Wall, she could have done so from Chersonesus Aurea or anywhere in the islands of the Kepulauan Riau, or the site of the massacre off the south coast of Sumatra.

Childress was English. She was also a Mask of the *avebianco*. Self-made, and powerful. Wang found himself ever more fascinated with the woman. *She* had thrown off the ties that had bound her within the world of the English. Now, in command of a ship, carrying secrets and power, her ability to find friends, money or aid would grow as she approached the heart of the British Empire.

She had to be making for the Gulf of Aden, bound for one of the ports there, or planning to pass through Suez and into the Mediterranean. How Leung planned to get a submarine secretly through those waters was beyond Wang's reckoning, but Childress and her mad servant could easily debark and take passage in the more usual way.

"I have a course," he called out to the locked door.

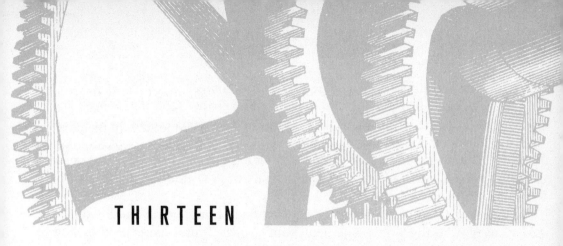

THIRTEEN

And falling into a place where two seas met, they ran the ship aground; and the forepart stuck fast, and remained unmoveable, but the hinder part was broken with the violence of the waves.

—Acts 27:41

BOAZ

Longoria leaned at the bow rail with Bosun McCurdy as Boaz climbed over the side. Their heads were tipped together. Several sailors huddled amidships, beneath the belly of the gasbag. A lone figure stood aft at the wheel.

McCurdy approached Boaz. "Midshipman Longoria tells me the skipper's been at the helm since putting us over yesterday."

"H-he was s-singing hymns all the n-night long," the lad said.

"How did you get him to come back here?" asked Boaz.

"Told him we n-needed the bosun. Finally he ordered the c-course. He hasn't spoken since. I d-don't know what to do with him."

"Relieve him of command." McCurdy spoke brusquely, as if he had not been agonizing over precisely this question.

"I c-cannot do that."

"You are the only other officer aboard," Boaz said. "Lieutenant Ostrander is long since bereft of his senses. It would be a kindness."

"There's a war on, *sir*," McCurdy replied. "You can do this much more easily than I. My testimony and that of John Brass here will back you up."

Boaz turned and stamped across the deck. McCurdy called after him, while the sailors amidships skittered away. Ostrander seemed to notice nothing.

:: *he was bound over in the tent of the King, where the snakes within his head were banished by prayer and the healing touch of the ruler* ::

Be careful.

"I am always careful," Boaz told no one in particular.

Ostrander gripped the helm so tight his fingers were pale. The expression on his face was unnaturally fixed, his skin wind-reddened and gaunt, eyes blank as those of the Brass dead in the encampment below.

"Sir," said Boaz. "I am come to take you home."

A single quivering tear ran down the lieutenant's face. His chapped lips parted as if he meant to speak. McCurdy and Longoria caught up, stepping to each side of the Brass to support their commander.

The lieutenant struck the midshipman a blow that cracked. Longoria staggered back with a cry. McCurdy grabbed at Ostrander. Another blow flew, this one misaimed.

Boaz bound Ostrander's arms to his body from behind and lifted him away from the wheel. The lieutenant struggled for a moment of boiling rage, then sagged like a punctured gasbag.

"Enough," the Brass said. "Bring everyone aboard that this ship will carry. I will stay with the rest until they can be settled in the tunnel. You return with aid, or at least food and ammunition."

"I'll do what I can." McCurdy turned to the midshipman. "Sir, the ship is yours."

Longoria sobbed.

: : *even as they cast them from the walls, the people cried for the deaths of their priests*: :

"This business grows ever more devilish," Boaz whispered to the man now slack in his arms. Monkeys were impossible. What had YHWH intended with these fools?

Paolina, where are you? How have I gone so far wrong?

WANG

The water changed where the Indian Ocean met the Gulf of Aden. Ever-deepening blue shifted to a greenish brown, as if all the sands of Arabia were trying to flee into the sea. The feel of *Good Change*'s hull in the water also changed.

A low, rocky coast fronting baked highlands rose to their right. This was a place where the desert met the water without any intervening kindness of green, growing things. Something sullen loomed on the horizon to their left, but whether it was the coast of Africa, a last glimpse of the upper reaches of Wall, or just a cloud bank, Wang could not say.

The monk had made no appearance, to his surprise. He kept expecting to smell her pipe, or see a flash of saffron, but ever since her ghost—a ghost of a ghost?—had steered them out to sea along the Goan shore, she had vanished. He wondered if she was even now afflicting *Five Lucky Winds*.

In any case, she was not bothering him. Wang spent the night alone in his bunk and had passed this day alone on the deck watching the ocean slide by.

Wu met him at the rail. "Are you rested?"

"Am I ever rested?" Wang's voice sounded querulous, even to his own ears. "No one has tied me down and beaten me today, so I must count that to the good."

"We take what victories we can from life," Wu said.

"You sound like that silly monk."

The mate braced his hand against the rail. "I should not talk to monks so much were I you, friend Wang. They are schooled in the arts of confusion."

"I was confused long before making her acquaintance."

Wu laughed softly. "Are you confused about our location?"

"No. This is the Gulf of Aden, to our right is Arabia, and somewhere to our left is Africa."

"Soon we will meet the British at their patrols."

"Our staff still flies their banner."

The mate nudged Wang, elbow to elbow. "We will use the same story we used at Panjim."

"So . . ." The cataloger looked Wu up and down. "Yesterday you beat me senseless for something I did not do. Today you ask me to speak for all our lives and safety. You still have something to learn of the ways of motivating men."

"Your life and safety depend foremost on your performance."

"I will speak," he said. "I have met this Childress twice, and greatly desire to meet her again."

One of the sailors called down from the wheelhouse. "Warship off the port bow."

The two of them looked. A white bulk loomed near the horizon.

"Now you will get your chance," Wu said.

"With hard eyes and ready weapons trained on me from both sides, no doubt."

Wu patted him on the shoulder. "One thing I like about you, Wang. You are a realist."

KITCHENS

Ottweill gave him a long, shrewd look. Then he turned wordlessly and trudged back to the barrier where the crew took their unexpected rest.

"Go back to base," the doctor announced. "In confidence will I confer with this fine bureaucrat. No guards will I need. When I return, the next shift may come on."

A muttered cheer rose, quickly aborted in the flickering shadows. "You wants us to shut the borer down cold?" someone asked.

"No, leave her idling. I will check her fire myself if too long we are here."

"Then be off, you lot," shouted a fat man with a rumpled face.

Kitchens followed Ottweill back down the tunnel until the doctor found a pile of tailings to his liking and took a seat. He tugged a small silver flask from within his coveralls. "Slivovitz?"

"No, thank you."

The doctor took a careful sip, then capped his flask and put it away again. "Only at special times do I myself this luxury permit. This Wall will be my grave, so not so much need for saving do I find. Still, a man must have discipline."

"Doctor," Kitchens said, "I have never seen you so slow to answer. On most occasions one must stand aside from the sheer velocity of your replies."

"I know your kind of person. You would not ask your question about the societies lightly. I will not answer lightly."

Which, right there, was more of an answer than Kitchens had truly expected. "I understand, sir."

"I studied at Heidelberg first," Ottweill told him. "Before I went to the Polytechnic in Berlin, then to the University of St. Andrews. There was a time when I imagined myself a philosopher."

Kitchens started a bit at that statement.

Ottweill raised a hand as if to ward him off. "No, true this is. Never had I abandoned my dreams of building in the earth, not since the first tunnel in my grandmother's basement I dug at the age of five. Such a whipping Papi gave me, you may be sure. But for a time, it took my fancy that there was a truth to the spirits of the earth, and that a man with a shovel could also carry a lamp of knowledge on his journeys. What might we learn from the flints among the chalk, from the tiny animals trapped in the seams of coal as if their bones had formed there? What might the shapes of the insides of the mountains tell us about the urges of Creation?

"These things I studied, even while I drank and fought and applied myself to classes in mechanics, in chemistry, in geology, in the applications of steam. In turn they led me to a study of other philosophers. Dr. Professor Gruene at Heidelberg had made a survey of the literature of these secret societies. They are not so secret, just quiet about themselves. He showed me how old the white birds were, those *avebianco* with their roots in the early days of Christian Rome. He showed me how the Silent Order grew from the dualistic faiths of Persia. There have been other societies, to other purposes, but long these two have struggled with different visions of God and His intentions for the world."

Ottweill tugged his flask back out, and took another slow, careful sip. He did not offer it to Kitchens this time. The clerk sat fascinated, wondering how much more the doctor would tell him.

"Behind thrones they do not stand, these societies, but often beside them. Just as a man might belong to a parish, or be an alumnus of a university, so he might be a white bird or numbered among the Silent. When you inquire if this digging is a project of one of the societies, I must of course say yes. In the same sense that the Royal Navy is a project of theirs, more *avebianco* than not if the truth we will tell. Likewise the entire Matter of Britain, and indeed almost anything of substance in this world."

Ottweill looked at the wall opposite them, seeming to study the textures of its shadows. When Kitchens was sure the doctor was not simply pausing for breath, he spoke.

"You would say this tunnel was not conceived or funded by the societies for their purposes, but that those who did conceive and fund it might share in those purposes."

Ottweill took his time in replying. "A fair enough statement. Imagine you might that the Rational Humanists are more interested in the expansion of the body politic and its attendant perquisites. But no, come this project did not from the secret halls of Valetta or Phu Ket."

Valetta? Kitchens had never heard that mentioned before. He wondered how much of this was known at Admiralty, and who in the Special Section answered to these hidden masters. Amberson? The Queen's mad doctor Stewart? "I should like to think I would have known if such a thing were true," he said, knowing that the opposite far more likely held.

"A vision of mine this tunnel was, untainted by those ancient agendas." Ottweill sounded both sad and angry, as if he were returning to his natural state of condescending energy. "What spirits in Whitehall moved it forward were almost certainly not untainted. Even the Queen herself blessed my work."

Kitchens felt his heart seize cold. "You have met the Queen?"

Ottweill's face hardened and he stared. "Yes. And you?"

"When she was at Osborne House?" the clerk asked, almost not daring to speak. "Or . . . later?"

"A man of many secrets you are, indeed." The doctor's voice very nearly crackled now. "Both, in truth. Once before, and once . . . later."

"Her condition must be a doing of the societies," Kitchens breathed.

"I will not speak of it further," Ottweill announced. He stood, shaking.

They marched in silence to the barred metal gate, then out to the handcart.

"You will be on your way." The doctor released the brakes. "Starving here we are, and at grave danger of continued attack. Do your job to summon a relief, and my job of tunneling I will do."

"Into solid brass?" Kitchens asked. He was certain this project was finished, no matter what the doctor said.

"A way in I will find. Through as well, damn your English eyes."

PAOLINA

A shallow bay, pilings dotting the mud that led out from the beach. A spit
to her right, ragged with familiar trees. A looming knee of rock to her left,
rising up like a tiny cousin to the stone immensity behind.

The shadow of the Wall eclipsed the water, a great squared cloud the size
of the world. The last quarter of the year was at hand, and so the sun had
moved southward. A vee of birds rose from the distant trees and crossed the
sky, heading for the light.

"We are here," Ming said in Chinese. "Our journey reduced as if it had
never been."

She unlooped the cord from his wrist and passed it to Gashansunu.
Wordless, the sorceress coiled the length. The other woman seemed
thoughtful, even drawn.

"That was the step of a moment for me," Paolina said. "How did the
transit seem to you?"

"I used my powers to follow your path," the Southern woman replied.
"It was . . . difficult. My *wa* cried out at the crossing of the Wall." She fell
silent.

Paolina tucked her gleam away along with the ragged angel feather,
then set to helping Ming look for their boat. They had passed through
here only weeks ago. They located the boat easily enough in the crowded
brush. Creepers had already begun to grow over the hull, and moss
bloomed along the inverted keel.

"I should scrape this before setting out," Ming told her. "Lest there be
hidden rot."

"Then I will help. I am not quite ready to bid you farewell."

They hauled the boat onto the muddy beach, leaving it overturned.
Ming hunted for tough shells or jagged rocks to do his scraping, while
Paolina went back for the oars and the rolled-up tarpaulin they had left
tucked beneath the hull.

Neatness, always neatness. Now it meant Ming's freedom.

She was unsure of the distance to Taiwan, but it seemed like he must
go very far indeed.

Paolina met Ming back at the boat, where he was comparing the worth
of several makeshift tools. "How will you manage the journey?"

"I must reach Sumatra in this boat. No farther than our original sea
journey to here. There I can find someone to take me to Singapore. Then

I will sign onto a vessel heading north, a little coaster or freighter. A competent man with a quiet mouth rarely lacks for work at sea."

"And on to Oluanpi?"

"Somewhere in Taiwan," he said. "I cannot go to Tainan. Surely we are all long since made outlaw. Admiral Shen might forgive, if he knew all the truth, but the Beiyang Navy cannot afford to. The Dragon Throne would never imagine doing so. My honor has been sold away, so I must live as I can."

"I am so sorry," she began, but he stopped her with a look.

"I followed Captain Leung. Even now I believe his purposes and those of Admiral Shen are not so far apart. If *Five Lucky Winds* can carry the Mask Childress to stop the Golden Bridge, as she has proposed to do, then our sacrifices will be worthy."

"Hopefully she can make the journey."

Ming shrugged. "I cannot conceive of how, but then I am neither a captain nor a mask."

"If I had her close by, I could take her." Paolina felt comforted by the weight of the stemwinder against her thigh.

"Advice is something I should not presume to give you," Ming told her. "You are near to a mask, or a princess of the Imperial house, and I am but a sailor from the provinces."

"Do not be immodest! You were chief among the sailors aboard *Five Lucky Winds*."

"As may be. But for you, step lightly with your powers. If you continue to pass across the world as we just did, you may awaken dragons."

She was unsure what to say to that, so she said nothing, but instead took up a promising stone and helped him in his scraping.

That afternoon, Ming was ready to set out. They had harvested some gourds to carry water for him, and enough fruits for the crossing. Sumatra was not far over the horizon.

Paolina helped him push the boat into the sea. Gashansunu watched from a distance. The Southern woman had spoken very little in the course of the day. Paolina touched Ming's arm, wondering if she should hug him, but he smiled and slipped over the gunwale.

"I go," said Ming. "Farewell, and may all the luck of the seas follow in your wake."

"Farewell."

With that, it was over. He rowed away, facing her in his seat, but with his head tucked down and focused on his labors. She wondered if he cried, for she did, and could not decide if that was an honor or unworthy of them both.

Paolina watched for a long time, until he was a gray-black speck on the water, then turned back to Gashansunu.

"You do not want to go to a place," the sorceress said. Her expression was almost wistful, which struck Paolina as curious. "You want to go to a person."

"To Boaz, yes."

They sat beneath the failing light of day. A fish baked on coals was spread between them on broad leaves. Paolina had plucked some tart, pulpy, green-fleshed fruit to go with it.

Gashansunu clicked her tongue. "Difficulties present themselves."

"I can imagine. You showed me your Silent World. It has correspondences to the real world. I—"

The other woman interrupted. "The Silent World *is* the real world. This is the Shadow World. When you traffic with the passage between the two, best to remember the difference."

Paolina wondered why the world of sunlight was the Shadow World. "In any case, the Silent World corresponds to the Shadow World in the matter of place. For all that they are not the same size."

"They correspond in the matter of persons, as well. I am my *wa's* shadow."

"Surely that is the other way around? Do you not call your *wa*?"

"No," Gashansunu said. "You are confusing effects and causes. There is not a single sun in the Silent World casting all shadows the same direction, and so the correspondences appear imperfect to us."

Paolina persisted. "This beach has a form in the Silent World, yes?" *What is the Silent World, stripped of this woman's very powerful metaphor?* "People have a form in the Silent World, but they move themselves through differing places and moments. It is far easier to step from a place to a place than from a place to a person."

"That is close enough to the truth," Gashansunu said in a guarded tone. "You surprise me."

"Thank you." Paolina realized that this woman was something of a female *fidalgo*, much as the Mask Childress had been.

Gashansunu clicked her lips again. Then: "How would you expect to pass through the Silent World to reach a person known to you?"

That question had been much on Paolina's mind since stepping to this beach from the other side of the Wall. "The simplest way is if the person's location is known to me. Were I to seek out Hethor, all I should need to do is step to his village. He will be close by."

"Go on," the sorceress said encouragingly.

"Likewise, if they go from a certain place to another place, in the manner of a hunter or tradesman, I might go between those places to look for them. But this is little more than a case of the first instance."

"What if you do not know of their location? As with this Boaz?"

"I know places he has been," Paolina said slowly, still thinking in terms of the correspondent geography of the two worlds. What *was* the Silent World? Perhaps a template for this world. "I could visit them, just as if I had walked or come by ship, and seek information in the usual manner. We have both been to Mogadishu, though that was a burning nest of violence on my last, brief visit. We have been to the Armory of Westmost Repose, the Brass city of Ophir, and Dr. Ottweill's work camp."

"That would be an ordinary search, using your powers of translocation to avoid the difficulties of travel in between."

Paolina took up a stick and began drawing in the mud of the beach a line map of the portions of the Wall she had traveled. "I wonder about finding the person directly. I expect that having walked in the Silent World together, I could locate you. I have seen your *wa*, and know your form in that other place. You were far more present there than the landscape was."

"Now you are closer to it," the sorceress told her. "We have powers of seeking and calling. But just as you need to have visited a place in the Shadow World to be able to return there through the Silent World, so you must to know a person that well. How well do you know this Boaz? Have you met his *wa*? What is his seeming in the Silent World?"

"We traveled for many weeks. We had, well, adventures together. Of the sort that pull two people closer." With a flood of guilt, she recalled their mutual betrayals on the cliffs below Ophir, when he had subdued her to carry her down the long stairs, and she in turn had simply *stopped* him with the original stemwinder. "I do not suppose he has a *wa*, for he is not human such as you are or I." Paolina wondered briefly if Gashansunu *was* human. "Likewise I have no notion of his seeming in the Silent World. However . . ."

She tugged the stemwinder free from its pouch, caressed it lovingly in her hand.

"I have," she continued, "touched him with my gleam. This means I have taken his measure. I believe that may be my equivalent to what you call 'knowing his seeming.' "

"This I cannot tell you," Gashansunu said. "Your way of reaching the Silent World is so different from my own."

"Not so different. You have been able to show me much I did not understand about the stepping through. The Silent World was invisible to me until you opened my eyes."

Thus the power of metaphor, she thought. *I may not be able to purge myself of this woman's perception.* Paolina was almost certain that Gashansunu's narrative of the Silent World and the Shadow World only modeled the underlying reality, rather than explaining it.

"Would you try this theory first?" Gashansunu asked. "Set your device to know me, if you have not already done so. Give me an hour's time to walk away from you, my direction and destination unknown. Then see if you can step through to me."

Paolina looked about at the long shadows of evening. She had hoped to go onward this same day, but Gashansunu had the right of it. She *should* practice her theory here where no one was around and the object of her search would be close by. Far fewer things might go wrong, and some might go well.

"Let us wait until morning, and good light," she told the sorceress. "If I am successful, we will make the attempt to reach Boaz."

"Fair enough."

Together they watched the last of the day steal off into history, while the wine-dark night overtook the world.

CHILDRESS

They steamed into the muddy waters of the Gulf of Aden on a gloomy morning. Low clouds over damp, thick air made heavy all of the banners now strung from *Five Lucky Winds*. The submarine lacked the gay enthusiasm she'd shown returning to home port in Tainan, or even the hopeful energy of their call at Singapore.

Hsu, the pilot, pointed out a vessel ahead. "British warship," Leung said in Chinese. He called down through the speaking tube for quarter speed. She could hear the tension in his voice.

As they approached the warship, the only sound was water breaking over their bow to rush alongside the hull. The world acquired an intensity, an edge to the light and noise and ocean scent and the whiff of Leung's perspiration and the nervousness of Hsu at the little wheel that served as helm up here.

The warship had definitely sighted them. A long blast on an air horn echoed over the water, reminding her suddenly of the great foghorns at the harbor in New Haven. The British vessel picked up speed, a wave breaking before the curved white prow. Turrets spun on the deck, bringing huge cannon to bear.

"He is already too close to use his largest guns." Captain Leung still spoke in Chinese, presumably for the benefit of the pilot. "We are almost certainly sailing toward a parley rather than a sinking, for he would have fired by now."

"One could always sink us after a discussion," she replied in English.

"You are a fountain of good cheer."

The two vessels closed their distance quickly enough. A loud hailer crackled, audible even across an intervening half mile of water. "Stand to for boarding!"

"All stop," Leung called down. "Bring us to a halt and drop the sea anchor."

Five Lucky Winds shuddered as if she wished to pitch nose forward and hide beneath the safety of the waves—which would be no safety to speak of in this narrow, shallow body of water.

"Mask," the captain said, "I believe this next moment belongs to you."

The warship loomed close, Maxim guns tracking from small stations along her midline, though her crew did not seem to be dashing to battle stations. She put a boat over the side, four men climbing down into it. It was a steam-powered launch, considerably larger than that now carried by *Five Lucky Winds*.

"I should go down to meet them," Childress said.

"No," Leung advised. "Make them come to you. You can descend to converse, but you will have more power if you are first seen above them."

This was no different from a librarian's podium, of course. People forced to look up were always at a disadvantage.

"I am torn between politeness and the ways of power."

Out of sight of the approaching British, he squeezed her hand. "You are not Miss Childress in this hour; you are the Mask Childress. Live your name."

"I am the Mask," she repeated, echoing his words. Once more she called upon the ghost of Poinsard.

Soon enough, three men were saluted by al-Wazir in proper Royal Navy fashion. "Welcome aboard, sirs," he bellowed.

"My good fellow, are you all madmen?" asked one of the officers. Hardly an auspicious preamble to negotiations, but by no stretch a declaration of violence either.

"No sir, Leftenant Commander," al-Wazir said, still shouting. "But we sail at the direction of a woman, and it's her you'd be speaking to."

The lieutenant commander glanced up at the conning tower. "A woman?"

"You would be well advised to take him at his word, sir," Childress called down. "I am a Mask of the *avebianco* on a critical diplomatic mission in this time of strife."

"Madam," the British officer said, enunciating his words with care. "I have never heard such a lot of balderdash in my life. Kindly present yourself on deck and provide an explanation."

Childress nodded to Leung, then took the ladder down to the deck hatch. At each rung she let some of the Mask Poinsard flow back into her, so that by the time she stepped out into the sunlight to meet the lieutenant commander, the offense of her dignity was a palpable thing.

KITCHENS

More of the doctor's work gang escorted him back up the tunnel. As they walked along the tracks, the grinding roar of the borer resumed. Ottweill's words about the Queen were much on his mind. The doctor had *seen* Her Imperial Majesty in that horrid tank of blood and fluid. He possessed some insight concerning her fate—who had done this to her, and why. All Kitchens had to go on was a dim instinct that one or possibly both of the societies were involved. That, and the Queen's request to him.

Remake what has been undone.
Break my throne.
Help me finish dying.

Why not *Undo what had been made?* he wondered. What precisely had been undone?

Then the little gang of roughnecks were at the gate.

"Them sailors is still out there," said one, vaguely familiar to Kitchens. Had they met at the quarry site back in Kent where the borer was tested? "We got another party on the stockade fence. Orders. You tells 'em you're coming through, lest they shoot you."

Kitchens was surprised to find any of dusk remaining outside. He'd somehow thought this the middle of the night. Being deep within the Wall had surely shadowed his thoughts overmuch.

A small airship, presumably *Erinyes*, was visible above the stockade wall, tethered low to the ground. People moved about on her deck. The group on the stockade watched him pass through the ruins of their camp without attempting to stop him. He knew how badly those men had wanted to be within their bolthole. Kitchens avoided the ruin of the gate, instead climbing the ladder. The ropes were still tied there.

"You going back to the sailors?" asked a blond man with a seamed face, clutching a rifle close as any lover.

"Surely if I am to find aid for your expedition, I will not do so from behind these walls."

"I'd get over and to your friends before full dark, then. A man shouldn't be alone in these jungles."

"Your advice is my command." The clerk nodded, grabbed the rope, and climbed down the outside of the stockade.

He stumbled across the field of fire, around bits of snapped bone, shattered Brass and the debris of repeated battle. Blood curdled in long, narrow puddles covered with flies. This was indeed not a place to be stranded.

Sailors crowded around the lines mooring *Erinyes*. Kitchens pushed through to find Harrow.

"What transpires?" he asked the chief.

"McCurdy took John Brass up with him to relieve Lieutenant Ostrander of command," the petty officer replied. "Bad business no matter which direction you slice the loaf."

Kitchens was amazed. "They want to give the ship to that Boaz?"

"I think McCurdy wanted someone who wouldn't hang for this to play the hard part. That Brass has some attachment to the men of *Erinyes* that I don't fathom."

"I must go for aid," Kitchens said. "Much here should be reported to London. If McCurdy can get me to Cotonou, I can send support back here while taking a larger airship back to England."

Harrow leaned close, almost intimate, as he whispered in Kitchens' ear. "We won't lift more than two-thirds of these men, and not even that many if Ostrander vented too much hydrogen. With the tunnel and the camp barred to us, there will be a hell of a fight over privilege."

The rope chair dropped over the side from above, swinging down into the gloom of evening.

"Let me up, Chief. I'll do what I can to take care of everyone, but I must report, above all else."

As well as find a way to aid the Queen.

One of the sailors pushed to Harrow's side. "Bugger it, Chief, they's asking for you up there."

"Send Mr. Kitchens first," Harrow said loudly. "He can speak for me. I plan to be the last man off the ground, when they're ready to take us all home."

The chair spun as it rose. *Chair* was too kind a word. This was barely a sling, as if he were a carcass being brought up for the galley. He kept his gorge in place even as rough hands drew him over the rail.

"You're not Harrow," someone said, then McCurdy pushed forward. A very frightened midshipman hung close off one shoulder.

"Where's John Brass?" Kitchens asked.

"Belowdecks with the lieutenant, sir." The bosun tried to look back at the midshipman, but the young man stepped away from his glance. "Someone has to sit on the poor bugger, and he won't likely scratch out that Boaz' eyes."

"We must lay in a course for Cotonou."

"I still got four men on the ground," McCurdy said quietly. "Harrow's boys number forty more, at least."

Kitchens glanced back at the ropes. "Are you going to be able to take them all aboard?"

"Could." The deck around them was very quiet. "We wouldn't make much altitude, and we'd be slow. That's four tons more than we'd normally carry, just body weight, plus the food and water we'd have to bring up, and the gas cells are down almost thirty percent thanks to some fancy piloting. A storm comes, Chinee raiders find us, more of them winged savages attack, we're dead men."

Kitchens retained his sense of ruthless duty. He had to get back to the Queen, to report on Ottweill's fate, and to answer her note. "Better to put almost everyone over the side and run for Cotonou with a minimal crew. More men on the ground will increase their chance of survival. More men up here will slow us down."

A muttering arose among the gathered crew, someone's voice quite clearly complaining, "I ain't going down—" until shushed by his fellows.

"You might want to watch your mouth there," McCurdy said. His eyes were pleading, though his voice was hard.

Kitchens shifted his attention to the junior officer quite literally hiding behind the bosun. "Midshipman, you are in command now, yes?"

The boy nodded reluctantly.

"I have no authority here. My writ runs only to the surviving crew of *Notus*. But I have the ear of the Sea Lords and the Prime Minister's office. I tell you now that our duty to Queen and country requires you to make all speed to Cotonou so I can send word onward of what has befallen, and mount an effective relief of these stranded sailors and the camp beyond. What are your orders?"

The midshipman gulped and began shaking.

"You are a British officer, lad. What are your orders?"

The boy fainted dead away, hitting the deck with a crack.

"Bloody hell," Kitchens said, almost shouting. He smashed his poor attaché case into the deck.

The Brass loomed out of the evening shadows. "Ah," he said. "It is you. Have you poisoned Midshipman Longoria?"

Kitchens stared at the metal man, vainly willing him to transform into a capable, competent Lieutenant Ostrander, then said, "I believe Bosun McCurdy is now in command of this vessel."

"Oh, sir," McCurdy breathed, appalled.

Shouting echoed from below, and a short scream.

"Then cut the bedamned lines and we lift," Kitchens said, hating the moment.

"I am not sailing away with you," the Brass man protested.

"Everyone else expects to!"

A series of quick ax chops, and the airship jumped away to screaming from below, and scattered rifle fire. McCurdy ran to the rail, shouting, "Stop, you idiots!" before staggering back with a bloody hole in his face where his right eye had been.

He spun once, blinked with his remaining eye at Kitchens, said quite distinctly, "Trust the Brass bastard," then toppled backward over the rail.

FOURTEEN

And she went, and came, and gleaned in the field after the reapers; and her hap was to light on a part of the field belonging unto Boaz, who was of the kindred of Elimelech.   —*Ruth 2:3*

BOAZ

Christ, man, get to the helm, shouted the Paolina–al-Wazir voice in his head. *Don't let them swing.*

The Sixth Seal shrieked as well.

::*binded him to the mast they did, and whipped him three times three days with a salt-crusted rope, for that was the punishment for mutiny in those days*::

Most of the sailors rushed to the rail like monkeys at a fruit fall. Boaz stumbled aft. A white-haired man clutched at the wheel, his seamed face drawn in shock.

"Get us away from the Wall," Boaz ordered. "Head west of north with all speed." Altitude, these airships always fought for altitude. "Take us up."

::*the very air is the kingdom of the birds. Do not challenge the will of the Lord by casting thyself into the skies*::

"H-how f-far, s-sir?" The helmsman clutched the wheel, not reaching for the engine telegraph or the attitude controls.

Boaz picked a number out of nowhere. "Five thousand feet, then level out."

Good lad. That was al-Wazir.

::*he shewed a span of a dozen dozen cubits, and dozen more of those, and claimed the tribes would climb that far*::

I am cracked. My crystals are damaged. Shadows of people I have come to love live in my head and tell me things I do not know in my own mind. The history of my kind lives in my gut and rants madly of ancient times and the brutal privilege of absolute power.

If he took the Sixth Seal back to Ophir now, what would become of the city? This monstrous voice would require only a handful of years to raise a mighty empire bent on conquest and destruction, in the name of biblical restoration. No wonder the ancient Kohanim had hidden the Seal away in a lost cave on a deserted coast.

:: *that we might beat even the sepulchers of our fathers into swords and drive the enemies of our God into the bloodred waters of the sea*: :

He wrenched his thoughts back to the present moment. McCurdy was dead, which saddened him. Kitchens' notion to race for help was plentifully sensible. But Boaz could not go with them.

Five thousand feet? What was he thinking? He could not get down from that height. Yet turning back toward Ophir seemed less and less practical, given the mad thing in his belly.

:: *you should not know the voice of the Lord even as He shouts thunder in your ear*: :

The rest of the crew were being driven to their tasks by the vessel's surviving petty officer. The helmsman had signaled for altitude and for speed, then resumed clutching his wheel for all the worth of his life. Kitchens stepped to *Erinyes'* aft rail and looked down across the night-dark jungle. Boaz joined him there.

The wreck of *Notus* still smoldered. Sparks were visible at the edge of the camp's cleared field of fire. Boaz realized they were the flash of a last few shots in their direction.

:: *they will defend the holy books, the consecrated oils, and the salt that we have harvested from the graves of angels*: :

"Harrow will have his hands full," Kitchens said. "That's a mutiny in progress down there, and one petty officer dead already."

"I should not know," Boaz said. The human voices in his head muttered at that. "My kind account authority differently."

"Not so different as all that, I think." The man studied him carefully. "I have read the reports. But now we have a pretty problem here aboard *Erinyes*."

:: *kings fail and fall; their thrones shiver empty; dark smokes hang over all the lands until even the olives wither in their groves*: :

That voice was so loud in his thoughts it threatened to flow from his mouth. He tried to concentrate on what Kitchens had been saying. "That problem would be what, precisely?"

"Midshipman Longoria is unfit for duty. Lieutenant Ostrander is not even fit to wander loose. McCurdy is dead. That petty officer working the deck now will not speak to me, or look at you. *Erinyes* is a vessel without a commander, but carrying great need."

:: *snatch up the banner and ride the fallen hero's horse into the fray, for ye shall be accounted holy and brave and the names of thy sons sung at temple for a hundred years*: :

'Tis nae mutiny when you have never taken the oath.

"You surely do not propose that I should captain this ship," Boaz said. This clerk had no idea how worrisome his thoughts had become.

"I have no warrants here. *Notus* was under my control, but *Erinyes* is posted to the East African station. I will take command if I must, but I will be years at hearings before they can unwind the whole business."

"Whereas I am an enemy of the British Crown," Boaz pointed out. "Or at the least my people are. You would surrender your vessel to an adversary?"

::*do not play at the game of captains and kings unless you are forged of their mettle*::

"It is not my vessel to surrender." The frustration in Kitchens' voice was evident. "If I am delivered to Cotonou as a hostage released, I will be made welcome and heeded. If I come to Cotonou at the helm of a ship over which I have no command authority, I will be arrested and bound over for transport back to England." His voice dropped to a nearly desperate whisper. "My duty requires me to be free and effective. Better that you seize the ship than that I take it."

Careful, lad. The Paolina–al-Wazir voice was gaining strength over the clamor of the Sixth Seal. Her sense infused him. *Walk softly, but be bold.*

"So they will arrest me instead? Better to put me down now along the coast and let me make my own way."

::*no man ever took a crown without a thought to the swords that might someday break down the door of his throne room*::

The Seal had become almost reasonable, Boaz realized.

Their further conversation was interrupted when a shout went up from the foredeck. "Lanterns in the east! The Chinee is upon us!"

Al-Wazir's voice gusted from Boaz' mouth. "Ring for battle stations. Man the guns, now. Deck division to arms!"

"By the blood of Christ," Kitchens swore. "This Wall will never let up."

"This is not the doing of the Wall. Your empire is at war with China." It dawned on Boaz that this man had traveled aboard *Notus* for some time. "Or do you not know that?"

"What?"

"*Erinyes* came east scouting after a great aerial battle over Abyssinia. The Imperial dragon and the British lion are savaging one another bloody in the east."

"We are undone!" The clerk's anger was palpable.

::*a messenger came with the dawn, riding on wings of wind, and cried defeat in the green vales above the city*::

Boaz' fingers scrabbled at his midsection, seeking to open the little doors the Sixth Seal had caused to be so firmly shut.

Stop! he shouted to the voices in his head.

"Fliers!" screamed the bow watch. "Them killer angels come off the Wall!"

"Mind the helm," Boaz shouted to Kitchens and the terrified sailor at the wheel. He stomped forward. This was a threat he could grasp in hand. "Rifles at the ready!"

WANG

The white warship drew nearer. She gleamed slightly pink in the light of the setting sun and flew more flags than any one man ought to be required to understand.

Shen brought *Good Change* parallel with the great vessel. A dozen sailors lounged at her rail high over his head, staring down. Raising his hand, he waved. Some of them waved back. On a balcony above them, another man stared at them through a pair of lenses. He studied them a while, but did not wave back.

That was it.

No guile, no stealth, no force. No signal. Just two ships passing in the late light of the day.

A strange lack of climax to a moment that could have claimed all their lives.

Wu reappeared from belowdecks once the warship was safely behind them. "We will make the smallest port we can find, and purchase fuel oil for our engines. You will be our buyer."

"Of course," said Wang. "You trust me with funds?"

"Your loyalty is not in question, only your good sense."

He wanted to ask, *Who are you to question my loyalty, who conspire with vanishing monks and claim to be a dead man walking?* There was no point. Wu was right. Wang would not escape into an English port here. Where would he go? Who would take him in?

Besides, he was still far too interested in finding Childress to give himself up to anyone else.

Anyone, he corrected his own thought. Not anyone *else*. Anyone.

Morning found the cataloger talking to a strange little man in grubby white robes. The fellow's skin was the color of the rocks above his port town, his eyes black, and he had a narrow beard that he was forever stroking as if it were a restless animal.

A handful of coolies wearing nothing but roughspun trousers and head-scarves wrestled a fuel line onto the deck of *Lucky Change*. Several of Wu's crew worked with them, bringing up a connection from below.

The man almost hopped from foot to foot in his nervousness. "How is it that your vessel full of the enemy is permitted to pass our water gates?"

"We are no enemy." The story was at risk of becoming too practiced. "We serve a prince of Serendip, who has sent us to secure some peace in this fighting that seems set to overtake all."

"I do not know the fighting," the wharfinger said. Quite clearly he cherished his ignorance.

"I might ask you a small question," Wang proposed.

"My answers will likely be small, as well."

"Have you seen another vessel here with a Chinese crew and an English commander? It would be strangely formed, for it is made to go underneath the waters at times."

"Ah, my friend." The port master patted his arm. "I, too, have been blessed with a boat made to go underneath the waters at times. By the virtue of the strong backs of my sons, and my cousin Mustapha who is a carpenter, we have remade her now and again, but still she sinks."

"No, no, I mean a submarine."

The man's eyes crinkled. "Some things are best unspoken. You ask if I have seen a sinking boat, and I tell you of my own misfortunes—a man of wit and discernment would read the lack of an answer in that sorry story."

"Speaking with you is like braiding the tails of three cats."

The Arab bowed. "Your words are a balm upon the memory of the Imam who had my schooling in my younger days, when I could be torn away from the date palms and the doe-eyed young women languishing beneath them."

Wang was uncertain as to the virtue of doe-eyed women. "I thank you, sir."

A boy ran up and whispered urgently into the man's ear. He nodded, said something in Arabic, then turned back to Wang. "One of the morning's first fishing boats is returned with news. HIMS *Inerrancy* has stopped a strange vessel lying very low in the water. Perhaps these are your absent friends come again?"

"Doubtless," Wang said. He glanced to the east, wondering if the lifting clouds would reveal *Five Lucky Winds* nearby. Even so, what would he do in the presence of the British, presuming the submarine was not simply sunk out of hand?

After an interminable time, the pumping was finished. The port master's coolies capped the hose and coiled it back under the supervision of the pump boy.

"We must be back at sea," Wang said. "To follow the course our friends set."

"The course on which you sailed ahead of them?" The port master clasped the cataloger's hand in both of his. "Watch what may come, and remember that sometimes there is silence in every house."

Wang was heartily sick of secret agendas. He stepped up the plank to the deck of *Lucky Change*. "Cast off," the cataloger said brusquely to Wu. "I have news of our quarry."

GASHANSUNU

Late in the evening Gashansunu had slipped into the Silent World to scan for hidden watchers, or even the heart-fire of some dangerous predator, but saw nothing except the flicker of life along the quiet strip of forest between the Wall and the sea. The ocean itself gleamed, as oceans always did in the Silent World. Saltwater circled everything, touched everything, flowed in the veins of everyone who had ever lived.

Paolina slept beneath a ragged palm near the last smolder of her fire. Gashansunu climbed the rotten knee of rock at the west end of their little beach. Using her ordinary sight, she followed the path. Her *wa* had absented itself since they passed the Wall, though not so thoroughly as to yet worry Gashansunu. She wished to look into the west, as her devotions at Westfacing House called for, and open herself up to invite her *wa* to rejoin her at its place in the Shadow World.

This rock had no top, as such. Just a place where the difficult path ceased climbing and began struggling among boulders and crevices full of thorns. She climbed a larger, squared boulder that seemed to have rolled from higher up on the Wall and set to her meditations. Here she was considerably higher than any point in the city, and so faced much more of the west than she would have at home. On her left, the Wall was almost close enough to touch, and consumed the south.

The Wall was just as dark and brooding in the Silent World as in the Shadow World. Great energies moved within it, as a clay kiln might be filled with sizzling coals. The ocean on her right glowed with the memories of life. The sky above was empty. The Silent World knew no stars, seemed concerned only with what was on the face of the Earth. She sometimes wondered why the moon, at least, did not intrude on that other place, but then the rules that governed its underlying magics were not something of which even the greatest of the house priests could claim a thorough understanding.

I am here, she told her *wa.*

Though its presence was not close, the words of her *wa* reached her.
THIS PLACE SEEMS SO EMPTY.

Gashansunu considered that a while before answering. *All places are empty, until someone comes to fill them.*

THE MIND OF THE WORLD IS DIFFERENT HERE, her *wa* protested.

What do you mean, the mind of the world?

Her *wa*'s answer was matter-of-fact, and also profoundly heretical: WHAT THESE PEOPLE OF THE NORTH CALL GOD—JUST AS THE SILENT WORLD IS THE MIND OF THE SOUTHERN EARTH.

Now it was Gashansunu's turn to protest. *But the Silent World is everywhere, behind and beneath all things.*

YOU DO NOT YET UNDERSTAND.

With those words her *wa* fell silent, even as it drifted closer.

Gashansunu watched the night a while, both within her own thoughts and through the Silent World. No further wisdom came, though she spent much time thinking on what her *wa*'s strange words had meant.

PAOLINA

She woke with the sun, feeling more rested than she had since, well . . . ever, perhaps. Gashansunu was not nearby.

After splashing her face with water, Paolina took the stemwinder from its pouch, tugged the stem out to the fourth stop and began to slowly turn it in search of the Southern woman's trace. They'd stepped together through the Silent World. Paolina knew her now without silver bonds or strange meditations. She would home in on Gashansunu and follow the sorceress wherever she had gone.

This was like spotting a particular spark from a distant campfire at night. Paolina had not tried to follow a person before, but she'd already seen how life could glow in the Silent World. Using the stemwinder, she didn't enter that other place as Gashansunu had done, but rather looked into it. The world of light became veiled, but also sharper; the ocean acquired a strange, glittering cast; and the sorceress came into a brittle focus. She was atop the knee of rock, which seemed some great, slow creature with thoughts that moved at the tempo of years.

Paolina focused her will on Gashansunu. Without considering the woman's *place*, she pushed off, projecting herself forward while also sending pressure back so as not to destroy the beach.

Between one footfall and the next, she was on top of the rising mass of rock, and nearly tumbling over the far side. Paolina dropped hard to a sitting position and braked with both feet and one arm while protecting the gleam with her other arm.

Gashansunu called out just as the slide came to an abrupt and somewhat difficult end. A sharp pain hurt Paolina's tailbone. Empty air stretched beneath her toes.

"Lean back against the rock," Gashansunu said from behind and above her.

"I know, I know," Paolina whispered. She had little fear of heights, but anyone could become trapped in the wrong place. Her first business was to take her eyes off the horizon and the long drop beneath her feet, to let her sense of equilibrium restore itself.

Vertigo.

"I will reach for you." The sorceress again.

"No, no, I must rest a moment." Paolina closed her eyes. "Besides, I am far more experienced than you at heights. I grew up along the Wall; you hail from a flatwater city."

"You may have grown up atop a pinnacle, but right now you are on a narrow ledge of rotten rock high above a stony beach," Gashansunu observed. "I do not think you have the advantage of me this day."

"A moment more, please. A moment more."

The scramble to safety was short and nasty. Paolina shivered from fear, glad enough of the sunlight.

"Now you see why sorcerers do not often follow people through the Silent World, even when we know them well," Gashansunu told her.

"Did you intend to test me to the edge of my death?"

"No." The other woman sounded embarrassed. "I was meditating and lost my count of the hours. I had thought to find some clearing in which to await you, but my understanding was that we would discuss the requirements of the effort beforehand."

Paolina felt shamed in her turn. "I did not intend to put either of us at risk. Please accept my apology."

"You have learned something this day," Gashansunu said.

"I have learned to be careful where I step." Paolina was a bit cheered by her own humor.

"Do you still wish to chase after Boaz?"

"Yes. Before I lose my nerve. I would go to Boaz, and I do not know where he is."

"At any great distance, the spark such as you saw in me will be a glow within your thoughts, nothing more. He could be atop a mountain or cast down into a pelagic abyss, and you will not perceive the difference."

"I will perceive that he is there, and alive, when I set myself to him." She tugged the stem to the fourth setting. Boaz she knew very, very well. When she had shut him down in the meadow below Ophir—her betrayal of him, for which she'd tried to make up ever since—she had taken his measure.

She found him, a faint glimmer very far away, somewhere well past the western horizon. Africa, then, where she had left him. Which likely meant a British cell, or back upon *a Murado*, as opposed to having been captured by the Chinese.

More to the point, he was *alive*. "Boaz," she whispered, a vast relief flooding her heart at the thought of reunion.

"I will come with you." Gashansunu took her other hand with a looping of the silver cord.

"Let us away, then." Paolina smiled, unwilling to contain her joy.

She dialed the stemwinder in, held Boaz firmly in her mind and stepped forward.

They tumbled into empty air, Paolina screaming as she fell.

CHILDRESS

"You are not of the peerage." Lieutenant Commander Bork was a big man, sun-reddened with the look of distemper about him. His tropical kit fit poorly, folded, rumpled and sweat stained. The men behind him held their weapons ready. She was all too conscious of the larger guns aboard Bork's ship.

"I am the Mask Childress," she repeated. "Of the *avebianco*. As you value your commission, and the peace of the Queen's realm, you shall let me pass with my ship and crew."

"Your *ship*, madam, is an enemy vessel designed for only one purpose— the destruction of British hulls. Even if you have overtaken her with a train of scoundrels, I can no more let you proceed onward with this craft than I could allow you to enter a church clutching a carbine."

Childress felt a rare burst of rage. "I am not a combatant, Lieutenant Commander. I am a diplomat bent on stopping this affair. With the aid of this good crew, I shall carry my mission to Valetta to represent the negotiations that have been undertaken with the Chinese Empire, as well as the Silent Order. A minister from London is even now traveling to meet me there." She leaned forward, compounding the outright lie with further exaggeration. "A very important minister. Prime, one might say." Her voice dropped to a whisper, so that Bork was drawn toward her. "Would you care to be the officer who must explain later why this voyage did not go forward?"

"Sir," al-Wazir barked. "If I might hae a word with ye."

Childress whirled on him, then stopped the hot words that sprang to her lips when she saw the expression on the chief's face.

"A Scotsman, to boot," the officer grumbled. "You insult me, madam, a boat crewed by coolies, commanded by a woman, with a bloody one-handed braveheart to speak for her."

Al-Wazir threw himself to full attention. "Chief Petty Officer Angus Threadgill al-Wazir, sir! Attached to this woman's mission by direct order of Admiralty and in consultation with the Prime Minister himself."

"Even if you had papers I would not believe you, man." The lieutenant commander slapped his swagger stick against his trouser leg. "I have half a mind to place myself ahead of the rush and give you a thrashing right now."

"You're damned right I've lost me papers, sir," al-Wazir said. "I've also killed two of the enemy's airships, escaped from the Chinese navy, and crossed all of Africa and most of the Indian Ocean to get here. Lost me hand doing it, *sir*. I can tell you what color the lampshades are in the Planning Room on the top floor of Admiralty's Ripley Building. You tell me, *sir*, how does the First Sea Lord take his tea?"

"How the First Sea Lord takes his tea does not matter," said Bork, but a nervousness darted within his eyes. "It is the brace of you fools with a damned lot of coolies and four forward torpedo tubes that cannot be permitted into the Suez Canal!"

"Then arrest us now," Childress announced loudly. "Sink our ship. Make your reports. You will enjoy commanding a coaling station in the Shetlands until your retirement, I am certain of it."

Bork's red face purpled. "Do not threaten me, you dreadful termagant!"

Childress wasn't sure, but one of his subofficers appeared to be trying to swallow laughter. She barged ahead. "You seem to feel quite free to threaten me, sir. I am certain that indicates your willingness to be treated just the same, by the simple rules of Christian charity."

Bork took a deep breath and visibly gathered himself. He closed his eyes a moment, contemplating his own frustrations, then said, "You sail into my waters under a ridiculous banner not to be found in the flag books. You command an enemy ship, filled with enemy sailors, in a time of war. You make bald-faced assertions of your authority without any written orders or charters to validate your claims. Do you expect me to believe all this?"

"Well, yes," Childress said, in her most pleasant speaking-to-theology-students voice. "What else is there for you to do?" She glanced up the conning tower at Leung, who was watching impassively. Time to take a step that would almost certainly give him dreadful pause. Childress had thought this through carefully but had quite deliberately declined to discuss it with the captain. "I shall offer you a compromise."

"You are in a position to offer me nothing," huffed the lieutenant commander.

"Of course I am, silly man." She smiled, letting her teeth show. "I am in a position to offer you the chance to save your own career, and possibly claim a hero's welcome on your return to London. Far better that than the ignominy that awaits you should my mission fail on the rock of your intransigence."

He spoke through gritted teeth, barely moving his lips. "Madam, what would this vaunted compromise entail?"

She pitched her voice so it would carry clearly to the captain's ears. "Send two of your men aboard. One may seal the tubes and stand by in the torpedo bay to ensure nothing untoward takes place in British waters, and most especially the vital Suez that you are so rightly charged with maintaining. The other may remain topside in the conning tower while I and my executive officer Mr. Leung pilot this ship through the passage and into the Mediterranean. Dispatch whatever hulls you deem necessary to serve as escort, and to clear us at Port Said so that I am not forced to renew this ridiculous argument with Her Imperial Majesty's Mediterranean Fleet.

"During the transit, Cap— I and Mr. Leung will keep the majority of our crew on deck so that you may know we are not moving to arms or committing some other untoward sabotage. On reaching the open waters, we shall resume our normal operations, but your seals may remain upon our tubes."

Bork appeared almost impressed. "If you are telling the truth, perhaps all will shine as a result of this plan. If you are lying, then I will have admitted a grave threat into the heart of the empire."

"Lieutenant Commander Bork, have you ever heard of a Chinese warship commanded by an Englishwoman? Or indeed, any warship, anywhere, commanded by a woman? Spin whatever wild tales you will about me, but rest assured that I am not the mistress of some one-ship attack force from halfway around the Northern Earth bent on domination of the high seas."

"She has a point, sir," the laughing officer said from behind Bork's shoulder. He seemed in full command of himself now. "There might be truth and truth, but this doesn't stand or fall on an act of war."

"You'll be the Cairo squadron commander's problem if I let you through," Bork grumbled. "Passevoy always was half a fool, and I know which half. And I'm almost ready to believe you. You've a colonial accent, and a wretched Scotsman besides, for proof." He turned back to the man who'd just spoken. "Lieutenant Ericks, you will remain here as observer. Take one of the men from the launch to watch over the torpedo bay of this benighted ship."

Childress' heart leapt until the officer's next words. "In the meantime, I'll take your man al-Wazir off for consultations. He's such a highly placed fellow, I'm sure he won't mind tea with my captain." Bork's eyes bored into hers. "You shan't miss a one-handed petty officer, I can't think."

She opened her mouth, and closed it. *Think,* Childress told herself, *and quickly.* She'd already taken too long, lost the air of habitual assurance that she had so carefully cultivated.

"I shall require his services once we reach Port Said."

"I am certain Captain Yalow will not mind a little trip up the canal on escort." Now Bork was grinning. "This man is under oath to the Crown. We'll hold a hearing, work through the details of his service to Admiralty behind closed doors. Chief, you will come to me."

Childress could feel al-Wazir's eyes boring into her shoulder. Leung's gaze would be heavy and angry from above. What could she do but say yes? Any other answer doomed the ship.

"Chief al-Wazir, I shall expect you in Port Said," she said crisply.

Lieutenant Commander Bork returned to his launch with a satisfied smirk, now that the exchange of hostages had been negotiated. Lieutenant Ericks approached Childress. "I'll have Seaman Spradley with me, madam. Sir. Ma'am." He seemed briefly lost in the honorifics.

"Mr. Leung will show you to your duty stations," she said absently. Her stare was fixed on the wild red hair of the man even now being taken away. What had she just sold him into? How would he resolve the divide between loyalty to his oath and the very informal but real alliance formed here aboard the submarine?

One wrong answer from al-Wazir and Bork would have *Five Lucky Winds* at the bottom without a trace.

She sighed, and turned to face the wrath of the submarine's real captain.

KITCHENS

Battle was joined in a rattle of rifle fire and the bark of the stern chasers. Obsolete weapons anywhere but in the air, he knew. Old habits died hard up here, and a good, solid bit of shelled shot was just the ticket for the predominantly wooden airships of both empires.

For these damnable winged savages, a Maxim gun would have been far more to the point, but they were quite difficult to keep cooled in aerial applications.

He crouched next to Tremblay, the old sailor at the helm, aware that at any moment the Chinese airships with their battle lanterns hung out could open up with their weapons. *Two*, both comparable to *Notus'* class. Barring a miracle, *Erinyes* was done for, even without the killer angels.

McCurdy's successor chivvied his men urgently, lining them up on the rail in firing parties while simultaneously shouting belowdecks. Boaz walked among them, giving orders.

The winged savages made several bloodless passes, just for the sake of terror, Kitchens realized. They certainly had that effect on *him*. A few lines parted at the flick of a blade, while the beat of their wings could be heard even over the drone of *Erinyes'* engines.

Altitude. She was smaller and lighter than her pursuers. He had no illusions about this little airship outflying the savages, but perhaps the Chinese threat could be reduced. Kitchens studied the telegraph, then rang for nose-up, dump all ballast.

She lurched with a thunderous whoosh as the tanks along the keel were opened. The deck jumped, the masts and stays groaning violently. Many of the defenders were thrown down with violent shouts. Kitchens only kept his feet by clinging to the telegraph's brass capstan.

"Usually they whistles that one around first," the helmsman groused.

"Keep us up and circling away from the Chinese," Kitchens snapped. "There's no time for niceties."

The sudden maneuver had done nothing to discourage the winged savages, but the airship was now visibly higher than the Chinese pursuers. The two airships were like dragons cruising the moonlit night, lazing after the desperate swallow that was *Erinyes*.

They'd circled far enough into their climb that the starboard battery could fire on the enemy. A ragged cheer went up from that rail, though Kitchens could not see what they celebrated—no sparks fountained, no flames erupted, and neither of the pursuing vessels staggered in their courses.

Then the winged savages came aboard in earnest.

Boaz was everywhere on the deck at once, laying to with a boathook. Sailors in their panic fired indiscriminately, both over the rail and across the deck to the mortal danger of their fellows. A dozen of the attackers pushed from the fore. Kitchens realized that he was unarmed, at least for this sort of work. If they'd come over the aft rail he'd already be dead.

He grabbed up a loose carbine with a fixed bayonet, dropped by whomever had also bled copiously on the oaken boards. Kitchens retreated back to the wheel only to discover Tremblay missing his head and one arm, while the helm spun free.

He grabbed at it once, twice, his blood-slicked hand stinging from the impact, before taking control.

Oh, Lord, heed a longtime apostate and show me Your mercy now. Kitchens brought the wheel back closer to true, to avoid bogging into a turn so tight *Erinyes* would waste all her momentum. He had no way to read the wind, no means to track the sky, so he steered away from the Wall. One way or the other they would all be dead soon.

Then the Chinese began to fire upon them. The dragons were gaining on the swallow, while killer angels bled her dry.

He willed them to more speed, to more altitude, wondering if airships slain in battle flew to a cloudless heaven of their own.

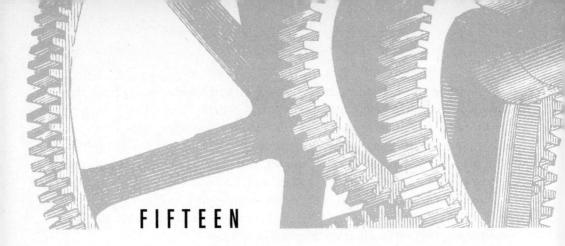

FIFTEEN

Then we which are alive and remain shall be caught up together with them in the clouds, to meet the Lord in the air.　　　　　　　　　　　　　　　*—I Thessalonians 4:17*

BOAZ

When the airship jumped up, his boathook swung wildly and tore into a sailor's jacket. Another three inches and he would have killed the man.

::*we will make a fort of the clouds and slay even the rain with our spears of lightning*::

Many fell cursing. Winged savages were over the rail in force now. They were stupidly fearless. They were also tough enough to take a bullet in the chest and continue their attack, where any monkey man would have either decently expired or at least moaned out his pain.

A seven-foot length of ironshod oak, on the other hand, these flying horrors definitely respected.

::*so he shewed them their own lights upon a stick, and their ambassador agreed that another path should be found*::

Shove.

Crack.

Tear.

Smash.

Yank.

Battle was full of short, sharp words, often repeated, never resolved, one death after another until eventually everyone fell.

He'd slain his own brothers, other selves of his self, defending Ottweill's stockade, and now he'd slay the armies of Ophir to fight for another few minutes of life before Chinese shot claimed them all.

A winged savaged loomed large, mouth bloody with someone's scalp. Boaz fed it the iron end of the hook for a chaser; then his implement jammed on a prominence of the jaw. The Brass cursed, pushed forward, and shoved both the flier and his own weapon overboard together. He turned swiftly to see what other wild-eyed madness was afoot.

::*then the Lord sent an angel with an inkhorn, and seven more of His host with swords of jet and chalcedony*::

"Get out of my head!" Boaz shouted as he slapped away a bronze sword in midswing.

The fight was tumbling rough. The winged savages were not going directly for the kill, but rather worrying at their prey. That the Chinese continued their pursuit was only a bitter lagniappe.

Boaz experienced a moment's respite as the attackers swirled away to regain their momentum. *Erinyes'* pitifully small complement of cannon spoke from the ship's waist, but they were little threat to the flying killers. He looked up at the gasbag and wondered when they would simply start slitting the cells. A few deft slices and a bit of flame would put paid to everyone's ambition.

::*flew he acrost the walls of the Garden with poison in his mouth*::

"I don't have any poison." The Brass man braced himself for the next wave of screaming flesh and flashing eyes and bloody blades. They were all too happy to oblige.

Sometime later—minutes or hours, he could not say—quiet prevailed upon *Erinyes*. Smoke eddied from belowdecks, but no one seemed alarmed at the prospect of fire, so Boaz reasoned it was from the cannon. The survivors were ragged, bloody, wild-eyed. The airship's engines shrilled. They ran so hot and hard he feared damage, but Kitchens had held the helm and was pushing them farther away from both the Wall and the pursuing Chinese.

::*the King sent four men down from the mountains of spring to treat with the devils and their strange boats*::

"You are a painful burden, my ancient friend," he gasped.

It is not so unlike us, said the Paolina–al-Wazir voice inside him, audible now that the noise of battle had died.

With that thought, a round of Chinese cannonfire battered *Erinyes*, and they were back at war. How long had he rested? Thirty seconds, possibly a minute.

Boaz leapt to the poop in three bounds to stare aft, where the larger airships were gaining.

All people hear the voices in their heads. They just understand them as thoughts.

::*the Lord is in all our thoughts, and His deeds cannot be disavowed*::

"'Tis the hydrogen," gasped the surviving petty officer, joining Boaz, Kitchens and the helmsman. It was the first time he'd spoken to Kitchens. Two other sailors readied the stern chasers—a pair of almost comically tiny breech-loading cannon. "We have lost too much, and the tension is out of the bag. We lift slowly, and we wallow."

"What can be cut loose?" Boaz asked.

: : *all may be cast aside when the Holy Fire comes, save that the Temple itself be ringed by twice ten men blessed with wine and oil*: :

Kitchens shouted for rifles aft as a rocket blazed from their pursuers and churned through the air. Everyone on the poop watched in fascination. The missile passed just beneath the hull.

"A little higher and we'd have been a ball of flame," the sullen petty officer said. "We are done for."

"Your name, man!" the clerk demanded.

"Martins, sir." He was breathing hard.

"This is your ship, Mr. Martins. I have just been minding it for you. I know nothing of aerial tactics." Kitchens' voice dropped to a growl. "What do we *do*?"

"Savages ho," shouted a tired sailor, and they were back at the fight without any response to Kitchens' question.

What we do, Boaz thought, *is what all life does. We struggle until we die.*

: : *death is but a hallway in the house of God*: :

That had been one of the Seal's more sensible observations.

They fought more. Night, moonlight, blood black as oil on the wooden deck, the Chinese ships following with the patience of sharks. Their battle lanterns were an uncertain constellation, always in the corner of Boaz' eye, always reminding him of where the Wall lay.

He fought. He killed. Men dropped around him from the blows of crude bronze swords, from the swipes of claws and teeth, from sheer fatigue.

They were *losing*. Kitchens continued to shout from the poop, screaming orders, curses, random nonsense. A sailor who had taken a clawed kick to the gut leaned against the mainmast trying to keep something long and damp clutched within his body.

Boaz was once more very glad he could not smell.

He would die with *Erinyes*. They were much too far above the ground for him to survive the fall, as he had done so long ago when traveling with al-Wazir. "Chief, I have failed you," Boaz whispered. "You as well, Paolina. Most of all."

There she was. Paolina stared at him in wide-eyed wonder for just a moment before the air beneath her feet claimed her and she fell screaming into the African night. Someone else tumbled with her. A flight of winged savages peeled away to follow them down.

Boaz nearly leapt over the rail to save his lady love, but Kitchens was shouting again about the Chinese and a respite from the deck fighting and there was still more battle to be joined, and still he prepared to dive overboard, hoping to think of something deeply clever to do as he plunged thousands of feet to the jungles below.

WANG

Good Change steamed slowly through the Bab el Mandeb waterway. The Royal Navy apparently were far too excited about their submarine to bother with a motor yacht. That huge British warship shepherded *Five Lucky Winds* from the Gulf of Aden into the Red Sea, and then north toward Suez. All they could do was trail along.

"You have lost her, I think," Wu told him. "You will soon lose us. We have no charts beyond the Gulf of Aden."

"How hard can it be to follow another ship?"

"Not difficult here. If Childress somehow talks them into the Mediterranean, well . . . Do you fancy seeing how well *Good Change* can slide beneath the waves and pursue them underwater? In any case, without charts of the bars and reefs and rocks, we will soon be done for."

"I am not interested in returning," Wang said shortly. He didn't look forward to the fate in store for him. Being under British guns seemed less terrible.

Where *was* she bound?

He watched the shore slide by on each side. Rocks tumbled down from the plains of sand that rose to both east and west here. This place was a dry ocean bottom, as if the water had drained away except for the trickle of the Red Sea. A man could lose his soul staring at those expanses of dun and ochre and rippled brown.

Wang realized that much to his surprise he missed Chersonesus Aurea. The green intensity of the island had always seemed overwhelming to him, maniacal even. The endless hooting of the birds, the nodding of the trees, the sweet heaviness of the flowers: It had been so much more like his home of Chiang Hsi than this desert-on-the-ocean ever could be.

The sun was pitiless, like a shovel opening a grave. On the islands there had been shade and fruit and occasionally cool water. When the light in the sky grew too much like a fiery lamp, one could go to ground.

Even the flooded library, with its stinking well of lost knowledge, was better than this boat. He could either stay below and bake in a stuffy cabin, or he could remain on deck to be broiled by the sun.

At least up top Wang could keep an eye on his quarry. *Five Lucky Winds* remained occasionally visible despite the huge ship in the way.

Even stranger, he realized he missed the monk.

"I am going to go sleep," said Wu, jarring Wang from his reverie. "Nothing will change for several days, at this speed."

The cataloger scratched at a pool of sweat on his back, beneath the rough white uniform they all now wore. "It is too hot to sleep."

"Hell is also warm, I hear."

They sailed on for two days and two nights. Wang ate little, and dozed on deck in the evenings, eschewing even the limited accommodations afforded to him. He was far more interested in whatever might be taking place ahead.

Which was nothing, so far as he could see.

They moved in a convoy, six ships in total. Two civilian freighters followed *Good Change* as they followed the British warship and her submarine charge. A smaller warship led the parade.

Twice British airships overflew, heading toward the war. Once a southbound convoy passed, a series of troop ships and escort vessels carrying what seemed to be thousands of soldiers.

They go to fight my emperor, Wang thought, but he could not summon outrage. Not when he traveled under a false flag. Waiting to be discovered as a spy seemed almost the least of his worries, but at the same time his most likely outcome.

He would find Childress; he would find the words to call her back to the east, to China and the Silent Order. In bringing her along, the net of warfare that had been cast across these oceans would be gathered, too, so that all could return to their rightful pursuits.

CHILDRESS

She walked to the foremost point of the grating, where the hull sloped away. Water rushed past, foaming and busy and gurgling to itself. Oceans by night were very different creatures, she realized. They reflected no burning sun, did not seem to birth storms so readily, and absorbed the effluvia of a million dreams from the cities along their coasts.

Something sharp tugged at her nostrils. Cigarette smoke? Leung allowed no tobacco aboard *Five Lucky Winds*, any more than he allowed opium or hemp. The fire danger alone was too great.

Childress turned, thinking to see Lao Mu with a cupped flame in his hands—the old man was a great trickster among the crew, she knew. Instead someone stood right behind her, jauntily smoking a small pipe.

"You—," Childress began in Chinese, then stopped. This was no sailor. A monk, in fact, of the Oriental tradition; in robes of color uncertain by moonlight. Bright, gleaming eyes peered at her from a grinning Asian face, beneath a head shaved bald.

A woman, she realized.

One she'd seen before, on Wang's yacht.

Finger to lips, the monk shook her head slightly. "Do not wake them," she whispered in English. "It is hard enough to keep myself unnoticed here without loud converse to attract their minds."

"Who *are* you?" Childress kept her voice low but urgent. All she need do was shout and sailors would leap to her aid. "What are you doing aboard my ship?"

"Your ship?" The monk seemed to find this a very amusing statement. "That would surprise Captain Leung."

Childress felt a twinge of guilt that she immediately dismissed. This monk was accomplished at the art of verbal sparring. She would not fall victim to rhetoric.

"It is certainly not *your* ship."

"No, but this is my journey." The monk tapped the ashes of her pipe overboard. Sparks flashed before vanishing into the waters of the Red Sea. "Every ship sails toward a multitude of destinies."

"Don't double-talk me. I toiled among theologians for forty years. I know better."

"Do you know that I am your friend?" the monk asked. "I have worked very hard to join you here."

The Mask reached out to touch the other woman's robes. They were dry, and soft. As opposed to, say, crusted with salt from the sea. She had not literally crawled out of the water and onto the deck, at least not in the past few hours.

"You have been with us for a while." *As you were before.*

A grin now. "I am always with you."

"No," Childress said, letting determination into her voice. "You most definitely are not."

"There are seventeen buttons on your black dress," the monk said, her voice hardening. "There should be eighteen, but one is missing, the third from the bottom. Captain Leung keeps a tintype of his parents and his sister in your cabin. The ship's wheel on the bridge is made of brass-bound teak from the forests of Siam, while the ship's wheel in the conning tower is polished steel that the captain has a man work over every day that you run upon the surface of the waters."

"Who *are* you?"

Another flash of a grin. "My name does not matter, even to me. But think you this: If the Silent Order and the *avebianco* pursue the interests of two factions of men in matters of importance to the Northern Earth, who is it that pursues the interests of the Earth itself?"

"God," she blurted.

"Your God is just your way of understanding the world," the monk said. "Can you point to him? I can point to the earth."

"More riddles." Childress looked up at the sweep of the sky. "There is far too—"

She stopped speaking when she realized the monk was no longer there. Nor was the other woman walking back across the deck among the sleeping sailors. Only a whiff of pipe smoke hung in the air, swiftly snatched away by the wind.

Childress went below. No point in raising an alarm. Still she bolted dogs on the hatch of her cabin, shutting herself firmly in for the night.

PAOLINA

She fell.

Air plucked at her with the hands of a mad thing. The night-dark ground spun below. Far below. Someone was screaming.

The screamer was using *her* voice.

That offended Paolina.

Above her, an airship receded. Gashansunu tumbled as well, but the sorceress was concentrating, not spending her energy in terror. Winged savages circled, plunged, following them down with mighty strokes through the air.

They will tear my throat out.

I shall strike the ground so hard there will be no bounce.

Fear will suck the air from my lungs and I will die on the way down.

Her left hand still clutched the stemwinder. The fingers of her right stroked the knurled stem. The body knew what the mind was too distracted to remember.

"Just because I am falling does not mean I am dead," she told the uncaring air. Talking took away the screaming.

Gashansunu opened her eyes and twisted in the fall, reaching for Paolina with an outstretched hand. Paolina released the stem and grasped for the sorceress. She had her calibration now, truly had not lost it before.

Even as they clasped together, hand to wrist and vice-versa, the winged savages caught up with them. Shadowed eyes gleamed. Bronze swords glittered by moonlight. Great leather sails on ribs of bone creaked.

She would die in three, two, one . . . and Paolina *stepped* on air, taking the sorceress with her even as the blades flashed.

A series of wet explosions echoed from below. Paolina and Gashansunu bounced up, slamming into the underside of something heavy and firm; then bounced down, slamming into wood that might as well have been rock.

Someone screamed. This time it was not her. A wooden beam slid past her face to knock a panicked sailor flat. This was followed by a moment of calm.

"What did you do to them?" shouted a man.

Boaz bent over her. His face was cast, impassive, immobile except for the flicker of the metal eyes, yet somehow she could read his concerned relief.

"Paolina." His voice stuttered and clicked a bit as it issued from the little grate within his pursed lips. The Brass had seen hard use.

Her heart flooded with light. She must have glowed from within, brightness leaking out of her pores like a bonfire deep inside a forest.

"Boaz."

"They are not all dead," said Gashansunu with a brutal practicality.

Paolina sat up. The deck was hard, and her body was a giant bruise. "Who is not all dead?"

The sorceress stood at the rail. Four sailors edged away from her with their rifles wavering. She ignored them as she looked down. "You transferred the force of your fall to most of those flying devils. A handful wing back toward us now."

"To the rail!" Boaz shouted, urging his crew into action.

Guns boomed in the night. For a moment, Paolina was glad, until she realized the firing had not come from this airship. Where *were* they?

She stood, staggering, and saw that two airships pursued. She recognized the battle lanterns and the shark shapes swimming through the moonlit air.

Chinese vessels, like *Shirley Cheese* she'd brought down on her voyage north aboard *Notus*. Like *Heaven's Deer*, which she'd destroyed over the Indian Ocean. Like the three whose crews she'd murdered off the coast of Sumatra.

"I will not kill them again," she muttered, mindful of the old doctor aboard *Heaven's Deer* who'd helped al-Wazir, of the sailors in *Five Lucky Winds'* complement who'd been so decent to her.

These were just men.

Boaz was at her side once more. Or had he ever left? "They will kill us," he told her. "As soon as they tire of this game and resume firing their rockets. Then we will die in a tumbling mass of flames, falling from this sky."

"I have done enough falling for one day." Paolina closed her eyes and thought on the matter of airships.

Her calm was a strange thing amid the surrounding violence. Though her heart rattled in her chest like a mongoose in an empty flour barrel, Paolina did not care.

With her eyes closed, the world was magnified. Every whiff of gunpowder and blood and splintered wood and fuel and the great, greasy scent of the gasbag seemed as a shout in a quiet cave. Likewise the noises of battle, the creaking of the hull, the popping from the hydrogen cells above, the individual screams and prayers and curses of the sailors.

Even the feel of the deck beneath her feet was different.

Our engines, she thought, and looked into their red-hot, pounding hearts. Too much heat—they would soon drive themselves to scrap. When they did this the airship would be nothing more than a thing of the wind.

She followed the engines' hot, pounding thread to find the similars poised in the air hundreds of yards to the south and east. Two pairs drove this airship's tormentors forward on wings of hydrogen.

Something roared nearby. Men panicked. The deck lurched. Still she stood with eyes closed, tweaking the stemwinder in her hand.

A dull thud. The deck lurched again, in a different way. A whimper for mercy, the answer a silence almost overwhelming in its indifference.

She reached into the first of the Chinese engines. Far simpler to starve its fuel, hastening the aging of the little vessels through which the spirits were drawn by fast mechanical pumps. A bubble in the wall, a breach, a spray—then the engine died hard and fast.

The remaining engine pulled the enemy airship into a tight curve. Paolina reached there and repeated her trick even as the men around her shouted out their luck.

In a moment, that airship was inert, sliding at an angle across the sky, an envelope of souls who had not been destroyed by her actions.

More racket, a series of booms, and she was nearly knocked to her knees. Without consideration she reached out to slow her own airship's

straining engines. That robbed distance between themselves and the remaining pursuer, but she was ready. This time she starved the enemy engines with a simple touch, slipping through them both so quickly that the
Chinese ship's acceleration died without slewing her about.

"Fire aboard the enemy, sir," someone shouted as Paolina opened her
eyes.

"Isn't that the general idea?" she asked, but then saw what the sailor
had meant by that. Across the gulf of air an engine blazed. The ruptured
spray of fuel had been ignited and now an entire nacelle was in flames.
The Chinese air sailors were growing smaller as her vessel gained distance
even on its reduced power. She watched them scramble, silhouettes against
the light of flames and moon, until they cut away their damaged engine
and *it* fell like a fitful orange comet toward the soil far below.

Then they were far enough away that the battle lanterns of the pursuit
were just lights in the sky. The winged savages had fled—or worse,
hidden—in the course of the battle.

"Welcome aboard Her Imperial Majesty's Ship *Erinyes*, Miss Barthes,"
said a man whose voice she didn't know.

Paolina opened up her eyes in the Shadow World, abandoning the
view of the Silent World to which she had been clinging, to see a man of
modest height and build. He wore the tattered remains of some dark, formal clothing now coated in a patina of grease, blood and dust.

"Where am I?" she demanded. "Who are you? Where is Boaz?"

She then sat down heavily, jarring the bruises of her body even harder,
and fell immediately asleep.

GASHANSUNU

The sorceress had not been so frightened since being sent into the Cave of
Sharks as a girl for her second passage. She had known then that she
might well die.

Tonight, falling through the sky like a stricken bird, she had known that
she would die. In Gashansunu's understanding of the Silent World, you
had to *be* someplace to *go* someplace. One did not simply step off of empty
air.

She had been falling, readying her soul for death while opening herself
to the possibility of a miracle. A miracle had come, but from the strangest of
quarters.

Now she watched Paolina slump on the deck as the Brass man and the
strange, dangerous, mad-eyed fellow in tattered black bent over her. Sailors
still kept an uneasy, armed distance from Gashansunu, but she had already

stolen the spirit of the spark from their weapons, and so they could harm her with nothing more than hard looks. Not that they knew that.

Yet.

The enemy airships had fallen behind. Gashansunu wondered who they had been. From what she'd learned in Hethor's village, the Northern Earth was divided between a few impossibly large cities that sent their power around the world on booted feet and soaring wings—unlike the Southern Earth, where the power stayed home and the few cities that existed took only what they needed from the lands around them.

She could easily count the cities in the extents of Africa—her city, of course, navel of the Shadow World; the Bone People and their small, strange empire on the desert coasts far to the south; the tiny men of the deep deserts who kept their magic in wooden sticks of lightning and spoke the elephant to his knees; the crystal mages on their table mountain at the southernmost tip of the land. More cities, as well, across the water of the girding ocean along the Shores of Ice and Fire.

Here there were two: England and China. Yet Gashansunu knew they were not mortal enemies, for Paolina had traveled with the man Ming. The girl had carried him across the Wall and sent him home in an open boat.

Now the girl had carried Gashansunu across the air, saving her from falling through a miracle that had shattered the backs of a dozen fliers. This was the thought that kept circling within the sorceress' mind, refusing to either take root or flee, until she snatched it with hands of silence. Paolina had pushed off the bodies of those winged savages to make her step.

How much of the girl's power lay in her gleam, Gashansunu wondered, and how much of it lay within her? Paolina was like no sorceress ever.

"Enough," she said, dismissing the thoughts. For now, she was alive against all sense and expectation. This airship was in distress, but it was not tumbling from the sky. Paolina was in distress, but she was not dying. Gashansunu walked to the bow, followed by shuffling sailors with their not-quite-aimed weapons, and watched the depths of night for the return of the fliers. Behind her, the Brass man and the madman revived the girl who had saved them all.

She stood for a long while. The deck had grown quiet except for the cries of the wounded. The engines rattled and coughed their distress, aided by the curses of the engineer-sailors. Africa slid by below, water on her left, land on her right. The sky was covered with wispy clouds that curtained the moon.

Gashansunu reached for her *wa*. It had been distressed by their passage of the Wall. She had not felt her other self since coming to this airship. Stretching out her mind, she called it to her.

Sister of my flesh, twin of my true self, silent self, return to me now.

Perhaps the falling had frightened her *wa* far away. It had nearly frightened her soul right out of her body. Gashansunu also knew that the *wa* was afraid of the Northern God. Finally, her people did not so often fly except on the strength of their power. The city built no airships or gliding kites.

Was her *wa* in truth a creature of stock and stone, becoming only a distant, uneasy spirit in the vaults of the air? That was not what she had been taught at Westfacing House. If true, it ran against much of city lore.

If untrue, then where was her w*a*?

Already she was lonely for her Silent companion. Gashansunu began to wonder if she should dread its fate. She already dreaded her own.

CHILDRESS

Five Lucky Winds slid into the harbor at Port Said. Her two escorts kept close, as if she were in danger of escaping. While Childress could readily face taking her hostages with her and setting them free later on, she feared mightily for al-Wazir. She would not slip the net now at the cost of leaving him behind.

A familiar boat broke from the back of the convoy, steaming for a set of docks populated mostly by yachts. She stared at it a long moment before realizing she saw Cataloger Wang once again.

What magic had he used to trail the British through Suez undetected? The same that had folded the monk away into thin air, perhaps.

Right now she wished she had some of that magic for her own.

"You will stand to along the naval pier," shouted Lieutenant Ericks, their British minder, from below. He pointed to six small white-hulled vessels anchored in a long row.

Childress turned to Leung, who nodded. "Captain," she whispered, "we are in the Mediterranean. Alive, well, unhurt. The cost for this was small."

They moved at quarter speed, then dead slow, until *Five Lucky Winds* had settled quietly into position underneath the British guns. Once the anchor dropped, Leung had his entire crew piped on deck for parade. Alone in the conning tower beneath the drooping flag of the two Earths, Childress understood this.

He wanted to be with his crew, waiting to see if their journey, and indeed their entire world, ended here.

Childress knew the feeling. By all the angels in Heaven, she would not leave here without al-Wazir. She wished for some hidden power, some secret prayer.

A whiff of pipe smoke from nowhere, acrid and hot, made Childress realize she might just have such a thing—secret power if not secret prayer.

Thank you, she thought, and almost heard laughter in return.

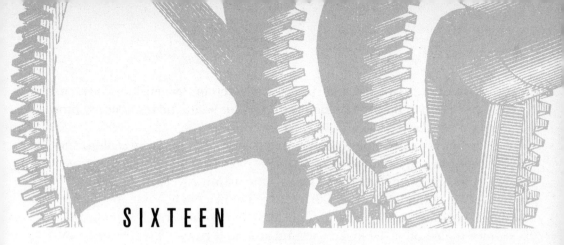

SIXTEEN

Thy borders are in the midst of the seas, thy builders have perfected thy beauty.

—*Ezekiel 27:4*

BOAZ

Paolina opened her eyes and coughed.

::*her beauty was as a dozen lambs newly freshened on the highest meadows of Mount Habba*::

"Hello," she said shyly. Her fingers brushed his hand, and he was lost.

"You live." Boaz was unaccountably pleased. The human voices inside his head purred. As for his gut, at least it seemed to be making sense.

"I live." She closed her eyes a moment.

He was losing her!

No, no, she was resting.

::*the maiden slept ninety nights and nine, and all the days between, on cloth-of-gold and cedar boughs*::

Hold her head up, boy.

The latter was al-Wazir, plainly as if he were speaking from a point just past Boaz' ear. The Brass lowered himself to a seated position on the deck and took her head in his lap.

People were shouting, Kitchens speaking urgently, the engines straining with an ugly rattle, the late-night air suddenly cold enough to lay condensation on him, but he held Paolina in the circle of his arms.

::*they bore her bridal-bright with yew poles beneath her sedan*::

She sighed. Her eyes were evening-dark, and full of stars. Or perhaps that was just the oil leaking into his.

"Those men want your attention." Paolina's hand closed on his.

Boaz looked up. Kitchens came into focus from somewhere very far away.

"That's the girl, isn't she?" the clerk demanded. "The one Sayeed lost in Strasbourg."

His vision sharpened, the springs and actuators within him coiling as for battle. "This is Miss Paolina Barthes of the Wall. She is under my protection, sir, and no subject of the British Crown."

::*a champion arose from the crowd, crude and loutish in the cast of his face but with shoulders to make a giant take pause*::

Kitchens laughed, almost a giggle—the man was very close to the edge of terror. "I should think, sir, that you might need to be under her protection. I require your aid, if you could leave her in the care of . . . of . . ." His voice trailed off as he looked around at a deck crowded with bloody, exhausted sailors.

"Call her companion over," Boaz said. The strange woman did not act as if she were a frustrated captor.

One of the sailors squatted next to him in the temporary absence of Kitchens. "You be taking us in to Cotonou, sir?"

"I am not your command—" The Brass stopped himself and thought for a moment. "What has Mr. Kitchens said?"

"His clerkship told us to wait for you to be done with the foreign chit."

::*struck them three and seven, then seven and three, until none of the water sellers could walk, or even cry for help*::

Boaz would have leapt from the deck and knocked the man cold, but for the fact that Paolina was still propped against him. He settled for words. "She is no foreigner, sir, for this is her land, and she is absolutely no chit. As you value yourself, address this woman with respect, for she saved us all."

That went without dispute, especially for anyone who'd seen Paolina plunge past the rail, then reappear moments later as so many of their attackers had tumbled broken-backed and shattered from the sky. All had noted her handling of the pursuing Chinese.

"Begging your pardon, your Brass-ship." The man screwed up his courage and tried again. "So is we going on to Cotonou?"

"Most certainly our voyage continues to Cotonou," Boaz snapped. If the airship could last that long. Damaged as she was, taking her back to the Wall was likely suicidal.

He had to consider Paolina.

::*you shall ring her with fine silks, and the flowers of the lower meadows, and the honey from four farms at each end of the land*::

Now you're getting it, laddie. Yes.

The sailor scuttled off to the poop to call out directions to the helm. Others organized the wounded and the dead. *Erinyes* was not large enough to have her own doctor, while the carpenter who served as chiurgeon had been killed in the attack, so the medicine was of the roughest sailor's sort.

Boaz could have done a better job.

"My dear," he said, trying the words in his mouth to see how they felt, to see if they landed flat and hard on the deck. "Have you skill in the setting of bones and the closing of wounds?"

She tried to sit up, but failed with a groan. Then the strange woman was close. Her face was strangely ornamented, adorned with white dots and tiny, eye-shaped shells. She spoke oddly flat English, as if she'd learned from a book with no one about to speak with. "I will watch over her. Her head is struck, I believe."

::*Jezebel! Temptress! Thou shalt not suffer*—::

"As for these men?" Boaz asked, ignoring the roar of the Sixth Seal.

Distaste flickered in her eyes. "Once I have seen to the girl, I shall see to their hurts."

"Let me go," Paolina told him. "For now. You must fly the ship with that madman in the ruined suit."

He stood, stiff and worn, to head for the poop. As Boaz mounted the short ladder, he turned. The foreign woman was just rising from Paolina's side, already looking at the gaggle of bloody, exhausted men gathering around her.

"We're hours out of Cotonou," Kitchens told him. "The crew is half dead, the gasbag is leaking, the engines are done for, and if we were set upon by a flock of sparrows, I do not think we could defend ourselves." He patted the helm that he now gripped tightly. "*Erinyes* is knackered."

"As well as everyone aboard her," Boaz said, feeling the pressure of monkeylike impatience. "What would you of me now?"

::*cut through the bindings which straiten you and make forward to the altar*::

"We must discuss command. I need you to seize this vessel, to save my freedom for larger concerns I am pursuing."

"Paolina is here now," Boaz said. "I will not have her arrested in Cotonou, nor anywhere else. Neither will I permit myself to be taken again."

There must have been an edge to his voice, because Kitchens gave him a troubled look. Even in the night shadows close beneath the gasbag the man was easy to read.

"No one is arresting you, John Brass. If I have my way, you shall be a hero from Cotonou to Cornwall. But they will most certainly arrest me if I arrive in command." Kitchens sounded horrified. "I am a *civilian*, after all."

::*him that taketh up no arms in time of war haveth no say in the making of peace*::

"I am an enemy."

"An enemy officer, commanding *Erinyes* under his parole!"

"Parole? To whom?"

"To *me*!"

Boaz was almost ready to allow the Sixth Seal to take control of his mouth. Let this madman argue with that. "You can return in control of *Erinyes* through my hand, but not your own? Your laws are mad, man. Simply mad."

Kitchens stood his ground. "You are an officer under arms. Better you lead the ship than I. I can give direction, but not orders."

"I am no officer," Boaz protested. "They will not take orders from me, this English crew."

The clerk leaned in close. "They already are."

: : *carrying the banner furled in bands of goat hide so they would heed his call but not his colors*: :

He was right, the Brass realized. So was the Seal, if it came to that. "You will swear this to me," he demanded of the Englishman. "That when we arrive there, Paolina and I will be free to go upon our way. We will not be taken in and chained by anyone, ever again."

"I cannot bind another man's honor," Kitchens said, "but I can bind my own. I pledge my place in the Special Section of Admiralty and my powers of persuasion to your cause."

So it goes, Boaz thought. Any commander serves at the will of his men. As long as he guided *Erinyes* to Cotonou and the British airship station there, Kitchens and this crew would follow him. If he turned away, south toward the Wall or east back toward the African interior, there would be more trouble.

Trouble from the deck, trouble from the winged savages, trouble from the Chinese.

: : *our fears rise within us like hunting birds on the wings of dawn, and their cries strike down across the meadows of our hearts*: :

The airship labored on through the remains of the night. Muttered consultation with the older sailors revealed that they should hail Cotonou sometime after dawn. Boaz had no idea what sort of presence the British might have there.

"It is a quiet base," Kitchens told him. "Reinforced since the loss of *Bassett*, to support a more forward fleet element along the Wall. We've neglected the West African station because there has been so little opposition here. In the past two years, Chinese incursions have grown far bolder. The Wall itself now fights us more vigorously as well."

"You will never prevail against the Wall," Boaz said quietly. "My own people built an empire for dozens of centuries, and could not control more than our small allotment. Rome could not do it; neither will Britain. The Wall is too great, too powerful, too much the barrier in the mind of the world to be overcome by a million men under arms, with all the airships of Heaven behind them."

:: *the angel came down to him on a chariot of fire, and spake in a voice carved from the thunderbolt*::

Kitchens chose his words with care. "It is not the Wall we fear. It is the Chinese. The Wall is a great, slow storm of stone straddling the two Earths, but it is just a thing. The Chinese seek to carve out the heart of the Empire and make us all bow down like savages."

Having known a few Chinese, briefly, Boaz considered this. "They would probably say the same of your English navies. You pursue one another about the world, looking to set fire to every ship in the air and every boat on the water. Who could have the right of such a thing?"

Kitchens made a small noise, somewhere between a sob and a laugh, then said, "I do not know, John Brass. I only know which sovereign to whom I am sworn."

"What of your queen?"

:: *she rules from a chariot of blood, riding dark miles over a land of emptiness*::

Kitchens looked about. Boaz had the wheel now, holding a course. No sailors were on the poop, only the two of them. "I must speak of something terrible," the clerk said. He seemed greatly shamed.

"What is your fear, man?"

"Our Queen is hostage to some dread combination of science and magic. She lies in Blenheim Palace, entombed in a cask of her own fluids, living in the dark while men make a pretense of heeding to her." Kitchens gulped air, a dry sob now. "She has asked me to . . . to . . ."

It *was* a dread, Boaz realized. Something well buried.

Inside him, al-Wazir stirred. The man's voice was deeper, softer, as if Paolina had left his head when she appeared, but a part of her had remained behind.

Do not prod him, laddie.

:: *they shall find their own souls within the fires of Baal*::

Which Boaz took to mean that the Seal agreed with al-Wazir.

"I must return to England," Kitchens announced, in control of himself once more. "Not just to seek aid for the tunneling project, but to return to

Her Imperial Majesty's side. I allowed my notions of duty to cloud the honorable truth."

Boaz watched the horizon a while. After an extended silence, he asked the next obvious question. "What will you do there?"

"What she asked me to."

Near dawn the foreign woman came to Boaz. He was surprised to have spent the night at the wheel without agitation over Paolina. A sense of progress, of the firmness of their reunion, had lent him peace even while she was resting.

: : *storms pass on over the sea, but still the flood remains behind* : :

"All is well," the woman said. "She slept long, and now looks into the problem of the engines with some of these . . . men."

Boaz glanced at the nacelles, but of course they were not out monkey-swinging over the gulf of air beneath *Erinyes'* keel.

"What about you?" he asked. "You are of the Wall."

"Of the Southern Earth," she corrected. "Gashansunu, a member of Westfacing House in the city."

"I am Boaz, a Brass of Ophir, along the Wall."

"Boaz, Brass of Ophir, I have followed this girl across the Wall to the waters of the distant east, then to here. In three days she has shown me more of the powers of this world and the other than I have seen in six decades of studying."

"Paolina has that strange talent of laying open the tightest-shut eye."

: : *she rides a steed out of Eden, bright white as the world's first sun* : :

"I would return soon," Gashansunu replied. "But my *wa* remains unsettled. I should allow this to heal before I once more stretch myself in the Silent World. Besides, I am curious as to the fate of the girl Paolina."

"Have you foreseen something?" A hard urgency leapt deep within Boaz.

"Only that." She pointed forward, just off the port side of the bow.

He looked a while, until he realized that a darker thread hung in the lightening sky of the last of night. Smoke, rising from a great fire on the ground.

Cotonou had been burned.

"The ship will not make the journey all the way back to England," Boaz said, almost to himself.

"She may not have to."

The battle lanterns of four more Chinese airships lit, one by one, bonfires to announce the coming of the enemy.

"Go and fetch Paolina now," Boaz said urgently. "Kitchens with her, if he can be wakened."

The ship's engines seemed louder, more strident, as if *Erinyes* knew that battle came to her one last time.

::dig the trenches before you fight, that the carriers of spears shall have a place to lay their bodies down::

You are in for it now, boy.

CHILDRESS

British tars working the decks of their idled ships stared at *Five Lucky Winds* with frank curiosity. A small crowd of mixed Egyptians and foreigners gathered along the base of the pier, where it met a public street. Clearly the submarine was the day's wonder.

The war, wherever else it raged, did not seem to have come to Port Said yet.

The morning grew so hot that even the seabirds retreated to crouch spread-winged along the verges of the pier, or simply huddled miserably in the glare. The city continued its bustle of noise and smell and squalor and plain, old-fashioned busyness.

All eyes were pointed at them. As were the Maxim turrets aboard *Inerrancy*. She wondered how those men felt, trapped in their little metal cages, aiming death at her unmoving crew.

At least Leung had caused the awning to be raised.

Bork arrived a few hours later, in the pounding noonday sun. He was piped aboard by an English bosun, from a flatboat filled with sailors in crisp, white uniforms with large sidearms.

Not quite a raiding party, but much more than a courtesy call.

She did not see al-Wazir among them.

The lieutenant commander appeared intensely pleased. Four of his sailors came with him, pistols depending prominently from their belts. "Mask Childress," he intoned with the righteous satisfaction of a beadle confronting a parishioner napping through the homily.

Something orange—no, saffron—flashed in the corner of her eye. Bork's flatboat issued a loud crack and began listing. Two of the sailors fell into the harbor, the other two struggling to clamber onto the sloping deck of the submarine.

Leung's crew began to laugh. Bork turned to his men, then lost his balance and fell.

That was a bizarre piece of slapstick, robbing the British officer of his dignity. Childress contained a smile as two of Bork's escorts helped him to his feet. The others fished their fellows out of the water, with assistance from the amused Chinese.

"Madam, if you somehow believe this moment to be accounted a victory," the lieutenant commander shouted, "then you shall indeed be sadly mistaken!" He spun to leave, then realized his error.

"A dramatic exit works much better, sir, when one has a usable egress," Childress said softly to his shaking back.

The crowd along the docks howled with laughter. The tars on the moored ships enjoyed their mirth as well, though they fell stiffly silent as Bork's gaze swept them.

"You will be hard pressed to explain to a promotion board how you allowed a woman and a pack of grinning Chinese to watch you swim to shore," she told him.

Bork growled, "You will kindly lend me a boat, madam."

"Of course." Childress turned to Captain Leung. "The launch for our guest, Mr. Leung. Also a crew to row it, lest our property be misplaced."

The monk would go ashore, she realized, much as the woman had come aboard—cloaked from observing eyes until she was ready to be seen. The Chinese would know better than to question such a one, should they glimpse a flash of her robe or a whiff of her smoke, while the British would never notice her.

Go, Childress thought. *Turn their commander's heart and fetch al-Wazir from his cell.*

The launch was winched up from beneath the deck grating and set into the water. "You will fare with my best blessings," Childress called out.

She hoped the monk's trick, whatever it was, would turn the business soon. They could hardly sit idle in this harbor, waiting for Wang and his fellows to come to some devilment, or worse, the war to catch them all.

Five Lucky Winds would fall victim to Chinese grenadoes just as readily, and likely with far more enthusiasm, than she would to the predations of the British.

The lieutenant commander and his party were rowed away in resentful order, taking their observers with them in the horribly overcrowded launch. The submarine was at last alone with her surviving crew. Except for al-Wazir, wherever he was.

As to whereabouts, *why* was Wang here? His purposes could not possibly be friendly to hers, yet Childress had not seen ill in the man's eyes in Panjim. At any rate, he would not approach the submarine while she was moored so close to the British. Not Wang, who didn't have nearly that kind of heat in his blood.

What an odd thing to think of a man.

KITCHENS

A man shouted in his ear. He'd dreamt of tumbledown shanties and a railroad that stretched around the world like barbed wire wrapping the skull of a martyr with rough rust and cold steel rain.

"Wha—"

The razor was in his hands, and a sailor stumbled backward with an expression of shocked panic.

A crisis was afoot, to be sure. Kitchens had not even gone below, just tucked himself behind an equipment locker on the foredeck. He knew nothing of *Erinyes* or the arrangements of her people.

Surely this was not an attack, for no guns fired, either in the hands of crew or from the turrets along the ship's waist.

He stood, rubbed his eyes and revised his opinion. Four Chinese airships loomed forward with glowing battle lanterns spread wide. A rising column of smoke testified to the state of the airship towers at Cotonou. A trap had been sprung.

The last sunrise he'd ever see blossomed in the east.

The girl! She could stop airships. She'd frightened Captain Sayeed silly with her strange powers before demonstrating them again right here on this deck.

Kitchens scrambled to the poop. The Brass man stood there, gripping the wheel as if it were his very existence. Martins, the surviving petty officer, was there along with two of the older sailors. Where the devil was that worthless midshipman? Longfellow? Longglory? This vessel was cursed by God, that much was certain.

"We will not live out the day," Kitchens announced flatly on reaching the helm. "Unless, friend Boaz, that girl you so delight in can work some magic against all our enemies at once."

"I do not think she likes that magic so much."

Kitchens bowed slightly. "Sir, I must inform you that my given word concerning your fate in Cotonou is almost certainly broken. We cannot fight four aerial cruisers together, even if the ship were in full trim."

"I am here." Paolina mounted the three steps from the deck closely followed by Gashansunu.

The clerk became painfully aware of the fact that almost half the effectives remaining to this stricken ship were crowding onto the poop. Between the wounded and the dead, they could not mount a decent firing party at either rail.

"Already there have been too many fights," Kitchens said. "We have not enough left to us. You I have seen fall through the air and return again as if strolling through an alder copse. Can you send *Erinyes* through some hidden path in much the same way? Or shall we wait here to be burned from the sky?"

"This pass is not my doing." Her voice was solid, though her face was pale and her body shook with fatigue. "You men piloted your ship into the gates of Hell, and now you wish to once again be pulled free by a woman." Paolina reached out and circled Gashansunu's arm with her own. She favored Boaz with a long, silent look. Then: "I could take my friends and step away from here, and never be troubled by the sight of your pyre."

No prison would ever hold this woman. Kitchens opened his mouth, seeking some words that might turn her heart.

Boaz spoke first. "You will not."

His words dropped like belaying pins. Some part of Kitchens noted that they were sailing uncaring into battle. They could slow; they could turn; they could delay the moment of inevitable reckoning in some form or fashion.

Or they could listen to two lovers argue until all were slain.

"No," Paolina said. Her voice was clear and hard. "I will not. Because that is what a *man* would do."

"And you are no man, my lady," Kitchens said, sliding back into the conversation. "Least of all a dead man."

"I—I do not think I can move this entire airship away."

"Stop the engines of those before us, as you did before," Martins said reluctantly.

"Why? They will only restart, and we could not escape a tired stork. We cannot sail close and snuff their lives with our mighty cannon. Furthermore"—she raised her hand—"I will not slay them. I have already killed far too many with my powers. This I will not do again."

"Then what?" snapped Kitchens.

"We land," she told them. "We land, and I find a way to help us escape on foot."

"No." Boaz' voice was flat. "We may do better than that. I have been aboard one of those airships before."

"As have I," muttered Paolina.

Boaz continued. "We shall take one of theirs, flee with a full gasbag and engines under all power. You can cripple the others for a short while. They will not make up the distance."

"Where then?" Kitchens demanded.

"Who cares!" screamed Martins. "Anywhere that does not require us falling to our death with skins afire will suit me." He took a huge, shuddering breath, then added, "Sir."

Kitchens nodded. "You have an excellent sense of priorities." He turned to Boaz and Paolina. "How precisely do you propose to undertake this misadventure?"

"I have a plan," she said slowly.

PAOLINA

She hadn't the least idea, but panic was edging into the exhausted faces around her. *Erinyes* and all her people would drown of fear before the Chinese could kill them. This was no time for indecision.

She most certainly did not intend to die with the dawn.

"Gashansunu, to the prow with me," she said. "The rest of you gather and arm such crew as can still stand and fight."

Paolina had no idea what they would do with any weapons, but that sort of thing always comforted men. The organization would give them purpose in the face of panic.

The sorceress followed her to the prow. "Go, now," the foreign woman said without preamble. "Leave these people to their fates. They are not yours, and you are not theirs."

"I will not depart without Boaz," Paolina said firmly. "And I will not condemn these men who have fought for our lives."

"You cannot move this airship; you said so yourself."

"I once called a submarine across hundreds of miles of ocean."

"What?"

"An underwater ship."

"How did you do this?"

Paolina almost screamed. "I don't *know*!"

"Even then," Gashansunu told her, "you had something to push against."

"Yes. I caused an earthquake that claimed many lives."

"You have nothing here to push against. We are in the air."

"I pushed against those horrid angels," she told the sorceress. "Their weight countervailed our rise. I could push against one of those airships."

"Without destroying the ship and crew?"

"I will not slay them. But for every action there is a precisely opposing reaction." Paolina turned that over. "Can I balance this passage by taking our crew there and moving their crew here?"

Gashansunu looked as if she were trying not to be impressed. "How would you *know*?"

"I can look at their ship. All life glows in the Silent World. How much else can there be in the middle of their air, in this world or the other?"

"Then look with my eyes," the sorceress told Paolina. The other woman proffered the braided silver. "Take my wrist and we will examine together."

"You will not step away with me?"

"You are right to mistrust," said Gashansunu. "But now is not a time for betrayal. Now is a time for swift action."

Together they slipped into the Silent World without ever leaving their few inches of deck.

The airships hung like flies trapped in ancient pine sap. Even in the Silent World, the spirit of their hydrogen flickered like a ghost within a ghost. Sparks swarmed below the belly of each fire.

Light and life in the middle of the atmosphere.

She looked behind her and counted the presences. Twenty-four remained alive on *Erinyes*—along with Boaz, who did not glow in the same fashion. She knew that the way she knew the length of her own hair, the shape of her own hand. Paolina stared once more across the airy gulf, trying to figure out how many Chinese there were. Could she so simply trade people from place to place, balancing the push of each translation like the numbers in a pretty piece of mathematics?

The world was never so clean and simple.

Or was it?

The principles of action were as basic to the universe as anything she knew of. God had designed the world to work clearly, cleanly, consistently. Apparent miracles like the stemwinder, or indeed the Silent World itself, were just a lack of sufficient understanding. That was so painfully obvious that she had always had difficulty comprehending why everyone else did not see it as such.

The Creator had endowed human beings with minds that they might think clearly about the wonders of His world, not so that they could cast aside reason just to prove some article of faith. Otherwise, what was the point of reason in the first place?

That argued for a world that was clean and simple, once you stripped away the shadows of faith and unreason and looked only at what was before you.

Before Paolina was a swarm of men bent on her destruction. Before her was the problem of setting one crew against another without slaughter or fire or plunging death.

If the *men* would let her.

Forty-seven souls on the airship she studied. Almost twice as many as remained aboard *Erinyes*.

But the balance of forces is physical, she realized. *Not spiritual.*

She patted the bow chasers. Small-bore cannon, on cradles with levers designed to level and aim them. They were recoilless to keep from interfering with the airship's course.

I shall bring the guns, she thought. *They will be toothless behind us.* Paolina turned to Gashansunu and tried to speak. Here in the Silent World her lips moved like a fish in water.

Paolina took them back into the Shadow World. The Chinese airships were closer, the men of *Erinyes* gathered for the last, exhausted fight. "Get everyone who yet lives onto the main deck," she said urgently. "Don't bother defending the ship. Have them all join hands or link arms, touching one line. I wish we had a silver cord, but rope will have to do." Bad enough she would have to account for all the men on the approaching vessel.

Gashansunu stepped aft while Paolina watched the impending battle. The east lightened. A few thousand feet below them, a beach gleamed, the ocean reflecting the last of night's stars. The interior was sullen mudflats and the textures of jungle, except for the scattering of fires that marked the remains of the British presence at Cotonou.

If she failed, if they fell or were struck down from the air, not much time would remain for repentance. Paolina wondered how many men she could step away with, as she had done on arriving. Could she break the backs and burst the hearts of some to save the rest?

Or would she only spirit away Boaz and Gashansunu?

It could not be much of a crime to murder someone who would be dead of falling moments later.

Oh, yes it could. Once again, she was thinking like a man. She hated that.

Paolina set to work with the stemwinder, finding the firefly-in-a-bottle glow of the men aboard the oncoming airship. This might be a kind of magic, but the principles of action would save them all.

It took far too long for Gashansunu to gather the men of *Erinyes*, even with Boaz and Kitchens chivvying them on. Tired as they were, staring at their approaching deaths, these men still knew how to stand and fight. They did not know how to cluster in a trusting circle.

Cannon boomed all too close before they were ready, but the shots went wild. She could hear the distant barking of orders after the first salvo. Boarding parties, or firing lines, or just the gunners re-laying their weapons.

Paolina gathered her chosen ship firmly in her mind, its people spread out along the waist and down inside the hull. Her people were close.

What would happen to them, so scattered? The ones too far from the center might simply plunge to the earth as she almost had.

Nothing to be done about it now. She would not take more lives, not with a purpose, but she was not yet ready to lay down her own either. This ship's company were not so much to her, but their loyal, fearful respect for Boaz was clear enough, and his for them unmistakable.

For the sake of everyone, she would take these Englishmen with her.

"We are ready." Gashansunu slipped her hand into the silver cord dangling from Paolina's right wrist. She had a loop of the rope wrapped around her free arm. Boaz was beside the sorceress, one hand on the rope as well. With the other he reached out to touch Paolina.

"You will save us all," he said quietly.

Her heart thrilled. He was here. They had no past, they likely had little future, but he was here now.

Paolina looked into the rising glow of morning and wished she'd known a better way. Praia Nova was never so difficult as this, was it?

Of course it was.

"Boaz," she said as she focused in on the effort that would take them all in a leap across the space between the ships. Too late to worry about how high the decks were or whether anyone would appear inside the unbreathable gases of the bag or whether the beam of the hull would be a problem.

"I love you." Her words were lost in another roar of cannonfire.

Then things changed.

WANG

He went ashore in Port Said with his story about serving a prince of Serendip close to his lips. Cataloger Wang soon realized that no one cared, not even the bored harbor master's clerk who'd pressed him for moorage fees.

None of the crew from *Good Change* came with him, of course. He did not believe Wu's tale about their being cursed from touching land, but *they* certainly seemed to.

Someone must buy the fruits and vegetables for the galley, seek a chandler for marine necessities, bargain for more fuel, listen to whatever street gossip an enemy foreigner might be able to pick up.

Port Said was a town of low, flat-roofed buildings that reminded him of Haikuo or one of the other sleepy ports of southern China, rather than the mad bustle of Canton or Singapore.

People here seemed to live on the streets. He wondered what they used the buildings for, given that every activity from cooking to vending to childbirth took place in public. The heat was different here, too: baked-rock solar violence unlike the drenched discomfort of Chersonesus Aurea. This place felt as if it never known a sea breeze.

Once again, Wang was tempted to just walk away. If he didn't return to *Good Change*, how would they fetch him back? By the time either the Silent Order or the Celestial Empire sent assassins, he would have moved on.

As before, he knew he would not jump the rail. Shen and Wu surely knew that as well, or they would not have sent him into the city.

He did the business of the ship, signed notes of payment for gold at the dockside—their scrip was dangerous here, very dangerous.

Once he'd finished marketing, Wang headed back for the docks. His goal was to get close to Childress and the submarine. Idlers there would be chewing over the rumors like back-alley mongrels.

Wang walked briskly. This was not a place to show himself overmuch, not so close to the British vessels, but he kept an eye on *Five Lucky Winds*. Sailors milled on the deck, and he thought he saw Childress among them.

He had to conclude that the Mask would prevail. She had gotten this far without being captured or sunk by the British.

"Psst."

Wang turned, against his better judgment, which was shrieking for him to walk on, *walk on, WALK ON.*

It was the monk!

"You must help me break them free." She spoke around the pipe dangling from her mouth.

"What!?"

Her hand snagged Wang before he could back away. "Come, now. We will go to their navy offices. You will pretend to be confused, and seeking aid. You have that same lie about the Indian prince, yes?"

"Well, yes," Wang began.

"Then use it."

Walking with the monk was an unusual experience. No one *noticed* her. Wang understood this at some level—he'd seen her do that trick before. Or more to the point, had *not* seen her.

The world didn't turn some strange hue; demons did not climb out of Hell; there were no colored smokes. She simply walked, and no one saw.

Arm clutched tightly in her grip, he followed in the same cloud of confusion.

Together they marched right past the marines guarding a two-story wooden building over which flew an oversized Union Jack.

The monk paused at the top, touched her lips for silence, then waited for the door to open. A group of suited English civilians came out. She slipped in, followed by Wang.

He supposed someone might notice if the door moved on its own, but he could scarcely credit that five sober men had filed past him at the distance of less than a foot, and noticed *nothing*.

Wang was desperate to ask the monk how she did this, but he already knew the sort of ridiculous answer she would give him.

Inside were polished wooden floors, high walls painted white, and electrick ceiling fans whicking slowly over rows of desks. The monk paused, closed her eyes for a moment, then threaded across the room. Wang hurried to keep up. If he fell out of her spell in *here*, that would be the end of him.

They passed within inches of diligent clerks, then ducked down a hallway to a door labeled "Chart Room." The monk moved as if she were born to this place, but Wang was beyond surprise.

She darted inside, necessarily dragging him along. The room was filled with large, flat-drawered filing cases. The monk swiftly rifled through them, searching for something specific, then pushed several sheaves of paper into Wang's hands. "Here, put these away," she said urgently, before stuffing more inside her own robes. "If you survive, you'll be glad you have them."

Moments later, they were back in the great hall, heading toward a little office of frosted glass. She stopped him just outside the partition and leaned very close to his ear.

"How fast can you run?" the monk whispered.

"Not very," he mouthed. Wang mimed a slap to his ample belly.

"Fear will move you." She spun a high kick and shattered the glass set into the door.

Everyone stared. Two dozen English clerks, an armed marine turning from near the front door, a man in a naval uniform springing up from behind his desk within the little office.

Run, her voice said somewhere inside his ear.

He sprinted as the shouting began, cursing as violently as his innocent childhood would allow.

GASHANSUNU

Her *wa* cried.

She had never considered that the denizens of the Silent World could grow lonely. They lived amid perfection of form, unchanging, blissful. Like the Northern concept of Heaven, an eternity of sameness in a state of grace.

Gashansunu had always thought that aspiration to be a special kind of madness, but she was not a Northerner. Nor was she a *wa*. Not in this life.

But her *wa* was, well, her.

And her *wa* cried.

I am here, Gashansunu told it.

YOU ARE LOST.

She could not see her *wa*, even as a trace of a presence. A gulf of air yawned beneath, the flat silence of the world far below, traceries of life sparking brighter as in the Shadow World daylight woke the jungles. The ocean surged, a sullen, glowing thing.

Gashansunu wondered why she was here, amid nothing.

I TRY TO BRING YOU BACK.

Imploring her, Gashansunu realized. *Here I am. Not gone from my head.*

Another cry, vacant tears from an eyeless face.

THE NORTH IS EMPTY.

THEIR IDEA OF GOD HAS SAPPED MY ILK FROM THE WORLD.

I AM BEING TAKEN UP.

Soon I will come back, Gashansunu promised her *wa*, as if it were a sobbing child.

SOON YOU WILL BE TOO LATE.

SOON YOU WILL BE LOST, CUT OFF, AS AN INFANT OR ONE OF THEM.

SOON I WILL BE NOTHING, AND YOU WILL NOT BE ABLE TO FIND YOUR WAY HOME.

She looked around. Paolina was nearby, in midstride, face set with determination and a strange grief.

A Chinese shell hung in the air. Though the metal was dead, and thus had little presence here in the Silent World, the energies of its discharge played around it. *Fire is a species of life,* she thought.

The airships were close. Their bags danced with light. A flurry of sparks fled the nearest one, that made Gashansunu think to turn and look at the ship they had left behind.

Twenty-two souls followed her and Paolina, clinging to the line like mussels to an anchor rope. Not enough time had passed for terror, or even a surge of their bodies, but in another moment mouths would be opening; then they would be on the Chinese deck.

Gashansunu belatedly realized where she was. She had sliced time between one heartbeat and the next, between one click of the Shadow World and the next. The Silent World did not have time, as such, but the minds of people who went there perceived it through the filter of time, just as their bodies did back in the Shadow World. Great power was required to step completely outside time and slice it open like a sacrificial slave.

I do not have this power, she thought. *I am no house priest.*

YOU ARE SWALLOWING MINE.

The sorceress finally realized that the distance of her *wa*'s voice was within her.

She could not conceive of what that meant. People sometimes lost their *wa*, or themselves, but no one she knew of had ever swallowed up their *wa*.

My poor soul, Gashansunu thought, then wondered why she had chosen that terrible, terrible word.

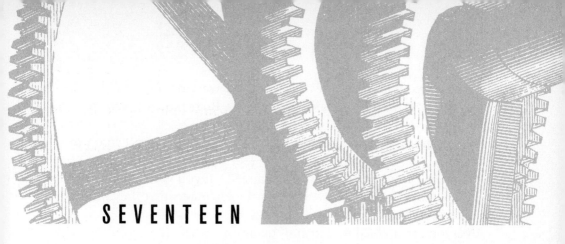

SEVENTEEN

And the second angel poured out his vial upon the sea; and it became as the blood of a dead man: and every living soul died in the sea.
—*Revelation 16:3*

BOAZ

He stepped heavily onto an alien deck. A knotted circle of men crowded around, gasping and stifling cries. Seven of *Erinyes'* cannon rolled loose.

Someone screamed out across the open air, their voice trailing away. A Chinese sailor who'd missed his footing.

:: *birds could soar no higher than the very angels of the Lord, yet here you have stood on the mountain with wings of wax and feathers upon your shoulders*::

Paolina, he thought, but survival came even before love. She and that sorceress were safer than any of them. Orders were needed, quickly. He spoke in a low, urgent voice.

"Quiet. These ships are similar enough to your own. Petty Officer Martins, take three men and find the engine control room amidships. Two from the gas division go up into the bag so you may see to learning the arrangements. The rest of you dump these loose cannon overboard. We will depart as swiftly and silently as we may."

"Someone should pull in the battle lanterns," Kitchens shouted as he loped away.

Another salvo of fire came from one of their sister ships. *Erinyes* bucked and splintered, a brief flame jetting from her hull. Already the men over there were yelling.

Boaz wished them the luck of it.

:: *one by one their robes were torn back, to shew each a man with his sword beneath his woman's cloak, and the deception was brake*::

He twisted the wheel hard to port. Levine, an old sailor from *Erinyes*, had followed him onto the command deck. "Here," the Brass said. "Figure how to call for more altitude. We must gain before they are on to our ruse."

Their airship turned away from the attack. Paolina had chosen the northmost vessel in the Chinese line, so they were not forced to cross the bows of their erstwhile enemies. *Small favors,* Boaz thought, *from the hand of the Divine.*

The sailor looked at the controls in bafflement. "Ain't like our'n, guvner."

"I know nothing of it, either," he snapped. "If you need to, run smartly and carry word to the gas division and the engineers that they must sort this out right away."

Everyone scrambled in a rush of panic and relief. They would survive another few minutes, and maybe beyond the day with both luck and skill.

::*watch the last horseman, for if he is taken, you will all be ate one by one, each by each*::

"I understand." Boaz raised his voice. "Two men here for a stern watch, quickly."

Kitchens popped up from a hatch in the deck and looked him in the eye. "Will we live, John Brass?"

"For now."

The Paolina–al-Wazir voice surfaced again. *And well done, laddie, well done.*

I did nothing, he thought, but did not say.

"Something's gone over the side of *Erinyes.* Looks like a strip of bag fabric. They're making a signal."

"Number two Chinee is swung toward us."

"Flames on our ship! Erm, their ship! *Erinyes,* sir!"

"Number three Chinee is standing to our'n."

"Number four is heading our way."

::*the false riders were diverted away by cunning, and so the trapper trapped*::

"The hoax is done," Paolina said. "It bought us several minutes' head start and a faster airship."

"Yes," Kitchens replied, "and we sail toward the heart of the Empire cloaked in the enemy's colors."

Boaz realized that his desire to reach Ophir had guttered out in Paolina's presence. He hadn't even noticed the death of that ambition. Just having her close to hand was sufficient. But to sail to England . . .

"We must alight, Mr. Kitchens," he said. "Neither Paolina nor I have any wish to approach London."

"I—" The clerk stopped, looked about. "You men, clear the deck a moment. I shall keep the stern watch a bit, but I must speak in confidence to John Brass and this sorceress."

The two men on the stern watch exchanged a glance, then scuttled forward. From the shouts, Petty Officer Martins was trying to organize a firing party with unfamiliar Chinese weapons.

Kitchens stared aft, avoiding both Boaz and Paolina. "Our defense is in speed and wit, not force of arms."

:: *the storm that crosses the desert spares no man, claiming the virtuous and the wicked alike*::

"That is your defense, sir," the Brass said. "Not ours."

"I will not go to London," Paolina stated flatly.

A sad, tired tension filled Kitchens' voice. "For my part, I apologize." He glanced at them, then returned to his study of the pursuit. "The fate of my country rests on what happens next. I can compel you to nothing, but I beg you to help see me safe to England."

"What is this fate?" asked Paolina.

:: *and a darkness rose over the plains of Absalom, while in her heart writhed the pain of two loves twined like snakes*::

Kitchens seemed to shiver as he glanced at the pursuing airships. "We are a nation at the edge."

Boaz marshaled his thoughts. "What, sir, is the edge on which the largest empire in history now abides?"

"The edge of madness." The clerk's voice dropped to a whisper. "I fear the Empire will fall."

:: *the flames of the furnace polished his bones, until on the third day the prophet rose up, gathered himself from the ashes and walked through the iron door to once more confront the king*::

"All empires fall." Boaz tried to think what the Sixth Seal had meant with those words.

"Maybe this is England's turn," Kitchens replied. "But there is already war to drag down the world with her. Look at the deck on which we stand right now. A month ago, this would have been beyond conception."

"It is my doing." Paolina's voice was bleak. "I carried the gleam into your empire. The Chinese pursued me to Mogadishu, where they snatched me away from Boaz, carrying poor al-Wazir with them. That was the opening salvo in this war. Because of me, and my stemwinder. If I had not come, they would not be fighting now."

:: *a maiden rode the shoulders of a cold wind, ice streaming from her hair, while death carried himself in her van*::

"Regardless, there is war today," Kitchens said, obviously impatient with the argument. "It pursues us at this moment; it spreads across Africa and the Wall. India must already be a battleground. A war that will take the lives of tens of thousands, and ruin millions more."

:: *as you travel among the distant forests, so the concerns of the forest dwellers become your own, for all that your heart abides among the sheep and their meadows*::

"This war is not my concern," Boaz told the clerk. "The Wall will not burn. It is of the Lord, and too large for your armies to encompass."

"Perhaps you are correct, sir. But that is not enough for me. This cancer grows at the heart of England. I have been charged with cutting it away. If I can do so, Government will change, and we will have cause to stop the fighting without seeming weak."

That gave Boaz long pause. Paolina gripped him more tightly. Their gaze met, though he could not read her eyes.

"Whom will you kill?" she asked.

"I will kill no one," the clerk replied almost absently. "But I would help a beloved woman finish dying."

:: *when you heed the counsel of women, and leave the priests idle in the dusty rooms of their temple, you will find a different nation at your feet*::

"The enemy is gaining," Boaz reported. "We are nearly at risk, if they are willing to fire on one of their own airships."

Paolina stared at him. "This is not their airship anymore."

WANG

Pursued by shouting men, he burst into another hallway. This was crowded with boxes, crates and a cluster of mops and brooms.

No time to choose. He ran right. Bellowing close by. A bell began shrilling *alarm, alarm, intruder, intruder.*

Double doors ahead. A place to bring in goods and equipment.

He raced into a marshaling yard. Wagons, a steam tractor with a flat trailer behind it. Surprised men, mostly Arabs but a few large-boned Britons.

"Fire!" Wang screamed without breaking stride. "Inside! Raise the alarm!"

He'd never run so fast in his life.

The crack of a bullet told him that being outside had been a poor choice. Nothing struck him down, while a babble of Arab voices rose louder and louder.

The outer gates of the yard stood open. The street beyond invited him. Already the people and traffic there swirled to focus on the happenings within.

"My pardons," shouted Wang. "Make way for the injured!"

Another bullet snapped overhead. The gathering crowd melted as fast as it had coalesced. He melted with it, the shouts of "Oi, you, 'alt," lost among the chaos.

Don't push, Wang thought. *Be one of them.*

He knew he was an idiot. There wasn't another Chinese man on this street. Everyone would mark him for a foreigner.

Yet a dozen styles of dress pressed around him, clothing skin colored from almost midnight black through nut brown to pale white. He was different, but not alone in his difference.

The alarm still shrilled behind him, fading with distance. Angry British shouts echoed, but few in this crowd would turn a hand to aid their masters.

This place was like Singapore, he realized. Whoever ruled held the power, but the people were their own and majestically indifferent. He would never see such a thing in the heart of China.

Wang's chest ached awfully. A stitch in his gut felt like he'd been knifed. His legs shivered, elastic and vague.

He slowed to a walk. Either he would reach the boat or he would not. Meanwhile, the monk had been doing . . . what?

Sometimes, Wang wished he had told the Kô to do his Imperial worst. Instead of chasing two magically impossible women halfway around the Northern Earth under the threat of his own death, he could be in his not-so-comfortable office, drinking bad tea and piecing through ancient documents so rotten they made his eyes burn.

He smiled as he passed through the dusty streets amid the donkey shit and the spilled fruit and the press of foreigners.

GASHANSUNU

She continued unmoored in time, even in the Shadow World. The new airship seemed little different than the old, but the men were strange. Here one moment, over there the next, then gone. Likewise the sun stuttering as it crested the horizon.

I am Westfacing, she thought. *That is east.* Unless the Northern Earth was so turned around even the compass stood untrue.

A magenta sliver jumped to an orange crescent between one moment and the next.

Worse, the voice of her *wa* had faded completely. She felt different, as if a hand had been sliced from her body. The sense in her head of always knowing gaped.

Yet something had been traded for that. She had gained. A fair trade?

A man looked closely at her a moment, opened his mouth to speak, but his voice was like distant thunder trapped in a cave. Just an echo, an echo, an echo.

Is this madness? Has some wall inside my head burst open?

Her *wa* did not answer.

Gashansunu tried to reach into the Silent World, to mark her place there. If she could, she would step home now, walking with the stride of leagues as Paolina had shown her.

To her horror, the Silent World would not open for her. That had not happened since her first bleeding!

"Where?" Gashansunu cried out in her own language, but no one on this side of the Wall would know the words, would hear the loss in them.

The city had abandoned her. She was already dead. She was become a *wa*, unknowing and unknown. She had lost the connection between her two selves, between Shadow and Silence.

The sorceress wept until a grubby little man brought her a cup of water and awkwardly patted her arm. He stood inside time with her a while, which comforted Gashansunu. Eventually she realized she heard the rage of voices in full quarrel.

Paolina, her Brass, and that strange, dark-suited madman who seemed to issue orders without authority.

She checked for her *wa* one more time, realized that she was indeed lost, and went to see what she could make of this bit of afterlife that remained to her.

PAOLINA

Two airships gave chase. The third tended to *Erinyes*.

She was so tired of being at the wrong end of someone else's gun sight. The Northern Earth was nothing but bullying, warfare and mad grabs for power. She'd found Boaz, finally, but instead of stepping away together they seemed trapped ever deeper inside this English war.

She wanted to go home. Wherever that was.

"Before you ask," Paolina announced, "I will not strike them down for you. I will not kill and kill again."

"You didn't strike down the last lot." Kitchens' voice was drawn tight. "You deterred them so we could flee."

"We fled into more enemies, despite your promises. I played my little tricks again." She felt something boiling up inside her. "When do I stop running? Is every hour of every day going to be another call for me to rescue more and more? *I am not here to be your guardian angel!*"

"Paolina—," Boaz began.

But she whirled on him, still shouting. "Let me find my way!"

Kitchens visibly gathered himself. "You claim to desire stability. In that case, help me do what I must. Then Government will be too distracted to prosecute this war in the East. Afterward, the Wall can go back to the Brass and their like, China can return to her own affairs, and Mother England may rethink her purposes."

She opened her mouth once, twice, then forced words out around the bitter laughter that threatened. "So all I need do is get you home, help you murder a queen, escape the retribution of your entire empire, await the progress of negotiations at half the distance around the Northern Earth, and *then* all will be well? You must think me a terrible fool, Mr. Kitchens."

"Not to put too fine a point on it, Miss Barthes, but yes, that is all you need do." Unshed tears glittered bright and savage in his gaze. "I have no better answer, except to let the servants of both empires continue about their killing ways. If you are going to magic yourself away, this would be an auspicious time."

She looked to Boaz, who still clutched the helm. He shook his head slightly before saying, "I will follow wherever you lead. But for my own part, I would not abandon these men and their purposes. Mr. Kitchens offers more hope than any other path I can see."

Paolina felt as if her heart would crack. "You will not come if I step away?"

"No, I will come." If Boaz were human, his smile would be lopsided and melting; she heard that in his voice. "I will come though I know it to be wrong, because what else can I do but follow you?"

Gashansunu touched Paolina's elbow, startling her. "There is no path behind us. I will follow you much as the Brass will, but set your direction well."

Paolina wanted peace, harmony and a good set of tools. Not a creaking deck and the boom of none-too-distant cannon, and the ever-changing word of a man little better than the *fidalgos* of Praia Nova who had so plagued her childhood.

Kitchens wouldn't look at her. "The helm, if you please, sir," he said to Boaz.

The Brass braced against the rising crosswind until the clerk had a good grip.

"Stern watch!" Kitchens bellowed. "Someone tell me where we stand on weapons. We're fighting for it again, boys, this one last time."

The few crew still on deck simply groaned. Someone began handing firearms up through a hatch. Paolina stood by the rail with Boaz and Gashansunu. The Brass had a weary set to his shoulders, as if even the metal of his body were sinking into fatigue. The sorceress appeared very troubled.

They could have their damned silly war. Once she was safely on the Wall, Paolina was never coming back. The two empires might battle one another to their proverbial knees and it would mean nothing to her. *Nothing.*

Try as she could to hold on to that anger, the surge kept slipping away. Would she condemn Ming and ten thousand of his fellow sailors to watery graves? She'd already slain half a fleet, off the coast of Sumatra. That they would go on slaying each other without her was no excuse.

Not when she had a chance to stop this war.

"I would leave with you," she said to Boaz. "To a place where we might find calm, and consider the times to come. I am afraid we will not find that place."

"No one will find that place," Gashansunu said. "It is lost."

Boaz answered them both. "We will. In time. Right now, I owe these men their lives. Mr. Kitchens has convinced me of the worth of his purpose."

"I cannot say if he is right or wrong." Paolina examined her conscience carefully before she chose her next words. She was letting go of something she barely understood: freedom, companionship, her life lived her way. "I can only know that the price of walking away is higher even than the price of staying. If we can stop a war with his mad idea to behead a government, then we will stop a war. But . . ." She looked at them both. "I *will* comprehend what storm it is we sail into. In every detail that clerk can squeeze out of himself."

Paolina drew the stemwinder from its pouch and stared down the Chinese airships sailing after them. She had disabled the last two such that pursued them, and caused a fire in the process. Now that she had moved men just as she'd once moved *Five Lucky Winds*, she wondered if she might more profitably remove the crews from their ships and let the altitude take the vessels.

Otherwise the men would simply effect repairs and continue their war.

Paolina focused in on the pursuing airships, finding their images in the Silent World. The gasbags glowed with the restless energy of the hydrogen within. The motes of souls swarmed below aboard both vessels, men at their oh-so-serious business of pursuit and destruction. Very briefly she was tempted to send them all to Praia Nova. Let the *doms* with their precious male wisdom deal with almost a hundred angry Chinese sailors.

But she could not do that. Such a gesture was too cruel, and the cost to the women of Praia Nova would be unbearable.

Ming would be disappointed besides. All those men over there were versions of him, just as all these men here were versions of al-Wazir. Similars, brothers, reflections.

Real to her. In a way that she had never been real to the *doms*.

Sumatra it was.

She could visualize that fatal stretch of shoreline very well indeed. The boat had been about half a mile offshore. Sufficiently close for these men to swim if she put them in that exact spot, though the beach would be safer.

Had she seen enough of the beach?

Paolina set the fourth hand to the rhythms of the first airship. That one closed slightly faster than its fellow. The men swarmed, each golden light, each heartbeat, each soul and mind.

They will know I am here, she thought. But they already did. Everyone seemed to. Even Gashansunu had come looking for her. Hethor was right—she could not hide. All that was left to her was to use her power as best she could.

"No more waiting," Paolina announced, and sent forty-seven very startled men halfway around the world.

A huge spray of saltwater spewed away from the airship. Something large fell with it, wriggling.

The now-abandoned airship veered off course almost immediately. Her helm had been fighting the same crosswind that bedeviled their own ship. Paolina swiftly turned her focus to the other vessel. Forty-nine men there. They already reacted to the change in the other vessel, moving toward the rail. She could imagine men calling out to their cousins or old friends on the other deck.

Maybe they would find Ming, and he would help them understand.

She simply could not kill more of these Chinese.

This crew vanished as well, traded for several more tons of seawater and a flashing silver rain of fish that glittered as they fell. The second vessel veered away from its course, nose pitching downward.

"I will let them wander," Paolina said. "I suppose the remaining airship could conduct a recovery operation, but they will be a long time about it."

"*Erinyes* will distract them, miss." That was Kitchens.

She hadn't realized he'd left the helm. "I am very tired," Paolina said, then sat down on the deck so quickly it was nearly a collapse.

Boaz bent close as Kitchens stared from the helm. "Do you need to rest below?" the clerk asked.

She peered up at him. His face seemed to almost glow in the orange light of morning, erasing the grime and pallor and half-starved gauntness. Privation, transformed into something edging on serenity.

"I will sit a moment," Paolina said, "and you will sit with me, and you will tell me *exactly* what it is you hope to accomplish on your return to England. If I am going to give up everything to aid you, I would like to know what I am buying at such cost."

Beside her, Gashansunu stared aft toward the drifting airships. "You are already buying many things at great cost, air priestess." Her voice was distant.

CHILDRESS

A great ruckus erupted ashore. An alarm bell shrilled in a building beyond the moored British gunboats. Most of the sailors visible on their decks vanished with some urgency. Even the attentions of HIMS *Inerrancy* shifted away from *Five Lucky Winds*.

She could have laughed. *The monk has done some grave mischief. If she does not bring al-Wazir out of this unharmed, I will do* her *a grave mischief.*

"Captain Leung," Childress called out in Chinese, "I should have the men strike the awning and stand by."

Orders were barked, and the crew hustled to their work. Ashore, a pillar of smoke rose from the building that bulked behind the gunboats.

Fire? The monk had set a *fire*?

If nothing else, Childress had to admire the woman's brazenness. The Mask Poinsard could have taken lessons from this one.

Another alarm joined the first. Her shore party emerged from astern the endmost gunboat, rowing with all diligence.

Something was different.

Childress counted.

Five men, not four, in that launch. Though he was hunched over an oar, the fifth was far too large.

She turned and scrambled up the conning tower. "We should sail as soon as the launch is aboard," Childress announced to Leung, who scanned the shore through a set of glasses.

He called down for the engines to be ready and the harbor anchors to be drawn up, then said to Childress, much more quietly and in English, "I see six gunboats moored, another anchored along with that heavy cruiser. Do you propose to leave this harbor in full view of them all?"

"Do you propose to await a better time? Keep the crew paraded on the foredeck, depart waving to the people of Port Said, and play the fool. If they send swift boats after us, we will stand to and claim ignorance. Our chances of accomplishing anything are better on open water."

"Then we are bound for Malta," Leung confirmed.

"Yes." Childress thought quickly, but there were no better answers. "All other routes are closed to us now. The only way to have done with this nonsense between the Middle Kingdom and the British throne is a path drawn straight through the inner corridors of the *avebianco*." Though she would dearly love to know what the monk had to say about this.

The launch came aside. Al-Wazir, red faced and huffing, climbed aboard first. "Get it up here now, lads," he growled, pointing at the boat.

Childress called down to him. "Go below, Chief, before you're spotted."

His upturned face met her gaze. "Am I glad to see you." Al-Wazir stepped inside the base of the tower and grunted as he climbed one-handed down the hatch.

Something exploded onshore, roofing tiles and timber fragments spinning into the air.

"That is our invitation to depart," Childress said.

"A magazine explosion. Bad business." Leung called down, "Deck party fall in. Salute our hosts." He lifted the speaking tube and asked for quarter power, then began directing the pilot out of the harbor.

Once on the open water, Leung ordered the crew below and the vessel secured to submerge. He and Childress and the pilot remained above, watching the sky for airships and the waters abaft for pursuit. Ships were setting out from Port Said in numbers, but thus far HIMS *Inerrancy* did not seem to be among them.

"I am concerned about those gunboats," Leung told her. "They move considerably faster than we can sail."

"This I would not know."

"It is your ship." Something mild but dangerous hovered in his voice.

Though it pained her to argue with this man who'd grown so into her heart, Childress knew she must face the problem squarely. Still a part of her held back. "No, Captain, this is your ship. I am at best a kind of admiral, saying what must be done. But when we are face-to-face with the enemies of your people, I will do anything I can to keep us all alive. Including seeming to throw you over as just another crewman." She paused to let her words sink in, thinking, *I am still a woman and you are still a man.* "Would you prefer that I yield authority in all things? Even in the face of an angry British officer?"

"This was not rightly done."

"No," she agreed. "But we have prevailed."

"There are new difficulties," Leung said, retreating from his stubbornness. "My chart of this sea is very limited, for reference only. A rational man could not navigate a vessel by its use."

"Malta is north of west of here. The Mediterranean is not overfull of reefs and sudden rocks. Avoid islands and the shore."

"You truly know nothing of naval navigation, do you, Mask?"

"No, I do not."

"Neither do I," said the monk from behind them.

The unflappable Leung started. Childress just shook her head.

"Who are you—?" the captain began, but Childress cut him off with a wave of her hand. "Welcome back. Your talents amaze me."

The monk grinned broadly. "Then be amazed." She reached into her robes and pulled out a very large sheaf of paper. "I trust you can read British."

Childress took the bundle. It was a set of charts, hastily folded and somewhat crumpled. "Captain, I believe we have our answer."

"Not all the answers we need." His voice was hard. "Your machinations are troublesome enough, Mask, for all that I have encouraged them and understand them. But this . . . woman . . . is aboard my vessel without my leave or knowledge. I would know who and what she is. And why."

The monk fished out a little leather sack and began tamping a jade pipe. Her eyes twinkled as she kept her gaze on the captain. "You, sir, are speaking to the miracle worker who drew British attention from your hull back in Port Said. I freed the huge man while I was about my business. If that is not ample evidence that our interests converge, then you are a greater fool than even the man who breaks his oaths and flees his nation in time of conflict, taking with him a valuable war machine."

"Please," Childress said. "I know a little of this woman."

"That you know *any* of this woman only proves my point about command authority," Leung snapped, finally losing his temper. He shouted into the speaking tube. "Bai! Dog all hatches tight. No one crosses into or out of the hull until I call down again."

A long, awkward moment passed. "Rumor will fill my ship from stem to stern before the hour has turned," Leung said quietly. Anger had already receded like a tide. "Discipline has long since been compromised, but the notion that I have lost all control of who comes and goes aboard *Five Lucky Winds* will be more damaging."

The monk was blatantly unrepentant. "It is time for a new order in the world," she announced cheerfully. "Surely the deck of one rogue submarine is not so bad a place to start."

"What *are* you doing here?"

She stabbed the smoldering pipe toward Childress. "Following her."

"You are a white bird?"

"Not in the least."

"A member of the Silent Order, then?"

Another insouciant grin. "They seem to think so."

Leung would not release the point. "Then whom do you serve?"

"The interests of the world." She took a long drag. "In the person of a quarrelsome old man of poor digestion who answers to the name of the Jade Abbot."

"Who?" Childress asked simultaneously with Leung.

KITCHENS

He could not squat on his heels next to the girl Paolina. His entire body was too tired, aching in every joint. Sitting on the deck as she was doing seemed simply undignified. There were no other options, though.

"Mister Levine," he called down to the main deck. "Find the galley and see who can manage a Chinese stove. We will need to eat soon, all of us."

"Mess it is, sir," the old sailor replied.

Something more for them to do, at the least.

Kitchens turned back to Paolina. "What would you of me, then, Miss Barthes?"

"Where are we bound?"

"England," he said. "To be specific, a place called Blenheim Palace."

She closed her eyes and sighed a moment. "What is at Blenheim Palace?"

"The Queen herself."

"I presume she lies in state." Paolina opened her eyes again. "Or some mischance is at stake to draw you there."

"A great mischance that has paralyzed Government, or drawn it into the hands of unscrupulous men. I cannot say which."

"We abandon all to flee into the angry heart of the Empire pursuing this mischance."

Kitchens sighed. He couldn't recall where his worthless writs had gotten too, in the attaché saved at the last moment from *Notus*. Three airships and a descent into Ottweill's private hell had left him with too little accounting even in his own memory. With the writs, or perhaps *Notus* herself, was lost his little set of words from the Queen, along with whatever testimony Captain Sayeed had tucked away in that forgotten envelope.

"She told me a thing," he said softly. "When I saw her, just before I came to the Wall. She said, 'Remake what has been undone. Break my throne. Help me finish dying.' "

"So does she now lie in state?" Paolina sounded almost sleepy, but Kitchens knew to be very wary of this girl.

"No, but she should. She floats in a tank of bodily fluid, a bloody oracle for the Empire. Lloyd George has struck me as too decent for such a blasphemy, but whoever has managed this has arranged the Empire to his convenience. Too much goes unquestioned. Her Imperial Majesty wants her country back, and herself to go on past the end of life's journey."

Paolina's eyes fastened on him. Glittering, hard, filled with careful thought. "If we strike down this queen, we shall be regicides. The most hated people in Europe. I have already been hounded from the heart of your empire. This price I will pay again for Boaz' sake, and Ming's, and al-Wazir's, and that of all these silly, foolish sailors on these very decks. But how do you know our actions will not simply worsen affairs?"

Again, Kitchens chose his words with care. "Prince Edward is no fool. He was never meant by God to be a governing sort of man. But neither does he stand in the sway of his mother's counselors. Whoever has made this scheme at Blenheim, they have almost certainly cut him out. Keeping Her Imperial Majesty alive at any cost argues they do not want the heir upon the throne."

The fierceness faded from her eyes. "You did not answer my question, Mr. Kitchens."

"If I could speak with him, I would, but the Prince of Wales has been a man of his own circle, far away from Admiralty and Whitehall. He prefers the smart set to serious gentlemen who study trade and industry and the affairs of distant nations."

"Then perhaps he does not so much favor war," Paolina said.

"He does not so much favor war, and neither does he hold close the advice from those who do. If we can pursue the Queen's will and somehow alert him to the matter, well, that will be enough to open this rotten business up. Not even the hardest elements in Parliament will pursue open war with China in the shadow of Her Imperial Majesty's death."

"Will our deaths even be counted?" she asked.

"Will you not just walk free, as only you can do?"

She could not walk free, not now. Anymore than she could just walk to Kitchens' queen, in a place she did not know among people she had never met and could not follow.

They stared at one another a while, like two cats contesting a doorstep before dawn. No claws came out, though, and eventually he turned away, feeling vaguely foolish.

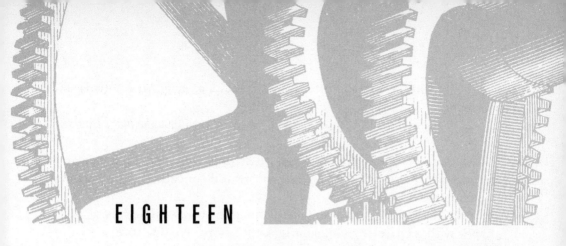

EIGHTEEN

The queen of the south shall rise up in the judgment with this generation, and shall condemn it: for she came from the uttermost parts of the earth to hear the wisdom of Solomon; and, behold, a greater than Solomon is here.   —*Matthew 12:42*

BOAZ

Eventually he was able to rest. Paolina slept next to him, curled on a length of rubberized fabric meant for patching the hydrogen cells. Her breathing was deep and regular, with a faint, periodic whistle that Boaz found most endearing.

::*thy breasts are as does at the spring, dipping their brown muzzles daintily to suck at the water*::

Boaz did not even know what to say to that, but the Paolina–al-Wazir voice chuckled inside him. Or at least the al-Wazir voice did.

::*clad in light with a sword of winds, the angel overflew the sleeping camp as secretly as a falling star*::

Right now, England was not his problem. His problem was shutting down far enough to allow his mechanisms to self-maintain, his lubrication stores to reinfuse his joints and relays, and his memories to settle into long-term storage. Boaz shifted a little closer to Paolina.

As for the Sixth Seal, and the voices in his head . . .

You're fine, laddie. We're not voices. We're just you, talking to yourself.

But I never talked to myself before now.

You never had a heart before, John Brass.

He finally settled into the torpor of self-repair, one hand touching his hollow, clockwork chest, the other resting on Paolina's hip.

The next day, hills of tortured brown stone rolled by beneath the keel. Kitchens and Petty Officer Martins met with Boaz on the poop. The Brass had the helm a while.

"We got the old girl running properly," Martins said. "She's a strange one, being Chinee and all, but a gasbag is still a gasbag. An engine is still an engine."

::*a man can pluck up the sword of his enemy, an he know the blade from the guard*::

A thought occurred to Boaz: Not all swords were created equal, nor were all sword arms. "I believe that we are still concerned with reaching England undetected."

"Yes," replied Martins, "and with this monstrous gasbag every jack-anapes with a spare eye will spot us long before. We'd best set down in Algeria or Portugal and make our way by boat from there."

"That will take too long," Kitchens said. "We should keep to the air while we may."

Boaz spoke again. "Then I have a proposal."

All eyes were upon him.

"We will rise to an altitude as high as possible without endangering lives aboard."

The petty officer shook his head. "You'll have men passing out. Ain't no one going to do their work right, you get very high up there. Not enough air in the air up there."

::*a flame may be borne from the lowest cave to the highest mountain, but withal it will still be a flame*::

"The ship runs now," Boaz said. "We'll push upward until either the men or the engines bid us go no higher, and I shall pilot her alone."

They still stared.

"I do not breathe," he explained patiently. "Thin air is merely thin air to me. So long as the engines fire and the crew can rest peacefully. Up so high in the sky we will be merely a speck to men on the ground, and possibly escape even the observation of aerial pickets."

"What is the highest this vessel can fly?" Kitchens asked.

No one knew the answer to that.

As the crew prepared for their uneasy rest in the thin, frosty heights of the sky, there was one more bit of business to attend to. Boaz was surprised that the English had not come to this themselves already, given how fixed they all seemed to be upon the forms of their society.

::*they built her strong and true to ply the shores of the west wind's home, and the king brake a jar of wine upon her prow and christened her Hope of the Day*::

He waited until Paolina mounted the poop to raise his question.

"What is the name of this vessel?"

"Something Chinese, I am sure," she said. "Ming taught me a fair bit of their language, but I have no skill at reading it. The words are little houses of meaning built from unknown timbers."

"I am of the opinion that we should give this airship a name of our own."

She laughed, her voice pealing in the cool morning air of this altitude. "Do Brass name their vessels?"

"Brass do not have vessels. We are a people of the Wall. Our last ship broke on the rocks of Abyssinia three thousand years ago."

"You are becoming an Englishman; I would swear to that." She laughed again, and this time the rush left a smile upon her face as it retreated. "What shall we christen this airship?"

"I do not know," he said. "Something meet and fitting. You and I have turned away from our own destinies. Our world is the Wall, but we head into the heart of Northern Earth."

"That is hardly the stuff of naming." She frowned, serious now, though he could still see the humor in her eyes. "I shall ask Mr. Kitchens and the crew."

:: *the goatherds do not rise as an army, neither do the maids march from their duties around the fire*::

"You may receive a regrettable suggestion."

The regrettable suggestion came back on the lips of Kitchens, actually, as he came to Boaz an hour later.

"Paolina is below, seeking materials for an oxygen concentrator."

"I suppose she wishes to stay with me at the wheel when we climb." Something inside Boaz thrilled.

Good lad.

"We have a name," Kitchens said diffidently.

:: *a staff he struck into the ground, which flowered then and there as a bush heavy with golden fruit, and there was an epithet upon his lips*::

Boaz suspected the Sixth Seal of developing a sense of humor. At the very least, it had been far less frantic of late. "What is this wondrous name?"

The clerk snorted, holding back deeper laughter. "*Stolen.*"

"*Stolen.*" Boaz had to admit, he liked the name. He'd feared far worse. "Have they discovered wine aboard?"

"Sailors? If so, it has been drunk in secret convocation. And what does a Brass need with wine?"

"To bless the naming of the ship," Boaz explained patiently.

"Of course." Kitchens snorted again. "We shall make do."

Within the hour, everything was ready.

:: *never walk strange paths without the armor of the Lord or the weapon of prayer*::

The surviving crew gathered around. Levine produced a beaker of brown fluid. "From the galley," he said, "for to spill across her rail in the naming."

Boaz continued to hold the helm, and so all eyes were upon him. Kitchens nodded slightly.

:: *he led the Haramites out of their enslavement, then in later years took up banners with the horse-people of the long valleys*::

Wondering who the Haramites might have been, the Brass began to speak. "This ship we have taken for our own will soon hold you as you rest. We climb to where the air is almost ice, and make our way up high safely to England's shores. There we will fulfill a mission of utmost delicacy, and release you all to your native soil. Our brave hull, taken from the enemy to suit our purposes, we name *Stolen*. A gift we will make of her to your queen."

The crew cheered as the petty officer dumped the brown fluid over the rail. Most of it sprayed back onto him. To general laughter, they returned to their duty stations until only Kitchens and Gashansunu remained with Boaz.

"Where is Paolina?" Boaz asked.

:: *though bruised beyond measure, the King paced by the wrack of his palace, fearing for the Queen and praying to the Lord for her deliverance*::

"Below yet," Gashansunu answered. "Do not worry after her."

Boaz adjusted the attitude controls. Ballast and gas balance had already been configured as best they could. The vanes and elevators had been holding *Stolen* at altitude until now, but she fairly leapt to rise into the sky. He would climb until the engines threatened to starve, then lose just a small amount of altitude. A rope had been rigged down to the poop so he could vent some hydrogen to bring the airship lower at need, lest an unexpected development occur, or the air grow too thin for the vanes to bite effectively.

Already he seemed colder, though Boaz was certain this was little more than his imagination. If they could overfly England's defenses, Kitchens might yet reach his mad, dying queen.

Everything Boaz wanted was still belowdecks, in the form of a young woman cooking up oxygen to pack away like weapons in an armory.

:: *the Lord put brass in the skies that we might always mark His intentions, and the moment of the day of His return*::

Indeed, Boaz told the Sixth Seal. *Indeed.*

If the Paolina–al-Wazir voice within him had any comment, this day they kept their opinions to themselves.

WANG

Good Change fled the harbor at Port Said amid a rush of vessels. The fire hardly seemed a threat to the entire city, but it definitely menaced the docks while sowing confusion. British gunboats were casting off. Dozens of narrow-hulled fishing boats scrambled for the Mediterranean. The Kô's yacht moved amid a flight of similar pleasure ships and small traders.

The cataloger stood in his usual place in the prow and watched the mess unfold. The monk had been here in Port Said, though he had not seen her aboard *Good Change* since they'd discharged Childress off the Goan coast.

What had she been about?

If nothing else, she had shoved a pair of charts into his hand. He tugged these out of his jacket now and uncrumpled them. The sheets were awkwardly large. Whatever the maps represented had almost certainly been too valuable to abandon.

Definitely maritime navigation. Shorelines he didn't recognize. While the mysterious monk had something of the Monkey King to her character, Wang could not see why she would have tricked him over this.

Wu would want to know what had happened ashore. Wang would give the charts to the first mate, then, and let the other man work out their significance.

"I am the hunter of spies," he told the water, "not the navigator."

The water had no answer, except for the distant tolling of fire bells.

Wu, Wang and Captain Shen gathered around the table in the wardroom. One of the sailors had the helm for a rare change. The sun played golden light across the wine-dark sea outside. If this had been Chersonesus Aurea, Wang would have thought a storm was coming. Here, who knew?

The two charts were spread out. One was a view of the entire Mediterranean. Useless, as Wang understood it, for any sort of real navigation, but it helped them plot their course. The boat's own chart drawer had nothing beyond the Gulf of Aden.

We have sailed too far from the center of the world, he thought. *Only barbarians and feral dragons dwell here.*

The other chart was of the harbor at Valetta, the chief port of the island of Malta.

"Why Valetta?" asked Shen. "This is some trap."

"The monk went to a great deal of trouble simply to lay a trap, sir," said Wang. "*Five Lucky Winds* left Port Said under the cover of the fires she set." His legs still trembled a bit from the mad dash through the city, but Wang still smiled. "There is too much connection here to pretend away. Besides, I can tell you she searched for these particular charts. If she'd meant to throw us off some trail, she would have grabbed for any map close to hand."

"This does not discount the possibility of a trap," grumbled the captain.

Wang noticed he did not avoid the subject of the monk, either. "Is she aboard now, sir?"

"Who?" A strange, almost feral gleam stood in Shen's eye.

"The monk," Wang said. A reservoir of angry patience burst. "That madwoman who crewed aboard your boat from Chersonesus Aurea to Phu Ket, then on to Panjim before she moved over to *Five Lucky Winds*."

"The Kô would never allow a woman to crew his vessel. Therefore it must not have been."

The cataloger looked to Wu. The first mate was trying to swallow a smile. "You know," he said. "You rowed us both to the landing at the palace of the Silent Order."

"I know that some things pass through the world unseen," Wu replied. "The north wind. Cloud dragons. Certain monks."

"You are not dead," Wang insisted. "She is not invisible. All of you are crazed."

Yet she *was* invisible, he realized. Or could be. She had walked him right into the heart of the Royal Navy in Port Said, past dozens of clerks and guards, unremarked.

Now it was Shen's turn to smile. "Those are powerful words coming from one whose life hangs in balance."

"Oh, leave off that silly pretense," Wang snapped. "We both know that my life was forfeit from the moment the Kô summoned me." The words surprised him, but he could not call them back, and so pressed onward. "If I live out this voyage, it will be by the favor of Heaven, and the miracle of certain people forgetting to silence me. All I have left is my purpose of finding the Mask Childress!" His eyes stung with incipient tears, but Wang knew better than to allow them to slip free before these men.

"Find her, then bring her back to Phu Ket, yes?" asked Wu.

Wang stared. What did it matter once he had located the English-woman? But he remembered his orders as the anger flooded away from him on a retreating tide. "Even with her aboard, you will need me to re-turn through Suez and the Gulf of Aden."

"The Indian Ocean awaits you," the mate told him.

Captain Shen tapped the chart table. "But first, this vile city of Valetta. Ordinarily I would put you ashore down the coast, and have you walk."

"Why not now? You don't trust me?"

His hand swept across the emptiness of the oh-so-tiny Mediterranean on the larger map. "I have no charts except for Valetta harbor itself. I should not like to risk my keel on hidden rocks. Bad enough that we transit almost three thousand *li* of open water. Four days in unknown shallows is madness enough. I will not risk some reef to put you over after all this distance."

"We fly their flag. This hull is European built. No one will question us." Wang said that with far more confidence than he felt.

"Your story about the Prince of Serendip carried some authority out in the Indian Ocean," Shen said in an acid tone. "Deep in these British waters, a boat full of Chinese will be much harder to pass off."

GASHANSUNU

She paced the deck as *Stolen* rose ever higher. Small noises emerged from below as the crew settled to rest, the shallow breathing of sleep their best hope.

Time had not stopped for her again, nor stuttered. She was coming unmoored; she knew that. Her *wa* was gone. Her theory in the moment was that she had died, and this journey of her body was simply force of habit from her earlier life, living out the last memories of people and places.

Who knew, after all? Her *wa* had never spoken directly of such things. No one's did.

Round she made a circuit, past Boaz silent as the coming night; along the starboard rail to stare northeast across the heart of the desert; to the prow where the late, fading sunlight stood off to her left side and the brass tracks in the sky gleamed with esoteric brightness; then back along the port rail to stare toward the glowering bulk of the Wall already slipping below the horizon of rationality.

That the Earth loomed large was a truism, simple as saying water was wet, or that stones fell downward. But the city, *her* city, was profoundly focused on the terrain of the Silent World, and thus indifferent to the Shadow World. What went on beyond the city walls had no great relevance. Even the Bone People, in their power and their horror, had pressed their way in.

She began to wonder if the comfortable limits of her people's existence constituted a trap.

They were *all* possessed of the elusive spark that marked a gleam. "Sorcerers" was a term of pride among the adepts and house priests and circle callers. It had always been so easy for the sorcerers to account themselves as towering above the world. That the churning sea of lesser souls on occasion turned out a wild sorcerer was seen as little more than an evolutionary process. William of Ghent had been mighty when he held the fortress at Zimbabwe, but once he had been swept away by the tides of unreason, no one stood to take his place.

When a sorcerer of the city fell, her power was never lost.

Gashansunu realized she had fallen. She'd left the comfort of Westfacing House behind, for the sake of pursuing omens. She'd thought this to be a campfire errand, something to pursue of an evening, then come back and spend a month being glad of her place in the city. Instead it had blossomed into a holocaust that threatened to consume her, cut her off from her past, and remake her future beyond recognition.

All because she had followed the spark of a girl who had, in truth, just been passing by.

If Gashansunu had fallen, who would take up her power? Baassiia, of course, the circle caller, would ensure that her duties were apportioned. Others might grasp the strands of her spirit and its purpose. Her *wa*, well . . .

That was the crux of it for Gashansunu. She quite literally could not envision living without her *wa*, yet it had slipped away from her—so far away that she could not even see its spark in her head—and had departed amid a mumble of words about how she had swallowed it down.

But one did not swallow a *wa*. The opposite, even, if one was both especially unfortunate and notably foolish in the Silent World.

Was she becoming Paolina's *wa*? Northerners did not possess a *wa*, even if they had opened a path to power as the girl had.

Yet she was fading, cut off so far from home and all the purposeful intents of her life.

Gashansunu cast away the mordant imaginings and looked back toward Boaz. The girl had not yet reappeared, while the Brass man seemed fixed at the helm, as if *Stolen* had climbed so high that they'd been transfixed in an eternal moment, frost-rimed and clad in the pale light at the top of the sky.

PAOLINA

She clambered up the bamboo ladder amidships. This vessel was nearly a twin to *Heaven's Deer*, which had carried her and al-Wazir from Mogadishu to a hard landing on the storm-wracked sea not so far from Sumatra. Paolina's time aboard that airship loomed large in her memory—she'd snatched the vessel from the hands of its own crew through mad-eyed recklessness.

Right now, she was not even sure she could touch a grenado. Yet that day not so long ago, she'd killed with them, and nearly brought an entire ship out of the sky.

On deck, the air was cold and thin and very disturbed. Engines labored, rumbling nearly to a stalling cough. Boaz could not drive *Stolen* much higher. She stopped and took a deep breath from the oxygen pot she'd crafted—air, its vital essences concentrated so that she could remain alert and in the company of Boaz as he brought them above all interception.

Except for the sorceress, they would be alone.

Her muscles stopped shaking. She felt warmer for the several breaths of purified air. Paolina made her way to her beloved's side.

That word.

Beloved.

It had popped into her head just before she'd circled her arm in his, just as his neck turned with a faint creak so their eyes could meet, just after the set of his face and body had changed oh-so-imperceptibly so that she knew he too was smiling, in the moments and minutes that followed.

"How high are we?" she finally asked.

He glanced over the rail. "I estimate four miles." A long slow pause followed, then he said, "These vessels rarely rise over two miles, outside the strange vertical atmosphere of the Wall. You can hear the engines labor terribly. Our headway is poor relative to our fuel consumption, but we have a powerful following wind. Moreover, a man cannot breathe decently here."

That reminded Paolina to sip again from her oxygen pot. Gashansunu approached as she pinched the valve and let the blessed, pure spirit of the air rush into her mouth.

The sorceress maintained the almost peculiar calm that had taken her lately. Something in the blankness of the woman's eyes made Paolina step closer to Boaz.

Gashansunu was not a friend, but at least an ally. Until now, too far from home, on a voyage none of them had meant to undertake.

"I have fallen." The Southern woman seemed to be resuming some conversation set down in the press of the moment.

Boaz glanced at her. "Did you harm yourself?"

"Too late. The air has taken me."

"You still walk among us, hale," said Paolina.

"Then where is my *wa*?" The sorceress glared. "I only meant to settle the worries of the day, not to come into chaos. I have outwalked my power and it has been taken up."

"I have no *wa*," Paolina said starkly. "I do not expect I ever shall. Yet I am in the world whole and unharmed."

Gashansunu looked as alien to Paolina in that moment as she had at their very first meeting at Hethor's village. Whatever words were on her tongue escaped without sound, and she turned away.

"You should sleep," Paolina called. "This thin air has robbed you of some portion of your heart."

She stopped and sucked again on the oxygen pot, then wrapped herself close to Boaz. Never mind that he was cold as anything she'd ever felt—like a midwinter night in Dickens' *Mystery of Edwin Drood*. Winter was one of those seasons she'd always marveled to see and likely never would.

Much later Boaz woke her.

"You must go below."

"Why?" she asked, querulous.

"Because you have used your air. You cannot break more water now with the ship's sparks; you will hurt yourself or cause a fire in the hull."

Paolina sat up, unaware she'd been rolled up tight in a length of rubberized canvas, propped close to the stern rail.

Had he tucked me in? she thought.

Boaz went back to the wheel and loosened the chocks. He looked over his shoulder at her. "We are along the westward belly of Africa, if I understand the map Mr. Kitchens sketched. I should think to see Spain at some point."

She heard the rattling engines, uncomprehending. The gasbag groaned, straining at this altitude it was never meant to reach. She felt the creaking of the hull, every board shrinking just a bit too far, as if the termites and woodworms themselves would drop away and tumble to their freedom far below.

Ice, my brain turns to ice.

"I will not go below," Paolina mumbled.

He beckoned her. She slipped once more within the chilled circle of his arm and tried to lay her cheek close against his chest.

"I love you," she told him.

"You do not know the meaning of that word," he replied gently. "Neither do I, for I have no heart. Intellect, yes, and courage when at need, but if I only had a heart . . ."

"Then we are made for one another." Her voice was a whisper now. "A witticism of God the Creator. You were made to be alone among a thousand of your fellows. I was made to be alone among any of my own kind. We can b-b-b-b-be alone t-t-together."

His arm circled her tighter.

Paolina tried to kiss his cheek, but her lips stuck to him, and she had to pull free with a small, tearing pain. She sucked one last time on the empty oxygen pot, then stumbled back to the ladder to lie below amid the warm, breathing mass of men.

She wondered where the sorceress was.

The rough thrumming of the air-starved engines lulled her all too fast to sleep.

CHILDRESS

The monk seemed almost gleeful at their bafflement. She dropped the ash of her pipe into the Mediterranean waters and set to tamping more weed. Her maddening grin flicked like a scissortail at dusk.

"Though no one seems to recall this any longer, I am still in command of this vessel," Captain Leung said in his mildest, most dangerous voice.

"You have charts to steer by." The monk glanced at the afternoon sky. "You will be safe at night, but right now there may be jolly tars close overhead in some nearby cloud."

"I will con my vessel as I see fit. Neither you nor this Jade Abbot have a say in the direction of *Five Lucky Winds*."

"Not I," said the monk. "The Jade Abbot directs nothing. Many days he is lucky that someone brings him tea. We all serve."

Leung's voice slowed even more. "What are you doing here?"

The monk was serious now, with the suddenness of a cloud masking the sun. "Seeing the Mask to her destination. Without the charts, you would risk too much."

Childress was stung by this. "I have found my way thus far well enough."

"Of course you have. Else you would not be the Mask." A puff on the pipe, a return to insolence. "But even the greatest thief must have someone to hold the ladder."

"I am no thief!"

The monk laughed. "What else are you? You stole your title from a dead woman. You stole the girl from those who would have her. You stole the lives of an entire fleet. You stole this submarine and the heart of its captain from the Beiyang Navy. Now you would steal power from the secret councils of the *avebianco* much as the Monkey King would steal Heaven's peaches."

More embarrassed than stung, Childress drew breath to fling a riposte. What stopped her was the realization that this woman knew far too much about her. *How?*

Leung stepped in. "I should despise you, monk. I should have you thrown over the side with iron bars chained to your hands and feet. But even if I did that, I am certain I would find you on my bridge an hour later, dry as the desert and smirking."

"I should not think it worth your trouble, no," the monk replied.

"But this is because I have worked out who you are." The captain bowed. "Welcome to my ship, Lan Ts'ai-ho."

Baffled, Childress asked, "Who is Lan Ts'ai-ho?"

The monk was laughing so hard now that she nearly swallowed her little pipe. The captain looked ahead, sweeping the horizon with his glasses as if this were all perfectly normal.

When she'd recovered her breath, the monk answered. "He believes me to be one of the Eight Immortals of Taoist legend."

That was no more illuminating than before. "Who?"

"Sages, purveyors of wisdom, priests who were especially good at shearing the wealthy temple-goers. I do not know *who*. And it does not matter. No woman walks the Earth for a thousand years. Heaven would not stand for it, and Hell would swallow her up!" The monk's eyes sparkled with an untold joke. "Perhaps the name is passed on, like a patent of nobility from father to son. Maybe the Immortals are reborn anew in every generation. Perhaps they are an idea so powerful that someone rises to fill each place without ever knowing what drew them forth." She leaned close. "Or it could be that I am just an annoying monk who has feasted her eyes on far too many *xiákè* epics in the temple library."

"It does not matter." Leung continued to scan the ocean. "You might be any of those things. Or all of them. Or even none. You are still Lan Ts'ai-ho, and you carry the banner of the Monkey King in these years of the world."

"You do not care if I am a peasant girl born beneath a harnessed ox in the fields of Fu-chien?"

"I do not care if you were born in the Forbidden City, of the body of an angel on a couch of ivory." He put down the glasses. "You are aboard my ship without permission, behaving dreadfully. If you are a divinity, then I will bid you welcome and make the best of my hospitality. If you are an insolent peasant girl from Fu-chien, then I will throw you into the sea and tell you to swim for that distant shore."

"In that case," the monk said happily, "I am most definitely Divine. I also hunger. I have not eaten a decent meal in . . ." She paused, counting on her fingers. "Weeks!"

With a sharp look at Childress, the captain escorted his guest below. That pained her heart in an unexpected fashion. She wondered what game he was playing at—surely this was payback for her brushing him aside before the British. Just as surely the monk's remarks about theft had stung Leung as they had stung her.

She did note that Leung had taken the maps.

How had the monk known so much of her affairs? Who had she been listening to? *Where had she come from?*

Fruitless speculation, at least for now. They were Malta-bound; that was enough. *I could have made much with this man,* Childress thought, *but I wish the journey to be at an end.* With a start, she realized she'd come nearly all the way around the world. From here she could almost go home.

Except somewhere along this voyage, she'd lost the notion that New Haven *was* home. She could not decide if that was a tragedy, or a liberation. The west beckoned, the island of her reckoning rising pale-cliffed from sun-drenched waters somewhere ahead.

Childress spoke quietly with the chief. Her guilt drove her to the conversation as much as her fondness for the great Scotsman.

"How was it aboard Bork's ship?" she asked.

He turned briefly away, pain flitting across his face. "A man should never swear too many oaths, Mask. In time, his word will come to break itself."

"Were you . . ." She was afraid of the word.

"Tortured?" He laughed, though it came out more as a retching. "Nae, unless you call a ration of rum and some good Royal Navy slop in a tin tray torture. They treated me far worse than that. They were *reasonable*."

Childress whispered, "What did you do?"

"Nothing."

"Nothing?"

"Nae. I did not speak of this vessel or her crew. I did not tell them of the Mask Childress, who I've come to call a friend." He paused, then said, "I did not ask help for the mad doctor at the Wall. That would hae betrayed too much of our intents. As well as Boaz."

At the misery in his voice, Childress stepped close, wrapped her arms as far as she could reach around al-Wazir's massive shoulders, and held on to him while he wept.

WANG

Much to his surprise, they sailed the North African coast unmolested. He'd expected airships to come droning out of the sky, a fleet from Port Said or Cairo or some Italian port to be hunting *Good Change*. Even just simple bad luck should have overtaken them.

Instead there was water, shoreline and a quiet sea. Weather threatened but did not appear. Dolphins followed the boat a while. The crew was surly and silent as normal. Wu muttered at him from time to time, but Wang even discovered some shrimp left in the pot when he went below after the crew's dinner mess.

He could not remember being at peace since before leaving the library at Chersonesus Aurea. Fear of one kind or another had driven him forward, darkened his soul, clouded his thinking, robbed him of too much of who and what he was.

Now, trapped in a boat amid angry men too far from their own waters, he was just Wang again. The son of farmers, a cataloger and an archivist, a subject of the Son of Heaven, a denizen of Northern Earth.

Wang wondered where this unexpected sense of peace had come from.

Wherever the war was right now, it did not follow them across the Mediterranean. He could well imagine the bombings, the shelling, the duels on the waves and amid the clouds, all raging from Singapore to the African coast of the Wall.

If the war stayed there and did not come into the South China Sea or the British Atlantic, then, well, this was the game of nations.

But the Golden Bridge project, fed by his work in the sunken library, would tip that balance. The fires, the killing, the dying would spread all around the world. Childress had the right of it when she argued against the Middle Kingdom building a broad path across the wall. Ancient magic or modern engineering, it would not matter once they'd opened that wound in the fabric of the world.

Her fear had been for what might come over from the other side. His fear was for what this side would take across.

Wang still did not know what he would do on catching up to Childress. Bringing her back to Phu Ket seemed unlikely. So far as the crew of *Good Change* were concerned, he could stand in the middle of Malta and their vengeance would not reach him.

No man was safe from the Silent Order—they were like the tongs of Shanghai and Hong Kong writ large across the world. But this boat full of dead men would trouble him little so long as he stayed away from the water.

Wang watched the sun slip magenta-bright below the horizon and contemplated how he might live through the coming fights, how the Mask Childress would receive him, what he might say to her, persuade her of.

Tell me, do the Masks truly believe they rule the world?

Let us fight the Golden Bridge together!
I have come to capture you, but I will not. Please do not send me home.

The sea held no wisdom, only the ever-closing *li* between his feet and the stony shores of Malta. There some of his questions might perhaps be answered.

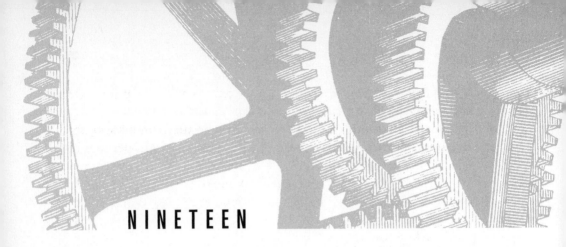

NINETEEN

And when they were escaped, then they knew that the island was called Melita.

—*Acts 28:1*

BOAZ

He brought *Stolen* down out of the upper sky a day later. The engines sounded close to failure, and the crew slept far too long. Boaz had rested at the wheel, staring sightless along their course and holding firm while the voice of the Sixth Seal ranted quietly deep within him. His constant companion had become like a heartbeat, though he was still all too conscious of its power.

Now the airship passed over sparse, brown mountains somewhere in Spain, according to Kitchens' hand-drawn map. Boaz hadn't succeeded in following the coastline, for there was too much air and sea traffic, so he'd kept inland except for passing high above a narrow strait busy with military vessels.

None of them had looked high enough *up*. A speck in the sky was just a speck in the sky, Boaz knew, but when your enemy flew, any such were as dangerous as rust specks on an idled joint.

That was all to his good fortune.

: : *wings of wax and feathers with which to challenge the very angels of the Host of Heaven*: :

They cruised low over ragged forests that gave way to long aprons of shattered rock and glum brown outcroppings. The air was crisp, but nothing like the misery of the upper altitudes.

Gashansunu had been among the last to go below, and she was the first to emerge. She seemed far less fey, as if whatever had troubled her before had passed in the unquiet rest below.

"Does the air agree with you now?" Boaz asked.

"Never did I starve for breath." The edge was gone from her voice, as well.

::*crammed with dust you are, and you eat the prayers of men as if they were broken stalks in the meadow*::

She would say no more. The rest of the crew began to stumble forth. Within the hour almost all were on the deck.

"We lost two men to the altitude," Martins said quietly to Boaz and Kitchens. Both the petty officer and the clerk looked worse for the wear. The Brass realized that he had become something of a judge of human beings.

"Whom?" asked Kitchens.

"Schoenhuth of the gas division, what had carried a wound from the killer angels. Also Gallaher from the engineering division." Martins grimaced. "He was our best mechanic. Only one left with real training. Klaw didn't make it off *Erinyes*, and Weiss died in the fighting."

::*the oldest warhorse in the pasture yet has the light of battle in his clouded eyes*::

"This will not matter much longer," Boaz replied. All eyes leapt to the horizon, seeking Chinese airships or winged savages or some new horror.

"Brass bastard," muttered the petty officer. Then: "We'll lose several more if we take those heights again."

Paolina joined them, bleary and stumbling from her time below. She carried another oxygen pot. "A number of the crew are ill." Waving the little device, she added, "This seems to aid them. I have a second one charging below."

"Mr. Kitchens," Boaz said. "This is your errand. We are beyond the boundaries of my purpose."

The clerk stared at his hands. That was, the Brass realized, an unusual episode of uncertainty for this man. Whatever doubts warred inside him, Kitchens always maintained a focused intent.

::*a Godly man, pursuing justice past all cost of reason, as a Godly man should do*::

The clerk's gaze passed slowly from eye to eye. "I must press forward, and not spend time in fighting or fruitless negotiation. If we are stopped, I will never be permitted to approach Blenheim Palace and the presence of the Queen. Her Imperial Majesty asks no less of me. I can ask no less of *Stolen* and her crew."

Boaz spoke. "This vessel will not fight again, true?"

Martins shook his head. "Our crew won't fire on a British ship, and we're much too far into our own territory for them Chinee to find us now."

Kitchens muttered agreement, as if it pained him.

::*set flame to your banners, cast away your armor, shear your heads and rub your faces with ash, for you are already lost to the living*::

The Brass ignored the voice this time. "Our last operation will be the landing at Blenheim Palace."

"Yes," the clerk said.

Paolina smiled at Boaz—she saw the line of his reasoning. Her approval thrilled him, sending an unexpected crackle through his crystals.

"We land now, and set to ground all but the few crew we need to keep *Stolen* operating for another day or two." He looked up at the tapered bag. "A gas man, whoever is left to manage the engines, and an extra pair of hands. We do not have sufficient company even now to work this ship in full. Let us make a virtue of our failings and travel as lightly as possible."

The petty officer looked to Kitchens. "Sir?"

"Best be done soon," said Paolina before the clerk could speak. "Let me know how many will remain aboard. I will create additional oxygen pots."

::*the King gave them back their oaths and set each man free with a coin and a sack of grain*::

Martins began counting out on his fingers. The crew huddled ragged and cold, sipping soup from tight-clutched bowls.

"I believe that this is your decision," Kitchens told the petty officer. "None of us know how to do more than grasp a wheel or guess at a map."

"I'll keep six," Martins said gruffly. "I'm off to tell the good news to them who have been volunteered."

Boaz turned to Paolina. "Go to the bow and watch for a place where we may approach the earth." He'd never landed an airship, did not intend to start now, but he understood what was required—a large patch of relatively level ground without nearby cliffs or other sources of disturbances to the air. "We shall want a good-sized meadow, or possibly the margin of a lake."

"Will you aid me?" she asked the silent Gashansunu. Together the two women walked forward.

He didn't want to bring the airship any lower. Already he was too close to the peaks of these ragged mountains. The airman's lesson that altitude was always your friend had not been lost on Boaz.

::*even a priest knows the ground over which he fights, workrooms of the soul where ideas labor at their patents*::

Forty-five minutes later, the old sailor Levine brought them low over a glittering tarn surrounded by meadows of blooming lavender. Boaz stared down at the pale purple haze of autumn blossoms mixed with the green-gray foliage.

"There is no point in trying to moor," Martins had shouted over the laboring of the engines. Instead they passed a pair of lines over the rail.

Most of the departing crew scrambled down like monkeys, swarming the fifty feet or so to the ground. Six would go over the side in slings, along with anything else deemed surplus to final requirements.

Stolen would be left with little more than a handful of crew, and no margin of error. Whatever happened would be the end of them—storm, attack, breakage, British interception.

::*uncovered by fate, they moved into the light, bathing in the gaze of their enemies*::

If he could catch a favorable wind at sufficient altitude, they might make Blenheim Palace undetected in two more days. The most dangerous portion of that journey would be the descent to the palace grounds.

An idea occurred to him. They could at least *attempt* to mitigate that. "Are there stores of cloth below?" Boaz asked Paolina. "Chinese silk, perhaps?"

"I have seen those. As well muslin sheeting."

"We are in want of a banner that we could lower so as to communicate with the ground upon our arrival. If we are lucky, this will slow the British from instantly burning us out of the sky for Chinese invaders."

"Ah," she said thoughtfully. "I must go see who among our remaining crew is a good hand with a needle."

::*for six days the maid Shulit sewed upon the standard of the King; on the seventh he called it finished and took her kiss for a seal*::

Soon enough they were off. Martins' six men had turned to nine, for not everyone wished to go over the side into the wilds of the Andalusian highlands. Boaz considered the fate of those aboard *Stolen* to be far more uncertain than those remaining on the ground, but each sailor's decision was his own.

WANG

Valetta lay before him. A little port in a little harbor, consisting of a rising array of formal sand-colored buildings in a European style—flat roofs, domes, spires, square windows of unfortunate nuance staring empty-eyed across the harbor. No one seemed to mind as *Good Change* approached.

Five Lucky Winds was not in evidence.

"Captain Shen says that we will not seek out a harbor master here," Wu told him. "I shall row you to a landing."

"How will you know to come fetch me back?"

"You will return to wherever I land you. A lookout will be kept."

Wang could imagine how effective this lookout would be. The crew, though no longer so mercilessly irritated with him, continued to treat Wang as if he barely existed. They were much too far from home, and perhaps worried about how to find their way safely down to hell from this distant place.

Then he wondered why he cared. He was come for Childress. The idea of returning to Chersonesus Aurea seemed alien. Going all the way back to China had become almost unimaginable.

The English Mask was his oracle now, his guide, his lodestone.

"I need a few moments," he told Shen. Wang went below to gather such small belongings as he had accumulated, along with the money allowed him by Captain Shen. All of this he placed in a canvas bag that had once contained onions and garlic. He tugged on the white robes of an Arab, so he would not be marked as so obviously Asian at a glance. Wang could not even pretend to pass for a European.

He wondered whether he would pass even a dozen paces down the street before being called out for a spy.

Wu rowed them across the harbor.

"Tell me," Wang asked, driven to seek some final sense of connection with this man who had both aided and tormented him. "What would become of you if you set foot on dry land? You might step ashore with me here and see a different world than the country of ghosts and ships that you have made your own."

"We are ghosts. I have explained this to you."

"A ghost on land is still a ghost."

"But he is not me." Wu crabbed water, bringing them close to a stone stairway rising from the slopping tide. "Come here; look for *Good Change*. If we have been forced to move, return periodically. Also, show a light if it is night."

"That's a stupid plan," Wang protested. "How will I see you? This harbor is full of boats, and half of them are white. Worse, the shore will be dotted with lights come evening."

"I will know." Some echo of the Kô's implacable, brutal indifference stood in the mate's voice.

"Then we shall see each other again." Clambering out, Wang wondered if he should have made a better good-bye.

"Little man," Wu called from the boat.

The cataloger turned from the top step and looked back down.

"You have done better than I might have thought." The sailor rowed himself away.

Wang was unaccountably pleased at the praise. He turned into the rowdy traffic of a busy port and was lost within moments. Not called out for a spy, not called out for anything at all, just a sun-darkened face amid sun-darkened faces, busy and anonymous and ever moving.

How would he find Childress in this?

CHILDRESS

Five Lucky Winds steamed into Valetta with flags flying and her crew on parade. This created a visible stir, from the decks of fishing boats to the balconies of the harborside buildings to the waterfront street traffic.

Childress stood in the tower with Leung. The monk was nowhere to be seen, of course. Al-Wazir waited on the foredeck with his raiding party, discreetly armed so as not to seem too much the invasion force.

As if a one-handed Scotsman and eight Chinese sailors were going to take on an entire island.

She wished them the luck of it. Right now, a thousand eyes upon her was much safer than anonymity. Already the British airship was casting off from its tower, moving swiftly enough that she figured panic at their helm.

Small craft skittered out of the submarine's way. Larger vessels gave long wails on their steam whistles. Somewhere in the city a bell began to clang. The noise was soon picked up and sent rolling across the harbor from a dozen church towers.

For a moment, everything inside her seemed to pause, as if coiled to spring. The iodine smell of the ocean, the rotten wrack of any fishing port, the scent of stone and roofing and animals; the golden light gelid as if to seize the harbor in an amber grip; the wind standing in her hair just so, to lift her away from the place and fly her to a better world; the coolth of the turning season on her skin, even here in the Mediterranean. A transcendent moment, as permanent in her *ars memoriae* as it would be ephemeral in the march of her existence.

Soldiers clattered down the waterfront, running too fast for the crowds, bayoneted rifles bobbing and swaying. The bells acquired an urgent clamor as the engines of the approaching airship raced. *Five Lucky Winds* glided into a mooring, her crew at attention on the foredeck, the world banner flapping.

Two men cautiously approached and took the lines thrown by Leung's sailors. They worked their way from fore to aft, tying off the submarine and laughing nervously. Childress descended the ladder, reasoning she would be far better positioned up on the dock.

Leung stayed behind. This was her enterprise now, though her failure would cost the captain and his crew imprisonment, and possibly their lives. *Five Lucky Winds* might well never sail again.

"This will not happen," she told the grimy ladder as she climbed.

Bai had repaired and polished Childress' old boots. Her dress was proper New England fashion, retailored by Lao Mu. Her hair had been done as neatly as any peasant's queue, though the fashion would pass no social muster. For the first time in a great while, Childress was conscious of her sun-darkened face, the marks of weather on her cheeks, her hands, her neck.

Such a scandal she would be to anyone who had ever known her.

Smiling, she reached the dock just before the puffing sergeant at the head of his little knot of men. The airship growled, pitching low above them.

"Ma'am," the sergeant almost shouted. His surprise was visible. "You, you, did you—?"

"This is my vessel, Sergeant," she announced. "I thank you for the honor guard, but it will not be required. My faith in the welcoming virtues of the citizens of Valetta is complete."

"Ma'am, I'm not . . ." The sergeant looked down at the deck. Al-Wazir grinned up at him, flanked by two sailors in dress whites, each holding a tray covered with small glasses of plum wine.

"Drinks for you and your men, laddie?" the chief roared, his voice thick with the fields of his youth.

"Sir, no . . ."

"You seem at a loss for words, Sergeant," Childress said pleasantly. "Perhaps you would care to escort me to the *avebianco*? I have much to report to the Feathered Masks in grand concilium, and a war to stop before it comes calling on your pleasant shores."

She was here. She was truly *here*. Where her journey would have taken her from the beginning, if *Five Lucky Winds* had not intercepted *Mute Swan* on the high seas and taken her off, to the cost of the lives of all others aboard the ship.

Such a long, difficult voyage.

"You're one, you're . . ." The sergeant glanced back over his shoulder at the crowd that had gathered thick and noisy.

"I am, my son," Childress said gently. "Now let us remove this business from the open."

The sergeant surrendered to the inevitable. He made a signal to the airship, then called his squad around and formed them up around her. Off they went, striding through the cobbled streets of Valetta toward a destination she knew nothing of.

Finding it herself would have been painful.

The crowds melted before them and re-formed behind, trailing a ragged tide of people. *Good,* Childress thought. The more public the better.

At one corner she saw Cataloger Wang, of all people, dressed as an Arab. Their eyes met a moment. He nodded slowly, then stepped into the thickest press to follow her toward the domed and spired structure that the sergeant seemed to have in mind for his destination.

She knew she could not look back, could not ask for him to be caught up, but still Childress wished she had some way to bring him with her.

PAOLINA

This time she stayed with Boaz even at the most rarefied heights. She'd made additional oxygen pots and had rigged the electricks to continue to produce more of the precious substance.

Others went below, all but Gashansunu. It seemed a point of pride to the foreign sorceress to remain with Paolina, which Paolina could understand. An airship was very much a male domain. Outlasting even the roughest swaggerer among the crew made a strong statement.

Although, in fairness, these men had been a fairly gentle bunch. Paolina was unsure if *Erinyes'* complement were cowed by the losses they had sustained, or if their essential natures were somehow less male.

In the crackling air that left small whiskers of ice on so many surfaces, only Boaz and the two women remained awake and moving. Once again, he had driven them so high that the engines sounded on the verge of expiration. The world below seemed strangely distant, as well.

"I continue alone," Gashansunu announced. She sounded gloomy.

Correctly divining her meaning, Paolina asked, "Have you sought your *wa* further?"

"Yes." A long, slow silence followed as words struggled from the sorceress' lips. Paolina waited in the silence—nothing would be rushed, not until *Stolen* descended over England and that empire's defenses leapt into action. Finally Gashansunu said, "I told you, I believe I have passed on."

"I do not think you are in the land of the dead," Paolina said politely. "This is the Northern Earth, not Hell."

"The Silent World is empty to me now. That my body still breathes in the Shadow World is testament only to the persistence of meat."

"This I cannot argue with. You take a point of philosophy that seems lateral to the facts of our existence. But I am not of your people."

"This is because you do not understand the nature of the real." Gashansunu glanced back toward Boaz. "He has no *wa*, nor even the possibility of one. He exists in this world without referent to the next. You, I believe, have the potential for a *wa* inside you—you can be unified, whole, a complete piece of yourself. Long have I thought our way in the city was the most right and natural, that our understanding with our *was* is the most proper way for a person to feel. Sooner would I have sliced away my thumbs than be as alone as I am now."

Awkward, Paolina pulled Gashansunu toward her embrace. The sorceress resisted for a moment, then stepped into the circle of arms. Paolina's head barely came to Gashansunu's shoulders, but for a long moment they were of a single purpose.

Paolina released the other woman. "I cannot counsel you on the fate of your *wa*, or what that might mean for you. I can only say that if you can sorrow, and shed a tear, then you are not yet dead in this world."

"We will be soon enough, I believe," Gashansunu said with a bitter laugh.

"England is possibly our grave, yes. There is a strange irony here."

After a moment, Gashansunu prompted her. "Yes?"

"When I first resolved to leave Praia Nova, the village of my birth, my greatest ambition was to reach England and present myself to the court of Queen Victoria. Now, well, finally here we are, reaching for England and the royal court. I find my intent so different from what it was mere months past. I am finally come to where I once set out to be, and I have no interest in my arrival."

Stolen passed over the south coast of England late the next morning. Paolina knew the lack of charts would be critical in finding Blenheim Palace. Kitchens had drawn a rough map, but they would require much more than that to locate their goal.

"That must be Portsmouth," the clerk announced a few minutes later, looking over the stern rail. "By the gods, I wish we had a decent chart. Blenheim Palace is in Oxfordshire, reasonably due north. The problem is finding the palace."

"You have been there?" Gashansunu asked.

"Well, yes."

She looked at Paolina. "I will not walk the Silent World here, with my *wa* gone and all the familiar countries of the Southern Earth too far away. You might be able to find this place of his desires."

"Could I walk there? No, for I do not know the place," Paolina answered her own question, "and no one whose light I can follow is there for me to pursue as I did Boaz before."

The sorceress shrugged. "In time, we might think on a way. Surely it can be seen from this height."

"It is a great, huge palace amid woods and fields," Kitchens said. "We might take note of it if we are close, but only if we know where to look. Up here the world is too wide as my gaze slides across the ground."

Paolina took out the stemwinder. "Think on this place, Mr. Kitchens. Remember it as well as you can. Let me see if I can find a path within."

"I shall hold my course northward," said Boaz quietly. "Until one of you tells me otherwise."

WANG

Valetta's people were far more interested in the submarine than they were in the procession jogging through their streets. Wang did not have difficulty following Childress.

She'd seen him as well, and they'd traded a significant glance. Wang could not convince himself of this being a disaster. He followed until the men escorting her crossed a wide plaza and hurried up the stairs of a great, domed building.

Childress stopped at the top, to the evident surprise of the soldiers, and turned to scan the streets. He resisted the urge to wave, but presented himself at the bottom of the flight.

She extended a hand.

Wang nodded to acknowledge the invitation and trudged upward to meet her.

The librarian greeted him warmly. "My friend," she said in English, and clasped his hands with a smile. She added in Chinese, "Are you crazed? This will be the death of you. You should have gone home from Goa."

"Going home would have been the death of me," he replied in the same language.

The sergeant leading her spoke reluctantly. "Ma'am . . ."

Even Wang could see that he was torn between duties and self-preservation. Childress was a formidable woman, slayer of fleets and leader of mutinies. This English soldier could not be aware of more than a portion of the truth, but still he knew trouble when he saw it.

"My man, who was not ready at our arrival," she said crisply in English. *I am come to take her away,* thought Wang. *Why does she bring me within?*

"Next time," she added, "pay attention. We shall not have these errors again." Childress turned to face the doors.

Two soldiers scrambled to throw them open. She walked slowly, with an expression of deliberate concentration as if she worked some spell. He quickstepped after her as they passed into the shadows, much as if he were her servant.

A messenger, carrying a belated dispatch from the far side of the Northern Earth.

Within was a dusty, empty room where soaring pillars supported the dome. It had once been a temple, Wang realized. Church, here in Europe—he'd seen churches in Singapore and Tainan. Now the floor was empty, innocent of the hard benches Christians seemed to favor. A raised section at the far end suggested there had once been an altar. Narrow windows with colored glass shed speckled light in long bands across the echoing silence.

The doors crashed shut behind them. A light shower of dust fell from high above. He looked up to see the interior of the dome, pediments that must have been meant to bear statues spaced around the band at its base.

"No one is here," he whispered.

"I know *that*." Childress sounded irritated.

Wang shut his mouth. The Mask looked about thoughtfully. Doors led out at the back, while darkened hallways extended left and right.

No one moved.

Even so, he had the distinct impression of being watched. People in the shadows? If this place was like the Forbidden City, there would be listeners hidden within the walls, under the floors, down inside the very pillars.

Somehow, Wang was sure that the foe here was not so hidden. If anything, they were too close.

"You may come out now," Childress called in a strong, clear voice, as if summoning children from a hiding place.

Wang jumped slightly as the shadows began to move.

KITCHENS

They'd passed above Portsmouth undetected. *Portsmouth!* He was almost to his goal. His body felt wretched, headache still stabbing, but at least the bright circles had faded from his vision. Paolina, that angel of mercy, had brought oxygen and water until he had turned both away.

A man could only take so much.

Now he watched the trees pass by far below, rougher green textures against the vague striations of farm fields. The girl manipulated her device, the small, strange magic that had driven all of them so far.

Without her, he would have failed long ago. Without her, the Queen would remain trapped endlessly. Without her, they could die in the sky even now.

"Think on the palace you seek," she said, the faint Portuguese lilt in her voice thrilling him.

He considered his memories of Blenheim Palace. An architectural marvel, a stone monstrosity, mausoleum for a not-quite-dead Queen, a hive of angry Scotsmen and serious fellows with a penchant for interrogation. Whispering marble-floored halls, cotton-draped furniture, the scent of blood, countryside full of sturdy English peasants who would protect their masters' secrets, a town occupied by a Highland regiment . . .

Something tickled in Kitchens' mind. Like prayer, but in reverse, as if a voice from beyond were reaching in. He imagined the palace as it had looked upon his approach, the road from Woodstock, where the turns had been, how the copses and belts of trees had been laid out. Were there walls? Was the drive graveled or cobbled? How far from London had he come?

A map of England shifted in his mind. His work had always been overwhelmingly concerned with what took place beyond Albion's shores. Home was mostly railway stations, offices, naval bases, manufactories—resources to be deployed, locations where important men must be visited to deliver reports.

That England was a *place* had somehow always escaped him.

Now he flew above the landscape, swifter than a bird, sliding past clouds, looking down on twisting country roads and the brick-lined cuts of railway embankments. Shadows seemed to fall in all directions, as if the sun spun in the sky above him. The world grew to a blur of color; then Blenheim Palace stood at the center like the trick of a display at an odeon.

"Thank you," she said, and he was shivering.

Gashansunu offered him more water. "Here, you will need this. If I but had the right herbs . . ."

Paolina was already off to confer with Boaz.

Soon, thought Kitchens. *Soon, my Queen. Though I am far later than I should be, I still come to your need.*

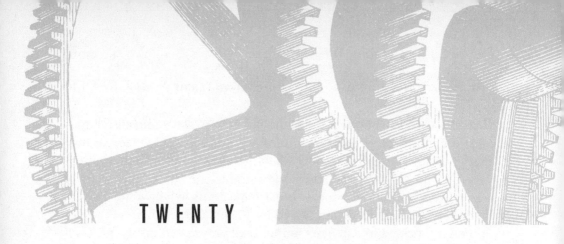

TWENTY

Curse not the king, no not in thy thought; and curse not the rich in thy bedchamber: for a bird of the air shall carry the voice, and that which hath wings shall tell the matter.

—*Ecclesiastes 10:20*

BOAZ

"A bit to the left," Paolina told Levine. The old sailor had the helm, a stoked oxygen pot beside him. The crew was roused for the imminent landing. "We should be able to see it soon," she added.

The Brass looked over the rail. "I do not know how you can tell one field from another here."

"It does not matter, dear," she said. "I know where Blenheim Palace is as surely as I know where you are. I will probably be able to see this place for the rest of my life, waking or sleeping."

::*he took them upon the mountain, and shewed them all the kingdoms of the Wall, and they were sore amazed*::

"It is a strange power you hold."

"I do not hold it." Her tone was absent as she peered over the rail. "I only use it."

"Still, here we are."

Kitchens tromped back to them, his face almost purpling. "I will not go ashore as an armed party!"

Martins followed close behind. "I do not propose to attack a royal palace, sir, but it is madness to land unexpected and have no response if we are met in force. Guns in hand will at least allow you time to negotiate."

Paolina glared at them. "What is this business with men and guns? Will you never lay down your arguments?"

"We sail unannounced into the heart of the Empire." Kitchens' voice was thick with frustration. "To arrive armed for attack only perpetuates the treason."

::*a king in madness is no more the man of his throne than a beggar who shouts murder in the streets of dawn*::

"There is no treason here," Boaz responded. "There is only need and action."

The clerk shook his head. "Admiralty will never see it that way. Whitehall neither. This is an *enemy* vessel."

"I have caused the banner to be slung," Paolina said.

Kitchens whirled. "Where was I?"

"Arguing over guns." She added, "It is still furled, but we will drop the cloth on our descent."

The final design was a length of white with a golden crown and the letters "UK" sewn upon it. That signified nothing in particular but seemed likely to be perceived as non-Chinese. Doubt was important right now, in the minds of the defenders of Blenheim Palace.

Boaz had been given to understand that anyone charged with the safety of the Queen could not afford uncertainties. He had not raised the question. This was a fool's errand at its best, taken on from loyalty rather from any rational expectation of success.

The Paolina–al-Wazir voice spoke up, almost all the old sailor's now that she was here in person. *Laddie, you've done well, but I ken you'll be doing little more.*

::*the majesty of the Lord shines forever, no matter whose hand lifts the ark from the altar*::

"I did not mean to start a war," he said, "but I do mean to stop it."

Paolina touched his arm. "You did not begin this madness."

"We all did," he told her. "The fighting commenced in East Africa, when they came for you, then strengthened when the Chinese returned. I had no small part in that."

"Could you have stopped them then?"

It had not even occurred to Boaz to try. First he had been running; then he had been obsessed with the Sixth Seal. "I might have acted differently."

She turned away, looking over the rail. "We should begin our descent."

"Armed!" shouted Martins.

"I will not have it," Kitchens shouted back.

::*coming dressed as traders in small goods and animal hides, they hid away their swords beneath the blankets of their mules*::

"Then let them carry small arms concealed," Boaz said. "You British always have some pistols aboard; surely the Chinese do as well. Do not threaten, but be prepared. To come this far, then throw away any chance that might aid you in reaching the Queen, seems simple foolishness to me."

The clerk stared, breathing hard. "Pistols, then. Holstered. No one fires or threatens except at my word."

"Aye aye, sir." The petty officer huffed from his own oxygen pot, then clattered away.

"We descend," Boaz told the pilot. "More oxygen all around; it does not matter now if we run out. Unfurl the banner."

Levine rang for emergency descent, which would release hydrogen from the cells. They could not fly away so well from Blenheim Palace, but it did not seem to Boaz as if that was a likely future for *Stolen* anyway.

GASHANSUNU

She looked at the countryside hurtling toward her and wondered if these people considered their land pretty. The stark beauty of the ocean was hers, the ever-present dark line of the Wall in the north, the musical clattering of the clockwork sky at midnight, the colors and sounds and shrieks of the jungle at dawn. This place was green, in a slightly dusty way, but the land had a sameness that disturbed her Southern heart.

The sorceress closed her eyes and imagined herself once more in the Silent World. It was closed to her now, with the loss of her *wa* and her distance from the Wall. She had ceased to struggle against the separation, though she mourned it.

Was this what had troubled the world, before she set out from the city? A knowledge that the end was coming all too fast, that a group of madmen in a stolen airship would drive with all their might toward the overthrow of one of the two great thrones of Northern Earth?

Surely war and revolution could not be what the world had wished for. Perhaps the skies had only cried to have this girl and her device removed from their purview. Southern Earth had wanted no part of this Northern problem.

Most likely, she was mistaken on all counts. Now she was lost in a place too distant to ever glimpse her home again.

Gashansunu was unsure that this ragtail crew managing an unfamiliar vessel would not simply slam them all into the earth. That would save the British defenders the trouble of killing them. Kitchens with his formless plan to break a throne was nothing more than a man driven past the edge of madness.

She was nothing more than a woman already at the same destination.

Around her, the sailors swirled, excited, crowding close, waiting to touch soil, to see how much trouble the toffs were truly in.

Humans never seemed to recall that they were made to die. Willful indifference was both their curse and their blessing. Her people did not lose sight of what was to come, not ever, but they folded that realization into their magic, their myth.

Dying here, far from her own *wa*, she was little more than a crying ghost to haunt the halls of this distant power.

At least she would see the girl Paolina to her fate, which was what she'd set out to do, with the blessing of Baassiia and at the request of omens circling high and low.

She wondered what omens circled now.

KITCHENS

Blenheim Palace spiraled below, unmistakable as *Stolen* shed altitude much too quickly. The sailors pulled away from the rail and braced themselves for a rough landing. Only Boaz, Paolina, Gashansunu and the mad old man at the helm still stood.

They had certainly been noticed. Men were hastily assembling in the forecourt, and more crept out onto the roofs in ones and twos. Snipers, to oppose the enemy.

"One of the inner courts, if you can," he shouted.

Paolina nodded and continued to stare downward.

Low, so low it seemed as if they would slam to earth in another moment, the ballast was released. *Stolen* bounced on the air, flinging upward hard perhaps two hundred feet. Kitchens was thrown down as someone screeched like a child at a midsummer carnival.

Engines roared. *Stolen* heeled over, turning across the rooftops. Rifle fire peppered, and somewhere nearby a cannon boomed. A chimney caught at their prow with a horrible splintering.

Stolen bucked, nose dipping to make a ramp of the deck, then pulled free to plummet into a courtyard beyond.

More gunfire rattled. The gasbag erupted with an explosive farting noise.

"'Ware hydrogen!" someone shouted. Kitchens tried to jump overboard, but a settling of the tortured hull tossed him forward before he could make his own leap. He tumbled to a bed of autumn plantings, narrowly missing a piece of statuary. His pistol spun away into a stand of hydrangeas.

The clerk looked up to see the hull heeling dangerously, boards splintering. The gasbag seemed torn between settling with the ship or rising on some final adventure of its own.

More crew dropped overboard, landing around him with curses and howls, even as the shouts of the men on the rooftop echoed.

"Inside, now!" Kitchens shouted. "Move! We must reach Her Imperial Majesty!"

PAOLINA

She jumped, tumbling toward the screaming clerk. Bullets cracked around her. Dirt fountained. Gashansunu ran, then stumbled, falling with a bloody bloom across her back. The petty officer scooped the Southern woman up, for all that she was a foot taller than he, as the crew ran in a thin tide toward a set of glass doors. A fellow in a dark suit stood within and screamed until Levine smashed through and threw him down.

Paolina raced after them, leaping over another bed of flowers as the glass began shattering with the impact of more bullets. She was in a sitting room, the screaming servant now a whimpering ball on the floor. Sailors bristled with pistols and makeshift weapons.

"The hallway beyond!" she shouted. "Away from the gunfire."

The group retreated through double doors. A crackling noise echoed from outside.

"Gasbag's ready to go up," said the old pilot.

Paolina checked head count. Gashansunu lay on the floor, groaning. Kitchens leaned against the far wall, his breathing labored. The petty officer was shouting at him about guns.

She whirled. *Where was Boaz?* Paolina raced back into the drawing room to see the Brass man out in the garden. He staggered, then staggered again. Boaz was being hit by bullets from the rooftop.

To these Englishmen, he was an even greater enemy than the Chinese. A creature of the Wall, come before their Queen.

Out the shattered doors. Across the broken soil. Flames, crackling and acrid. The gasbag settled, mercifully blocking some of the lines of fire. Smoke issued from *Stolen*'s broken hull. The engines, or at least their fuel, burned.

Boaz stepped toward her. A deep dimple punctuated his face. Two more wounds puckered his chest. His left arm flailed, creaking and whirring.

She was at his side. The bullets seemed to have stopped, or at least Paolina noticed them no longer. Tugging at his right arm, she tried to lead him toward the safety of the building.

He resisted one step, then two. She heard more gunfire. That did not matter. Getting him away from the explosive hydrogen mattered.

Shouting. Soil fountaining. Swift lead fingers plucked at her clothing, raising a line of pain along her right thigh. Everything had gone wrong, horribly horribly wrong.

"Come *on*," she shouted.

The Brass seemed to awaken to her voice. "I am here," he croaked. Something was the matter with his voice box, and the words buzzed strangely.

"Inside."

He followed as she tugged, stumbling as another bullet struck him in the back. Then they were through the broken doors, across the little room, and into the hall where the sailors were already diving to the floor. Levine grabbed Paolina's ankle and tripped her. She fell hard, Boaz collapsing beside her. The world became noiselessly loud and burning-bright.

WANG

Figures stepped out of the darkness in a peculiar array, distorted by shadows and the colored light until he thought they might be a troop of demons. He drew a sharp, fearful breath, then forcibly reminded himself that this was not one of China's temple graveyards.

A moment later, the light shifted, and he saw instead a line of people with tall masks like a festival processional. Their leaders wore feathers sweeping down from their faces to dangle low across their chests, brilliant displays of plumage.

"A Mask comes among us," intoned one of the feather-faced demons.

"A Mask of the *avebianco*," Childress replied, her voice firm and strong. Wang wondered what she might really be feeling in that moment.

The white birds gathered around her in a circle. "By whose authority was this Mask raised?"

"My own."

It was the wrong answer. The processional stirred. Hands moved; steel slid almost noiselessly from twice a dozen sheaths.

"You carry no authority." The shadows seemed deeper.

Childress glanced sidelong at Wang. She appeared worried, the first time he had seen her so. "There is ritual," she said. Her tone did not betray her, whatever her inner thoughts. "I have come through fire and death. Not elevation by ritual."

"Whose death?"

Even Wang could see her relief.

"I carry the authority of the Mask Poinsard," the Mask Childress complained. She stepped close to her interlocutor. "I stand in her place now and forevermore, by right of blood."

A murmur ran around the room. The tension did not relax, but neither did it tighten.

The feathered leader stepped forward, and in a much more ordinary voice asked, "What is your name, woman?"

"The Mask Childress."

"So you were Poinsard's Childress."

"The Mask Childress," she repeated firmly.

Now the gathered Masks relaxed. Wary, not on the point of violence.

"You are come aboard a most unusual vessel," the interlocutor continued.

"Consider for yourself the meaning of that vessel, along with the fact that it sails at my command." She gathered herself. "It is not the way of the *avebianco* to set all power on the wing, but I have been forced to such measures in my travels to reach you. I have visited the Golden Bridge project at Chersonesus Aurea. Now I bring word of what the Silent Order would accomplish there in partnership with the Dragon Throne."

Wang started at that, but held his tongue. Whispering began among the assembled Masks.

She went on. "I have seen the beginnings of the war between England and China. It will be the death of far too many, and bring down our own ambitions as well. I have seen the stemwinder, that will change the order of the world. I have treated with men from Singapore to Port Said to set our council to finding the path to save us all. You will not gainsay me now, not after such trials. I am a Mask. Accept me, or never hear what I know."

The Feathered Mask swirled and met the look of his fellows. One by one their faces emerged. They were demons no more, just men and women playing games of identity and purpose.

Wang was surprised to find his heart slowing.

"What say you, brothers and sisters?" asked the interlocutor.

Their whispers rose to a murmur, then a babble, speaking first to one another, then to their colleagues farther away.

Childress patiently awaited their response. Wang stepped close to her. Then the monk appeared, as if stepping from behind a pillar. The Englishwoman winced as silence infected the room.

"Greetings," the monk called loudly in English. "I bear a message from the Jade Abbot."

The interlocutor bowed low. "His Prominence has not sent word to us in over a century."

"He would not now, except that the course of madness here on the Northern Earth has extended too far." She flipped her pipe between her fingers. "Too far to be sensibly reversed on its own, it would seem."

After a moment, the Feathered Mask stepped into the hanging question. "What is this message, oh monk?"

She leaned forward. Her pipe smoldered, though Wang had seen no spark. "In so many words, he has instructed me to tell you, and I quote, 'Cease your fecking about.'"

"What?" Wang demanded, the word slipping out of him. He continued recklessly. "The centennial wisdom is to 'cease fecking about'!? I refuse to believe that."

"I could rephrase it." The monk grinned insolently as ever. "I could tell you that the hour grows late and hope dims, that the very fate of men and the Grand Design imposed upon us all hangs in the balance, and that without prompt, swift action on your part the future intended for us all will fail."

"It would mean the same thing."

"Sounds better," Wang muttered.

Childress laid a hand on his arm, but he caught no warning glare from her.

The Feathered Mask seemed torn between laughter and red-faced anger. "He is never changed, the Jade Abbot. As it happens, we have been clever enough to understand that the world is transforming in some profound ways yet to be understood. There are too many engines, too many machines, and now a mechanism for bringing adept magic into the word has been built. This war is a symptom, not a cause, of change."

The monk did not seem impressed. "The difference is that the Jade Abbot can create transformation of his own, should he deem that necessary. Better to solve your problems yourselves than to regret a solution imposed from far away."

"It does not matter," Wang said, ignoring Childress' increasingly ungentle tugs on his arm. "You all seek the same goal. Me, as well. The Mask Childress would stop this war; the *avebianco* would oppose the designs of the Silent Order; this Jade Abbot would restore balance to the world. You have *no argument*."

Now he was beneath the full force of the gaze of the Feathered Mask. "Then what do you propose we do, servant?"

"You are the council of the *avebianco*," he snapped. "I should hope that you are wiser than me. Direct your agents within both empires to ease military actions and accelerate whatever peace is under discussion. Send messengers to the Silent Order with assurances of cooperation and request further discussion." *Childress, to be specific.* "Call a halt to the machinations, before the momentum proves too great to resist the processes of war. Surely you have read history?"

"This man speaks," Childress finally said, "as an officer of the Chinese Empire, and an agent of the Silent Order." Her tone asserted her claim to her authority. She gave Wang a strange smile. "His courage in traveling here to carry this message cannot be denied, nor his role in what must come next."

"On this moment, on your bare word, we should leap headlong into action?" someone called from the ranks of the Masks.

Childress' voice went hard. "If I am a Mask, then my bare word is sufficient. If you do not judge me a Mask, then why do we treat now?"

CHILDRESS

She was afraid they could see the uncertainty plain upon her face. This council was not like she'd ever thought—a thing of theater and dreams, rather than something resembling a faculty senate meeting back at Yale.

Even more strangely, they began to file through one of the side doors of this vast, empty cathedral. One by one the Masks and Feathered Masks slipped away from her, each carrying their totem. Childress followed, Wang in her wake, the damnable monk walking alongside as if this were all happy coincidence.

Yet the woman had cemented her all-too-flimsy claim to authority here.

What lay beyond was not some closet or meeting room, but a stairway descending into the chipped, pale foundation rock.

They spilled out into a limestone cave. Torches guttered, and the space reeked of old damp and aggressive slime. A crude statue loomed in the center—no, not crude, Childress realized. Just a style so foreign to her that it was almost unrecognizable as art.

Whoever had carved this had seen the world through very different eyes. A woman with a wide, heavy-lipped face stared blankly at Childress, but her body was much too big. As if a sow had borne a human head, or a woman had carried a hundred children at once as in primitive myths. Her belly rose like a hillock, then fell away again to her feet. Pendulous breasts were rendered faithfully in the stone.

An earth goddess of the most chthonic sort. Doubtless of great interest to the Comparative Theology fellows back at Yale, but now the focus of a circle of chattering Masks. Except here where she might have expected cloaked identities and ritualistic language, they behaved more like the faculty senate she had thought to see before.

"Janklow worked the Istanbul people for two years. . . ."

". . . we saw the reports on the first battles along the African coast."

"If the British had paid more attention to that Tesla fellow, they might now be . . ."

". . . don't know. Nothing from Shanghai since well before the fighting."

". . . was buried secretly because better his death go unreported and let them all wonder."

"Besides, we might just bring him back . . ."

The interlocutor turned to her. "It is like prayer, you see. We respect the word of God here amid His Creation, but Rational Humanism does not come naturally to many. Simply setting aside the storms of the soul is difficult. This goddess is very old, more ancient than most of what now stands on Malta. She is part of the catacombs passing every which way beneath. Our focus on her is not hierarchical, but she serves to draw in what we say and reflect it back to us."

"Literally?" Childress was incredulous. Somehow the *avebianco* had always seemed to her to be an order of bureaucrats and clerks, building their networks of information to more properly model the happenings of the world and thus advance the case of Rational Humanism. Not a bunch of costumed gabblers in an ancient cave.

But she continued to listen.

"Admiralty did not want to confirm the arrests . . ."

". . . that unfortunate tunneling project will breach . . ."

". . . we don't know where the girl went after that, but the Listeners have been disturbed."

"Here is the final summation of Chinese casualties off the coast . . ."

They were not gabblers. Masks moved from one knot to another, so that the composition of each group changed and changed again. Each shared with the next, and then with their newest neighbor, until understanding was everywhere, like a stain in water.

A very strange arrangement, yet oddly effective.

Beside her, Wang shifted uneasily. She squeezed his arm again, whispering, "Wait, this will soon be done."

"I do not fear it be done, Mask," he replied in Chinese. "I fear it not be done well."

Eventually their voices died. Everyone but the interlocutor had found a knot in which to stand, their shuffling back and forth at an end. They all faced the goddess.

"We support the Mask Childress," said someone from the first knot. Her fellows nodded.

"Our support is provisional, but affirmative," announced a man in the second knot.

"We cannot support her," the third knot's spokeswoman said, but two of hers shook their heads in disagreement.

Thus it went around, eleven groups of four or five Masks each. Eight stood with her, two against, one in an undecided draw.

The interlocutor turned to Childress. She shook, chilled by the stone and the waiting and the strange, swift efficiency of these people who were her own.

"We accept your report. Our agents will take their word as swiftly as possible to London and Beijing, and to the field commanders wherever they may be reached. In certain places we will not be heeded, but in many others your words will find sympathetic ears. An ambassador will be named to both the Silent Order and to the Dragon Throne, plenipotentiary with the power to loose and to bind, in order to make formal agreement with the intent of setting aside attempts to breach the Wall. We will also see to the girl Paolina, for we believe she may be back on this Northern Earth."

"Of that last I am confident you are in error," Childress said, struggling to hold her voice firm. "As for the rest, I welcome your voice in these matters. We may yet stop this madness." She felt in the moment the tumblers of history shifting, as if the logic of some profound and painful decision had finally made itself apparent to her heart.

"You will carry our word back to the East." The interlocutor seemed almost grim. "Go to the Silent Order first, and instruct them to leave off their plotting at the Wall. If we must cross over, then we may consider such an effort together, for there is little point in exporting our struggle to those virgin, unchurched shores. It can surely hold no significance there except what we carry with ourselves."

"No—," Childress began, then broke off as the Feathered Mask continued.

"After that you will go to Beijing and carry the same message to the Emperor on his Dragon Throne. Tell him no one will win at this game of war. The English have found themselves in error due to a rogue magician with whom he should no longer be concerned."

"What will you do to Paolina?" she asked, worried by that threat.

"We will aid her in finding a way to be less of a danger to herself or the seats of power," the interlocutor replied. "Your business is in the East."

"Why me?"

"Because you are a woman who can bend the very ships of war to her will, and have the friendship of half a hundred others who may help."

It would not be safe for Leung and *Five Lucky Winds* to return to Chinese waters, but that choice was not hers to make. Not right now. "I will need to speak to the crew of my ship," she said. "I must sort out what is best for them."

"I can take you home." Wang's speaking up surprised her. "I am here with the yacht *Good Change*. My vessel may pass under British guns and their watchful eyes without creating alarm."

"What of *Five Lucky Winds*?"

Beside Wang, the monk smiled and blew a cloud of smoke. "Go speak to that nice Captain Leung. He threw over a lifetime of loyalty and discipline for the sake of you. I am sure he will agree to be sent home."

The interlocutor handed Childress something. She took it, briefly uncomprehending. His feathers, rising above a hidden domino as seen from the back, longer pinions trailing below.

"You are a Feathered Mask now," he told her. "You have proven beyond question your loyalty and capability, and will rise high in our councils upon your return from the East."

She looked at the monk, then at Wang. "I should return to *Five Lucky Winds*, I think."

"Go," said the interlocutor. "We will come with seals and documents to delight the Mandarins of the Eastern courts, but you already know what this is and what must be done."

"Yes," the monk said. "What must be done."

She seemed pleased, which in turn pleased Childress. The librarian turned to climb the stairs, trailed by Wang and the monk.

None of the *avebianco* followed them upward, so once they had regained the street, they were alone except for the usual traffic.

"Do you know the way?" Childress asked Wang.

"Follow me," the monk said, then strode off in a cloud of smoke.

TWENTY-ONE

The arrow cannot make him flee: slingstones are turned with him into stubble.

—Job 41:28

BOAZ

He stumbled through a country of black lands and bloody rivers. The sky flashed in stuttering arcs of lightning and memory. A voice shouted.

: : *rising from the grave trench with wisdom in one hand and justice in the other* : :

No, Boaz thought. *Not that.*

: : *each step made as a carving, so that the statue walks beneath the noon sun* : :

Fire? Heat, at any rate.

: : *burnt offerings placed at the points of the compass, until the Kohanim is done propitiating* : :

He didn't feel pain. Not as monkey men did. But something was badly, badly wrong.

: : *rising from his ragged bed, the dead man walked through the temple doors and cried havoc upon the enemies of the king* : :

One arm seemed to be stirring of its own accord. The other would not move. Boaz envisioned himself in chains.

: : *and so the spirit of the Lord came into his body and seized him with a violence* : :

Boaz realized his legs flexed without his command. The Sixth Seal . . . ?

: : *spake he in a voice of unreason that shouted from the far side of the law* : :

He rose, unseeing, unhearing, skies boiling in inner vision, locked within the metal arches of his own head. Only the movements of his body transmitted themselves to his sensorium, though he had no volition.

: : *striking them down in anger, he walked past the gateposts and drowned himself in the bloody river* : :

Everything felt stiff and strange, as well, beyond the sense of wrongness in his motion.

: : *breath of the Lord like rain in the desert* : :

YHWH, Boaz thought, addressing the absent God of his first creation, *if this is Your hand, please release me. If this is the hand of another, please strike them down that I might fall away free.*

Something hit him hard, but he did not fall.

The Seal screamed.

: : *faithless and foolish both, you will give up your soul and sense alike for the sake of duty gone wrong:* :

"I have given up nothing," he said, his voice box hissing and crackling. Paolina, al-Wazir—for their sake and the sake of the people from whom they sprang, not for his own, he had moved across the face of the Northern Earth. He gave everything, but he had not given up.

: : *now brace the left wall, that it not tumble:* :

Boaz realized his left hand stretched out. Something was there, unyielding, durable. A wall.

: : *drop the scales from your eyes and see the light before you:* :

He looked, and saw a cluster of men with rifles peering through a doorway, shouting silently. Carpet before him smoldered and guttered with flame. Furniture was shattered to polished splinters.

: : *stand firm before them, that they may not pass:* :

"Boaz," Paolina shouted from behind him.

He wanted to turn and answer her, look to her safety, ensure that she would be well and whole and hale, even when these men burst into the room and struck them all down in a hail of bullets.

: : *that he threw himself across the fire:* :

His mouth opened and words stormed out, not his own, but the Sixth Seal's, in full control of Boaz' body.

BY THE HAND OF THE LORD AND THE WILL OF MY MAKER, I ABJURE THEE, ABSTAIN FROM VIOLENCE AND STAND BACK BEFORE YOU INTERFERE WITH THE HOLY WORK— ELSE YOU WILL BE STRUCK DOWN AND BROKEN ON THE ALTAR OF THE LORD.

Their faces were shocked. Their guns wavered. Somebody behind him shouted. Footsteps echoed as they ran.

Only Paolina cried out for him, before shrieking as someone unseen forced her away.

The bullets began again.

: : *never will you know:* :

WANG

Their passage through the streets of Valetta was quieter this time. Almost as if they were invisible. The Maltese simply turned their faces away. Even the British soldiers they passed did not seem to take note of the three of them.

He had to ask the monk. "Are you doing this?"

She shrugged. "No more than you are."

"Consider from where we emerged," Childress said. "The *avebianco* clearly have a curious relationship with the society here. They are much more present than I would ever have thought. I suspect the Masks—the other Masks, I should say—walk the streets unnoticed until they choose to draw attention to themselves."

"That is all I ever do," the monk told them. "People see not what is before them, but what gathers in their attention."

They crossed a plaza, passing by whirring flights of pigeons and a fountain smelling of old pipes. The buildings were a bit smaller than the imposing windowed cliffs of limestone and granite lining the waterfront. The monk took another turn, surefooted and swift, that Wang had no notion of. The docks could not be so hard to find.

Soon they approached *Five Lucky Winds*. The crowd watching the submarine had not noticeably dispersed. Wang and Childress were forced to push people aside. The monk simply threaded, as if she were smoke moving through trees. Maltese and British stepped aside, murmuring.

The monk strode the gangplank. Childress followed. Wang trailed behind.

As they reached the deck, al-Wazir leapt forward to sweep the old Englishwoman into a bearish embrace. "We didna know when you'd be returning!"

Leung stepped forward with a sidelong glance at Wang. "Mask, how did you fare?"

"We must go up to discuss this," she said.

The captain nodded. They climbed the iron ladder inside the tower, Wang trailing behind in the smoky wake of the monk.

GASHANSUNU

Her body was dying.

She knew this the way she knew her own heartbeat. She knew this the way she knew that a bloom of flame and pressure had washed overhead. She knew this the way she knew her place in the city—instinctive, unquestioning, *right*.

That was fitting enough. She had been dead for a while, with the loss of her *wa* and the distancing from everything in her world. The Wall was not just an artifact of the world's working, it was a barrier that kept the soulless violence of the Northern Earth well away from the verdant, quiet Southern Earth.

People died all the time there, too, but they died of things one could understand: fevers from the rivers; accidents on the streets of the city; an argument between Houses raised too high, beyond the distance of reason. When they died, their spirits moved to the Silent World and transformed into *wa*, to come back again and again among the hearts and minds of the sorcerers.

Gashansunu had never imagined death to be such an orderly process. Someone called out numbers. Rattles, thumps and sharp reports echoed, as if building were being done with tools of iron and lead. Voices chimed; people groaned. She lay flat on the ground, facing down, and saw nothing but a bit of messy carpet that smelled like death.

The antechamber of disaster, struck down in the middle of all the business of the world.

Her back was numb, and so were her legs. She was far too warm, except where she was far too cold, and the slick heat on much of her body suggested significant exsanguination.

She tried for the Silent World one last time. Though it had been barred to her since the loss of her *wa*, Gashansunu still wished she could go back and spend her ultimate moments in that place.

Much to her surprise, it opened at her will. The noises and the pain faded as she found herself in a quiet hallway that stretched beyond the bounds of vision in both directions. She could see the other souls of *Stolen*'s company around her. Bright knots of wrath burned more distantly.

Her *wa* cried.

YOU ARE HERE!

HELP.

She whirled, casting her gaze from point to point, place to place, desperate to see where her poor *wa* had gotten to. That was not apparent to her, so Gashansunu called out again.

Where?

HERE.

Something flickered to her left. She rose, defying the impossibility of torn muscle and broken bone, and followed the crying.

KITCHENS

Everything was a disaster. They had attacked Blenheim Palace, seat of the Queen, and failed. He could only pray for a swift death.

Their little band had retreated around another corner. Clothes still smoldered from the hydrogen explosion. That they had been a pair of rooms away saved them, but still two more of the men were dying. So was Boaz, apparently, until he rose to walk into the fire of their opponents.

"Back, back again!" Kitchens shouted to his handful of survivors.

The Brass was distracting the palace defenders, so the intruders dragged themselves and their wounded around another corner. This branch of the corridor had been unharmed by the explosion. It appeared strangely normal, in the way of an English great house shuttered for a season. He spent the briefest moment basking in the scents of furniture oil and carpet dust before focusing on what would happen next.

Kitchens could not imagine how to reach the Queen now. He'd hoped to have some time to move through the halls of Blenheim Palace—it had been virtually empty on his last visit—but the defenders had responded too swiftly and effectively.

Those defenders did not *know* what was wrong, what was at stake; they had not heard the Queen's wishes. Even if there was not an open battle raging right now, Kitchens could not imagine these men paying any heed to his explanation.

Martins had been right that they should approach well armed. Now they were down to a few shots, nothing more, with no time, no direction, and their lives at an end.

He would not be allowed to walk away from this.

Then Gashansunu stood, her body creaking oddly, dark blood seeping from the gunshot wound to her back.

"What the blazes are you doing?" Kitchens shouted, then realized it did not matter. He turned to Paolina, who was crying.

"It is wrong, it is all wrong," she told him. "You've killed everyone."

"My *wa* is with the Queen," Gashansunu moaned, then shuffled down the hall.

Kitchens' mind blazed. Maybe there was a chance. "Follow her!"

The surviving sailors moved. Paolina grabbed at Kitchens. "We cannot leave Boaz. He will die, be broken for scrap, pulled apart for study, reduced to nothing but metal and dust."

"Then *help* him," Kitchens hissed. "Help us all. We are out of men; we are out of weapons; we are out of time. Use your magic machine and buy us some of all." He shook her loose. "Help us or leave us to die in peace, woman!"

PAOLINA

She stared after Kitchens, who chased his ragged band of men as they followed the lurching sorceress.

Her loyalties were clear. She peered around the corner. Could she save Boaz? If she could just get to him, they could step away, all the way back to the Wall. She would not even push off, send the energy elsewhere. Better to level this part of the palace, let them wonder what had become of her and her Brass lover, teach these English *men* a lesson in manners.

Boaz stood in front of a group of armed defenders, arms wide, just as the Brass Christ had done when strapped to the wheel-and-gear of the Roman horofix. His voice echoed, though she could not make out his words. What-ever he was saying, the British had stopped shooting for a moment.

Almost forty feet of smoldering, bloody carpet, with three scattered bod-ies between them, separated her from Boaz. She couldn't cover that distance and manage the stemwinder, not with the threat of weapons firing at any second.

She could pull him to her, as she had once so disastrously done with *Five Lucky Winds*, but they would still be here, too close to ruin, for her to do more.

Five Lucky Winds . . .

It was a *submarine*. A ship full of men and weapons; and when last seen, al-Wazir, who was Boaz' great, good friend. She would buy all the time in the world if she called them *here*.

Much worse to have tons of warship dropped on your head than a single undermanned airship.

The sheer audacity of the idea stole her breath. She only had moments, but it might work. And now she knew how to move things without leaving a trail of destruction behind. All she need do was push off with a sufficient countervailing mass.

How many sailors had there been? Dozens? As well as that Captain Leung, and the chief. They would know what to do, how to hold off these defenders, how to save her and Boaz.

Paolina tugged the stem out to the fourth position. The submarine was the largest thing she had ever called, by a vast margin. But she'd done it before, so she could do it now.

A half-step back from the corner to shelter her work. Closed eyes, re-membering, remembering. How to push when pulling something so large. Where could she send the energy?

She focused on the Atlantic Ocean below Praia Nova. That was water she had seen every day of her life until she had walked away from her home. The force of calling the submarine would be like a bomb in the sea. Unless the boats were out, it would harm no one. That was an empty place. The only risk was to the *doms* and the men of the village who served them.

Well, that and the risk of doing this at all. Violating once more her oaths to leave off.

No time, no time, no time, her thoughts screamed. *He must live!*

Regrets were for later, Paolina realized. Ignoring her qualms, she continued to focus. She had the image of *Five Lucky Winds*, she had the place where the energy would go to dissipate the effort of the translation, and she would put the vessel down in the courtyard where the airship still burned.

Paolina turned the knurled stem and called the submarine to her.

The noise was indescribable. A presence, a force, a shattering of air, of ears, of mind. Paolina raced around the corner as seawater burst through the drawing room doors, flooding the hall between knee-deep. Boaz fell into the swirling foam. The men beyond scattered from their position.

He had fallen, but he would not drown. Her love could wait a moment, though it tore at her heart. She needed al-Wazir, Leung, the old librarian. She needed them *now*.

Paolina raced through the destroyed drawing room, splashing amid water that had already receded to her ankles. A great curving metal wall loomed in the garden beyond—the hull of the submarine.

Shouting in Chinese already echoed.

She burst out the empty doorway, screaming for al-Wazir.

CHILDRESS

The world slipped.

Valetta vanished.

The deck dropped from beneath her feet.

She fell, trying desperately to catch herself on the metal half-wall of the conning tower.

The tumbling stopped, slamming her into the deck again. She, Leung, al-Wazir and the monk were a tangle of bodies as the tower began to lean hard to the starboard. A great, wretched groaning of metal echoed through the hull.

Above her, Childress saw the gable of a *roof*.

Men yelled in Chinese. She heard al-Wazir begin to curse above the rushing of water. Then a girl's voice shouted the chief's name.

Paolina.

The girl had called the submarine with her gleam, again. Only this time they were not cruising a stormy sea.

A man popped up on the gable, stared at them wide-eyed a moment, then retreated. She heard a gunshot.

Leung climbed up, pushing against the two women to peer over the side of his little cupola. "We are in a garden," he said in a strange voice. "With the wreck of an airship."

Childress struggled to her feet. "Paolina."

The monk was already shinnying down the ladder.

"Below," Leung ordered.

If she is one of the Eight Immortals, Childress thought, *now would be an excellent time for her to show her power.*

The librarian scrambled after the captain and the monk.

Firing erupted from the rooftops. This wasn't a garden; it was a courtyard enclosed on three sides, in the manner of a great mansion. Childress had no idea where they were.

Sailors under the direction of both Leung and al-Wazir were tossing rifles down as the weapons were passed through a hatch. A party already returned fire, keeping the defenders at bay. They had plentiful cover among the chunks of a shattered wooden hull onto which *Five Lucky Winds* had dropped.

She looked around for Paolina. The monk had reached the girl, and was speaking to her urgently. Heedless of the bullets, Childress raced toward them.

". . . and Mr. Kitchens has gone to kill the Queen," the girl said, almost sobbing. "We must go now, before they destroy him utterly."

"Go where!?" Childress demanded.

"To fetch Boaz! He has been struck down. I fear he is dying." Her eyes were red, and mad with tears.

"Lead," she told the girl.

Paolina raced back through a ruined room that had recently been both burned and flooded. Childress followed, the monk hot on her heels.

Bodies were scattered in the corridor beyond, which was drenched in seawater. Boaz gleamed supine to their left. The rest seemed to be British.

"Are you two here alone?" Childress shouted, following them.

Sliding to her knees next to Boaz, Paolina looked up at the librarian. "No. I am with Gashansunu, who helped me find my way back from the Southern Earth, and Mr. Kitchens and all those sailors. But *he* is dying."

She tried to lift Boaz' head, but he was so much inert metal. The monk leaned over and flipped the heavy Brass body. He crashed onto his back. His eyes flickered open. The irises flexed, while something crackled from inside him, as if he meant to speak. His face was bullet-punctured. So was his chest.

One hand twitched. The three of them stared in shocked silence as his fingers dragged across his belly to touch a spot. A little panel popped open.

Boaz' eyes flickered. "Take it," he whispered, his voice a groan of distressed metal."

"No," Paolina said, pressing the panel shut again. She didn't *care* what he had in there. "We are removing you to safety."

A blast echoed from outside, shaking dust from the ceiling.

Safety didn't seem to be an option anymore, Childress realized.

"I will help you," the monk said. "There is only one place you can be safe, foreign girl."

Paolina looked at the woman desperately. "Where? What? How?"

The monk's voice was urgent, rushed. "The Jade Abbot will guide you and protect you. He watches and guides the world, as he once did for the boy Hethor. His temple is full of automatons and machines; he can repair your metal man. That is the work of his hands when his spirit is in need of rest. You will not be pursued there. Atop the Wall, his defense is mighty."

"Wait," Childress began to protest, then stopped. She was not sure she should speak now—the choices in this moment were not hers, the power not hers. As for the Jade Abbot, his name had protected her in Valetta. Maybe he could protect these people now.

With a glance at Childress, Paolina turned back to the monk. "Where do we go? How do I know to believe you?"

"You do not know. You have no reason to trust." The monk shrugged, and for a moment, all the irony fled from her voice. "All you have now is hope."

"Would you go with me?" It took Childress a moment to realize that the girl had meant *her*.

"No," the librarian said gently, certainty flooding her own thoughts. "I must stay here and die with Captain Leung and Chief al-Wazir."

"No one has to die," Paolina argued.

"They already have." Childress shook her head. "Whatever errand your friends are about has stirred this place to anger. There is a dead servant in that outer room, dead sailors in this hallway. Your Boaz . . ."

"If I depart, you will die."

"We will be killed whether or not you go. Whatever army defends this place cannot allow us even the success of living out this day. We have invaded someone's heart."

"This is Blenheim Palace," Paolina told them. "In the midst of England. Mr. Kitchens came here to help the Queen die." She turned to the monk.

"Show me where you would go. I will send you and Boaz, that your abbot might see to him. I will follow when I may."

"I cannot do that," the monk said, her voice very unhappy. "I must return with you."

"I shall not ever come if you do not do this for me now. He is more precious to me than even my own life."

"How do you know where to send me?"

"Can you tell me somehow?" Paolina sounded desperate.

"I can open my thoughts to you, in a way that most cannot. You can see the place, send me, and follow when your time is right." The monk bowed her chin and began to pray. Childress watched Paolina work her little device, setting one of four hands as she muttered to herself. Gunfire cracked outside, and another explosion, but the girl kept on. Childress wondered how soon they would be interrupted from one side or the other.

Then Paolina glanced up again. "I have it."

She bent to kiss Boaz, clutched her stemwinder close, and sent both the monk and the metal man away with a pop of air.

"Now what?" asked Childress.

"We locate Kitchens," Paolina said. "We help him finish his business, and we find a way out of this for all of you. Then I will go to this Jade Abbot. We will place my stemwinder among his automatons as just another decoration in his temple. I shall never use this power again once that has happened, for its burden is too great for any one person."

"You would be free from both Northern Earth and Southern Earth atop the Wall," Childress observed.

"I was born of *a Murado*; it is fitting I should die there."

They walked down the hall. "A moment," Childress said at the doors. She stepped through to pass into the garden and call the men of her broken-backed ship to her.

WANG

He crouched among unfamiliar bushes, surrounded by sailors. What had just happened to them? No one around him seemed terribly surprised, but Wang was shocked beyond measure. One moment they were in the harbor at Valetta, the next they were falling out of the sky . . . where?

No wonder the Silent Order feared this Mask Childress so.

"Can you shoot?" Someone shoved a short rifle in the cataloger's hands.

"No," he whispered. It was something to do, though. He pointed the gun at the rooftops and tried to pull the trigger.

Where *were* they?

"We have died and gone to Hell," said the sailor who'd just handed him the rifle, as if Wang had spoken aloud.

"Is Hell full of Englishmen?" asked another. "In any case, I have not yet seen the Judges of the Dead. Have you?"

"Here," someone shouted at Wang. A hand reached out to shoot home the bolt on his rifle.

Maybe it *was* Hell.

Al-Wazir, unseen to Wang, roared about death and Scotsmen. Then the Mask Childress walked into the garden. She seemed to glow, and stood tall as if apart from the battle.

Probably not Hell, then, he realized.

"With me," she called in Chinese. "We have our purpose, and must follow the girl Paolina one last time."

A man with captain's tabs on his uniform looked up from behind a chunk of hull. The traitor Leung! Wang had not realized he was so close. "Purpose?" the captain shouted. "You destroyed my ship for a purpose?"

"I did nothing," Childress said calmly. Two bullets sprayed dirt at her feet, then were answered by a hail of Chinese gunfire. When those echoes died away, she added, "If you wish to live, you will come with me."

Leung called out, "You heard the Mask!"

The call to fall back echoed around the garden. Another Beiyang officer slid down a rope from *Five Lucky Winds*, wires trailing from behind him. "Scuttling charges ready, sir!" he shouted. "I have warheads from the torpedoes hooked in as well."

"Everyone after the Mask," Leung said. "Including you, Sun-Wei. I shall slay my own ship."

The sailors raced for shelter, heedless of the fire from the rooftops. Some returned covering fire, and two of their men fell to be dragged along, but in moments the garden was empty except for Wang and Leung.

"You should have gone with them," Leung said sadly.

Wang saw the grief in the captain's eyes. That woke him to the truth of the moment. What would Childress say to this man? He tried his best: "Why? So you could die alone with your ship?"

"*Five Lucky Winds* is already dead. This is her funeral to carry her into the next world." He slid something on a little box, grabbed Wang's arm, and rushed the two of them indoors. They passed a ruined room, into a ruined hallway, and followed the echo of running feet until the explosion behind them rocked the building so hard that both men tumbled to the floor.

"I never want to see a firecracker again in my life," Wang moaned.

"I will never command the sea again." Leung picked them both up, and they followed the sounds of the panicked crew.

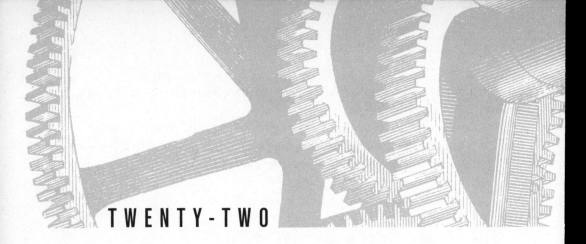

TWENTY-TWO

. . . of the hope and resurrection of the dead I am called in question.   —*Acts 23:6*

BOAZ

He opened his eyes.

His head was blessedly silent.

A high ceiling above, dark blue painted with gold and red. Phoenixes?

Vision was curiously strained and flat. Only one eye seemed to be functioning.

A face loomed. For a moment, Boaz thought he was among Chen's sailors again, along the Abyssinian coast, but this was a much older man than any of those warriors. He seemed far too calm as well.

There had been fighting.

Boaz tried to lift his hand, but it would not come.

"You have been in a very bad way, my metal friend," the man said in Adamic.

"No monkey alive speaks that tongue," Boaz whispered.

"I am no monkey; I am a man." A wrinkled smile. "And I have been alive a very, very long time. You would be amazed at what you learn if you stay around."

"I am Brass," he replied, this time in Hebrew. "We live on from the days of the first Brass."

"You are Brass no more." The old man followed his change of language, then touched Boaz' forehead, marking the spot where al-Wazir and Paolina had laid their chrism.

Paolina!

His rescuer continued. "You are something more. Just as the world is now becoming something more than it has been all these divided years of Creation."

"If I am more, then why can I not move?"

A sad smile. "Because I repaired your processor first. There is a dangerous beast in your belly."

"The Sixth Seal of Solomon."

The old man seemed surprised. "Ancient of days?"

"From a cave in Abyssinia." Boaz reflected for a moment. "Sealed there by a Kohanim of King Solomon's reign."

"Such times those were."

Boaz asked the paramount question. "Where is Paolina?"

The old man's face wrinkled into a delighted smile. "The girl with the gleam. I am afraid that I am neither all-seeing nor all-knowing, so I cannot say."

"Where am *I*?"

"A question from the musings of every thinking being down the ages of Creation." He leaned close. "In this case, you are in the Jade Temple atop the Wall."

A woman loomed into Boaz' vision. After taking a long look at him, she said in Chinese, "Your Holiness, I would go back, but I lack the means." Boaz understood her well enough.

"As would I," Boaz urged. He willed his body into motion, but he had been reduced to a talking head. "I need to return to Paolina."

"All will resolve," the old man replied in Hebrew. "You are going nowhere, my metal friend."

The woman gave him another long look, switching to Hebrew. "You saved them all, I believe. You stopped the British long enough for help to arrive."

Disjointed recent memory stirred. "No," Boaz said slowly. "The Seal did. I was . . . gone . . . from my head. I had been wounded too gravely. It picked me up and carried me forward those last minutes."

The old man laid a gentle hand on Boaz' forehead again. "Then perhaps it has served its purpose in this matter. Perhaps you have served yours."

KITCHENS

Gashansunu had led them in a broken-backed gait down one hall and up a grand corridor. When she stepped around a corner, a storm of gunfire brought her down.

Kitchens slammed back against the wall, breathing hard. He squeezed his eyes shut, fighting tears.

"What now?" whispered Martins.

He looked around. Levine, the old pilot. Three other sailors. The petty officer. Himself. Six men, with empty pistols and burns upon their faces.

In short, they looked like people who'd wrecked an airship.

Gashansunu was surely dead now. Paolina was gone, run after Boaz. Boaz was broken. The rest of his crew were dead or missing.

They were out of options.

"I do not know," Kitchens said. "At this point, they will not negotiate."

"Can't imagine there's much retreat, sir."

An enormous explosion rocked the building. Plaster dumped from the ceiling, setting up a roiling cloud of pale dust that floured them all.

Kitchens took advantage of the moment to duck his head around the corner where Gashansunu had died. Definitely the hall to the Queen's chambers. Fifteen or twenty men were positioned before her doors, rifles bearing from behind overturned tables.

He ducked away again before they could sight in on him. "No retreat, no advance, no surrender."

Her Imperial Majesty's words echoed in his head.

Remake what has been undone.
Break my throne.
Help me finish dying.

He'd done nothing she asked. All he'd accomplished was the deaths of dozens and a terrible disturbance among her guardians. This war would intensify, for surely Government would see their airship as evidence of Chinese complicity in the attack. China, and the Wall in the form of Boaz.

England would go to war against the world in mistaken vengeance for his mission to do the Queen's bidding.

"I have failed." The razor hung heavy in the lining of his sleeve. Kitchens wondered how it would feel kissing his neck.

"Sir, I don't know if we did right or not," the petty officer said. "But you believed it, and I believed you." He turned to the surviving sailors. "You lot find linen closets or something and hide till the fighting's over. I can't think you'll escape this, but if they take me and Mr. Kitchens here, maybe they won't be killing mad by the time they find you."

Levine growled. "No point in stopping now."

"It's at an *end*!" Kitchens shouted, then was ashamed of the violence of his voice. "We have failed, and we will be brought down for it."

A racket of men moving fast sounded through the double doors behind them. The other defending party had broken past whatever last magic Boaz had been working. The Brass and Paolina were lost, too, then.

Sobbing openly, Kitchens slipped his razor into his hand and waited to die.

A wave of Chinese sailors broke through the doors, Angus Threadgill al-Wazir at their head.

CHILDRESS

She had never been much for running, but this was a time for nothing else. Al-Wazir took the doors ahead without stopping, leading with his left shoulder so that they burst through in a cloud of plaster dust. Childress heard him bellow, "Kitchens, my lad!"

There was a brief moment of further confusion as the running mob skidded to a stop and sorted itself out. She and Paolina pushed forward to see a body in the cross-corridor. The girl let out a short, shuddering sob.

"Fifteen, twenty oppose us," Kitchens gasped to al-Wazir. "Around to the left. We must break through them before the regiment at Woodstock arrives in force."

Al-Wazir looked sidelong at Paolina. Childress followed his glance. She knew what he was thinking.

"Do not use it," she said in a low voice, gathering Paolina into her arms.

The girl wept into her shoulder. "I cannot," she whispered.

The chief had already seen this, and turned back to his planning. Leung and Wang caught up as well.

"Captain," al-Wazir said. "Are we up to rushing a score of armed men in a prepared position? We'll lose half of us at the very least."

Leung looked sour. "What do we gain?"

"An end to the war," Paolina said, pulling away from Childress' shoulder. "Even more so, an end to all this madness."

"An end for the Queen, who desires it most rightly," Kitchens answered. "But I must do this thing, or we will have failed."

"None of us are getting out alive," said Martins. "You going to surrender and let them shoot you like a dog, or try until the last?"

Now Leung looked back at Childress.

Was this truly up to her? There could only be moments before more defenders arrived.

Why was it her decision?

Because she was the Mask.

This was a game of secret societies and dueling thrones, and most properly her business. She had taken up the Mask Poinsard's role with her original pretense. Now it was time for her to accept the full responsibility of that elusive, hidden power.

Men would die. Many men. She came in that moment to an enlarged understanding of Paolina's distress at being forced to use the stemwinder again and again, begetting ever more violence to stop other violence.

Where did it end?

Not here, not now, not today.

"Make the attack," she ordered. "Let us give Mr. Kitchens his chance."

Leung barked out orders. Al-Wazir pulled his assault team together. "I'll go out first," he announced loudly. "The lads will be confused by me. That might buy us a few extra seconds."

They all shouted in Chinese, counting up to ten, then—waving carbines and pistols, sweeping Kitchens' few surviving sailors with them—poured around the corner.

PAOLINA

She stood trembling in the empty hall. Only Childress was with her. Even that chubby civilian—Wang, someone called him?—had run shouting into the gunfire. The noise of battle bordered on the deafening, bullets shattering the walls in their corridor. Childress pushed her against the left wall, where she was least likely to be hit except by a ricochet.

"I sh-should have used the stemwinder," Paolina said. Hethor had told her the world was dust and gears, that the stemwinder was an instrument of man's free will. Why was she ever so plagued by power? "N-now they're all g-going to die. All of this is my doing. Look, they have even trampled Gashansunu's body."

The sorceress was unrecognizable, a broken corpse spread too far.

Something banged loudly.

"You must calm yourself," Childress said. "Can the stemwinder take you away now?"

"Y-yes. I could abandon all of you to your deaths and walk free."

"Then go," urged the librarian. "Enough has been done here. Just depart."

"To Boaz." Paolina was miserable. Every fiber of sense told her to flee. Her love for the Brass man urged the same. She was trapped here only by a sense of loyalty to choices Boaz had made. This was the culmination of Kitchens' mad errand.

Abruptly, the shooting stopped. The building was strangely quiet, except for the crackle of a distant fire, and muffled voices shouting. Servants to battle the flames, or more soldiers, to battle *them*.

"Do we look?" Paolina asked.

Childress shrugged.

Then Wang leaned around the corner. His face was bloodied and feral, with a darkness in his eyes. "It is a disaster, but we have won the moment. The price was too high."

Paolina shuddered, then summoned her courage and stepped out to see what had become of her friends.

Bodies were scattered everywhere. Chinese and English, attackers and defenders. Some groaned or breathed in slow red bubbles. Many more were broken, shattered. Al-Wazir stood amid a small knot of Chinese, his red hair torn and bloody where something had snagged at his scalp. Everyone else was mess.

"Leung is fallen," Wang told them.

Childress shrieked, then covered her mouth. Paolina's heart curdled at that.

The knot of men broke up, stumbling backward. Kitchens she spotted now, and thought she recognized a few others; then the doors broke open with a blast of light and sound.

Everything seemed to happen out of order. Childress on her knees, crying over a body. Al-Wazir slumped against the far wall, looking surprised. Kitchens pressing into the next room, men with guns at his back.

Could she heal them? Where could she take them?

Did she have the *right* to?

All here had chosen to reach this moment, to live or die in this place.

She could not simply whisk them away.

Paolina knelt next to Childress.

Leung's mouth was open as if he had some final wisdom to impart. Hs forehead was marred by a gaping third eye, bloody and strange, that had swallowed all his words and left him with nothing but a blank and clouded gaze.

"I do not think he was ever out of Admiral Shen's orders," Childress said in a strangely calm voice. "They played a long and careful game, even with the mutiny and the deaths of the Nanyang fleet." Her voice drifted to quiet for a moment, then she said, "At the least, I should like to think this, for it means everything he did from beginning signified more than this foolish death."

She leaned forward and kissed his cooling lips.

Paolina helped Childress to her feet, and they looked to see if any of the wounded might likely live. She could not go to Boaz until this was done.

WANG

The women were with the captain. He knew no other duty to follow, and the will of both the Silent Order and the Kô had been cast away. He passed beyond the doors to see what prize they had won.

A spacious room, mostly darkened, a great pair of bellows flanking the door, with a big tank standing just at the edge of the lit area beyond them. Hoses and cables extended from it. A woman lay crying on the floor beside an empty rocking chair.

Of the forty or so who had entered this fight, eight remained standing alongside al-Wazir. They had their weapons pointed toward the man Kitchens as he faced off with a red-cheeked Englishman who held a long, flexible rod tipped by a glittering knife.

". . . not the Queen!" the last defender shouted. His accent was similar to al-Wazir's.

"This insanity is over, Dr. Stewart." Something metal glinted in Kitchens' hand.

The two circled like cocks in the fighting ring.

He wondered where the monk was. She would have tripped this fool, tied his shoelaces together and blown pipe smoke in his face.

Wang stepped next to al-Wazir. He felt a curious kinship to the big, one-handed man. "Why do you not shoot the crazy one?"

"I'm about to," al-Wazir grumbled.

Kitchens tried again. "Dr. Stewart, be reasonable."

Stewart glanced at the sailors. "*I* did not bring the enemy here." He jabbed his weapon toward Kitchens, who stepped around it with ease.

"You *are* the enemy here," the chief called out.

Wang sidled behind al-Wazir's men, along the wall, past the rocking chair, to the tank that was obviously the prize. He bent to study the pipes and hoses, wondering what they might mean, whether they were properly labeled.

This day had passed so far from strangeness that he could believe he had already descended into Hell.

KITCHENS

The razor was comfortingly familiar in his hand. He had learned to use it as a child in Savoy, then much later trained further in the killing arts at the Black College. Kitchens knew he should just shout for al-Wazir to shoot Dr. Stewart down, but here before him was the man who as much as anyone was architect of all their troubles.

The troubles of the Queen.

Stewart's surgical implement flashed again. The doctor might be a great one for cutting into bodies on the table, but he had no notion of fighting. Kitchens stepped inside the jab to bring his razor around and lay open a slash on the man's cheek.

"Are you finished?" he asked.

Stewart gasped, put one hand on the wound. "You're cracked!"

"I did not keep the Queen alive past her time!"

Another jab, another step—then the doctor lost his footing. Kitchens moved quickly, drawing the razor across the side of his opponent's neck.

Like all real knife fights, the combat was over in moments.

Stewart fell in a spitting, spinning rush of blood and cried out.

Kitchens kicked him in the head, then stepped to the Queen's tank. Behind him a single shot echoed as someone ended the doctor's moans.

He did not even know how to open this. Latches and locks presented themselves around the edge of the port he'd looked through on his previous visit, alongside a panel of stuttering gauges. He was loath to have them fire into the tank.

If the Queen must be helped to die, it would be he who committed the ultimate treason of regicide.

Kitchens began flipping toggles, trying to release the port. There must be a larger opening, a way to crack the entire chamber so Her Imperial Majesty's person could have been laid in the fluid bath in the first place.

The little hatch popped loose. He tore it free, sending it clattering to the floor. A bloated, pale face, still familiar from a lifetime of coinage and posters and duty and loyalty, stared up at him with a gelid, unblinking gaze.

"Your Highness," Kitchens said, a moment of cold fear stabbing his heart. "I am here to remake what has been undone. I can break your throne if I can help you finish dying. Is this truly your will?"

Bubbles popped from her lips.

He raised the razor still slick and scarlet from the death of Dr. Stewart.

Another bubble, then a long, slow blink.

Would he be a regicide, a name to be condemned through the ages? Or was he an angel of mercy?

"I am but a clerk, my Queen," Kitchens whispered, filled now with dread of the enormity of what he contemplated. "This is not my place."

Her head shook slowly. Voices called outside, demands for surrender, fearful shouts in place of the angry pursuit they had met before. Another red bubble popped from her lips.

Kitchens believed for a moment that he could see desperation in her eyes.

He reached down with the razor.

Queen Victoria tilted back her chin and smiled.

With a firm movement of Kitchens' wrist, history ended and began anew.

TWENTY-THREE

And the wall of the city had twelve foundations, and in them the names of the twelve apostles of the Lamb.
—*Revelation 21:14*

BOAZ

His eyes opened again. This time he had some sense of his body. The ceiling was still above him, in the strange view of only one eye.

The Brass lay quietly and listened for the voices in his head.

They did not shout at him, but somehow they were there. Threads within his own mind, as the Paolina–al-Wazir voice had already mostly become before everything went so wrong. The blood and thunder of the Seal were there as well, now submerged in his own thoughts.

Someone cleared their throat.

Boaz found he could turn his head. An old man in saffron sat next to him. *The Jade Abbot.*

"Welcome once again." His deep brown eyes twinkled with some emotion Boaz could not read. "I do not think you are Brass anymore. Your thoughts are divided, complex. I believe you have become human."

"Why would I want to be human?" Boaz asked.

"Why does anyone want to be human? To love a woman, in your case." The Jade Abbot smiled. "You will not be free to walk about for a while, but I have done work to make you more comfortable. I am afraid you may be here some time."

"What of Paolina?" Boaz realized he *did* want to be human, if being human meant being with Paolina. The thought of going on without her was too much to bear. They could not lie together as husband and wife, in the way of monkey men. Too much had already passed for any innocence to remain to their love.

He would give anything for her to be back with him.

"That is up to the girl," the Jade Abbot said. "She knows she has a place here."

"Atop the Wall, between the earths."

"The earths are coming together. I believe she may be the joining between them."

"Here at the hinge of Heaven." Boaz closed his eyes. "I am lost, sir."

He felt the hand on his face again, a gentle touch that brushed softly then slipped away. "We are all lost, my Brass friend. We are born alone, we die alone, and if we are lucky, we find a path of the spirit that carries us through life in pleasing company."

His eyes burned. Tears? That was not possible. "Can you bring her here?"

"Only she can bring herself here. You cannot call her to you, no matter how great your love. Only she can choose to come to your side."

Boaz realized he had no choices, only desires. She knew how he felt; she knew how to find him. All was on Paolina.

The threads within his mind were a chaotic stir, not unpleasant, but not simple. He tried to listen, to pick out what they were saying, but just as he'd wanted them quiet before, now he wanted them to speak out.

Was this what it meant to be human? To wish for the impossible, to never clearly hear the tenor of one's own thoughts?

If that was the price of love, he was willing to pay it.

GASHANSUNU

The Silent World seemed much brighter now. Lives burned like bonfires around her, so many spirits guttering away even as she looked toward them.

A greater fire burned nearby. Gashansunu followed it.

As she approached, she saw a familiar light. Paolina, the girl who'd come from beyond the world. Her color and texture was clear even in this place. Gashansunu came close to the comforting glow.

The greater light rose beyond, like the oldest of house priests in the Silent World, great power and potential and the paths of history and story and love and hate bounded together in a swirling knot. A chief with a golden crown lay here in state, ready to release her energy to form a new generation of might in the Shadow World.

She slipped into Paolina's light and felt a comfortable settling in. Like her own *wa* had come home.

No, Gashansunu realized. *She* was the *wa*.

The great light spilled open, a thousand snakes trailing bright-smeared into the wider extents of the Silent World, leaving behind glowing spoor. Some leapt into Paolina, some into others of the spirit-lights around Gashansunu's host, but most sought their destinies beyond.

Someone cried out, and a silent bell the size of the world began to toll.

CHILDRESS

The Queen shrieked once, then burbled. Kitchens turned away from his butchery with a crimson spray across his chest and face. His eyes shone with bright madness.

The blinded maid on the floor drummed her heels and howled like a kennel bitch at the death of her master.

Wang stood up from behind the end of the tank. "There are tubes here for oil, blood, spiritual aether and pulmonic fluid. Also electrickal mains. If you wish this work to be done beyond recovery, we should cut these."

"I have slain her." Kitchens' voice was brittle.

Paolina stepped forward and stared into the tank. She seemed graver, more settled somehow, here at the death of everything.

"Now that you have finished, I want to go to Boaz." Her tone was distant, a marked contrast to Kitchens'.

"Can you take the survivors with you?" Childress asked.

Paolina's gaze was far away. The stemwinder was already in her hands. "Yes. Who will come?"

"Not I," Childress replied. "I must stay and face whoever comes. I am here for the *avebianco*. In truth, for Admiral Shen as well."

"I'm an Englishman," said the old pilot. "I shall face English justice."

Kitchens nodded. "As will I."

Wang spoke up. "I should stay with the Mask Childress. I am set to a task that cannot be parted from her."

Paolina looked to al-Wazir, the one man she would have taken if she could. He was touching his right side, fingers scarlet with blood. "I do not think I should be going anywhere, Miss Barthes. You see, I am mortal wounded."

The seven of Leung's sailors who survived looked confused. Childress spoke to them in their language. "The girl is leaving for the Wall by magical means. I strongly suggest you accompany her, for while these English may negotiate with us, you will be slain as mortal enemies."

The old cook, Lao Mu, was one of the remnant. "May we gather as many of the wounded as we can?"

"Paolina," Childress said, "these should leave with you, but they wish to claim the fallen. The hallway is almost certainly too dangerous now, though."

"I shall take them with me, and reach outside for those who still live," she replied. "Good luck to you all."

PAOLINA

She set the stemwinder to follow Boaz, wherever he was. Whether they would emerge into empty air was no worry to her now. Gathering the sparks of the sailors and the wounded in the hall outside, she simply stepped, pushing off sufficiently so as not to further devastate Blenheim Palace in her wake.

From one moment to the next, she was surrounded by an orchard shrouded in mist. The hour was late here, so she had moved farther east. A building in the Chinese style loomed nearby, an ornamental pond before it. Something vast towered beyond as a formless gray presence in the fog.

The monk walked out of the mist as if she had not been there even a moment before.

"Welcome. You were expected."

"Where is Boaz?" Paolina demanded. "I should have reached him."

The men crowded around her began gathering up the wounded in order to help them toward the building. Al-Wazir groaned among them.

"You have," said the monk. "This is the Jade Temple, which cannot be passed within so easily. This is where he and I came, when you sent us. You are atop the Wall, close as you can reach to your lover by the ways you followed."

Atop the Wall. She'd been to the top once before, when passing over with Ming on her journey after the death of the Nanyang fleet. It had just been a place, an obstacle to be crossed. She'd never considered its true meaning, nor the idea that there were places in the Shadow World she *could* not walk.

Had Gashansunu understood that?

Her crew shuffled past her. Paolina longed to rush after Boaz. Only the monk's words held her.

"The top is different," she said. "Neither Northern Earth nor Southern."

The monk shrugged. "Where a river meets the sea, to whom does the water belong?"

"This is more important," Paolina replied. "This is the world. God's Creation. Each side with its own path. Even a mockery of one another. Angels to the North, winged savages to the South. Farms and factories on the one side, jungled Eden on the other. Industry against magic. Separate but not inviolate. A bit of each passes over to the other."

The monk nodded, grinning her encouragement.

Paolina followed the thought toward its logical conclusion. "The world is divided much as the human mind, filled with contradiction, with logic and imagination, with image and word. Like the human mind, it works best when those contradictions are blended."

"Do you now know what the Golden Bridge is?"

"Yes." In that moment it was all so obvious. "The Wall itself. It is not a division; it is the joining of the two halves of the Earth, as the dreaming mind of God awakens to the thoughts of what might come next."

"The Wall," the monk said. "And you. Every bridge has a keeper."

"A troll," Paolina replied with a laugh. "And here is where the free will Hethor spoke of begins. From the middle of the bridge between faith and reason." It almost made sense to her now, in a way that promised more, once she'd had time to consider the problem. Years. "The gleam belongs here, in neither world. A fountain of free will."

"Yes." The monk's face was tight and fierce.

"Now where is my beloved Boaz?"

"Let me take you to your Brass." The monk extended an arm. "He is in the care of the Jade Abbot, a monk even older than I am, which is something of a trick, I can tell you."

They followed the last of the stumbling wounded through the forest, watching drizzle curtain the world in wide swaths. "This Jade Abbot . . . I hope he is not so much of a fool as so many I have met."

"Who do you think has kept the Wall this long?"

Her feet were wet, her body aching, and she did not care. Boaz waited, and with him perhaps a destiny within the shelter of a power old and great enough not to covet her stemwinder. Something whispered in the back of her mind. Alien, familiar. Gashansunu?

Not the sorceress, she realized. Or not just Gashansunu. Paolina's *wa* had found her.

WANG

A handful of Englishmen in patterned skirts peered into the room. Only four of them remained—Kitchens, the old English sailor, the librarian and Wang.

The soldiers burst in with rifles swinging, but they did not fire. A tired officer was among them, narrow bodied with a brush moustache. He tugged at the hair above his lip as he surveyed the carnage.

"It is done, I see."

"This thing is done," the clerk said. "Bernard Forthright Kitchens, special clerk to Admiralty. Her Imperial—"

The officer stopped him with a raised hand. Somewhat to Wang's surprise, Kitchens fell silent. "She has asked these last two years for help from a select few. The Cameron Highlanders were posted here in hopes that a way might be found."

"Posted?" Kitchens asked, his voice suspicious. "By whom?"

"Gentlemen." Childress cut them both off. Her voice was cold and miserable. "If the executions are not going to proceed right now, I would prefer an adjournment from this abattoir."

"No executions, ma'am. Not today." The officer looked her over. "I am Major Sharpe, of the regiment. Who might you be?"

"The Mask Childress, of the *avebianco*."

Sharpe glanced at the opened tank. "Here to oversee murder done?" His voice was mild, but he shook with passion. Wang began to wonder anew if they could possibly leave this room alive.

"Here to meet with Government to bring a halt to the war burning in the east," she snapped. "I did not come for your queen, though I do not dispute Mr. Kitchens' deeds. It is not murder to finish a death long-delayed. In any case, you shall not end me today with a bullet to the head, for I must meet with the Prime Minister."

"In that case, your patience will soon be rewarded," Sharpe said. "Lloyd George hastens even now from London by special train. The entire Oxfordshire lines have been stopped to clear the track."

"Good," Childress said. "Then England shall hear how best to sue for peace." Wang stirred as she pointed to him. "My companion will speak for both China and the Silent Order."

"I . . ." He fell silent. This was not China, where power was acquired through descent and heavenly mandate. He could beg away this moment and surrender his life to an English prison, or he could claim to be a kô, an agent of both the Dragon Throne and the Silent Order. How would these men know the difference?

She has done no less.

Wang tried again. "I will treat with your Prime Minister." His tone was crisp as Childress', though he told an even greater lie. He wished the monk were here. "There is no need for war."

How to take the message home? At the first, he would have them intercept *Good Change* at Port Said. Captain Shen would be enraged, but then Captain Shen was always enraged.

"You are a most unlikely ambassador," Sharpe replied. He and his men bustled the four of them away.

We may live a little longer, Wang thought. He would have to invent whole new lies, very quickly—large ones he could use to persuade a halt to the war, and thus render himself important enough to survive to go home and deliver the message.

His library seemed so far away now, but the distance mattered less than ever. His own man, Wang had to force himself not to sing as he walked the ruined halls.

KITCHENS

He sat on a narrow chair before a massive oaken desk. It had the look of something just now swept from under a furniture drape. A reek of burning tinged the air. The world outside was finally quiet after hours of fire-fighting noise and the occasional gunshot.

Wang and Childress had been separated from him. Kitchens devoutly hoped the shots had not been for them. He reckoned himself for the noose, unless they chose to make his execution a private and unofficial affair. Something to round out the evening, perhaps.

Minutes ticked by with the rhythms of a long-case clock on the wall to his right. Empty shelves reached fourteen or fifteen feet to the ceiling, except where the windows opened onto a garden. The chandelier was missing, though its mounting hook and gas pipes were visible in the middle of a plaster rosette. Once the last of the daylight faded outside, he would be in the unquiet dark with his ghosts.

The clerk studied his grubby fingernails in the waning light. Blood royal stained the little striations and clung to the corners of each nail. He'd killed almost two entire crews getting here—first *Erinyes'*, then the Chinese sailors following al-Wazir and that insane woman from New England.

Apparently they'd arrived at Blenheim Palace by submarine. Kitchens' grasp of that was tenuous at best.

Two dead crews. At least a dozen members of the Royal Household dead defending Her Imperial Majesty. That doctor, Stewart. All the men he'd failed down along the Wall under Ottweill's command.

One queen.

The door opened behind him, then clicked shut again. Footsteps echoed across the uncarpeted room. Kitchens was unwilling to turn and look.

The Prime Minister walked around the desk and sat in the large leather chair. He laid a revolver down.

That riveted the clerk's attention. "Sir?"

"Mr. Kitchens." Lloyd George's voice was slow, careful, lacking his usual witty eloquence. "I see you have returned to England."

Kitchens watched the pistol, wondering if it would somehow spring to life. In the deepening night, the Prime Minister was little more than a shape with some dimensionality.

"Sir, yes . . . sir."

"The Mask Childress tells a remarkable tale. As does that, ah, ambassador of hers."

"Sir." He could add no wisdom to their story, for he did not know it himself. They had appeared in the company of al-Wazir by the will of

Paolina Barthes, but they might as well have dropped in from the Iro-
quois Nation for all he could say.

Lloyd George studied his own hand. "I do not suppose it signifies
whether Mr. Wang is in fact accredited as a high commissioner. By the
time that woman is done with him, they will never admit otherwise in
Beijing. This pointless war may yet be over, and our friends in Valetta and
Phu Ket can return to their hall-of-mirrors vendettas with each other and
the Lord God Almighty."

"Sir." That was rapidly becoming a comforting syllable.

"Do you believe in God, Mr. Kitchens?"

"Sir?"

The Prime Minister leaned forward, his suit rustling as his shadowed
silhouette bent. "You heard me."

"Of—of course, sir. Who does not?"

"You might be surprised." Fingers drummed on the surface of the desk.
"I have been strongly advised to allow you to do yourself a fatal mischief.
This would save the Crown the bother and expense of a trial, with all its
attendant public humiliation at our many failures in protecting Her Imperial Majesty's life and person." More drumming, then: "Are you perhaps
interested in this option?"

"Sir."

"I shall take that as a negative. I am quite serious, you know."

Despite the oncoming chill of evening, sweat poured down Kitchens'
back now. "Sir, yes sir."

"God ordained the passing of the Queen at her appointed time. Bad science and worse judgment prolonged her life, at the urging of . . . certain
elements in Government and society. Even a man in my position, perhaps
especially a man in my position, is not privy to all decisions. There has been
a very quiet argument over the meaning of certain subtle communications
emanating from Her Imperial Majesty. You, sir, have resolved what was
becoming the most vexing issue of state in modern times, as well as the
most direly secret." Another round of finger drumming. "So, while you are
invited to be a suicide, you will not hang. I should not think to describe His
Imperial Majesty, recently the Prince of Wales, as grateful for the killing of
his mother. Neither is he blind to what has transpired."

A long silence followed, the two men facing each other in deepest
shadow.

Finally Kitchens could not stand the wordlessness. "Wh-where does
that leave me, sir?"

"You are free to depart. No one would ever believe your story anyway,
but should you choose to repeat it, there is a quite accommodating mad-

house in my home borough from which politically inconvenient lunatics never emerge." Lloyd George leaned forward. "A necessity of the modern state, I am afraid."

Summoning his courage, Kitchens shook his head. "She has finished dying, but she asked for her throne to be broken, and for what has been undone to be remade. I would know if her wishes have been carried out."

"You are also free to stay." The Prime Minister's voice grew even more slow and careful. "But your place in Government may be quite different. Few enough will know the truth. Many will never see you as anything but a lunatic."

What of al-Wazir? Or Ottweill and those unfortunate men slowly breaking through the roots of the Wall?

"I will bear my ghosts, sir, if I can serve out the terms of Her Imperial Majesty's desires in this matter. And my commission to the tunneling project remains unresolved."

"The world spins ever faster, Mr. Kitchens. Men of your . . . unusual . . . experiences shall be quite valuable in the days to come. War or no war. The Wall abides, as you say."

"Sir."

Lloyd George stood and walked out without a farewell. The Prime Minister left the revolver behind.

After a while, Kitchens picked the weapon up to check if it was loaded.

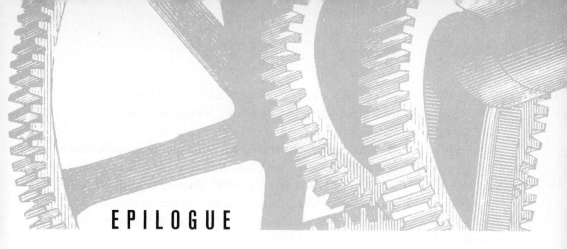

EPILOGUE

... so have I loved you: continue ye in my love.   —*John 15:9*

BOAZ AND PAOLINA

They stood along the rail of the Onyx Terrace. When the mists were gone, the view seemed to stretch all the way to the Mediterranean. She knew that was not true; she could do the math on the curvature of the Earth in her head without conscious effort. He knew that was true, for he knew that with the light in his heart, he could see the far side of Creation.

They were both right, and neither was wrong.

An airship slid slowly across the sky well below them. Vertiginous, steep, a sky that fell as sharply as a collapsing stair yet wide open as God's unblinking eye. They knew from the shape of the gasbag that this one was Chinese, but already two British ships strained at the makeshift masts near the Jade Temple. Plus a third vessel, alien as a shark, familiar as a tooth, risen from the country of the Bone People far into the Southern Earth and come now to this place.

This was not a conference. The Jade Abbot wouldn't hold with such. Rather, it was a dinner party, involving two librarians, one staying very close to a wounded, one-handed sailor; a very young but retired clock-maker; several veterans of the airship services of both great powers; as well as sundry submariners, denizens of the Wall, Correct People, sorcerers and other, stranger folk from distant lands, including a strange albino named William of Ghent who kept his distance from Hethor.

Should these sundry folk have occasion to speak over dinner, which in all its ramifications would last the better part of a week, so much the better.

Should an angel sweep down from the silver deserts and forests of the moon to pronounce some unknowable benison, so much the better.

Should Paolina and Boaz enter the red-lacquered halls of the Jade

Temple and sit among the assorted princes, admirals, special clerks, and stout-hearted warriors, so much the better.

For now they stood on the sun-warmed terrace and watched the Indian Ocean curve away toward the all-too-round horizon and enjoyed the simple, silent pleasure of one another's company. Alone, as everyone in this life was, but alone together. That one person complete and whole could multiply another's whole completeness was nothing short of a miracle.

Her heart thrilled, throbbing in her chest. His mind raced, while the new-brazed seams in his face and body yet ached a bit. Their arms twined, their hands clasped, their heads close as the familiar sound of labored engines drifted from below and a solitary hawk harried the orchards lying to the West. Voices drifted from the temple building, argument mixed with the sizzling scent of cookery and the clink of wineglasses.

"It's only just begun, hasn't it?" she said. A warm echo from the Silent World agreed with her.

His hand gripped hers a little more tightly. "It will only ever be beginning."

She turned into his embrace, kissed him tightly, and marveled once again that a man made entirely of Brass could have such a pounding heart.